THE LEGEND OF
TEPHRA

CAROLIN J.V. MILNER

Copyright © 2023 Carolin J.V. Milner.

All rights reserved. No part of this book may be reproduced, stored, or transmitted by any means—whether auditory, graphic, mechanical, or electronic—without written permission of both publisher and author, except in the case of brief excerpts used in critical articles and reviews. Unauthorized reproduction of any part of this work is illegal and is punishable by law.

ISBN: 979-8-89031-243-3 (sc)
ISBN: 979-8-89031-244-0 (hc)
ISBN: 979-8-89031-245-7 (e)

Because of the dynamic nature of the Internet, any web addresses or links contained in this book may have changed since publication and may no longer be valid. The views expressed in this work are solely those of the author and do not necessarily reflect the views of the publisher, and the publisher hereby disclaims any responsibility for them.

One Galleria Blvd., Suite 1900, Metairie, LA 70001
1-888-421-2397

*In an ancient village, an old woman utters a prophecy
of discord and bloodshed; a young shepherdess unwittingly
becomes the catalyst for the fulfillment of that prophecy.*

This book is dedicated to my husband Perry, to Adrienne and Sarah, to my children, and to all my family and friends who supported me in this endeavor with their love and encouragement. Thank you and God bless you for helping me realize my dream of turning what began as a short story into a published novel.

To my readers, I hope you enjoy reading *The Legend of Tephra*, a story that was inspired by names and terms heard in a college Physical Geography class. Due to the unusual names of the characters and places, a glossary with pronunciation key follows the text.

ENDORSEMENTS

"Following Tephra along her mystical journey will enchant the minds of both teens and adults. Milner beautifully paints an undeniable landscape of the Drumlin Village under Nunatak Peak along with the themes of staying true to oneself and treasuring the gifts of unfeigned friendship."

Veronica LeGrange,
Masters Degree in Educational Leadership,
Middle School Literature Teacher at a 2013
National Blue Ribbon School of Excellence

"The Legend of Tephra is one of the most delightful books I've read. Growing up on the customs and traditions of her heritage, a young girl is taught to be strong and independent. When she uses that strength and independence to question her own individuality and dreams, she then has to make some very difficult decisions. Whether fiction or not, long ago or today, this story exemplifies how much our heritage, traditions, and customs impact our lives and who we are.

Patricia V. Clifford,
Bachelor of Science in Social Work;
Medical Certification Specialist II –
Imperial Calcasieu Human Services Authority,
Developmental Disabilities Division

"The Legend of Tephra is appropriate for all ages and I am so excited to share this story with my grandchildren. What a lovely way to send the message that being strong through adversity and doing what is right, even if society says differently, will bring you through tough situations and help you find your heart."

***Maggie Wilson,**
Optical Manager,
ABO-NCLE Certified,
Costco Wholesale

PROLOGUE

In the soft, lavender light of morning, eleven hooded figures gathered in a circle on a massive flat stone. The stone, which the villagers called the Hammada Stone, was the sacred center of village life. Each hooded figure held a staff upwards towards the center of the circle; the tips of each staff were ornamented with a crystal the size of a small pear. As the sun rose on the distant horizon, the crystals reflected its light, casting an eerie glow over the figures and the Hammada Stone. One of the figures, an old woman, moved to the center of the stone. She closed her eyes, lifted her face and arms upwards toward the sacred mountain Nunatak Peak, and chanted in an ominous tone:

> *Beware of changes in the now!*
> *The rock will split, the rift will go deep.*
> *Fast the streams will flow;*
> *then the shift and blood will flow!*
> *Blood will flow like the streams!*

Kame, the oldest woman in the Drumlin village, spoke words that foretold alarming days ahead. Kame had outlived her mate, Adar, and had taken his place with the Wise Ones—a place customarily held by males. Since assuming Adar's role, Kame had represented her clan well, and her soothsaying had earned her the respect of the village—that is, until now.

For the past three mornings, as the Hammada gathered at sunrise for prayers, she had uttered her warnings, but the others had paid no attention. This sunrise she stood in the midst of the Hammada, her straight back denying her many years. "Turn not away your ears! When have I spoken falsely?"

Shael, a well-revered male, confronted Kame by saying, "A woman must consult the Hammada before proclaiming a prophecy so that we may consider its validity. You continue to ignore the custom."

"You speak of blood-shed when we have known only peace. You warn of a split, a division, but do not explain," said Karst, the oldest male member and leader of the Hammada. "How is it you see what we do not?" he questioned.

"I do not see things in Nunatak alone," Kame responded, "but in the eyes of the young ones of the village. They are restless. If you would but attend—"

"If you would but attend to the young ones of your own clan, old woman—" began one of the Hammada.

"It is to all the young ones of our village, now and those to come, that I am attending!" shouted Kame.

"No! There shall not be anger amongst the Hammada," another of the Wise Ones spoke up, "Our sacred gifts must flow together in peace; only then can we lead our people in the path of The Always."

"Your words are true," Kame answered quietly, "I will be silent—for now—but soon you will heed my counsel." With a deep sigh, she took her seat.

Moraine, another of the four female members of the Hammada, stood and faced Karst. "I cannot judge the truthfulness of Kame's words," she said, "but we all know the regard with which her prophecies have been held in the past. She has spoken with assurance and eyes unblinking three times now. Her prophecy is worthy of more reflection before we just set it aside."

Kame looked up at Karst to see how he would respond to Moraine's statement. He bowed his head in a gesture of prayer and pointed his staff towards Nunatak Peak. He then took a deep breath, raised his head, and addressed the Wise Ones, saying, "I put the words of Moraine before you. Can we be of the same mind on this, and wait upon The Always to lead us to a right judgment regarding Kame's prophecy?"

One by one, the members of the Hammada tapped their staffs on the stone three times, signifying their agreement. When all had agreed, they raised their staffs high, allowing the sun's rays to catch on the crystals, thereby forming a circle of light. The Wise Ones held their staffs upward with their right arm, each reaching out their left arm to help support their neighbor's staff. This circle symbolized the Hammada's unity and solidarity. Karst said a closing prayer, and together the Wise Ones made the ritual bow of leave-taking before each made their way through the village to his or her own dwelling.

The village was set in the smooth Drumlin Hills that formed the southern-most tip of a crescent-shaped, glacial mountain range. Nestled in the lower arc of the crescent was Mosken Lake, into which spilled the two waterfalls of Hanging Valley. One of the waterfalls, Nunatak, cascaded into the far northern edge of the lake, while the other, Cambria Falls, tumbled gently into the lake near the edge of the village. The large, irregular-shaped lake formed the north and east borders of the village; on the western edge, forests of hardwood trees covered rolling hills that later flattened into wind-swept plains. A mix of evergreen and hardwood trees grew on the southeast edge of the village, and continued up into the mountains where they converged with the Great Boreal Forest on the forbidden Barchan Mountain. Below the village, the southern hills gave way to broad sweeping plains, where one of the village clans cultivated the millet that served as food for villagers and livestock.

Several glaciers glistened between the peaks of the mountains. The highest mountain, Nunatak Peak, crowned the northern arc of the crescent, and was known in the village as the "Footstool of The Always." Its crystalline summit reflected the first rays of light from the east, and the last rays from the west. The Hammada—the Wise Ones of the Drumlins—based their prophecies on the color patterns reflected by the many ice facets of Nunatak. The crystals on their staffs, legend held, had fallen from the summit of Nunatak and could summon the spirit of The Always. Ancient prophesies formed the foundation of deeply ingrained laws and rituals that governed the villagers' daily lives. For the Drumlins, these laws were unquestionable.

CHAPTER

1

As soon as the snow melted on the eastern slopes of the Drumlin Hills, the sheep of the village would be taken to graze on the new spring grasses. Tephra, a young shepherdess, awoke on the morning of the First Grazing with a sense of heightened anticipation. She quickly dressed in the typical spring attire of a young village maid—a simple long-sleeved, knee length, light woolen shift. After arranging her long, light-auburn hair into two braids, as was the custom for young maidens, she joined her family in the cooking yard outside their dwelling. There she breakfasted on dried peaches and millet cakes.

Her mother, Caldera, greeted her with a smile. "You are impatient to be out on the hills again it seems."

"It has been a long winter, Mother. It will be good to be out in the sun with the sheep."

"Yes, but even in the early spring sun you must guard your skin. Did you use the esolis butter?" she asked. She was referring to a special ointment prepared by Hevel the Healer. It had been developed by one of Hevel's predecessors several generations ago, and was used as a cure for burns and as protection against the midday rays of the sun for the fair skin of many of the Drumlins.

"Yes, Mother, and I will have my shawl," she said, and with a loving smile, touched her mother's cheek.

"Your father is already at the sheep pens, clearing them for the shearing. Be sure to take him an extra flask of water."

She walked over to where her young sister, Breccia, was sitting with their brother, Sedi. Grinning, she gave him a playful tap on his head, and bent to kiss Breccia on her cheek. After picking up her shawl, her shepherd's staff, and two sheepskin flasks of water, she made her way to the sheep pen. There she found Tarn, her father, just as her mother had said.

"Good morning, Father! Mother has sent extra water for you."

"She takes good care of me. See that you learn well from her the ways of a good mate," Tarn said sternly, and then turned to her with a reassuring smile. "I have no worries that you will be a good mate, for you have a tender heart."

"Like Mother?" Tephra asked, smiling fondly at her father.

"Yes. The Always has shown favor to me in such a mate." Tarn paused a moment, as if to say more, but simply gave her a pat on the shoulder, and turned back to his work saying, "Tell Elos to hasten back here after you relieve him on the hills. He took the sheep out early so I could start on the shearing pens."

She looked around for her cousin, Esker, who tended the flock with her. After a few minutes, Tephra saw no sign of her cousin and assumed she was probably going to be late as usual. Esker was a good shepherdess and a good friend, and Tephra enjoyed working with her, but her habitual tardiness was trying at times. Tephra opened the gate and walked toward the pasture and her sheep. She smiled as she recalled the short conversation she'd just had with her father. He rarely talked to his children in words. He showed how much he cared for them through his attitude and gestures. By a touch, a smile, or a nod, he had a way of communicating his pride in his mate and his children.

Tephra walked past the work shed of the village toolmakers on her way to the pasture. One of them called out to her teasingly, "Sing for us, Tephra. Waste not your songs on the sheep!"

Tephra often sang gentle, soothing melodies to her lambs, and entertained her young sister and the other small children of the village with playful tunes. She also loved to sing the old songs of the village and the poem-songs from the ancient writings that told of The Always, and how he had led her people to the Drumlin Hills.

"Yes, Tephra, a song, a song!" cried another villager. A bit timidly at first, she began one of her songs as she continued to walk to the pasture. After the first two lines, her voice became clear and strong as she sang.

> *The kindness of the Always fills the hills of Drumlin,*
> *while His wisdom guides our ways.*
> *His glory is on the mountain peak*
> *where he guides us night and day.*

As she neared the hills where the earth-tillers were busy tending their crops, she heard a familiar voice call out, "What is the cause of your joyful song this early morning?"

Tephra shrugged her shoulders, smiled, and continued her song as Graben came to walk beside her.

> *Oh sing all of Drumlin, play on your strings.*
> *Give thanks for the harvest, the grain and the lambs.*
> *We are His people, O sing, Drumlin, sing!*

"Whatever the cause, I am grateful. Your voice is most pleasant," Graben said.

Tephra felt the warmth of a blush on her face and responded to Graben's compliment with only a smile and a slight bow of her head. The previous spring, during the annual Festival of the Fifth Moon, Graben was granted beginning courtship rights by Tephra's father. Tarn had been pleased to grant these rights to Graben, as he was of one of the largest and most prosperous Drumlin clans—the clan of earth-tillers. With a chaperon following a few paces behind, Graben and Tephra were allowed to walk together in the village after sunset. At the Harvest Festival in early autumn, Graben had asked for the Rite of Formal Courtship, announcing that he was preparing for the time when he would be ready to enter into the betrothal rites with Tephra.

For the past year, Graben made the prescribed calls to her dwelling and brought gifts to her family, as was the custom of the courtship rites.

"Tephra, I see you have no food with you for the mid-day meal," Graben said. "My cousins have a fine strawberry crop this season. It would be no trouble to bring a meal with some fresh strawberries, bread, and cheese to you on the hillside."

"That would be very pleasant," Tephra said with a polite smile, "but you must bring enough berries to share with Esker as well, for she is bringing the bread and dried meat for our meal today." With a playful grin, she added, "She is very fond of strawberries, you know."

"It seems I rarely speak to you alone. Your cousin Esker or your friend Olivine is always with you. Will you choose a chaperon and walk with me along the lake tonight?" Graben stepped so quickly in front of Tephra that she stumbled in her effort to avoid colliding with him. He reached out to steady her, and kept his hand on her arm as he said, "Before now it would have been unseemly for you to reveal your happiness that I had asked to court you. But surely you are aware that the entire village whispers their certainty that we will be mated before summer. It would not be unseemly now, and it would please me to hear you say how delighted you are."

"It is an honor to be chosen by you, Graben," Tephra replied quietly, not meeting his gaze, but looking at his hand on her arm instead. Yes, she had heard the rumors of the villagers.

With his free hand, Graben reached for Tephra's, and his voice became serious and low. "Remember Tephra? Remember when we were children—playing games, teasing each other, acting out our childish ideas of grown-up roles, even the Mating Ritual? You once told me I would forever be your chosen friend, and you hoped one day we would be 'mated for true.' I thought you foolish, for I was only eight and you, not yet six years. I desire that you might say those words to me again. I will not think you foolish now."

As they resumed walking toward the pasture, Tephra thought about what Graben was asking of her. There were many times when he had declared his pleasure that her father granted courtship. Now he expected a similar response from her, and she knew that it would not be improper for her to say what he wanted to hear when they were alone. Still, she could not and would not say what she did not truly feel. Both of their clans had long expected they would mate one day, and Tephra simply accepted it. They would be mated whether or not she said what Graben wanted to hear. It was the Drumlin way.

Graben had been her friend for as long as she could remember, and she was fond of him. Her family knew him well, as he was often at her dwelling visiting with her older brother, Sedi. She, too, fondly recalled their childhood games, but now there were no more games to play.

Tephra stopped suddenly, looked off in the direction of Nunatak Peak, and said, "You brought great honor to my clan when you asked my father for courtship rights. But even if you had not, Graben, you would forever be my friend, and I, yours."

Esker caught their attention by calling out to them. Tephra gave Graben a weak smile and waved at the young shepherdess skipping toward them. When Esker arrived, Graben repeated his offer of fresh strawberries to add to their midday meal.

"We will wait for you under the white oak tree near the shallow spring. The grasses there are soft," Esker responded excitedly.

In the customary gesture of parting, Graben bowed his head to each maiden and returned to his garden. Tephra walked quickly over to where her cousin, Elos, was watching the sheep, gave him the message from her father, and then turned to Esker.

"Esker," she began in a tone that was half-teasing, half-scolding, "you have been apprenticed to me for four years now. You know how to spot the bitter weeds and the dill grass, and how to lead the flock to sweeter pastures. You have learned the ways of the shepherdess well, except for one thing—you are always late! That is not a good model for young Creta." Last spring Creta, Esker's younger sister, had joined Tephra and Esker each afternoon as a part-time apprentice. After the upcoming Festival, she would join the two older girls for the entire day, in preparation for the time when Tephra would be mated and Esker and Creta would assume care of the sheep. Tephra loved the gentle animals she shepherded and was concerned about Esker's dedication to the task.

"I was playing with the baby, drawing funny pictures of animals to make him laugh and—Oh! Mother said to tell you Creta may not be able to come after the midday meal, she has to watch the baby because mother … oh, I forget! But Tephra, I will try harder. You will have no concerns about your dear lambs when you are mated to Graben. Ah, Graben! How favored you are!" Esker rambled.

Esker was right. Tephra was gifted with a high, clear singing voice and grace in all her movements. With those gifts, along with her long-lashed hazel eyes, light auburn hair that sparkled with honey-colored highlights, and her rapidly developing curves, Tephra was considered one of the fairest maidens in the village. Everyone knew she would be highly desired as a mate, favored as she was by The Always.

When the sun was at its highest point in the sky, the two maidens made their way to the place Esker had suggested. The sheep lapped water from the spring before turning to graze on the soft grasses and wildflowers on a nearby hill. After handing Tephra the cloth packet that held the food for their midday meal, Esker carefully spread a large cloth on the grass beneath the tree, and then began climbing the tree.

"Esker," Tephra laughed, "what are you doing up in the tree?"

"Watching for Graben," Esker answered matter-of-factly.

Tephra smiled, shook her head, and teased gently, "You are a young maiden, and still you climb trees like a child." As she sat cross-legged on the soft grasses, she picked some of the nearby wildflowers and daydreamed about the up-coming Ceremonial Dance for the annual Festival of the Fifth Moon. She, along with three other maidens, had performed the dance for two years, but this year a slight variation in the steps had been added to the routine. As she hummed and mentally danced through the recently learned movements, she unbound her braids and then began re-braiding them, weaving flowers into her long tresses.

After a few moments, Esker called down from her perch in the tree, "A man approaches. From the size of him, it is Graben." Tephra looked up as Esker easily made her way down and hopped from a low limb to stand in front of Tephra. She stood staring at Tephra with her hands on her hips and a puzzled look on her face. "Tephra!" Esker exclaimed, "You've loosened your braids!" A young maiden's hair, and even a mated woman's, was always kept braided and bound according to a long-honored custom. The only time their hair was allowed to hang freely was in the company of their family, but never outside their own dwelling, except at specific times of ceremony.

"Oh! I only loosened it to weave in the flowers. Help me finish braiding it before Graben sees. He is so very strict about such things." With haste, the two maidens plaited Tephra's hair.

As Graben approached, he nodded to Tephra and Esker, but did not offer a greeting or a smile. Tephra noted the hard set of his jaw and wondered if he had caught a glimpse of her hair flowing about her shoulders. He seated himself next to Tephra and placed his own contribution to their meal on the cloth; then taking the small loaf of bread, broke it into three pieces, performing the ritual that began every meal. The breaking and sharing of bread in this way honored the alliance of all the clans of Drumlin. The three leisurely consumed their meal as they talked of ordinary things—the sheep, the vegetable crops, the next market day, and then, the up-coming Golith Huntsman Trials.

This fierce competition among the young men of Drumlin Hills was in honor of Golith, who—according to the folk tales and legends of the people of Drumlin—was the greatest of all huntsmen. Golith could run as fast as a deer. Using a slingshot or bow and arrow, he could hit the head of a squirrel or rabbit so that no meat was bruised. With his spear, he could hit whatever target he chose.

"Sedi will be handing the Arrowhead over to me this year," Graben boasted. Tephra's brother, Sedi, had won the trials last year and now held possession of the Crystal Arrowhead. Legend held that the arrowhead was carved by the great Golith himself—carved from a large crystal found in a cave beneath Nunatak Peak.

"Are you so sure you will win?" teased Esker. "It is said that Noll has improved much in his skills with the bow and the spear over last spring, when his scores were almost as high as yours."

"Humpf! That is to be seen!" Graben answered, crossing his arms and tilting his head to one side. "And what about my skills with the axe? My knife throwing is always accurate, and I can out-run him too!

"Ah! Perhaps you *are* Golith returned to us after these many, many lifetimes," Tephra said giggling.

"Tease me, if it pleases you, my lovely one, and Golith I *will* be to you," Graben proclaimed confidently.

"Hah!" exclaimed Esker, "and what of Tor? He has greatly improved his spear fishing. How many fish have you speared? Easy to hit a still target, but ...."

"Esker, careful you do not provoke Graben," Tephra warned with a teasing smile. "He won't bring you more of his tasty strawberries and then you will have to buy them at market."

Esker stood, mockingly bowed toward Graben, and said in an impudent tone, "For your strawberries, I will be silent!"

"You will bow to me in tribute when I am holding the Crystal Arrowhead," he declared. Tephra noticed that although he was smiling, his tone was quite serious.

Esker shrugged and said, "We shall see. For now, I must take care of the meal cloth and see to the sheep."

Tephra picked up their water flasks and went to the spring to refill them, for the day had turned warm and they would be moving the sheep deeper into the pasture. When she turned around, she saw Graben was leaning lazily against the tree. He was grinning broadly; his gaze locked on her.

"What amuses you, Graben?" she asked, taken aback by his intent stare.

"Not amused, but pleased that soon you will be betrothed to me. I am the envy of every male in the village, you know." With a satisfied smile he continued, "I was remembering the first time I saw you in a ritual dance and watched the way you moved in perfect time to the music of the strummers. I knew then you were the mate for me."

Tephra realized Graben would not be saying those things to her if Esker was nearby, and that he had lingered until she left. Not knowing how to respond, she changed the subject. "My father has told me you are helping him repair the fences at the sheep pen. That is very good of you, Graben. It is very difficult for him since Sedi...."

Graben nodded in understanding, and Tephra did not need to say more. Her older brother, Sedi, who was one of Graben's closest friends, was still recovering from severe injuries received last autumn. When trying to rescue a pregnant ewe that had fallen into a steep, rocky ravine, he himself had fallen, badly breaking his leg. A stubborn fever set in, and the village healer began to doubt Sedi would ever walk again without the aid of a walking stick.

"Sedi is my good friend. After we are mated, our clans will be as one. He will be my brother, your father as my own. It is my duty to help him. Besides, Sedi insists he is getting stronger every day, and I know he will prove the healer to be wrong."

Tephra shook her head slowly, "I have not observed much improvement, but I know Sedi can be very persistent. If he is determined to walk again, perhaps The Always will shine favorably on him. But not, I am afraid, soon enough for the Trials. It will be difficult for Sedi to miss the Huntsman Trials this year, and then have to give up the Crystal Arrowhead to someone else." Graben said nothing in reply. Tephra knew he wanted the Arrowhead more than any man in the village did, but she guessed that he was uncomfortable with the circumstances. After a moment of awkward silence, Tephra suggested, "Come, let us see how Esker is faring on her own, and then perhaps follow the path to the orchards. The peach trees must be in bloom. If the orchard tenders are nearby, I will ask to pick a few blossoms to adorn our table at evening meal. I am sure your mother would be pleased if you brought some blossoms for your table as well."

Graben shook his head in reply as he stood and said with an air of authority, "I must return to the vegetable garden. There is much work to do, and I cannot leave the apprentices alone for long. They tend to get lazy if I am not there to watch them." He bowed in farewell, then turned and walked briskly toward his gardens.

When Tephra joined her cousin, Esker smiled mischievously. "You are quiet. Thinking of Graben?" she asked. "You know he will declare you as his betrothed. How delighted you must be!"

"Graben will be a very good mate," Tephra replied matter-of-factly. "He is a hard worker, skilled at many things, and handsome. We have been friends since we were babes on our mothers' laps. Come Esker, let us tend our sheep. That small one is wandering a little too far."

Tephra was uncomfortable with Esker's comments. In the Drumlin custom, all the choice of a life mate was granted to the male, deeming it most improper for a maiden to express a preference. Only after a certain time of courtship was a maiden allowed to show her pleasure at being chosen. Tephra knew that it would not be improper to speak of her feelings at this time, especially as the two were friends, and hoped she did not offend Esker by her matter-of-fact statement.

As the sun began to set, Tephra and Esker herded their sheep back to the night pens. After securing the gate, they bowed as they bid each other good night, and each walked toward her own family dwelling.

Along the path, Tephra met Olivine, a maiden of the clan of orchard tenders and her closest friend. The two had been playmates since they were old enough to toddle about the common yard of the village. There were many times Olivine's bossiness and competitiveness had threatened their friendship, yet their close bond remained, due in no small part to Tephra's gentle nature. They were intensely loyal to one another—a bond born of the years of sharing girlhood confidences that was nearly unbreakable.

"Te!" Olivine called, using her pet name for Tephra, "I've just been to your dwelling. The ribbons—oh! There are wilted flowers in your hair, and it is clumsily braided."

For a moment Tephra was confused by the reference to her hair, then remembering, she laughed softly, "Come help me put it in order. Esker has not your skill with braids, and we were hurried." Grasping her friend's wrist, she led her into a small, nearby grove of willow oaks, and confided to Olivine the earlier events of the day. "For a few moments today I felt most strange. I was thinking about the new steps for our festival dances, and if Esker had not been with me, I think I would have danced on the hills where my sheep were grazing. Instead, I braided flowers into my hair!" Tephra giggled, then sobering, said, "And then Graben came to share the midday meal with us and I think he saw me with a good part of my hair still unbraided. He did not look pleased."

"Ah! So there is the reason for your feeling strange and being so reckless—the handsome Graben!"

"N-No," Tephra said, "I was not thinking of Graben when I abandoned the hair customs. I told you. I was daydreaming about dancing at the Festival. But—ouch! Do not twist the braid so tight! Why were you at my dwelling?"

"Oh! Mother has completed the ribbons for our hair, so I left yours with your mother. But Tephra, dancing on the hills? Unbraiding your hair? I cannot believe you were so very bold!"

Tephra only shrugged her shoulders and grinned. "I wasn't dancing on the hills, just thought about it."

"Well, why shouldn't you feel like dancing? Soon you will be betrothed to Graben, and Ogen has hinted he will ask for solemn courtship, which means within a year...!" Olivine sighed deeply, "Ogen," and then she whispered, "I feel nothing but happiness when I think of him! Do you not feel the same about Graben?"

Tephra had always been completely honest with her dear friend, but was unsure of her feelings, and what to say to Olivine, so she replied simply, "I know I am the envy of not a few maidens. Graben will be a good mate. And he has always been my friend."

Olivine stepped back and inspected Tephra's freshly bound hair. "Now your hair is very neat. Except for those little curls which so prettily frame your face, and you know I envy those."

"Yes, as I envy your perfectly clear skin and the shape of your brown eyes. Why is it you do not freckle as I do, even with the healer's esolis butter?" Tephra commented, complementing her friend's clear, creamy complexion.

The two giggled at their oft-repeated comparisons, and then Olivine shrieked, "Oh! I almost forgot! I have named the time for us to practice the dance movements with Siluria and Mica. Even though it is their second year to dance with us, they are both a little awkward on some of the turns. The clearing is secured and one of the Hammada will watch over us as we practice." It was customary that practices were held in secret, as public dance was strictly forbidden except for the ritual dances that were performed at ceremonies and festivals.

"And I am sure even the Hammada would not challenge the time *you* named, so of course, Siluria and Mica have agreed," Tephra teased her assertive friend, as she often did, feeling assured Olivine would take it would good humor. They agreed to meet at the clearing at the appointed time, bowed to each other, and Olivine walked quickly toward her dwelling. Excited about the prospect of practicing the ritual dances, Tephra skipped lightly toward her own dwelling.

After she helped her mother clean up from their evening meal, Tephra helped Sedi walk outside where they sat enjoying the deepening twilight. There they talked about the upcoming Huntsman Trials and the Festival, and sharing memories of past events. "Sedi," Tephra spoke gently, "does it pain you much that you are not able to compete this year?"

"Yes, a little," he said soberly, then grinned playfully, "but I will return next year, and take back Golith's Arrowhead from Graben."

"Oh, so you, too, are sure Graben will win?"

"He has told me how much he has been practicing, and I have been able to watch some for myself."

"Giving him advice?" Tephra teased. "Is that allowed?"

"Our secret," Sedi said with a secretive grin.

"One of many?" Tephra quizzed, her eyes wide as she tried to hide a smile.

"Almost as many as you and I share," Sedi said with a wink. "Will you remember them when you are mated and have children of your own? And will you not be too hard on them when they are mischievous?"

"Ah! Like the times you took me berry picking on the terrace trails without telling Father? And the time you and Graben jumped off into the lake and gave me a terrible fright, leaving me stranded on the trail?" Tephra retorted, trying to sound angry, but failing.

"You weren't stranded," Sedi corrected her, with a suppressed grin. "You simply had to follow the trail back down to the pasture where we had started!"

"I was frightened when you jumped into the water, and a little confused. I was unsure of which way to go, as the terrace trails wind up and then down again in some places! And, you and Graben had been trying to scare me by telling me that we were already *halfway* to the Forbidden Mountain!"

Sedi chuckled, "We jumped to show the fastest way down!"

"I did not know how to swim then!"

"No, not then, but we taught you later that summer, remember?"

"Of course, I remember—by throwing me in the water!" Tephra laughed, slapping at her brother playfully. "If you recall, we were given a stern lecture and could not play outside for two days because—"

"Lads and young maidens do not bathe together!" they said together in mock severity, while stifling the urge to laugh out loud for fear they would be overheard and then reprimanded for mocking Drumlin customs.

Sedi's voice suddenly took on a serious tone, "It is strange, and then again not so strange, that you will surely be mated to one who is like a brother to me."

"What do you mean?"

"He has always been like a brother to us both, and I wonder when that changed for Graben. I did not know until he asked to court you that he might think of you as a mate."

"Neither did I," Tephra said softly, looking down at her hands. To avoid further conversation on the subject, she suggested, "I should help you inside, and then go see if Mother needs help with Breccia. Maybe if I promise to sing one of her favorite songs, she will not fuss about having to go to her sleep mat 'before everybody'!" As Tephra handed Sedi his crutch, he laughed at her perfect imitation of Breccia's nightly complaint.

After helping Breccia wash up, Tephra sang the promised song as she sat next to her and stroked her light reddish gold curls. Later that night as she lay on her mat, she thought back over her growing-up years. She recalled times both Sedi and Graben seemed to avoid her company, and the times they teased her almost to tears. She was thinking specifically of a few times she had heard Graben complain that she was always following them around. After the midday meal earlier today, he had told her that while watching her dance he had decided she would be his mate. Yet, she still was puzzled that she could recall no change in his attitude toward her until the day he had asked her father for courting rights.

CHAPTER

2

The time of the fourth moon began with warm and pleasant days. The two waterfalls poured the melted snow from the mountains into Mosken Lake; then rains, more abundant than usual, pelted the Drumlin hills. Soon the lake widened and streams overflowed, threatening the stone, sod and sheepskin dwellings built too close to its banks. The Hammada were summoned to beg The Always to slow the melting of the snows and ice in the mountains, and protect them from the spring storms. As they gathered around the stone, Kame reminded the others that she had foreseen the flooding of the streams in her earlier prophecy. She urged them to heed her warnings and that this was only the beginning of the prophecy's fulfillment.

Karst shook his head of long auburn and gray locks. "It is only a too-soon spring, old woman," he said, pointing his finger at Kame. "You seek notice by claiming to see what the Hammada do not. Although we have gravely considered your prophecy, Nunatak does not show colors that alarm us!"

Kame looked at each of the Wise Ones in turn, but most would not meet her gaze. Some shook their heads in agreement with Karst. "Then our strength must go into prayers for our village," she responded, covering her frizzled white hair with her prayer shawl and bowing her head.

The Wise Ones sang the old songs and chanted the ancient prayers, channeling their energy to something they could agree on—the well-being of the villagers. They watched the color patterns on the facets of Nunatak—the peak that was so close to The Always it never thawed. When the peak reflected the colors of light golden honey and the skies in the distant west turned a soft violet-blue, the Hammada announced that The Always had heard their pleas. The village would not be further harmed.

Three days passed and the prayers of the Hammada were answered. The earth was dry and a soft warm breeze caressed Drumlin hills while the villagers prepared for the two-day Festival of the Fifth Moon. On the first day of the Festival, the Golith Huntsman Trials were held on a broad open field at the edge of the village. Any male who had seen his fifteenth winter could enter the trials, although the competitors usually ranged in age from seventeen to twenty winters. The day before the Trials, preliminary matches were held in each skill: axe throwing, knife throwing, spear fishing, tree climbing, spear throwing, bow and arrow, and a foot race. The young men could compete in as many events as they desired. For the villagers, the matches that were the most exciting to watch were the final ones, where the competition was often fierce, and the judging had to be very precise. Women and children sat on one side of the field, the men and older boys on the other. Many of the women and maidens held flower garlands to wave as they cheered on their favorite competitors.

Spear throwing was the first match, and Graben was the first contestant. He had done well in the preliminaries, so he calmly took his stance on the mark with his chest out and his head held high. Glancing over to where he knew Tephra would be sitting with her family, he grinned broadly as he saw her—the sunlight turning her hair to red-gold, the small soft curls framing her delicate features. She looked up, smiled at him and waved her flower garland in a gesture of encouragement. He raised the spear into position and hurled it toward the target at the end of the field. When his spear hit the center precisely, he turned and beamed at Tephra. Again she smiled and waved her flower garland, and further encouraged, he squared his shoulders as he picked up another spear. Two more times Graben's spear hit the exact center, and each time he turned to observe Tephra's reaction. She had waved her garland enthusiastically each time, and he reacted with a deep sigh and a satisfied grin. Graben stepped away from the mark and with a wide sweep of his arm, gestured to Noll, the next competitor.

Noll stepped up to the mark, grinned and shouted, "So, he *has* been practicing!" The villagers laughed, and then were suddenly silent as Noll raised his spear. Graben held his breath as Noll's first spear shot toward the target. There was much excited murmuring among the villagers as the spear pierced the center of the target. Noll's aim on his second throw was just as true, and Graben forced a smile and rubbed the back of his neck. Noll's third spear missed by two fingers' width, and Graben let out a long, slow breath of relief. He received Noll's congratulatory pat on the back and gave his friend a consoling pat on the shoulder in return.

Graben stood with his hands resting loosely on his hips as Malik now took his turn. He had to suppress a smile when only on his third throw did Malik's spear hit the center. Ogen was next, and his throws were only marginally better than Malik's, and Graben's confidence strengthened.

As Tor picked up his spears and walked to take his stance, Graben could feel the excitement in the crowd grow. He heard the shouts of "Tor! Tor!" and "Graben! Graben!" as the villagers cheered for their favorites, and he could not help but try to determine which was louder. Graben watched intently as Tor raised his first spear. The cheers ceased, replaced by a tension-filled silence. The first spear hit as precisely as Graben's had, and he heard both cheers and moans from the crowd. When Tor's second spear was as accurate as the first, Graben swallowed and took a deep breath. As Tor threw his third spear, Graben watched anxiously as the spear seemed to move in slow motion toward the target. Suddenly the villagers were all on their feet and cheering wildly. Graben realized he and Tor were tied for first place in the spear-throwing event. He turned and was delighted to see Tephra was standing and waving her garland excitedly; to her right, Siluria was also waving her garland for Tor. With a forced smile, he turned to Tor and held out his hand.

In the knife-throwing event, which Graben had felt assured he would win, he was dismayed when the first competitor, Ogen, was able to hit center on all three of his throws. On his first two throws, Graben's knife had hit dead center, just as Noll's and Malik's had done. He clenched his jaw in frustration as his third knife-throw missed the target by a small margin, and only hoped it was close enough that he would at least have enough points for second place.

As he walked to take his stance for the axe-throwing match, Graben rolled his shoulders, flexed his arms and looking over at Tephra, flashed a smile and a confident wink. His first throw hit the center cleanly, and he repeated that accuracy in the second throw. However, immediately after the axe flew from his hand on his third throw, he grimaced and grabbed at his shoulder. Seeing that he had missed the mark by half a hand-width, he lowered his head and blew out a sharp breath of frustration. He heard the groan of the crowd as he walked over to where Hevel, the village healer, was standing by in case of any injuries. The healer felt all around Graben's shoulder, checked its range of motion, and massaged a soothing ointment on the tender area. When Hevel signaled that the young man would be fine, the villagers responded with loud applause, and Graben waved to show his acknowledgement.

Ogen proved to be exceptionally adept at axe throwing and Graben was certain he would earn first place. Noll and Tor each hit center on one throw, and Malik on two. Graben was slightly encouraged when, although he had not hit the center on his third throw of the axe, the others had hit no closer on one or more throws, and he assumed he had earned enough points for second place.

Graben joined in the good-natured taunting with Tor, Malik, Ogen, and Noll as they lined up for the foot race along with Col, a young man new to the Trials this year. In the preliminaries, Graben had finished last of the five, barely qualifying for the Trials, and was trying to ignore the slight fluttery feeling in his belly. As one of the judges approached the starting line, Graben concentrated on his strategy for pacing himself throughout the course. As the gong sounded once for the men to take their mark, Graben stepped up to his mark and took several deep breaths. The gong sounded again, and the men sprinted down the trail.

Noll was quickly several paces ahead of the rest, with Col closing fast. Graben kept Noll in sight for much of the race, but fell back as he stumbled slightly on one of the sharp turns on the trail. With a shake of his head, he set his jaw and focused on increasing his pace, pouring all his energy and thoughts into closing the distance between himself and Noll. When he crossed the finish line behind Noll, Tor, and Col, he was breathing hard and berating himself that he had not trained harder.

Malik had easily won the archery match the past two years, and Graben knew many of the villagers favored him. As he gathered with the other competitors for the archery match, he knew the scores in this match would be close, and watched anxiously as each man took aim at the targets. There were three targets: one was straight ahead at a fair distance, one had been secured high up in a tree, and the other was a swinging target suspended on a rope and set in motion by one of the judges of the Trials. Malik began the match with two perfectly aimed arrows, which brought a cheer from the villagers. When his third arrow hit the swinging target half a hand-width from the center, a collective groan was heard. Malik shook his head and grimaced as he walked toward the other contenders, while Graben suppressed a smile of relief that his toughest competitor in this event had likely been eliminated.

Young Col was up next, and Graben gave him a supportive pat on the shoulder, as it was obvious he was nervous. In spite of his nervousness, however, Col's first arrow hit only a knuckle-width from center. His second shot was perfect, and Graben held his breath. When the young man's third arrow hit even closer to center than Malik's, the crowd gave a loud, encouraging cheer, and Graben rolled his shoulders to keep from tensing up.

Tor's arrows hit close to center on each target—but not quite close enough. Then Ogen hit center on both of the first two—but on the third target did no better than Malik had done. Noll's arrow hit no closer than any of the others had, and Graben breathed a sigh of relief.

Graben was the last archer to compete. Taking a deep, calming breath, he walked to take his stance. He picked up his bow, placed the arrow, sighted, and then lowered his bow. After rolling his head to ease the tension in his neck, he again raised the bow, sighted, and took aim.

He sensed the sudden hush that came over the villagers and his pulse quickened. The first arrow hit the center of the target precisely, and the tenseness in his shoulders began to ease. With increased confidence, he lifted his bow, fixed his arrow, pulled back, let go, and watched as it cut through the air and hit the second target, high up in a tree, clean and true. As the villagers cheered excitedly, he grinned and turned toward the swinging target. He flexed his arms, took a deep breath, and placed the arrow in the bow. The judge set the target in motion, and to Graben, it seemed to be the only thing moving. The villagers, even the air, seemed to grow still. He wanted to steal a glance at Tephra, but dared not take his eyes off the target. Pulling the arrow back, he carefully took aim, and let the arrow fly. It whistled through the air, hitting the swinging target in dead center. Graben threw his head back in relief as the cheers of the villagers roared in his head. He then turned to look at Tephra who was standing and waving her garland and cheering with the others. Resisting the urge to go to her, he smiled broadly, waved his bow, and strutted to where the other competitors stood. Malik gave Graben a pat on the back and said something, which Graben could not catch because of the cheers of the villagers.

In the next match, tree climbing, Graben watched uneasily as the others made their climb. Again, Graben was the last contestant, and he knew his time in the preliminaries was not his best. The other competitors had done well, especially Ogen, and he would truly have to prove himself now. Stretching and flexing his leg muscles, he tried to clear his mind of everything except climbing the tree and retrieving his assigned token. The judge sounded the gong and called for Graben to come forward.

Graben reached up, grasped the two short wooden stakes that had been driven into the lower trunk of the tree. As he waited for the gong to sound again, blood was pulsing in his ears, threatening to drown out the sound. A heartbeat after the sound he began pulling himself up by his hands, reached the second set of stakes, and found his foothold. Tension was replaced by fierce determination and Graben quickly fell into a rhythm, climbed the tree, and retrieved his assigned token in the fastest time. After descending even more swiftly, he ran toward Tephra and tossed her the token he had retrieved—a small bell adorned with a ribbon of his clan's colors. He was rewarded with a wide smile as she caught the token, and he returned her smile with a self-satisfied grin.

The field events over, the competitors and the judges moved to the river for the spearfishing event. As he walked with the others to the river, Graben recalled the times he had watched the Golith Trials before he was old enough to be a competitor. He could almost feel the sense of excitement as the villagers eagerly waited to hear the results of the spear fishing match, and ultimately, the announcement of the one who would be named Golith and awarded the Crystal Arrowhead. When they had reached the river, Graben turned his full attention to the judges as they reviewed the rules. Each competitor would have three tries to spear a fish. Points would be awarded for each fish speared, according to its size. Each young man took his assigned position along the bank of the river, and at the sound of the gong, began watching the water intently, waiting for just the right fish to come into sight.

Graben's first attempt missed a large fish by a hand-width, and he blew out a breath of frustration. Widening his stance and relaxing his shoulders, he took a deep breath and held it as he spotted a large trout. He aimed his spear at its head, pulled back, then hurled the spear into the water. Suppressing a yelp of pleasure as the fish struggled against the spear, he waded into the river to retrieve his catch. The urge to check on his competition was strong, but he resisted, quickly put the fish into the bag provided, and picked up another spear. He edged slowly to his right and peering intently into the water, thought he saw a large trout swimming lazily in an area shadowed by a nearby tree. Yes, he was sure of it now. Harder to see in the shadow, and a little farther away, but the fish was barely moving—so it could be an easier target. Risky, he thought, but a chance he had to take. He moved as far to the right in his assigned position as he could, raised the spear to his shoulder, adjusted the tilt, reared back, aimed carefully, and let the spear fly. Sprinting toward the target area, he clamped his lips together to restrain a cry of triumph as he saw his spear had hit the fish right through its gills and speared it to the shallow river bottom. He retrieved his spear with the wriggling fish attached and walked with long strides back to his position. As he placed the fish in the bag, he shook his head in amazement as he noted the second fish was much larger than the first. He signaled one of the judges, and then allowed himself to glance at his competition. A few appeared confident, but Graben was certain he saw frowns on at least one or two faces.

The spear fishing trials over, the competitors returned to the field for some refreshment while the judges compared scores. Each young man exclaimed that he was certain he had caught the biggest fish. As Graben joked and laughed with the others, his mind was on that big fellow he had speared in the shadows. That was the biggest fish he had ever seen; but he did not share this bit of information. He looked up toward Nunatak Peak, assured The Always was smiling on him.

When the judges had reached agreement on the winner, all the competitors gathered in the center of the field for the awards. One of the judges, Esker's father, Elek, had been selected to make the presentations. He held up his hand for silence and the crowd grew silent. Graben felt and heard the pulse in his neck beating, and was certain those around him could hear it also.

"People of Drumlin," Elek began, "this year's competition was very close. These young men will make fine hunters and providers for their clans." He paused as the villagers broke into cheers and applause, and Graben joined the other competitors as they waved to their fellow villagers. Holding up his hand again, Elek continued, "I will announce the winners of the individual matches, and then will pronounce the name of the young man the judges have decided best deserves to wear the victor's wreath and take possession of the Arrowhead of Golith for the upcoming year."

Graben and Tor were both awarded medals that carried an image of a spear and target for placing first in these matches. These, and all the medals presented, were hammered out by the blacksmiths of the village. Next, medals with the appropriate images were presented to Ogen, winner of the axe throwing and knife-throwing matches. When Graben received his medals for the bow and arrow match and the tree-climbing match, he marched proudly over to where Tephra was sitting and with a smug grin, held them up where she could see. She smiled broadly and waved her garland in response.

"If Graben is ready to join us again—" began Elek, which brought on good-natured laughter from the villagers, "—I'll announce the winner of the spear fishing competition." Graben grinned and waved at the crowd as he walked back to stand with the others. "It seems we have another tie," Elek announced. "Once again it is Graben and Tor!" After the cheers had died down and the medals presented, Elek teased, "Graben, with your hands busy planting, when have you had time to practice spearing fish and still court one of the prettiest maidens in Drumlin?" There was more laughter from the villagers, and Graben looked over in time to see the deep blush that formed in Tephra's cheeks. He frowned slightly as he noticed she was not smiling, and had lowered her head.

Graben was not surprised when the judges announced Noll was the winner of the footrace, and after he received his medal, he could hear the anxious whispers of the crowd. Softly at first, then louder and louder the crowd chanted, "Golith, Golith, Golith!" After a nod of encouragement from the other judges, Elek held up his hand and when the chanting ceased, he cleared his throat and began, "I say again, the competition was close, very close. But adding each young hunter's points in each of the matches, we agree that the winner's garland and the Arrowhead of Golith must be awarded this year to—Graben, of the Earth-Tillers!" Graben threw his head back and raised his fists triumphantly over his head. As the villagers stood cheering their approval, Graben watched as one of the judges trotted over to where Tephra stood. He knew that according to Drumlin customs, the judge was asking Tephra if she remembered the words of the proclamation and would crown the new Golith. Graben stood, legs spread, fists on his hips, shoulders back, filled with pride as she nodded her assent and walked with the judge to where he and Elek waited.

Elek handed the garland to Tephra. Graben knelt on one knee, and looked up into Tephra's lovely face as she placed it on his head. Elek placed the coveted arrowhead in Tephra's hand and she tapped him on his right shoulder with it, saying, "I, Tephra of the Clan of Shepherds, by authority of the honorable judges of this year's Golith Huntsman Trials, proclaim that you, Graben of the Clan of Earth-Tillers, are Golith for this season. Arise and claim the Crystal Arrowhead, carved by the great Golith himself. May you carry it with honor; may it bring honor to your clan."

He stood and as he took the Crystal Arrowhead from her hand, leaned close to her and whispered in her ear, "Remember, now I *am* Golith to you!" He then turned to where her father sat with the men of his clan and asked politely, "Tarn of the Clan of Shepherds, will you grant your permission for Golith to escort your daughter, Tephra, to the celebration with his clan?"

Tarn stood and waved his permission, and the new Golith grinned as he took Tephra's arm and proudly walked with her towards his clan's yard for their celebration of his victory. He lifted the arrowhead and waved it towards the villagers, savoring their cheers and the fact that the most desireable maiden in the village was walking beside him. The earth-tillers clan welcomed Tephra warmly, as was natural, for she had visited the clan many times as she and Graben were growing up.

Tephra offered to help Graben's mother with cleaning up after the meal, but Vena shook her head and insisted she go be with Graben, where he was telling once again how he had speared the large trout. When the moon was large and bright over the distant hills, Graben escorted Tephra home, taking the long path near Mosken Lake. His sister, Beda, served as their chaperon, following at the proper distance behind them. As they reached the lake, Graben paused a moment, pointing out the reflection of the moon upon the water.

"It is a beautiful night," Tephra sighed.

"Tephra," Graben whispered, standing close, his hand on her arm, "tomorrow night we will be betrothed."

"And today you were Golith, just as you said!" Tephra said with a nervous laugh, attempting to keep the conversation casual.

Graben took her hand and whispered in a voice husky with emotion, "Only the day of our mating could bring me more joy than this day."

To hear him speak of their mating day in such a tone made her feel uncomfortable. She turned her head to look down the trail toward her dwelling, cleared her throat and stammered, "It-it is getting late, and—and tomorrow is the Festival Feast and the Ceremonial Dances. I—I should get some rest."

As they turned from the path along the lake toward Tephra's dwelling, Graben gave a low chuckle and said, "When I saw you dance at the Ceremony last spring, I knew I had to ask your father for courting privileges. I had known you since we were babes, but I did not think you could grow up to be so graceful or so lovely."

Tephra was glad that the only light was from the few torches along the village paths and that the deep blush on her cheeks was hidden from him. Her emotions were conflicted and she nervously chewed on her lower lip as she struggled with how to reply to Graben's words. To Tephra's relief, they had reached her dwelling and she was spared from having to say anything. Graben bowed and with a proud smile said, "The great Golith bids his lovely maiden a good night."

As Tephra lay on her sleep mat, she pushed aside the memory of Graben's words by mentally reviewing the added steps of the dances she would perform the next day. She had diligently practiced all the steps, and knew them so well that the other dancers depended on her to keep them in step. Still, there was always that fluttery feeling in her stomach before any of the ritual dances, even though this was her third year dancing at the festivals. As much as she loved to dance, she had to admit she was still somewhat uncomfortable dancing before the entire village.

CHAPTER

3

The next morning began the preparations for the Feast. Throughout the village, the maidens wove field flowers into garlands that would crown their braids, while the young men hung branches fragrant with blossoms on the tall posts surrounding the clearing where the villagers would gather. The Hammada Stone, the large flat stone in the center of the clearing, was encircled with torches of sheep's fat scented with fragrant oils. The men brought tables to the clearing that would hold the food for the feast, and they carried the two vats of wine provided by the vine-growers clan. Near twilight, the villagers gathered in a clearing on the north side of the village where they shared a communal meal of lamb stew, honeyed wine, bread seasoned with special herbs, and a variety of other foods prepared by the matrons of the village.

Strummers began a slow rhythmic tune on their varied instruments fashioned from gourds, sheep's entrails, and skins. The ceremonial dancers—Tephra, Olivine, Mica, and Siluria—were dressed in white flowing shifts. Their long unbraided tresses were crowned with garlands and colorful ribbons as they danced through the village in tempo with the music. As they drew closer to the clearing, the tempo increased steadily, and by the time the dancers reached the Hammada Stone, they were a whirl of color and fragrance. Each maiden arrived at her designated place around the stone and dropped gracefully to her knees.

When all were in place, the music stopped abruptly, and then the strummers began a slower, more restful tune. The maidens rose from their positions, turned, gracefully stepped up onto the Hammada Stone, and began the ancient Dance of Fertility. The dance represented a prayer that the crops would produce an abundant harvest, and that the wombs of those mated and soon to be mated would produce many healthy children.

The music, which was soft and meditative at first, gradually swelled in volume and tempo, and the movements of the dancers echoed the mood of the music. It ended in an abrupt crescendo as the maidens lightly skipped off the stone and toward the nearby stream while the villagers cheered and applauded. The maidens tossed their garlands upon the water in thanksgiving to The Always for the flowing stream that brought fresh water to the village; then each made her way back to her own dwelling to prepare for the next part of the festivities—except for Tephra.

She felt exhilarated from the dance and remained at the edge of the stream for a while, savoring the feeling of freedom she had experienced while dancing. She smiled, shaking her head as she recalled how nervous she had been about her performance. With a deep sigh of relief, she recalled that after a few steps, her confidence had returned, and she felt assured she had danced and twirled in perfect rhythm to the strummers. Back at the clearing, the musicians had resumed their playing and the villagers clapped out the rhythms as they sang the ancient tunes. As the music reached her ears, Tephra began to sway in time to the rhythm, and then the swaying became dancing. She softly sang along with the villagers as she danced, enjoying the freedom of her unrestrained, impromptu movements along the water's edge. Thoughts of her family waiting for her at the clearing, and her upcoming betrothal to Graben, faded away as she moved her body to the tempo. There was no real rebellion in her; but rather, an overwhelming urge to move to the music that seemed to pulse through her blood as it did through the night air.

"You are graceful, and lovely to watch, even though your movements are not according to custom."

Kame's voice startled Tephra, causing her to whirl about and stumble, then she felt a hand on her arm as Kame reached out to steady her.

"Grandmother!" Tephra gasped, her feeling of freedom replaced by fear and guilt.

"Pray that no one else observed your foolish abandonment of our traditions," Kame said, her voice quite serious. "It would be an insult to your father, and to Graben. I am surprised that you would be so careless, my child! Rearrange your hair."

Ashamed that Kame had witnessed her illicit dancing, and at the same time disappointed that those moments of exhilarating freedom had ended so abruptly, Tephra had nothing to say. She ran her fingers through her hair to brush it back from her face, and simply bowed her head, waiting for the scolding she was certain she would hear.

"All things are done as to a purpose. Nothing that our people do is without guidance, without meaning. There is ritual and a *way* in all we do. You have always known this, child. I will keep your small offense to myself, but I will say again, I am surprised that you would be so careless." Kame paused a moment, then continued, "Yes, yes. You are gifted with grace of movement and loveliness of voice, and it is good that you use them, for The Always bestowed them upon you. However, even such a gift can be used wrongly and bring dishonor. When you were younger, your parents and I had to scold you often for neglecting your chores in favor of practicing the steps you had learned. You are of an age now to be more mindful of your behavior. You will soon take part in the ritual that will begin your sacred betrothal. I am troubled ..." Kame broke off, shaking her head slowly.

Tephra tried to swallow the lump in her throat as tears of remorse formed in her eyes and her hands fell limply at her side. "Dear Grandmother, I am sorry that I have troubled you! It is just that, well, if Graben does claim me as his betrothed, I will no longer be allowed to dance, only to teach the young ones," she said, admitting for the first time, even to herself, a reservation towards her mating. "But, I will attend to my ways so that I will not trouble you again."

"Ah, I am troubled by darker things, dear child. I see things that are to come, fearful things. But the Hammada do not listen. They think I am just a foolish old woman, and that my inner sight is failing me as are my eyes."

"You are not old, Grandmother. You will never be old. You are like the ancients in our folktales. You will live to see my grandchildren! Oh! You look so regal in those robes!" Tephra exclaimed.

"My eyes are getting old, but I'll look upon my great-grandchildren, that much I know," Kame winked, smiled, and hugged her granddaughter in a sudden demonstration of affection as she said, "Now hurry, child, go wash your face. You must change for the Token Ceremony." Tephra kissed her grandmother on the cheek and ran to her dwelling, still feeling the warmth that came over her as she sensed forgiveness in Kame's hug.

Tephra donned a new garment and made her way back to the Hammada Stone where her grandmother and the other members of the Hammada were waiting, all dressed in robes of gold and crimson. The villagers watched in respectful silence as Tephra, Olivine, Siluria, and Mica were each escorted up to the stone dais by their clan's representative to the Hammada. The maidens had changed from their flowing shifts worn during the dance into simpler ones belted with a sash of their clan color, and each maiden carried a token of her clan.

As the girls stood in the center of the kneeling Hammada, Karst intoned, "Apprentices, come forward!" When the apprentices, including Esker, had entered the circle, he admonished them to continue in the work that their clans had trained them to do. He reminded them, "Now that you are full members of your clan, you are honor-bound to carry out your duties faithfully. Never forget that in doing so you please The Always, and bring favor upon the Village of Drumlin. Tephra, Olivine, Mica, and Siluria, you will now hand over your tokens to your apprentices." The maidens did as instructed and Karst intoned, "People of Drumlin, welcome these young maidens as full members of their clans!" The villagers cheered and all of the maidens went to join their respective clans.

Tephra barely heard the words Karst had spoken. Her thoughts kept straying as she tried to absorb the reality that if Graben spoke for her, as she was sure he would, her days as a shepherdess were almost over. She would be spending very little time on the meadows with her sheep, but instead would be going to Kame's dwelling to receive instructions for the Mating Ritual and preparing to be Graben's mate. After their mating, she would assume the responsibilities of a matron of the clan of earth-tillers. As she sat with her clan, she waited with mixed feelings for the part of the ceremony she knew would come next.

Karst stepped to the edge of the stone and asked in his booming voice, "Is there any young man who wishes to claim a maiden as his betrothed? Come forward now and state your intentions."

Tephra was not surprised when Graben was the first to approach the stone dais.

"I, Graben, of the Clan of Earth-tillers, ask to enter into the betrothal ritual with Tephra, maiden of the Clan of Shepherds."

"Have you petitioned the leader of her clan?"

"I have paid the required visits to her family and presented her father with the ritual gifts."

"Tarn, leader of the Clan of Shepherds and father of Tephra, come forward and grant or deny your blessing to the betrothal."

She watched as her father stepped up to the stone dais, took the blessing-stick from Karst, and struck Graben lightly on the shoulder as he said, "Graben of the Clan of Earth-Tillers, you have the blessing of the Clan of Shepherds." He turned to Tephra and motioned for her to come up to the stone. When she stood before him, he struck her in the same manner and said, "My daughter, I bless you and bid you into the care of your grandmother, the wise Kame, as she guides you through the final preparations for the Mating Ritual. May you serve Graben and his clan as faithfully as your mother, Caldera, has served me and mine."

Tarn handed the blessing-stick back to Karst, and resumed his place with his clan. Graben, following a long-established custom, stepped up to Tephra and untied her sash from around her waist. He then knotted it around his upper arm, and raised his arm to show the village. "I, Graben of the Clan of Earth-tillers," he shouted as his gaze traveled over the villagers, "proudly claim Tephra as my betrothed. Let no man touch her from this day forward."

"Now that you are betrothed, Drumlin daughter," proclaimed Karst, "you will not touch or be touched by, speak to or be spoken to by, any man until after the Mating Ritual is completed and you are presented to the village as Tephra, mate of Graben of the Clan of Earth-tillers."

Tephra then crossed the Hammada Stone to stand next to her grandmother. Kame draped her own prayer shawl over Tephra's head and shoulders and led her to the opposite edge of the Hammada Stone. There Tephra watched as another young man approached the stone and called out, "I, Ogen, of the Clan of Tool-makers, ask to enter into formal courtship with Olivine, of the Clan of Orchard-tenders."

Karst questioned Ogen as he had Graben, "Have you petitioned the leader of her clan?"

"Yes, I have paid the visits to Olivine's family as required, and I have presented her father with the ritual gifts."

Olivine's father was summoned to the dais and asked to grant or deny his blessing for Ogen to enter into formal courtship with his daughter. After he gave the blessing, Olivine turned toward Tephra, grinned happily, and walked with Ogen to be received by his clan.

"Are there any more young men to claim a betrothal or to plead for courtship privilege?" Karst inquired.

Two young men petitioned to enter the beginning courtship ritual with Siluria, of the clan of weavers. One was Noll, whose clan planted and harvested millet, and the other, Tor, of the clan of fishermen. Both young men had competed with Graben in the Huntsman Trials. Siluria, once an awkward, timid girl with pale, stringy hair, had blossomed over the long winter months into a lovely young woman. Her hair was now a shimmering golden color; her once-thin body now showed the prospect of perfectly proportioned curves.

Karst called the maiden's father, Topo, to the dais. "Honorable Topo, your daughter is honored by the request of these two young men. Will you allow them both the first privileges of courtship, until the time when one is deemed more worthy to receive formal courtship rights?" Topo walked to each young man in turn, and placing his hands on their shoulders, gave his consent, and then escorted his daughter to their clan's place on the hillside.

Tephra, watching from the other side of the Hammada Stone, breathed a sympathetic sigh for her friend. She suspected Siluria was dismayed that Noll would be a petitioner, even though he was one of the most handsome males in the village. He had often teased her during their childhood, sometimes with a touch of cruelty.

The third young man, Talus, of the clan of woodsmen, approached the stone dais, putting forth his petition to enter formal courtship with Mica. Karst called upon the maiden's father, Lahar, to give his consent. He did so, and allowed Mica to join Talus and his clan.

Karst now turned to where Tephra and Kame were waiting at the edge of the stone, speaking the words that awakened Tephra to the gravity of the moment, "Young maiden of Drumlin, you will now begin the sacred Time of Preparation. The prayers of the entire village go with you." She swallowed hard, hoping to rid her throat of the lump that had formed upon hearing Karst's command.

"Come child, it is time to begin." Kame spoke softly to her granddaughter as she lifted a torch from its holder at the edge of the stone dais. Eolia, another matron and one of the Hammada, joined Kame as she led Tephra down the path to Kame's dwelling.

Once inside, Kame motioned the now-betrothed maiden to take a seat on the mat she had prepared for her. She addressed her granddaughter solemnly, elaborating on the words of Karst, "You are now betrothed. To prepare for the Mating Ritual, to be certain that you are chaste and untouched, you will have nothing to do with any male, not even your betrothed. You may not greet the male villagers or acknowledge their greeting, and of course, they will not touch you in any manner. You are permitted, of course, to speak with your father and brother. The day of your next woman-flow, you will stay here with Eolia and I until you have had the cleansing bath, then you will go to the Caves of Solitude for the solemn preparation for the Mating Ritual. You are to rest here tonight. Tomorrow morning we will escort you to the dwelling of your parents, and you will continue to be a help to them and your clan during the day."

Eolia continued, "At night you will return here for instruction and preparation for the Mating Ritual. It is late. Rest a while now, while we seek unity with the Always." Tephra reclined on the mat and watched the prayer ritual. The ceremonial herbs—special herbs known only to the Hammada—were crushed and heated, creating a type of incense. A tea was brewed with the herbs and the two women sipped it slowly as they alternately murmured the prayers. Tired from all the activities of the day, yet anxious about the days to come, Tephra closed her eyes and listened to the prayers of the two elder matrons. Allowing the rhythm of their murmuring to wash over all her disquieting thoughts, she was finally able to fall asleep.

The next morning, after breakfast with Kame, Tephra was escorted to her family's dwelling. She changed into her day shift, applied the esolis butter to her skin, and took her staff to join Esker and Creta on the hills tending the sheep. They did their work as usual, and when the sheep were returned to their pen, Tephra helped her mother prepare the evening meal, ate with her family, played with her younger sister, and sat and talked with Sedi—just as before.

"So, who will I tease now?" her brother asked as he reached out and gently pulled her braid. "Breccia? Mama fusses if I tease her!"

"Yes, I know. Mama protects her too well. It has been so since the fever," Tephra said, referring to the fever that struck their five-year-old sister last summer. Several children of the village had become ill with an unexplained fever, yet all but Breccia had recovered fully. The child still had not regained her former strength, even though the Hammada had summoned the Always and the village healer had brought several herbs and draughts known to cure a fever and to restore health. Caldera rarely allowed the child to play in the common yard with the other children her age unless the weather was ideal. That left Sedi to amuse the child while Caldera took care of the household chores. A special bond was beginning to form between the two despite their age difference.

"Do you think she will miss me when I am...?" Tephra paused, finding it difficult to complete the sentence. She knew that in a week or two her woman-flow would come, and she would leave to go to the

Caves to prepare for being mated. It was difficult to imagine that so very soon she would no longer be a part of this household.

"When you are mated to Graben?" Sedi said quietly, completing her sentence for her. "But the clans are close. You and Graben will be with us often."

"I suppose, but, it will be different," Tephra looked down at her hands.

"Yes, for you will have your own dwelling to care for," Sedi stated, then continued jokingly, his voice cackling, "and you'll be an old matron, and then will become an old crone, frightening all the children! Ah-hee!"

Tephra giggled, "Ah, Sedi! You are always able to tease me and make me laugh! And I will come and help mother with the potions for your leg, and we will still have our talks, and we will laugh together at the comings and goings of our villagers that you see as you sit outside your dwelling." Her time with Sedi made her feel a bit better, and Tephra was determined to enjoy the next couple of weeks with her family and her sheep.

CHAPTER
4

Late one morning, less than three weeks after her betrothal to Graben, Tephra quietly approached Kame and announced that her woman-time had come.

"Ah, it is a good time," Kame responded and then continued, her tone serious and low, "Tonight you will return here before sunset. You will not have your evening meal with your family. You will remain here in my dwelling until your time is completed. After your cleansing bath, at midnight while the village sleeps, Eolia and I will lead you to Cambria Falls. Go now to your mother and tell her that you have entered the sacred Time of Preparation so that she can complete her own preparations for your Day of Mating. Go to Esker and give her a blessing, for you will no longer be with her on the hills. Now you leave your childhood behind. This time of preparation is your journey toward true womanhood. Mind all that you have been taught, and be attentive to each part of the journey. Only then can you bring joy to your mate, and contentment to yourself."

Tephra nodded in understanding, but as she walked to her family's shelter, she tried to make sense of the overflow of conflicting emotions she was experiencing. She felt anxiety, which was not unexpected for a young Drumlin maiden just days before her mating; but she also felt doubt, and more than she knew was appropriate.

"I should feel nothing but happiness," she thought, absently chewing at her bottom lip. "Graben has much respect in the village. He has always brought honor to his clan, and my own clan holds him in high regard. My closest friends tell me I am the envy of many maidens." She swallowed, took a deep breath and blew it out, trying to force all feelings of uncertainty from her mind as she arrived at her family's dwelling, aware that this was a time for saying goodbye.

She found her mother in the cooking area, cleaning vegetables with help from Breccia. "Sister!" the child called happily when she saw Tephra, and began chattering, "See? I am helping mother with the vegetables. And soon I will go to the hills with the sheep like you did. And I will sing the psalm-songs for them, but I will need your help on some. But don't worry—I do remember two of them very well. Would you like to hear me sing them?"

Tephra knelt and held out her arms to her little sister. The two embraced, Tephra fighting back tears as she stroked the child's red-gold curls. "No, not now my lamb. I have instructions from Grandmother Kame. I must talk to Mother, and then go to Esker on the hillside."

"It is alright. I know," Breccia said, looking into her big sister's face, "You are to be mated. Mother has been preparing, and I have helped her by taking care of Sedi."

Caldera looked at Tephra and smiled, then turned to her youngest child, "Yes, our little Breccia is really growing up. Now, Breccia, go practice your songs for Sedi. He knows them almost as well as Tephra."

Breccia kissed Tephra on the cheek, and skipped off to sing to her brother.

Tephra stood and Caldera quickly enfolded her in her arms. Touching their foreheads together, Caldera said softly, "It is your time, yes? Go to Sedi, then to Esker. I will send your father to you on the hillside."

Tephra could not hold back the tears, letting them stream down her face. She heard her mother sob, trying to hold back her own tears. "Oh, Mother!" Tephra choked, wanting to confide her doubts to her mother, but not knowing how and afraid to try, afraid to disappoint.

"My child!" Caldera said softly, "It is hard to give my first-born daughter to another, although your father and I could not be prouder of you, and happy that you have been chosen by one of Drumlin's finest young men. Now I know how my mother felt when your father chose me as his life-mate. I know you will be a good mate, for you have been a good daughter." Caldera held Tephra at arm's length and closing her eyes, whispered, "May The Always be with you, and grant that you and Graben find love together." Then, with a shaky smile, she stroked Tephra's face and said, "Wipe your tears, although they are natural on such a day, and go with my love, my Tephra."

Tephra went to the wash basin, splashed water on her face, and dried it with the cloth her mother handed her. She then walked to the porch where Sedi reclined with a poultice on his leg. Breccia was sitting in a sunny part of the porch, playing with her dolls made of wood and clothed with scraps from Caldera's sewing basket. Sedi looked up as Tephra entered the porch and made room for her to sit on the cot where he reclined. She sat down and he pulled her head down to his shoulder in an affectionate gesture, then gave a slight yank to her braids. Placing a hand on each side of her face, he turned her head to look at her. "Are those tears, when so near your mating day? Ah! Women!" he jokingly scoffed.

Tephra forced a smile and replied, "It's all Mother's fault! She got all weepy remembering her own time of betrothal."

"So, mating day will be soon?"

"Yes, soon. I go now to Esker, and then to stay with Grandmother Kame."

"Be sure to find me at the Mating Feast," Sedi reminded her, "I won't be able to join in the circle." At the Mating Feast, the villagers formed a circle around the newly mated couple. The couple stood in the center as the circle of villagers danced around them, singing a psalm of blessing.

"Of course I will find you! And you know Graben will bring you a cup of his uncle's wine!" Tephra kissed her brother on his forehead, blew a kiss to Breccia, and made her way to the hillside to share the news with Esker.

She knew she would find Esker and the sheep in the grassy meadow below the hills. Tephra reached the top of the hill nearest the meadow and paused to look out over the flock. "This is my last day in this meadow as a maiden," she thought. "I will miss walking over these hills to this meadow. I will miss being here with Esker and Creta." Tears moistened her eyes, and she shook her head in annoyance at herself for thinking sad thoughts. She recalled how Olivine was already looking forward to the day she would be betrothed to Ogen and preparing for their mating day. Taking a deep breath Tephra walked down into the meadow and to her cousin.

"I saw you on the hill and waved to you," Esker said as Tephra approached her, "but you seemed to be looking far off into the distance. Thinking of Graben and your Mating Day?"

Ignoring the teasing tone of her young cousin, Tephra simply smiled and said, "Thinking of the blessing I must give to you today, for soon I enter into the most solemn preparation time." She placed her hands on Esker's head, and whispered a shepherd's blessing. "May The Always guide you to fresh waters and to the greenest grasses, and may The Always keep all danger from you as you tend the sheep entrusted to your care."

Tephra kissed her cousin on each cheek, and then turned and walked toward Kame's dwelling before her eyes became filled with tears again. She had only gone a few paces when she saw her father coming towards her. She stopped and took a deep breath to compose herself so that he would not see her tears.

"My daughter, your mother tells me you will soon be going to the caves," Tarn said tenderly. Tephra nodded, and Tarn placed his hands on her shoulders, pulled her to him, and leaned his head so that their foreheads were touching. After a moment he removed his hands, took a step back, and said, "The next time I look at your lovely face, you will be a mated woman." Placing his hand on her head, he closed his eyes and whispered, "The blessing and protection of The Always be upon you, my daughter." Then he turned and walked back toward the sheep pens.

As Tephra watched him walk away, she felt her chest tighten with emotions she could barely control. However, she knew Kame was waiting for her, so she walked quickly to her grandmother's dwelling.

There, she and her grandmother shared a light meal and spent the evening in meditation as was prescribed by the laws of the village.

Tephra tried to be attentive as Kame gently instructed her concerning the rituals she would follow in the next few days. "You will spend two nights and two days in the Caves of Solitude behind the falls. During the two days in seclusion and meditation in the caves, you must faithfully complete all of the prayers and rituals at their appointed times. Just before midday of the third day, I will come with your mother to the cave. We will anoint you and dress you in your Mating Garments." Tephra listened expressionless, as Kame continued her instructions. "You will walk between your mother and me to the dwelling Graben has been preparing for you. At the door of the dwelling, you will be pledged to each other for life, with your mother and me as witnesses. Many villagers will be surrounding the Hammada Stone, and led by Karst, will chant the ancient mating prayers. After the setting of the sun, after Graben has fully claimed you as his mate, you and he will dress in colorful ceremonial robes, and he will escort you to the Mating Feast prepared in your honor. Graben will address the villagers, saying, 'Greetings fellow Drumlins! My mate, Tephra, now of the Clan of Earth-tillers, bids you welcome to our dwelling!' For the next several days, villagers will pay brief visits to your dwelling, bringing small gifts. You and your mate will, as is our custom, serve your guests berry wine and fruit-filled cakes that are now being prepared by the matrons of Graben's clan."

Tephra nodded that she understood what would take place during the Mating Ritual. However, although she understood the ritual, she wondered how she was supposed to rid herself of the doubts she was experiencing in only two days and two nights. "I will pray to The Always," she thought to herself. "I will meditate as Grandmother has taught me so that I can bring joy and contentment to—" she hesitated, and then swallowing hard, her mind formed the name, "—Graben."

CHAPTER 5

On the night Tephra was to go to the Cave of Solitude, Eolia arrived at Kame's dwelling. Tephra and Kame had just returned from the ritual cleansing bath, and now Eolia and Kame would participate in the ritual of drinking tea and chanting prayers for the soon-to-be mated couple. Tephra sat quietly as they did this, observing the older women with a sense of acceptance. She was dressed only in a simple robe that represented this brief stage between maiden and matron. At midnight, Kame motioned to Tephra that it was time to begin. Eolia picked up a basket from the corner of the room, and the three walked silently to Mosken Lake. The night was clear, and the moon was bright, so there was no need of a torch. The maiden and the two matrons approached the edge of the lake where several small canoes were moored to a narrow wooden dock.

Eolia placed a hand on Tephra's shoulder as she explained what Tephra would find in the cave. "The cave has three chambers. In the one with the spring, you will find a woolen coverlet and a simple shift. There is also some hay for you to rest upon."

Kame motioned for Tephra to disrobe and gestured toward one of the canoes. Even in the light of the moon, Kame could see the deep blush on Tephra's face and neck as she dropped her robe from her shoulders and handed it to her grandmother. Kame nodded her approval. Tephra had been made aware that this disrobing at the lake was a prelude to the Mating Ritual. After the vows at the door, Graben would take her into their dwelling. Disrobing symbolized shedding the clothing of childhood and entering the Cave of Solitude where a maiden puts on the clothing of preparation. When she and Graben are mated, she will don the garment of a mated woman—a mark of respect for all to see.

As Tephra knelt in the canoe, she looked up into Kame's eyes as she was handed the basket Eolia had brought. Again Kame nodded with approval, proclaiming, "You are lovely, and Graben will be assured The Always has favored him with such a mate." Closing her eyes, Kame continued in a low, chanting voice to give further instructions to Tephra. "Away you must go. Behind the waterfall are two caves. Row to the right side of the falls. Enter the cave there. Alone you must be. Aware of your true self you will become. In your solitude The Always can teach you. You are frightened and anxious, and that is as it should be. The joining of a man and a woman is to be with much thought and prayer." Then in a softer tone, she said. "Ah, but you are shivering in the late air. Go, my child, to the comfort of the Cave of Solitude."

Kame handed Tephra an oar for the canoe, then joined Eolia on the path. Eolia placed her hand on the other woman's arm. "My old friend, something troubles you?"

Kame turned to gaze back towards the lake. "Perhaps I am a foolish old woman like some are saying, but as she knelt in the canoe, my dear Tephra looked into my eyes and for a moment I felt a tremor of unease."

"Hah!" Eolia responded, "Everyone knows she is your pet. Your heart trembles to see her grown up! But wait till she and Graben present you with grandchildren!"

Kame forced a smile, "Your words may be true, old friend. Ah! This night air, this late time! My old bones need the comfort of my mat, where I will fall asleep saying my prayers!"

Kame and Eolia remained silent on their return, until they reached where the path divided. Placing their hands on each other's shoulders and giving the customary blessing for a restful night, each went to her own dwelling, ready to sleep after the draining ritual and the late hour. However, contrary to her words, Kame did not fall asleep right away.

She stayed awake until morning's light, asking The Always for guidance and protection for her granddaughter.

The abandon Tephra exhibited in her dancing had sent a shiver of warning through Kame, even though she had to admit, at least to herself, that Tephra's movements were very graceful and a pleasure to watch. And then, what did she see in Tephra's eyes as she knelt in the canoe that sent a second tremor? Was Tephra having doubts about being mated, or about being mated to Graben? She cherished the girl above her other grandchildren, for reasons she could not name, and felt a special protectiveness towards her.

CHAPTER 6

Dipping the oars into the darkening waters of the lake, Tephra paddled toward the right side of the softly falling waters. She knew that every betrothed maiden underwent this same ritual, but still she felt abandoned and frightened, and had to blink back tears. There was a mystery about the caves, and tonight it was heightened by a soft mist above the water. As she neared the falls, Tephra maneuvered the canoe far to the right, as she had been instructed by Kame, and placed the basket on a ledge. Thick vines grew from the rocks near the falls, and she grasped one to pull herself up onto the ledge that was just above the level of the water, and then used the vine to tie off the canoe. Easing her way behind the cascade of water, she found the cave Kame had described. She had to stoop only slightly to enter, but after a few steps, she found she could stand upright. The central chamber was not large, so Tephra was able to walk the depth of it in a dozen or so paces. It was wider across, tapering to the two small caves on each side. Crystals grew in the rear of the central chamber, giving off an eerie light, which illuminated a good part of the chamber, and even penetrated somewhat into the smaller adjoining chambers. Tephra placed the basket near an underground spring that bubbled in one of the adjoining chambers. Shivering as the night air chilled her bare skin, she found the shift and coverlet Eolia had said would be there. She quickly donned the knee-length shift and sighed in relief as her chilled body slowly began to warm.

Wrapping the coverlet around her body for more warmth, Tephra knelt by the spring and inspected the contents of the basket Kame and Eolia had given her before they left the lake area. Inside were a loaf of bread wrapped in large cabbage leaves to keep it fresh, a small earthen jar of honey, another jar filled with dried peaches, a small basket of fresh berries and an earthenware cup. At first, she wondered why there was no cheese or boiled eggs, but then considered that since she would be spending all the time meditating and praying, the supplies were sufficient.

Tephra sat on a large flat stone sipping water she dipped from the spring and thinking of Kame's warnings. She thought of her cousin Esker, and the sheep that were once her responsibility. She thought of her mother Caldera, and the lessons she had learned from her: how to weave the wool into soft threads; how to fashion a broom that would sweep the floor of their dwelling smooth without raising the dust; how to dig for the roots that when brewed would heal a bellyache and those that would heal a fever, and how to tell the difference. Tephra thought about the lessons, too, that she learned from the matrons of the village while she was shut away once a month—lessons concerning the Mating Ritual that aroused curiosity mixed with a little apprehension. After a while, her stomach rumbled and, although she had little appetite, she nibbled on a few berries and a small chunk of bread. She then arranged the pile of hay into a heap that would accommodate her body, wrapped the coverlet around her, and lay down upon her new resting place. Tired from all the emotions of the day, and the late hour, she had very little time to reflect on the purpose of her seclusion in these caves—to be open to The Always—before she drifted into sleep.

The next morning, Tephra awoke at first disoriented by her new surroundings; then as her eyes adjusted to the dim light inside the cave, she remembered where she was and recalled her purpose for coming to the Caves of Solitude. Stretching and sitting cross-legged on the pile of hay, she folded her hands and began reciting the poem-prayers asking for guidance from The Always. When those were completed, she went to the underground spring to wash her face and hands before eating a piece of bread dipped in honey and a handful of the fresh berries. As she tasted their juicy sweetness, she recalled the many times she, Sedi, and Graben had picked berries on the other side of the lake. She recalled the time Graben had playfully smeared her face with berry juice, which had dripped onto her shift, and Mother had scolded her for staining it. "That was a long time ago," she whispered to herself, "long before I knew he wanted me for his mate." She stood staring out over the lake as she thought of how in two short days her life would change.

After a time, she realized she should return to her prayers. Carrying the woolen coverlet and the earthenware cup out to the ledge at the entrance to the main cave, she filled the cup with water from the edge of the waterfall. After draining the contents, she filled it again, this time carrying the cup of water and the coverlet into the chamber of glowing crystals. Following Eolia's instructions, she spread the coverlet on the floor of the cave and sat cross-legged upon it, placing the cup of water nearby. Taking a deep breath, Tephra placed her hands palms up on her knees, and reverently began the ancient chants that asked for blessings upon her mating. She paused a moment in amazement as she heard her voice, sounding beautifully soft and reverent, echoing eerily in the shallow cavern. As she gazed at the glowing crystals, she was suddenly aware that her mother and her grandmother, and so many other women had sat here before these same softly glowing crystals and had chanted these same prayers. It was an emotional moment and she felt her eyes fill with tears. Blinking away the tears, she continued her meditations until her stomach growled from hunger and her legs began to numb from being so long in one position. Rising from her prayer position, she went to the ledge and stepped out to observe the position of the sun, marking the progress of the prayer rituals. She was pleased to note that her meditations were done as prescribed.

That day and night, Tephra followed the meditation rituals with no interruptions, and little distractions, softly singing the prayers with deep reverence, until mid-morning of the second day. During a rather long meditation, a worried bleating noise interrupted her prayer. The sound was like that of a frightened lamb, alerting her shepherdess instincts. She stood and stretched, longing for the thick sheepskin mats and the warm woolen coverlets back in her family dwelling. She walked out to the edge of the cave, and warily stepped across the ledge to the falling water. Seeing nothing, she filled her cupped hands, drank several gulps of the cool water, and splashed some on her face. Suddenly the tremulous bleating started again. Shielding her eyes with her hand, she tried to see across the lake, but still could not see the source of the sound in the bright sunlight. The rumblings of her stomach caused her to return to the shelter of the cave, where she had a meal of bread and dried peaches. Her hunger satisfied, she went back to the crystals, ready to focus on the rest of the day's meditations.

Resuming her prayer posture, she placed her hands on her knees and, in a soft voice, continued the ancient chants for guidance. Again and again, the distant bleating of the animal broke her contemplation. She began to wonder if she was imagining the sound. She folded her hands together, bowed in apology to The Always, and then resumed her chanting more loudly, hoping to drown out the noise. Her prayers were continually interrupted and resumed in the same manner. After several frustrating attempts to achieve the desired level of meditation, Tephra admitted defeat, arose from her position of prayer and returned to the cave entrance.

Tephra again looked all around the surrounding area, wondering where the distressed cries of the animal were coming from. With the soft echoes of the valley, the sound was hard to locate, but she was certain it was nearby. The shadows began to deepen in the valley around Mosken Lake, and Tephra quickly noted places where a lamb might wander. There were only a few and she eliminated most of them as they were too near the Boreal Forests and therefore forbidden to her. By now the animal's cries were more insistent and Tephra was convinced it was not only frightened, but in pain. Once again, her eyes scanned the slopes for any sign, and then she saw it—a tiny patch of white entangled in the vines and brush on a narrow terrace, dangerously near the edge. Her breath caught in her throat and she prayed it would stop its thrashing about before it fell. If the lamb fell, she hoped it would fall into the water where she might be able to rescue it, and not onto the sharp rocks of the terraced slopes.

Tephra returned to the cave and attempted to resume her prayers, but it was useless. She even moved to the chamber with the spring, thinking the sound of bubbling water would distract her from the bleating sounds. Still, the distressed cries of the animal prevented her from the concentration necessary for meditation. She tried all of the methods she had been taught—letting the sound become part of a mantra, acknowledging it as a distraction and forcing her mind to go beyond it, even attempting to sing so loudly as to drown out the sound of the animal; but none of them worked. She had been taught to care for and love animals, especially sheep. No amount of prayer could cause her to surrender her shepherdess instincts. Finally, she abandoned the ritual prayers, and prayed that somehow the lamb might free itself. She desperately wanted to go after the lamb, but that would mean abandoning the Mating Preparation Ritual.

As the cries of the animal became weaker, Tephra went again to the ledge behind the falls. Gazing across the lake, she could still see the animal, and it seemed to be even more entangled in the briars and vines. A new worry crossed her mind—wolves. As darkness descended, so would they. It was still early enough, she reasoned, that she should be able to reach the lamb and get it and herself to safety before dark. She could care for the animal overnight, then, as she knew no one would be in the lake area the next morning, the morning of her mating day, she could row the lamb to the shore near the pasture where it would stand a better chance of surviving. Tephra remembered the trails that led from the far pasture up the terraced slope of the low mountain. She felt certain that she could row to the ledge nearest the pasture, and with the aid of the thick vines, climb up quickly and rescue the lamb. It would take too long to navigate the winding trails of the terraced slope up to where the lamb was ensnared, but she could use the trails to descend quickly enough once she had the animal. She said a prayer of apology to The Always for breaking her meditation, as well as one for help in rescuing the animal, and climbed into the canoe that had brought her to the caves.

Tephra rowed quickly to the edge of the terraced slopes and tied off the canoe using one of the vines. She was easily able to climb up using the vines, and was grateful for the strength and agility she had developed as a dancer. Once she reached the lamb, she cooed to it softly and stroked the back of its head, calming it enough to untangle the briars and vines that held it. Cradling the animal in her arms, she began the trek down the sloping trail to where the canoe was tied. She was feeling confident she would find her way back to the cave and be able to care for the animal when the path ended abruptly, blocked by mounds of rocks and dirt. She realized the earlier heavy rains must have caused a small landslide, leaving her with no way to descend to the canoe and back to the caves, except perhaps the way she had come—using the vines.

Looking over the ledge, she knew it would be difficult to descend the rocky, vine-covered slope while holding an injured and frightened lamb. On the first try, the lamb had almost wriggled free from her arms as she tried to get a firmer grasp on a vine. When she secured her hold on the animal, she unintentionally loosened her grip on the vine, and slid downward a few feet. Her knee slammed into a jagged rock and she cried out in pain. Frightened and hurt, fighting back tears, she eased herself onto a nearby ledge. Flattening her back against the rock wall, she sobbed from both relief and pain.

Once she was safely seated on the ledge, and had eased her own shaking from the near fall, she attempted to calm the still frightened lamb. As Tephra petted the lamb and sang to it, her soothing voice calmed it, allowing her to focus more clearly on its injuries. It looked a bit odd, somehow different from the lambs in her own flocks, and its wool felt course compared to that of her lambs. There were deep scratches on its legs and shoulders from the briars, but nothing severe, even though some cuts were still oozing blood and fluid. Now that the lamb had quieted somewhat, Tephra concentrated on their situation. Her knee was lacerated and becoming increasingly painful, her hands were raw from the rough vines, and her body bruised and scratched from the near-treacherous fall. Somehow she had to get down to the lake and back to the cave behind the waterfall where she could tend the animal's wounds as well as her own, complete the day's prayers, and make reparation for abandoning them.

"I do not know how you came to be on this ledge, strange little one. If you can be still, maybe I can find our way down," Tephra said to the animal. She recalled that when Sedi and Graben were younger, they and several other boys had found a second trail, narrower than the one used for berry picking. They would take the trail to reach an area above the deeper part of the lake, and would use the vines to swing out over the lake, let go of the vines, and plunge into the deep part of the lake. Hoping to find the trail, Tephra continued to talk to the animal in soothing tones while inching her way along the ledge, feeling for secure footing. She reached an old, twisted pine tree that grew out from the weathered rocks. There was just enough space between the tree and the rock wall to allow her to slip through. Once past the tree, the ledge became wider and began to slope slightly downwards. Tephra breathed a sigh of relief as there was a little less stress on her knee, and she thought perhaps that the downward slope meant she was going in the right direction. The scrub trees grew thicker, and soon Tephra could no longer see the lake through them. She continued to walk along the rocky path as it leveled out, stopping every now and then to rest as her wounded and bleeding knee became more painful with each step.

The worry of being on the rocky ledge after dark and the fear she would not complete the ordered prayers and meditations of the day kept her moving along, with the hope that she would soon make her way back down to Mosken Lake. Even if she did not end up near the canoe, she was a good swimmer, and thought perhaps that the cool water of the lake would feel soothing to her injured knee. For a very brief moment, she thought she would have to leave the animal and climb down using the vines. She did not dwell on it though, as once again her training as shepherdess told her she could not abandon the injured lamb; instead, she resolved to find a way to get the animal to safety and care for its wounds.

As Tephra turned past a large boulder, the trail began to gradually slope upwards, increasing the stress on her injured knee and slowing her pace. She stopped to rest at a clump of small fir trees and carefully observed her surroundings as she fed leaves from a nearby plant to the lamb. Proceeding along the path, she soon lost sight of the waterfall and the lake as the growth along the outer edge of the path became more and more dense. As the sound of rushing water became less noticeable, Tephra realized she was moving away from the falls. The path ahead became more and more difficult to travel as it wound between large boulders and the inclined more steeply. Often she came close to losing her balance as she stepped cautiously over large rocks.

After struggling to climb over a particularly large rock, Tephra found herself at the edge of a wide plateau carpeted with thick, lush grasses. Off to her right, beyond the grasses, were fields of grain; to her left, a small grove of what appeared to be fruit trees. She walked toward the grove in answer to the rumblings of hunger in her stomach. At the first tree, she gingerly touched one of the round, deep purple fruits. It felt ripe, so she plucked it, sniffed it, then bit into it. It was sweet with a somewhat grainy texture similar to the peaches that grew in the orchards of Drumlin Hills. She bit off a piece, offered it to the lamb, and it ate greedily. Then she plucked two more, eased herself to the ground to rest her knee, and shared the fruit with the small animal. The fruit was tasty, but now she longed for a sip of water. She had had to sing and coo to the animal repeatedly to keep it calm on the climb up to the terrace, and now her throat was dry.

Although her knee was throbbing painfully after the arduous climb along the path, she pulled herself up and limped through the grove. Beyond the fruit trees, a wide, fast moving stream glistened in the noonday sun; beyond that loomed a dense forest of towering boreal trees, larger than any that grew near the Drumlin village. Limping along the edge of the stream, she searched for a place to rest and to bathe her rapidly swelling knee. She found a shallow side pool where large boulders slowed the current, hiked her shift up to mid thigh with her free hand, and stepped gingerly into the water. Lowering herself onto a large smooth rock, she was able to bathe the aching wound on her knee. At first, the water on the injury gave a brief shock of pain, but after a moment the coolness of the water eased the throbbing in her knee and she sighed in relief. Scooping water into her cupped hand, she drank thirstily and then scooped some for the struggling animal to drink, while cooing to it softly. The lamb became less agitated and Tephra attempted to bathe its wounds, even though it continued to complain loudly.

Suddenly she heard a noise and a strange voice said, "Greetings! It seems you have found Gabbro's lost kid." Tephra jerked her head toward the voice, and clutched the lamb closer to her in panic. Her mind whirled in a tumble of fear, anxiety and confusion, and she found it hard to breathe as she saw a tall, dark-haired man approach from the forest side of the stream.

"I mean you no harm, maiden. There is a crossing but a short way up the stream. I will cross and give you aid." Before Tephra could gather her thoughts, he was at the pool reaching for the animal and attempting to take her hand. "Let me take the kid, and give you a hand out of that pool."

Tephra handed him the animal, but refused the offer of his hand to help her out of the cool water. When he reached for her, she pulled away from him, lost her balance and fell into the water. She shook her head slowly as she looked down at her shift that was soaked to her shoulders, wishing she could disappear into the bottom of the pool. He moved closer and held out his hand, but Tephra shook her head violently in protest, hugging her arms tightly to herself. The man backed away and Tephra stumbled out of the stream, shivering from both fright and embarrassment, as well as the cool mountain breeze on her wet garments.

"Ah! You are shivering! You need a dry garment before you catch a chill," the man stated plainly, as he set the lamb down and pulled his tunic over his head. "Here, remove that wet shift and put this on." He tossed the tunic toward Tephra. She caught it, but only stared at the ground in front of her. As if noting her hesitancy, he turned his back to her. She limped over to a large boulder and squatted behind it for some privacy. Quickly removing her wet garment, she slipped his tunic over her head, while never taking her eyes from the stranger's back. "Are you robed now?" He turned back to face her, not waiting for an answer. His gaze traveled from her damp disheveled red-gold hair down to her bruised and scratched ankles. "Your knee is badly injured. Are you able to walk?" Tephra nodded shakily. The stranger scooped up the wounded animal in one large hand, and invited, "Come with me to my settlement. You will be welcomed there, and will find food and a poultice for your wounds." He motioned her to follow him as he turned and headed upstream.

Cold, tired, hungry, and aching from her wounds and bruises, she was tempted to follow him. However, the teachings of her village and the requirements of the Preparation Ritual forbid such an action. A man had spoken to her, which was forbidden, and she had broken the prayer discipline. As the realization of her circumstances enveloped her, she clamped her lips together to keep from crying out. She wanted to run, to flee from this place as quickly as possible, but knew by the throbbing in her knee she would have to move slowly. Taking deep breaths, she then turned and began limping along the stream toward the orchard and back the way she had come. She reasoned that without the lamb, she would be able to use the vines to climb down to the canoe and back to the Cave of Solitude. Once there she would resume her meditations and chants with full fervor. She would even add fasting as a self-imposed penance for leaving the cave, no matter what her intentions had been in doing so. She had taken only a few steps when the man called to her, "Little maiden, do not be foolish. It will be dark soon."

CHAPTER 7

Bruised and wounded from her journey up the mountain, Tephra was deeply distressed from the realization that she had violated her pre-mating seclusion. She forced herself to ignore the pain in her knee and keep walking. The appearance of the dark haired man confirmed that she was indeed on the 'forbidden mountain.' Now that the strange little lamb would be cared for, she could put all her thoughts and energy into returning to the caves. She would use the vines to lower herself down to the lake and row or swim back to the caves.

Go slowly, she told herself. Her knee was growing stiff and more painful from the swelling. As she limped over the uneven terrain in the deepening twilight, she stumbled and could not regain her balance. Pain shot through her wounded leg as she fell against a large rock, and she cried out involuntarily. Moving into a position that she thought would ease the pain in her knee, she decided to take a moment to rest, now that she was out of sight of the man from the forbidden mountain.

"You should not walk further with your knee so injured." Tephra's head jerked up as she heard the voice of the man, and she quickly wiped away her tears. She would not further humiliate herself by letting this strange man see her weeping. "I did not think you would get very far," he said as he handed the injured animal to her. She held it gently in the crook of one arm and petted it; then, to Tephra's astonishment, he bent and scooped her up in his arms, ignoring her silent protests. Heat flamed from her neck to her ears at the forbidden intimacy, and she attempted to cover her face with her free hand. "Do not be afraid. I will not harm you," he said in a calm, gentle voice. "I am Strata of the Barchan Settlement. You have nothing to fear from me or my people, little maiden. I will bring you to my grandfather's hut where he will tend to your wounds, and you will have food and rest."

Tephra was silent as the strong, dark-haired Barchan carried her and the animal almost effortlessly through the winding forest trail. Her mind was echoing repeatedly the words of Karst at her betrothal ritual, "You will not touch or be touched by, speak to or be spoken to by, any man until after the Mating Ritual is completed." By the time they were well into the forest, she had removed her hand from her face and, although she had to keep biting at her lip to try to stop its trembling, she began to observe her surroundings cautiously. The Boreal trees towered high above them so that much of the forest was in deep shade. A heady scent, from the trees and the flowering bushes that also grew in the forest, lulled her somewhat, and although still fearful, the sense of panic had decreased.

The tall Barchan asked, "What are you called? And how did you come to be on Barchan Mountain?" With her focus on the strange, exotic environment, Tephra had—for a brief moment—ceased to dwell on the consequences of violating her required time of solitude and the prohibition against contact with any male. "Do you have a name? Can you speak?" His deep, resonant voice once again broke into her thoughts. She shook her head, and compressed her lips together in an effort to convey the fact she was forbidden to speak. He belonged to a different village and contact between their villages was prohibited, and she was betrothed. Strata spoke again, "Welcome to Barchan Settlement, silent one. My grandfather's hut is just across the square."

Tephra saw several Barchans look up from their chores and stare as Strata carried her and the injured, bleating lamb through the settlement. She felt awkward and held the lamb closer as she thought, "They are the forbidden people!" A shudder of fear ran through her as she recalled the tales she had heard since childhood.

The man entered a small dwelling and laid her gently on a mat of thick furs. Taking the kid from her arms, he spoke in a reassuring tone, "Rest here. I will return this lost kid to my cousin, and send my grandfather to you." Tephra wanted to protest, but the mat felt quite comfortable to her tired and aching body, so she only nodded and watched as the tall Barchan left the dwelling. She hugged herself, curling her body, except for her painfully throbbing knee, into a ball in attempt to stop trembling. With her lips clamped together to keep from crying, she silently begged the favor of The Always.

Still trembling with fear and pain, she looked up as Strata and an elderly man entered the hut. Without saying a word, the man quickly examined her bruised, cut, and swollen knee, then spoke to Strata, "Bring bread and milk, then go to Uluru's hut. Ask her for a clean and proper shift for the maiden." Strata brought the food, and then left promptly. The old man arose and went over to a counter. Tephra could see he was busy there with some jars, pots, and bags. Looking back at her, he said, "You have not touched your food. Eat," he gently commanded. "You will be strong again soon. Eat. Eat." Tephra nibbled at the bread, and sipped cautiously at the milk. The taste was different, but not unpleasant.

The old man dipped a thick cloth into a small bowl containing a fragrant mixture, then knelt and wrapped the cloth around her knee. Tephra flinched in pain when the cloth was first placed on her knee, but after a moment the mixture in the cloth did its work and the intense throbbing was soothed. "This poultice will help your wound to heal, and the binding will keep the wound closed," the old man explained. "I am called Foehn. I am a healer of sorts and will prepare a brew to help you rest. The morning will find you stronger." As Tephra warily observed him, he sprinkled a pinch of powder into a mug and poured in steaming water from a kettle that had been heating on a grate over glowing coals. He handed the mug to Tephra, who sat huddled in the corner, feeling frightened and uncertain. The brew was pleasingly fragrant, and the old man had been quite gentle as he tended her knee, so she decided it was safe to take the mug from him. She carefully took a small sip and found it also had a pleasant taste, and both warmed and calmed her somewhat.

The older man looked up as Strata returned. "Ah, Strata is here. See child, he has brought a clean garment for you. We will wait outside while you freshen yourself. There is warm water and a cloth there next to you. The oils in the water will clean and heal your small cuts and scratches." Foehn gestured to a basin that sat next to the mat where Tephra rested, then he and Strata left the hut.

Tephra examined the garment Strata had brought her. The texture and style were much like her everyday shifts, but the fabric, though now faded in places, had been dyed a deep blue. Drumlin women did not wear dyed garments except at certain ceremonies; they considered it a waste of dyes that were often difficult to obtain. She washed her face and arms, quickly changed into the clean garment, and with trembling hands, clumsily braided her hair. Then, as the potion was beginning to take effect, she eased herself down onto the fur mat. She did feel somewhat refreshed, and was thankful for the time to clean herself; yet, her mind still raced with the thought that she had broken her mating preparation and was on Forbidden Mountain. She had so often been biting at her lower lip to stop its trembling that now she tasted a drop of blood.

As soon as they were outside the hut, Foehn frowned, squinted his eyes, and poked Strata in the chest with one finger.

"Granpoppa, I will explain," Strata shifted from one foot to the other and attempted a grin. "I was at the edge of the plateau near the stream, and I heard bleating. I saw the maiden bathing in the stream and holding the kid. She was trying to clean its wounds. From its markings, it is one lost from Gabbro's herd. I returned it to his yard before going to find you."

"Was it alright?" Foehn asked in response.

"The wounds were not serious," Strata replied.

"Gabbro was pleased, I am sure." Foehn paused a moment, then put his hand on his grandson's arm. "Strata, the maiden is not one from our settlement."

"No, Granpoppa. A Drumlin, I think, with hair like—a color I've never seen before."

"Yes, likely a Drumlin," Foehn agreed, "but Strata, a Drumlin would not venture on this mountain. They would be placed under banishment for doing so."

"I cannot think one so young would so defy their laws that she would risk being banished."

"And thus, you bring this Drumlin maiden into our midst," Foehn gave Strata a stern look.

"Her knee was badly injured and she could not walk on it. How could I have left the maiden all alone on the plateau?"

Foehn nodded as he stroked his beard, then warned, "Be aware, if she is a Drumlin, we Barchans are of the 'forbidden ones' and she will not trust us, and very few of our settlement will welcome her."

Strata nodded his understanding as he mentally recalled the stories his great-grandfather had told concerning the Drumlins and the Barchans. The stories contained many mysteries, for each of their laws forbade both the Barchans and the Drumlins to speak of certain things. Over the generations, many retellings had transformed the facts into legends and myths. At one time—many, many winters ago—there was frequent contact between the two peoples, but a fierce conflict had arisen, pushing the two villages forever apart. Some tales were of fierce battles fought by neighboring villages; some were of an insurrection so severe that it caused a terrible rift in a once united people. Several attempts had been made at reconciliation, the last being when Foehn was little more than a babe nursing at his mother's breast. There were only a handful of Barchans and Drumlins still living who remembered the incident. They did not speak of the renewed hostility that had risen from the attempts at unity. All the later generations knew was that the villages were now more segregated than ever before, each barely admitting the existence of the other.

While they waited for the Drumlin maiden to change, Foehn and Strata discussed what to do about returning her to her village. "It will be very difficult, I agree," said the older man, "but she cannot remain here."

"Well do I know the obstacles of both, Granpoppa. But for now, we must see that she is healed," Strata reminded him.

"We must go to Augur the Chief regarding the maiden, my son. I will care for her tonight, then, in the morning, your cousin, Kaoli will come to care for her while we go to Augur." Strata nodded his assent.

From the doorway, Foehn called out to the maiden, "Have you changed your garment?" When there was no answer, he asked his grandson, "Is she mute?"

"No, for I heard her crooning to the kid as I first approached her. Must be she is forbidden to speak to any outsiders, as we once were."

Foehn nodded and called out, "Tap on the jug if we may enter." Upon hearing a response, the two men entered their dwelling.

Foehn squatted on the floor near the mat the maiden occupied. "You are Drumlin, are you not?" The maiden nodded slowly and looked up warily. "So my grandson guessed. It is known that our mountain is forbidden to your people. So how is it that you were bathing in a stream so near our settlement, and holding one of our kid goats?"

The maiden looked up at the mention of the word 'goats'. "I understand, little one," Foehn said sympathetically. "You are forbidden to speak to us. Well, no matter. We will care for you and get you safely back to your own people."

The frightened maiden nodded and gave the old man a small, tight-lipped smile. Strata noticed she was having difficulty keeping her eyes open, likely due to Foehn's potion, and said quietly, "I will take my rest in Uluru's hut. After sunrise, I will return to see how the maiden has healed."

Strata watched as Foehn covered the sleeping maiden with a thickly woven cloth. "The mountain air at night would feel quite cool to a Drumlin," Foehn said quietly as he walked toward his own sleeping quarters.

Strata smiled, "Goodnight, Poppa," and made his way to his sister's dwelling.

CHAPTER 8

Tephra awoke just before dawn, feeling thirsty and disoriented. At first, she thought she was in her family dwelling, nestled in the rolling Drumlin Hills. She sat up quickly, quite startled as she remembered she was in the hut of a Barchan. Her chest tightened and she took several deep breaths to try to calm the feeling of panic that arose. Recalling the incidents that had led her there, Tephra was filled with apprehension about what consequences she would face. She worried what her mother and grandmother would think if she was not in the cave when they came at midday to prepare her for the Mating Ritual. She knew that by being away from the cave and her prescribed meditations, she had broken a very serious ritual and the Hammada would not be pleased. After taking a few deep breaths, forced her mind away from considering what actions they might take. Instead, she resolved to put all her energies into getting back to the cave. Gingerly she stood and tested her bandaged knee. It was still quite sore, but she was encouraged by the improvement and began to plan carefully her escape from Barchan Settlement, and her journey down the mountain trail and back to the caves.

A faint shaft of moonlight revealed a bucket and a drinking gourd on a counter inside the hut. Hoping it contained water, she limped over to it, took several sips to refresh herself, and then walked very cautiously out of the hut so as not to awaken Strata's grandfather. Though she was limping more and more with each step, she made her way through the settlement, finally reaching the forest trail. It was still dark, the moonlight occasionally hidden by windswept clouds. Realizing it would be even darker in the forest, she glanced at the horizon, looking for the first rays of sunlight, but saw only distant lightning. Once inside the forest she found several fallen limbs alongside the trail, and selected one that was sturdy and just the size to aide her as she walked. As she feared, the darkness was more intense under the lush canopy of the trees. With the thickening clouds, she was finding it increasingly difficult to see her way. When the trail branched out in three directions, she hesitated, having no idea which path to take. Refusing to become alarmed, she determined that if it were not the correct path, she could simply retrace her steps and try another.

In spite of her aching knee, she made good progress along the trail, and her eyes were beginning to adjust to the shadowy light. Then, two nearby flashes of lightening and a loud rumble of thunder caused her to stumble as she instinctively closed her eyes against the intense flare of light. She righted herself and continued down the trail with increased caution as more dark clouds obscured the light of the moon. Suddenly, rain started to fall in huge drops and the trail, which she could now just barely make out, soon became slippery. She tried to steady herself by reaching for a small overhanging branch, but it broke in her grasp and she tumbled over a shallow ledge and landed in a clump of leaves and boreal needles. She was unhurt, except for her knee that began bleeding once more and was now throbbing painfully. Guided by the glimpses of light from the intermittent lightening, Tephra inched her way to the rocky ledge from which she had fallen, and huddled under the outcropping of a large boulder. There, somewhat sheltered from the pounding rain, she waited out the thunderstorm shivering from cold and pain. With increased uncertainty that she would be able to return to the caves before midday, she wondered if The Always was punishing her for abandoning the Preparation Ritual.

After what seemed like hours, the rain ceased and Tephra could see light penetrate the cover of leaves and hear birds chirping their early morning song. Tephra sat up and eased from under the protective boulder. Her injured knee throbbed with heat and pain, while the rest of her body felt numb from the damp and cold. The bandage and blue robe were stained with blood, mud, and forest debris. She brushed her hair from her face with her hands to discover it was matted with bits of leaves and mud. She would need more time to clean up before Kame and Caldera arrived. Using a small leafless branch to assist her, Tephra attempted to walk. As soon as she put weight on her injured leg though, a wave of pain and dizziness overcame her, and she all but fell to the ground. She sat hunched over her injured knee, attempting to find some position that would ease the pain. Overwhelmed by her situation, tears flowed down her mud-stained face, and sobs shook her hunched shoulders.

At the sound of a snapping twig, her head jerked up and she drew in a quick breath, silencing her sobs. In her eagerness to escape from the Barchan settlement, she had given no thought to the dangers that might be in the Boreal Forest. Now the snapping of the twig alerted her, and the deep forest sounds, which were unfamiliar to her Drumlin ears, added a new fear. Looking up towards the ledge from which she had fallen, Tephra considered how to get back on the trail. She tried to hop on one foot, but found she could not keep her balance on the uneven, debris-strewn forest floor. Frustrated and tired from the exertion, she sat down on a nearby log.

Hearing a soft whistle, she looked around cautiously, and then gasped as she saw the tall Barchan who had carried her to his settlement. "Do not try to walk further. You will only cause more pain in that knee," he said as he jumped from the ledge. In two long strides, he was standing next to her, knelt, removed the soiled bandage, and was examining her swollen knee. He handed her the water gourd he carried, motioning her to drink, then pulled off his tunic and slipped it over her shivering shoulders.

As he stripped off his undershirt, she closed her eyes and lowered her head at the sight of his bare chest. As a few tears slipped down her face, she whispered in anguish, "It is hopeless, I am to be banished!" She felt him gently wiping the dirt and tears from her face and looked up, her hazel eyes meeting his deep blue ones, her face turning red with embarrassment.

His smiled and spoke in a kind voice, "I do know something of the ways of your people. I know that you risk banishment by being on Barchan Mountain among 'the Forbidden Ones', but you have nothing to fear from us."

She watched as he used a part of his undershirt to clean the dirt and blood from around the wound on her knee, and then poured water over the wound. The water was cool and the throbbing in her knee was eased somewhat. As he tenderly wrapped her knee with a dry strip torn from his shirt, she wondered why her people were so afraid of the Barchans. After a moment, he asked her, "Why did you climb to our mountain, and now seek to return to your village, when you will likely be sent away?"

Her only response to his question was to lower her head. Her eyes felt hot, and there was a sick feeling in her stomach.

"Very well," he said, "but you cannot walk until that knee has had a chance to heal, so I will bring you back to the settlement. My cousin will loan you another shift, Grandfather will make a fresh poultice for your knee, and my venison stew will warm and strengthen you." He lifted her so quickly into his arms that she was startled and instinctively reached her hands and clung to his shoulders. Almost as quickly, she withdrew her hands from his shoulders and folded them over her chest. She swallowed hard and squeezed her eyes shut as she realized, "I have touched the bare skin of a Barchan male!" Tephra bit her lip and tried to stop the tears that filled her eyes as she recalled the directives of the Preparation Ritual, and now was quite certain that her mother and Kame would not find her in the caves. As the Barchan carried her back toward his settlement, she tried to imagine what Graben would do, for surely he would be distraught. Frowning in concentration, she attempted to recall what happened when someone of the village was missing, but she found it hard to think clearly.

As they approached the settlement, a young man ran up to Strata and said, "I will go tell Foehn. The little lost maiden has been found."

He sprinted up the trail and by the time Strata and Tephra arrived at the hut, Foehn had a mat and poultice already prepared.

He motioned for Strata to place Tephra on the mat and spoke to her gently, "I've sent Pingo to collect a warm robe for you young maid, but these furs will warm you for now." He set to work gently cleansing her knee with an herbal bath. "More damage has been done. I do not think this will be able to take any weight for several days," Foehn said with concern, then addressing Strata, he said, "Put those furs behind her so that she can sit up. Some hearty stew is what she needs, and rest." Turning back to Tephra, he said gently, "We do not keep you against your will, little Drumlin. We only offer you rest, food, and healing ointments for your injuries. Stay here until you are well enough to travel, and Strata will lead you safely back to your people."

Strata looked at her and barely suppressing a grin, teased, "I have many responsibilities. I cannot carry you back to this hut every day. Do as Granpoppa says, for next time it might be a hungry bear or wolf that finds you huddled in the leaves. Although, perhaps it is true, as Augur has said, you are protected by the Almighty One." He gave her a broad grin and a wink as he left the hut.

At Strata's last words, Tephra looked up, puzzled. She did not understand some of the words he spoke. Bewildered and frightened, weak with exhaustion and pain, Tephra fought back tears, and tried to make sense of the conflicts within. She was among the forbidden peoples! She did not really know why they were forbidden; like all the Drumlin villagers, she had never questioned—it had simply always been so. She remembered the teachings of the Hammada and felt an unfamiliar, deep sinking feeling in the pit of her stomach. She had wandered into the Forbidden Mountains; a man had spoken to her and touched her during her time of seclusion before mating; she had seen and touched his bare chest—and that man was one of the forbidden ones! Yet, she had experienced nothing but kindness and genuine concern from Strata and his grandfather. Her confusion was almost too much to process; she could not stop trembling, or stop the tears that rolled down her cheeks.

"Do not weep, little one," Foehn said gently. "No one here will harm you, and you will soon be returned to your people." Next to her mat, he placed a wooden tray that held a bowl of water and a cloth, a small bowl of stew, and a few berries. Tephra washed her face with the cloth and water Foehn had provided, glancing up every now and then to observe him as he puttered about the dwelling. He appeared to be at least as old as Kame. His hair was long, like Karst's, but instead of auburn streaked with gray, it was snowy white and fell straight to his shoulders.

She ate a little of the warm venison stew, watching as Foehn scooped something into a shallow bowl and brought it to her mat. He removed a small leather bag out of his tunic, opened it and measured out what appeared to be ground leaves into the bowl. With his fingers, he mixed the contents of the bowl into a paste and applied it to Tephra's knee.

"This is clabbered goat's milk and a few herbs," he explained in a soothing voice. "It will help to send the fever out of the wound. You must eat apples and berries, and drink lots of the spring water I will give you. Soon your wound will heal. Now you rest." Foehn poured a little warm water into a cup and dropped in a pinch of something from another, smaller pouch. He handed it to the maiden, motioning her to drink. Tephra obliged, sensing that he indeed intended to help her. Fatigued from her ordeal and sedated by the draught Foehn had given her, she soon fell into a deep sleep.

Foehn looked up from the herbs he was grinding to see Strata standing at the entrance to the hut with a worried look on his face. "You are full of thoughts, where have you been?"

"To Augur."

"Ah! You must be very troubled to seek out that old hermit."

"Poppa, the maiden does trouble me. What do we do about her? Augur says if she goes back, she will be shunned by her village for perhaps a very long time, because she is considered soiled by her contact with us. He says they may have already declared her as among the dead.

If that is true, he says it is likely she can never go back." Frowning, Strata ran his hand through his hair.

"What do *you* think we should do? You know that the elders will agree we should at least attempt to get her back to her village. Many of our settlement will not accept her, you must know that." Foehn cocked his head to one side and stared at his grandson.

"Pingo and I could bring her back to her village and explain how we found her."

"You would likely be clubbed to death before you could say a word," warned Foehn.

"Augur says we must go to the leaders of the village first. Tell them how we found her. Make them understand she came to *us*."

"Yes, perhaps that would be safer," Foehn agreed, "but first, we must see that she is able to make the journey. And, I think we should move her to Uluru's dwelling. It is not wise for the maiden to stay in the hut of two men."

"I will go to my sister and ask her to prepare a place for the maiden. Uluru has a kind heart, and I am sure the maiden will feel more comfortable there," Strata said, then left to go to Uluru with his request.

Foehn shook his head and muttered, "What has Strata brought upon us? There has not been a Drumlin on this mountain in countless seasons." As he covered the sleeping maiden with a light coverlet, he smiled and whispered, "No, Strata could not leave anyone to perish on the plateau, not even a Drumlin."

CHAPTER 9

A world away from where Tephra was sleeping in the Barchan Settlement, Graben was in the dwelling he had prepared to share with Tephra upon their mating. His closest friends had arrived early to wish him well.

"This day, my friends," he said as he held up a mug of ale, "I am the envy of every male in Drumlin Village."

"Tephra does have many charms. The Always must hold you high in his favor," Ogen assured him, lifting his own mug.

Graben had bathed in one of the springs, had rubbed his skin with oils, and had dressed in a newly woven tunic and trousers, which were dyed to a deep, rich brown. Now, in an ancient Drumlin tradition, he tied Tephra's sash—the one he had removed from her waist when they were betrothed—around his forehead. He was grinning with self-satisfaction, knowing that everything in the dwelling was in good order and ready to receive his betrothed. When he checked the garland he had placed over the doorway for the third time, there was much good-natured teasing from his friends.

"I guess this means you will no longer be part of the Golith trials. Tephra will keep you tied to this dwelling, I am sure," Tor said jokingly.

"He won't be any competition for me now," teased Noll. "He'll grow fat and lazy."

Graben laughed, taking their joking in good humor. "Jest with me if you must, for I know it is envy that makes you say such things to your friend!"

"You will envy me when I take the Arrowhead from you next Trials!" Ogen boasted with a laugh. Then, in a serious tone he said, "Now we must raise our mugs to our good friend Graben, and take our leave as it is near midday and his betrothed will be arriving soon. He will need time for meditation." Without saying another word, the three young men raised their mugs of ale, drained them, and left Graben to await the arrival of Tephra, Kame, and Caldera. As soon as the door closed behind them, Graben once more checked that everything in the dwelling was in perfect order, then knelt and called upon The Always to bless his Mating Day. He recited the ancient prayers that had been handed down from father to son for many generations. According to Drumlin custom, he was to remain kneeling in prayer until his betrothed arrived.

Graben had recited all the required prayers, and still had not heard the expected knock at his door. He wondered if perhaps he had said them too quickly, so he said them again more slowly, but still his betrothed had not arrived. Now puzzled and concerned, he paced back and forth to the door wondering what he should do. He was startled from his thoughts by voices outside his door, and then heard an urgent tapping. In two strides he was at the door, opened it, and was quite shaken to find not his beloved, but Karst and Ogen standing outside, their expressions quite grim.

Karst went to Graben and placing his hand on the young man's shoulder in a sympathetic gesture, said solemnly, "My son, the Wise Ones have been informed that your betrothed, Tephra, is missing. When her mother and Kame went to the caves to prepare her for the Mating Ritual, she was not in the caves."

Graben felt his heart beat rapidly, the sound pounding in his ears. "What do you mean, not in the caves?" he asked incredulously. "Where else could she be?"

"When Caldera went to the caves, Tephra was nowhere to be found," Karst informed him. "However, Kame saw a canoe tethered near the rocks on the other side of the lake, and Caldera ran to the blacksmith to have him sound the alarm. Many villagers are now searching the surrounding areas, and fishermen are dragging their nets across the bottom of the lake."

Graben untied the sash from around his head and said to Ogen, "Go bring Tor and Noll." Turning to Karst, he said, "Honorable Karst, I trust the Hammada will be offering prayers for the safety of my betrothed. Thank you for coming to tell me she is missing. Now I must go in search of my beloved." Graben gave a slight bow, and as soon as Karst turned away, closed the door, and quickly changed from his mating garments into more rugged clothing. He was deeply troubled that Tephra was not found in the caves and could only think that something dreadful had happened. Taking a few deep breaths to calm down, Graben walked briskly to the lake.

When he arrived, he was told that some men had found broken vines and snapped twigs in some places, but they had seen nothing that told of Tephra's fate. Within moments, Ogen arrived with Tor and Noll. With Graben urgently leading the way, they followed the narrow winding path up the rocky slopes; however, they were forced to turn back when they encountered a rockslide. Upon returning to the small wooden dock on the village side of the lake, Graben learned that other men of the village had searched the nearby woods and ravines, and a group of women had searched the clusters of scrub trees that grew in the low hills, but still there was no sign of Tephra.

Graben saw Tarn speaking with two of the villagers who had joined in the search and went to him. "Father of Tephra," he said respectfully. Tarn turned to Graben and with a nod acknowledged his greeting. Graben swallowed hard, trying to keep the panic out of his voice as he asked, "Has anyone seen anything that would tell us what happened to Tephra?"

Tarn shook his head sadly, "No, no one has seen anything. Caldera searched every part of the caves. She could only report that she saw no signs that showed Tephra might have been in danger. A canoe was found across the lake near the rocks, but nothing else."

"But, why would Tephra leave the caves?" Graben asked, bewildered. Tarn, with a sad, worried look on his face, just shook his head.

Graben went back toward the lake where he met Caldera and several other women. Caldera ran to him with outstretched arms, her face wet with tears. "Oh, Graben! My daughter is nowhere to be found!" she cried.

Graben took her hands in his and said, "Karst and Tarn told me you searched the caves. Do you know when she left?" He was finding it difficult not to weep with Caldera, but knew he had to be strong—after all, he was Golith.

"There is no way to be certain. But, some food was still there, and the coverlet, too. Ah, Graben! Her grandmother and I were talking of how lovely she was going to look in the mating garment that my mother and I had worn. Suddenly Kame stopped and pointed to the caves, saying that Tephra's canoe was not at the cave where it should be…." Caldera closed her eyes and shook her head as she wiped away tears. "We then noticed the canoe near the rocks. Now I must tell Sedi and Breccia that their sister is still missing. Sedi, poor Sedi, was so upset. He wanted so much to help search…" Caldera's hand covered her mouth as she sobbed. Graben patted her shoulder in a gesture of comfort, and Caldera gave him a weak smile as she turned to walk toward the village.

"What reason would she have to leave the caves?" Graben wondered, as an overwhelming sense of dread filled him. His whole being cried out, "Where are you, Tephra? We should be alone in the dwelling I prepared for you!" Nothing seemed real, and he struggled to keep control of the varied emotions that arose as he tried to imagine all the reasons why Tephra would not be in the caves.

Darkness settled and Karst advised the searchers that it was too dangerous to continue the search, even with torches. Rather than risk anyone being injured, everyone agreed to resume the search early the next morning—except Graben. "No!" he argued, "we must keep searching. She may be injured, and leaving her till morning would—"

"Graben, we understand, but Karst is right. It is too dangerous even with torches," Shael said sympathetically. "Clouds cover the moon tonight. Go rest. You will need your strength to continue the search."

Ogen took Graben's arm and said gently, "Your uncle is giving good counsel. Come, we will go to your family dwelling."

"No!" Graben jerked away, "I will return to the dwelling I made for my mate."

"Then we will go with you," Tor said firmly.

Graben let Tor, Ogen, and Noll lead him to the dwelling that he was to have shared with Tephra. With their help, he managed to wash up and change into a clean tunic and trousers, and even took several bites of some stew his mother had sent. He insisted he felt better after the stew and was determined to take a torch and continue searching for Tephra, but Noll blocked the doorway, sternly reminding him that after a few hours rest he would be more helpful in the search. Reluctantly, Graben agreed and went to his mat; however, to his annoyance, Noll and Ogen stayed with him. He sat on his mat leaning against the wall with his arms folded across his chest, pointedly ignoring his guardians. Ogen spoke to him sternly, "We are staying to make sure you do nothing foolish."

Tor said he was going to his own dwelling, but assured Graben he would return at first light to help with the search for Tephra. Graben looked up and nodded, then stretched out on the mat, and turned toward the wall. He had to admit to himself that he was tired and that he would need to be rested to find Tephra. His eyes grew heavy and he slept, only to be frequently awakened by disturbing dreams.

CHAPTER 10

Teams of Drumlin men and matrons searched the woods and meadows all around Mosken Lake, covering every accessible area, no matter how small or unlikely. Graben was dauntless in his search for Tephra, often plunging through brambles, tramping through ravines in water up to his knees, and even climbing trees to scan an area. His friends tried to keep up with him, but soon realized they did not have the motivation he had, and therefore could not keep up with the pace he set. However, working as relay teams, they made sure Graben was never alone, and was kept supplied with water and dried meats. At sunset, when Karst called a halt to the day's search, Graben was so exhausted that Noll and Ogen had little trouble convincing him to return to his dwelling. His mother, Vena, had a large pot of stew waiting when the three men arrived, and insisted they each have a large helping of stew washed down with a mug of ale. Graben grabbed for the mug of ale first, drinking thirstily, then wolfed down the stew, splashed water on his face, and stumbled to his cot. Vena told Noll and Ogen that she would stay with Graben, and they could return to their own shelters.

At dawn of the following day, Tephra's clan, the shepherds, along with Graben's clan of earth-tillers, gathered with the Wise Ones at the Hammada Stone. Kame, Caldera, Tarn, and Graben were seated at the edge of the stone, their heads bowed. Karst addressed the clans solemnly, "The men of the village will continue to search for the maiden Tephra. Even the boundary areas will be searched, as far as can be done without endangering the men of Drumlin. The Wise Ones will offer prayers and song all through the day. If the maiden has not been found by dark, we will begin the Ritual of Parting."

The ritual involved three days of mourning that ended on the last day with the Closing Ritual. The first two days were for the family and clan of the deceased as they shared memories, offered prayers, and consoled one another. On the third day, the entire village would gather around the Hammada Stone where the body of the deceased would be displayed on a bier. The body would be wrapped in layers of spice-soaked woolen cloths, covered with a cloth of fine linen, and adorned with flowers or greenery. The family of the "departed one" would accept the condolences of the villagers as they filed past the bier, then the body would be entombed in the village burial cave. A torch, which would burn for one moon, would be lit near the entrance to the cave tomb.

When the sun had set and the torches along the village paths and around the Hammada Stone had been lit, men representing each of Drumlin's clans returned to the stone. Their defeated expressions and drooped shoulders told Kame that her granddaughter had not been found. Tears of grief spilled unchecked down her face as Caldera and Tarn arrived at the stone. Kame looked at their grief-stricken faces and realized they knew as well what was coming next.

Karst, in a controlled voice, proclaimed, "We will prepare for the Ritual of Parting for the maiden Tephra of the Clan of Shepherds. It is believed she has fallen into the dark waters of Mosken Lake, even though the fishermen found nothing by dragging their nets. There is no body; however, a bier will be adorned with some of the maiden's possessions. Tarn and Caldera, the Hammada will assemble here at tomorrow's first light to chant the prayers beginning the ritual while you make your own preparations. Kame will light the fires that will burn for one moon. Guardians will be appointed to keep the fires burning. Since she did not live to be mated, her belongings and her mating gift will remain in her clan. She was an undefiled maiden, so her Robe of Ceremony will be placed—"

Kame interrupted Karst by her sudden chanting:

> *Beware of changes in the now!*
> *Fast the streams will flow;*
> *then shift, shift, blood will flow!*
> *Dark will come to us....*

"Silence, old woman!" Karst commanded.

Kame stood, shook her gnarled cane, and proclaimed vehemently, "My granddaughter will not have the Ritual of Parting."

Kame tried to ignore the stunned gasps from those assembled, and the few villagers who were saying loudly, "One does not deny the Ritual of Parting!"

Giving a deep moan, she looked toward Mt. Nunatak and chanted once more,

> *Beware of changes in the now!*

Then she looked straight at the villagers and said emphatically, "Tephra will be returned to us. She is not below the waters!" Once again, she began her chanting, this time with more emotion.

> *Shift, shift, blood will flow ...*
> *Dark will come ... turn ....*
> *Turn from the rift.*

Kame swayed back and forth as she spoke, "Not departed, no, not departed!"

"Enough of your ramblings, Old One," Karst commanded, "We do not see blood and darkness—"

"That is true, Karst," Kame interrupted. "You do not see. You have closed your eyes."

Another of the Hammada broke in, "There must be no more quarrels in the assembly. We must offer prayers and prepare for the ritual."

"Kame," Eolia said gently, "we feel your grief. But, if Tephra is not below the waters, it can only be that she is in a place forbidden. And it would be far better that the maiden be below the waters."

With drooping shoulders, the clans silently returned to their dwellings while the Hammada chanted prayers in preparation for Tephra's Ritual of Parting. After the final prayers, Kame drew Karst aside, imploring him to listen. "I have seen more signs—no, please listen, for the sake of Adar, my departed mate whose friendship you once held so dear."

Karst nodded, so Kame continued, "Last night the crystal in my staff—the one that Adar carried for many years as one of the Hammada—began to glow as I was chanting the poems. Then I heard his voice—not out loud but in my mind, my heart—telling me our beloved Tephra was safe, that she would be returning to us."

"Kame, ah Kame," Karst shook his head. "And if she does return, where has she been? To places forbidden? If so, and that is the only possibility, she will be soiled, unclean, her spirit tainted with evils The Always alone knows. And what will be her life here then? As nothing. She will be banished, at least …"

Kame interrupted, "I know my granddaughter. She would not willingly go where forbidden."

"If that is true, well, it will be for the Hammada to decide her fate. But, old friend, do not let your heart rule your head in this matter."

"Can we not then rule that the Parting Ritual be delayed a day or two?"

"The Hammada has ruled according to the Laws of Nunatak."

Kame walked to her shelter with a heavy heart. Tephra was alive, she knew it. Surely she would feel it if that dear child had departed this earth. "No," she said to herself, "The Always speaks to my heart, and there have been no words of consolation, only words of hope. My Tephra will come back to us, but—why is it I fear what her return may bring?"

CHAPTER 11

Tephra woke up feeling groggy and disoriented from the draught Foehn had given her. She sat up and realized that she was no longer dressed in Strata's tunic, but in a soft, woven shift. She wondered who had removed the tunic and dressed her in the shift, blushing with embarrassment and shame. Ever since she had decided to rescue the small animal from the cliffs, her actions had taken her farther and farther away from her clan, her village, and all that was safe and familiar. She reconsidered her actions, but could not see how she could have left the animal trapped there on the ledge to either fall to its death or die of starvation. Yet now she was lost on this mountain, and all that she had known was lost to her. She assumed that by now her mother and Kame would have gone to the caves for her. What would they have done when they realized she was not in the Cave of Solitude? She tried to fight back the panic she felt and think clearly, even though she still felt a little lightheaded from the draught. Of course, there would be a search for her. When they did not find her, then what? If the canoe was still floating by the rocky slopes, what would they assume? Surely, they would not climb the slopes? And even if they did, they would not venture past the pool where the Barchan had found her. Her stomach was churning with anxiety as she tried to think of the possibilities.

Somehow, she must find her way back to the lake—but how? She knew her knee was badly injured and that it would not support her weight long enough to walk back to the terraced slopes and down to the lake. How long would she have before the Hammada would declare her as departed? She tried to recall the rulings she had been taught, but her circumstance was so uncommon, she could recall no ruling that fit. Frustrated tears flowed down her cheeks, and she angrily brushed them away, determined to concentrate on a way to get home and explain to the Hammada how she came to be on the Forbidden Mountain of Barchan.

After being left alone with her thoughts for several hours, Tephra heard Strata enter. He informed her that it was time to go to Uluru's hut, gently picked her up and carried her there.

"Uluru is my sister," Strata explained. "She is a kind woman, and she will take good care of you."

When they arrived at Uluru's hut, the woman greeted Tephra with a tender smile as she directed Strata to the mat prepared for her. Uluru brought her a mug of water and asked if she wanted something to eat. Tephra's stomach felt a little unsettled, so she shook her head and attempted a smile of gratitude. The woman left and returned with a coverlet. "You must have caught a chill. You are trembling," she said with concern. "Likely there is fever in your wounds. Foehn will be here soon. Try to rest."

For the rest of that day and into the next, Foehn, accompanied by Strata, returned often to Uluru's hut and administered his healing mixtures while Strata alternately paced and hovered.

Uluru often heard the Drumlin maiden mumble in her sleep, and she caught words that concerned her. She spoke to her grandfather and Strata about this. "I have tried to talk to the maiden, for she seems so upset. Often she sheds silent tears that she tries to hide from me, and she turns away when I try to talk to her." Uluru paused, sighed deeply, and continued, "She often talks in her sleep, and seems much troubled. She keeps repeating the words, 'Grandmother Kame, forgive me,' and

'Not departed, not departed!' She says she is defiled, shamed. What does this mean?" She looked at Foehn pleadingly.

"It means that soon Strata and Pingo must journey to the Drumlin Hills to let them know their daughter is safe," Foehn said with a sigh. "When her wounds have healed, we will deliver her back to them. We must assure them we mean only kindness. Tell them how it was Strata found her on the plateau. All caution must be taken, as they are a superstitious people."

"I fear I will be attacked as soon as I enter their village. Surely they will not listen to me," Strata exclaimed.

"Take Kaoli with you. She is to ask to see the one called Kame, for she is one who will listen."

"Grandfather, how is it you know of one of the Drumlins? There have been no words between our peoples …"

"There are some who have tried to mend that which was torn so long ago, but do not think on these things now. Prepare for your journey, for it is a long one. You must arrive when their leaders are gathered for their morning prayers."

When Uluru brought the maiden some tea, bread and jam that afternoon, she tried once more to talk to the maiden. "My child," she said gently, "can you see that we mean you no harm? We are trying to help you. I know what you have been taught about Barchans. The same as we were taught about Drumlins for many, many lifetimes. I know you want to go back to your village, but you cannot do so without our help. Strata, Pingo and a young woman named Kaoli, are preparing to go to your village to let them know you are alive, but injured, and that as soon as you are able to walk, they will bring you back to your village."

The maiden bowed her head, shaking it slowly from side to side, and said softly, "You have been so kind to me, a Drumlin." Then looking up she said with a timid smile. "I would be so very grateful if you could help me return to my village."

Uluru gently placed her hand on the maiden's shoulder and said, "We need to know your name, and why you were on the plateau when Strata found you. It is to ensure the safety of my brother, and Pingo and Kaoli."

Tephra took a deep breath, looked at her hands as she twisted them nervously, and began hesitantly, "I am called Tephra. I saw the lamb was caught by briars on a ledge. I climbed from Mosken Lake to untangle it, for I feared it would fall onto the rocks, or be eaten by wolves. I was unable to return the way I came. When I tried, both of us nearly fell, and my knee hit hard against a sharp stone. I tried to find another way back to—" Tephra bit her lip, and frowned. Uluru waited silently, sensing there was something Tephra was afraid to say. Tephra cleared her throat and continued, "I tried to find another way back to the lake, but the path was blocked by huge boulders and the other path led up to the plateau. Your brother found me with the animal. I thought without the animal I would be able to climb back down, but in my haste I tripped and fell, hurting my knee again. Your brother carried me to… his grandfather?" Tephra looked at Uluru questioningly.

"Yes, to Foehn's hut. He is a healer, and is grandfather to Strata and me. I understand you tried to return to Drumlin the next morning, but Strata found you after you had fallen into a ravine during the rainstorm. That is when the fever set into your wounds, and you were brought here."

Tephra nodded. "Thank you for caring for me. I did not mean to seem ungrateful. It is just that …."

"It is just that you are Drumlin, we are Barchans, and contact has been forbidden for too many lifetimes." Uluru smiled at the Drumlin maiden, who shyly returned her smile.

CHAPTER 12

The sky was barely beginning to lighten, and Kame and the other Wise Ones of Drumlin had gathered on the Hammada Stone to chant the prayers to begin the Ritual of Parting for Tephra. The Wise Ones had just bowed their heads when a voice called out, "Honorable Hammada, Wise Ones of the Drumlins, I am Kaoli. Two of my kinsmen and I have come from Barchan Mountain to beg a hearing. We have word of one of your people." Karst and Kame turned toward the voice at the same time, while the others drew closer together—some murmuring in fear and others pointing their crystal-tipped canes towards Nunatak.

Kame moved quickly to the edge of the stone and addressed the young Barchan maiden who was kneeling on one knee, her head bowed. "Is it my granddaughter you bring word of?"

"Are you the one called Kame?" Kaoli asked as she looked up at the old woman.

"I am. You who are called Kaoli, what word do you bring?" Kame struggled to keep her voice even.

"The one called Tephra is being cared for in the dwelling of my cousin. May my kinsmen approach?"

Karst moved to stand next to Kame and asked, "Is it true? The maiden Tephra is alive?" At Kaoli's nod he said, "Your kinsmen may approach."

At Kaoli's signal, Strata and Pingo walked from where they were waiting a short distance away, stood next to Kaoli and bowed to show respect. "This one is called Strata," Kaoli said, "It is he who found the maiden injured on the plateau. The other one is Pingo, who has also helped take care of her."

Kame heard the astonished gasps and murmurings of the other Hammada behind her. "Tell me, one called Strata, how it is you found my granddaughter?"

Strata related how he had heard the bleating of an animal, and after following its sound, found Tephra trying to care for it. "I offered her food and rest in the Barchan settlement, as I could see her knee was injured. She refused, and tried to run away. In her haste, she tripped and fell over some stones, further injuring her knee. She was then unable to stand. I carried her to the hut of my grandfather, one of the healers of our settlement."

As the mutterings of the shocked Wise Ones became louder, Karst motioned for silence, then turned his attention back to the Barchan. Strata continued, "She tried to return to Drumlin early the next morning, but fell into a ravine where I found her later that morning. I carried her back to my grandfather who again tended her wounds and gave her a draught for her fever. That evening I carried her to the house of my sister, Uluru, who has been tending to her the past three days."

Kame was both weak with relief that her granddaughter was alive and overcome with anxiety for what the Hammada would rule concerning her contact with the forbidden ones. So much emotion was hitting her at once that she staggered over to a stool and sat down heavily. Karst moved to stand beside her, and placing a hand on her shoulder, whispered, "Are you alright, old friend?"

Kame nodded and patted his hand, "My Tephra is alive."

Karst now addressed the Barchans, "What is the nature of the maiden's injuries? What does your healer say?"

At a gesture from Strata, Kaoli answered, "Her knee has been injured several times, the wound re-opened, and a fever has set in. It is badly swollen and she is unable to put any weight on that leg."

"How long before she would be able to make the journey?"

"It is difficult to say for certain, but the healer thinks no less than five or six days before she can stand on it at all—and as for the journey, perhaps not for two weeks."

"Is there no way to carry her down in a litter?" Karst questioned.

Strata answered, "Wise One, I assure you it is not possible. The journey was difficult enough for us to walk down. The trail is rugged and steep, and one must cross the Cambria River. It is dangerous at this time of year, and the bridge is narrow."

Another of the Hammada asked, "What of the terrace trails that lead up to the plateau?"

"Tephra said she tried to return by the terraced trails, but was unable to," answered Kaoli. "When we tried, it seemed there had been a landslide that took out part of the trail."

Karst nodded. "That is true. Several men of Drumlin were forced to turn back when searching for the maiden." He turned to the Hammada, and spoke quietly, "What do you suggest? This is unheard of. There is nothing in our laws by which to judge this."

Shael, of the clan of earth-tillers, spoke up, "This maiden has been among the forbidden ones, and is therefore defiled. If the Barchan's words are true, she went there on her own. The Ritual of Parting has already begun, so let it be completed. It is the simplest way—the way most favorable to The Always. If she is returned, she will have to be banished. The village may suffer the displeasure of The Always for accepting her after the Ritual of Parting has been declared, for her spirit may not be whole."

Kame stood up and pleaded, "Shael, if it were your grandchild, would you be so lacking in compassion?"

"And what of my nephew? Your granddaughter has broken her betrothal vows, and defied the rulings of the Hammada!"

Karst held up his staff and instructed, "Let us be silent. We will be united in prayer and meditation. We will seek the guidance of The Always. Hevel, your shelter is near. Would you allow the young Barchans to rest there and take refreshment while we meditate on all that has become known?"

Hevel the healer turned to the three Barchans, "Come, I will lead you to my hut. Kinber, my apprentice, will give you refreshment. I will return for you when we have decided." Kaoli looked at Strata questioningly, and at his reassuring nod, the three followed Hevel to his hut.

Once Hevel returned to his place on the Hammada Stone, the Wise Ones spent half the morning in prayer and meditation. Hevel suggested to Karst that they all needed some refreshment, and at Karst's agreement, he went to his hut and brought back a basket of bread, smoked meats, berries, and mulled wine. After they had eaten, and felt like they had clearer heads, the Wise Ones reviewed and discussed the sacred decrees of The Always. Moraine was called upon to read the decrees that applied to the situation. "One who ascends to Forbidden Mountain, also called Barchan Mountain, is declared unclean. The length of the chastisement is dependent upon the length of association with the Forbidden Ones, the Barchans. The accepted form of chastisement is… banishment," Moraine paused as she read the last word, and looked at her friend Kame with sympathy. She then continued, "The time of Preparation for the Mating Ritual is to be undertaken with utmost sincerity. A maiden who does not fulfill the Preparation Ritual as defined may be banished, or declared as defiled and without honor. She is to remain unmated for the rest of her days."

Karst called upon any to state why the decrees should not be enforced. Kame rose shakily to her feet and addressed her fellow members of the Hammada. "I know full well what our laws decree," she stated firmly. "However, as Tephra did not willingly ascend to the Forbidden Mountain, but was found injured on the plateau, I beg for leniency."

Raising his staff, Karst addressed the Wise Ones, saying, "We will meditate and ask for guidance from The Always. This a difficult decision we face, and we must declare a ruling soon, for the Barchans cannot be allowed to stay here longer." The Wise Ones bowed their heads as they raised the crystal tips of their staffs towards Nunatak. Karst chanted the ancient prayer for wisdom, then announced in an authoritative voice, "The Always has spoken to me."

"What wisdom do you have, revered leader?" asked one of the Hammada.

"I propose that we allow the Barchans to return to their settlement, and that the same three will come to us when the maiden Tephra is able to make the journey back to Drumlin. At that time, we will send an escort with them, and bring her home."

Some of the Wise Ones were appalled that the maiden would remain on the forbidden mountain for so long, while others expressed misgivings about any other Drumlins ascending the Forbidden Mountain. Karst tried to calm their fears by pointing out that Tephra was ill and injured, so there would be little chance of further defilement. He assured them that those who were to bring Tephra home would be chosen for their maturity and wisdom in the ways of Drumlin Village. After some discussion, they reluctantly agreed, and Hevel went to his hut and brought Strata, Pingo and Kaoli to hear the ruling of the Hammada.

"If you are honorable, and we are giving you our trust, the three of you will return to us, here at this sacred stone, in eight days. Three chosen Drumlins will return to your settlement with you and will bring the maiden back to her village."

Kaoli stepped forward and bowed, saying, "We will prove worthy of your trust." She turned to Strata and Pingo, and they also bowed and repeated her words.

Pingo and Kaoli turned and began walking toward the trail that had brought them to Drumlin and to the Hammada Stone, but Strata turned back and addressed the Wise Ones, "What will happen to the maiden when she is returned? We have heard that one who comes among the 'forbidden ones' is banished. Is this true?"

Shael shouted out before Karst could answer, "What happens to the maiden is not your concern!" Kaoli put her hand on Strata's arm, giving him a harsh look, and the three Barchans walked briskly toward Barchan Mountain.

Kame faced her fellow Wise Ones and asked, "Will Tephra be allowed a hearing before the Hammada? Surely it is clear that her being among the forbidden ones was not of her choosing."

"Yes, we will hear what the maiden has to say before she is banished—a hearing before the whole village of Drumlin, to set an example!" answered Shael fervently.

"There will be a hearing before the Hammada," Karst replied with authority, "and then the judgment pronounced before the village, with the essentials of her testimony given by one of the Hammada."

Kame bowed to Karst, "With your permission, wise leader, I will go to Tarn and Caldera and tell them that our daughter is alive and being cared for by some kind Barchans. I am sure Tarn will want to be one of the ones to make the journey to bring her back to her village."

"Yes, go to them. O Wise Ones, I charge you all, there is to be no discussion of what was witnessed here today. The villagers only need to know that we have discovered she is alive, and will soon be brought home. Say any more and too many questions that cannot be answered at this time will cause discord among our people. All will be made known soon enough. Go now in peace."

As Kame made her way to Tarn and Caldera, the other Wise Ones walked wearily toward their dwellings, some in groups of two or three, some alone. Kame could sense that all were troubled over the knowledge that one of their own was now among the forbidden ones, none more than she was. When she arrived at the dwelling of Tephra's family, she sent Breccia on a made-up errand as she wisely determined the child was too young for such news until they knew more. Tarn greeted her, his voice flat as though drained of all emotion, "Mother Kame, welcome. You can help Caldera and Sedi decide which of Tephra's few belongings will go on her bier."

"Come, sit down," Kame said, her voice shaky with emotion, "I have much to tell you."

"Sedi is resting on Tephra's mat," Caldera said, "We can go sit near him."

Kame nodded and Tarn held her arm as they followed Caldera to where Sedi was resting. He looked up and greeted Kame, "Grandmother! It is good you have come to us this early morning."

Kame walked over to Sedi and brushed his hair tenderly with her hand, then sitting next to him said, "I have come from the Stone. Our Tephra has been found. She is alive—"

"What?" Sedi and Tarn asked at the same time.

His voice quavering with emotion, Tarn asked, "But what of the Parting? The Rituals have begun. What will the Hammada say?"

Kame looked up to see tears of relief streaming down Caldera's smiling face. She returned her smile as tears filled her own eyes and explained, "A Barchan found her on the plateau. Her leg was injured and she was unable to walk, so he carried her to the hut of one of their healers. She now has a fever, but is being cared for in the dwelling of the man's sister. Tarn, you and two of the younger men of the Hammada will go carry her down in a few days."

"She is alive! Oh, Tarn, our daughter is alive!" cried Caldera.

Tarn went to Caldera and putting his arm around her, said anxiously, "My mate, I too am happy she is alive, but she is now with the Forbidden Ones. I will go to Karst and ask to go bring her home right away."

Kame explained about the rough trail, and the difficulty traveling with Tephra's injuries. She then suggested, "Perhaps you would be allowed to escort one or two of the matrons, ones that are mature yet strong enough, to stay with Tephra until she can make the journey."

Tarn nodded and said in a voice hoarse with emotion, "I do not want my daughter to be at risk of further defilement."

"She won't be banished when she returns, will she Grandmother?" Sedi asked as he wiped at a tear.

"Tephra will have a hearing. That is all I know. For now, we will give thanks to The Always that our child is alive and will return to us, and then Tarn and I will go to Karst." Caldera and Tarn knelt and Sedi bowed his head as Kame began a chant of thanksgiving to The Always.

While Caldera began to gather provisions in the hope that Karst would grant Tarn's request, Tarn and Kame went to visit the leader of the Hammada. Karst insisted their request be put to the entire Hammada when the Wise Ones gathered for prayer the next morning, but assured them their petition would likely be granted. Tarn was impatient, but bowed politely, and thanked Karst for hearing them.

Tarn walked with Kame to her own dwelling, took her hand, and said in a quiet, yet stern voice, "You must understand I mean no disrespect, but I will go after my daughter, no matter what the Hammada say. I will ask other men to go with me, for how can we be certain the forbidden ones are truthful when they said she was badly injured, and not just being held against her will."

Kame nodded she understood, placed her hand on his shoulder and said, "My son, I am certain those who came down to the Hammada were being truthful. They risked much to make the journey and to approach the Wise Ones. Wait until tomorrow, then decide what you must do."

"I will wait," Tarn said resignedly, then turned and walked toward the sheep pens in long strides. Kame stood watching until he was out of sight, knowing her son and Caldera were feeling the same mixture of joy and anxiety that she was experiencing, and her heart ached for them.

CHAPTER 13

Over in the village vegetable gardens, Graben was struggling to keep his mind on overseeing the harvesting of a crop of beans. There were several young apprentices working in his section. It was Graben's responsibility to be certain they were picking the beans that were at the right degree of ripeness and were handling the tender plants carefully. Thoughts of the approaching Ritual of Parting for Tephra came unbidden and at times overwhelmed him with grief and too many unanswered questions. "Why did she leave the caves? What was she thinking? She was supposed to be preparing for our mating!"

Suddenly a voice called out, breaking into his thoughts, "Graben! I must speak to you."

He looked up to see Kinber, Hevel's apprentice, approaching at a fast walk. "I am in no mood for company," Graben said, giving him a sour look.

"Come aside," Kinber said quietly, "I have news for you." Graben begrudgingly walked with Kinber until they were out of hearing of the harvesters. "Graben, Tephra is alive. She is living with Barchans. It seems she was injured and a Barchan man found her and carried her to their healer. Three of the forbidden ones came to the Hammada during their morning prayers."

Graben was so stunned by this information that he could not speak. Running his fingers through his hair, he turned and walked a few paces from Kinber, then stood looking off into the distance. He took a deep breath, blew it out and returned to Kinber. In a controlled voice he demanded, "What do the Hammada intended to do about her?"

Kinber's explanation was that nothing was to be done for several days, maybe two weeks. Graben sighed deeply, realizing that he needed to be alone to think about what he had just heard, but also knew he could not leave the workers unsupervised. He thanked Kinber, walked back to the bean patch, and attempted to hurry the harvesting. When he spoke harshly to one of the young boys, and received puzzled expressions from the other apprentices, he decided to call an end to the days harvesting. With more cordiality than he felt, he commended them for the day's work and reminded them to return early the next morning.

Graben went into his dwelling—the one he had prepared for Tephra—grabbed his sheath of knives and his spears, and set out for the game field. Once there, he threw knife after knife, and spear after spear at the targets until he was physically exhausted. He fell to his knees and beat his fist upon the ground, repeating over and over in a hoarse whisper, "Tephra, Tephra my beloved! Why? Why did you leave the caves?"

"I thought I'd find you here."

Graben jerked his head toward the sound of Tor's voice as he let drop the clumps of grass and dirt he had been clutching in his fists, and angrily brushed at a tear with the back of his hand. "So, you have heard?" Graben asked, struggling to control his emotions.

"Shael told me, and sent me to find you when you were not in the gardens. How did you hear?"

"Kinber came to me in the gardens," Graben answered flatly, then looked up at Tor and clenched his fists together at his chest. "She is alive, Tor!" he said hoarsely, "yet, lost to me still."

"Shael only said she was found on Barchan Mountain, but—" Tor reached out to steady Graben as he struggled to stand.

Graben grasped Tor's shoulders firmly and exclaimed, his voice raspy, "She is still on Barchan Mountain in the dwelling of the forbidden ones!" Graben repeated what had been told to him by Kinber.

When he had finished, Tor shook his head in disbelief, sighed deeply, and said, "Graben, your mother is very worried. Shael sent me to find you. It is getting dark on this field and we have no torch. Come. We will talk tomorrow." Tor walked with Graben to his mother's dwelling, and Graben was grateful for his company and his silence, for he was lost in his own troubled thoughts.

By evening of the next day, the entire village knew that Tephra was alive, and the rumor that she had, for some unknown reason, sought shelter on Forbidden Mountain was beginning to spread. Tor went with Mica and Siluria to visit Tephra's closest friend Olivine, to see how she was taking the news. Olivine was pacing back and forth, weeping and smiling one moment, then stomping her foot in anger the next. Her friends tried to calm her and persuade her to talk to them about why she was so upset.

Mica was growing impatient with Olivine's senseless babbling, so she poured some wine into a mug, put the mug into Olivine's hands, and ordered her to take a drink.

Olivine stared down at the mug, then up at her friends, and took a long drink of the wine. "I am certain Ogen was going to ask for betrothal at the Mating Feast for Tephra and Graben," she cried. "But now, even if he does, Mother is afraid for me to go to the caves. Tephra's mother insists her daughter would not have left the cave on her own. Many of my clan think there is some danger there now! Te was—no, she *is*—my best friend, and I rejoice that she is alive. I am worried for Tephra—Graben told me she is injured and is still on that mountain. Then Mother tells me our clan believes it is not safe in the caves. Until they know for certain—oh! I so wanted to be mated to Ogen!" and she began sobbing again.

Puzzled by Olivine's reactions, Tor decided to let Mica and Siluria try to console the distressed maiden.

CHAPTER

14

Uluru had a meal ready when Strata, Pingo, and Kaoli returned late the next evening from their visit to the Hammada. Kaoli went immediately to Tephra and told her that the Wise Ones of her village had been informed that she was alive, but that a severe injury to her knee had kept her from returning to her village. Strata assured her that when her knee was healed, men from her own village would come to take her home. Uluru had come to understand that she would not speak in front of a male Barchan, and was a little surprised to see the maiden flash a warm smile of gratitude at Strata. Uluru sent one of the older children to let Foehn know the three had returned, and to invite him to join them all for the evening meal.

After the meal, Foehn inspected Tephra's knee to see how it was healing. He smiled as he assured her it was healing as it should. Strata found a stool and pulled it near the mat where Tephra was resting with Uluru's children cuddled around her. She often played games with the children and told them stories, and they had quickly grown attached to the pretty maiden. Uluru was grateful for her company and for her help with the little ones.

Strata suggested that if Tephra was going to be with them for a while, she might want to know something of the lives of the "forbidden ones" beyond what her people's legends told. He began to tell her about the lives of his people, such as, how the grain for the bread she had eaten was grown on the side of the mountain that faces the rising sun, and about what animals they trapped for their meat and skins. He informed her that the leader, or chief, of their settlement was called Augur. A council made the laws, and stewards helped to see that they were kept and reported any violations, while Augur served more in the role of judge and advisor. At Uluru's suggestion, Strata also explained some of their everyday customs and shared stories about life in Barchan Settlement. She did not seem so fearful of them as when she was first brought to the settlement, but it was evident to Uluru that she was still somewhat uncomfortable when Strata was around. Uluru wondered if it was against Drumlin laws for her to even listen to him. Gradually she became more at ease and seemed to enjoy Strata's stories. One, about his encounter with a protective mama goat, had even made her laugh out loud.

When she had a moment alone with Strata, Uluru confided, "She is wonderful with the children. She tells them stories about the sheep she tended, and how she often sang to the sheep to calm them. She teaches the children little songs, and they adore her!"

Later, after Strata had told a story to amuse the children, he turned to Tephra, "Uluru tells me you sing to sheep!" Grinning he teased, "You truly sing to sheep?" Uluru sent her brother a warning look as she saw Tephra's cheeks turn pink.

Paleo went to her and pleaded, "Tephra, sing one of the songs you sang for us this morning," but Tephra glanced at Strata and shook her head. Paleo then turned to Strata and said, "She also told us about some of the crops raised by her village. Oh," he giggled, "and she made us laugh when she told about how one of her sheep strayed into a vegetable garden and almost caused a fight!"

Strata smiled broadly, "I wonder it did not. One of our goatherds had his ears boxed by the vineyard owner when two goats chewed some vines. I would like to hear more of your people, Tephra."

Pilli, Uluru's youngest daughter, said quietly, "I think we have made Tephra sad. Don't be sad, Tephra," and leaned over to give Tephra a hug. Tephra smiled at Pilli, stroking her hair.

Uluru noticed the way Strata was looking at Tephra and thought, "Hmm. He is growing fond of her, as am I, but with him, I don't know …." Her thoughts were interrupted as Strata stood up quickly and announced that it was late and he and Foehn needed their rest, as did Pingo and Kaoli. He accepted the hugs from the children and followed Foehn, turning to give Tephra a smile and a wink as he walked out the doorway.

Uluru sent the children to get ready for sleep while she finished clearing things away. She looked over to where Tephra rested and saw her wipe at a tear. Her heart went out to the lovely Drumlin maiden her brother had rescued. "She is so loving and gentle with the children," she thought, "and she is so grateful for even the smallest things I do for her." Uluru had a sudden impulse to go to Tephra and hold her as she would Pilli, but realized she might be embarrassed to know Uluru had seen her crying. Instead, she looked in on her little ones, and went to her own sleep mat.

The next day as Tephra was helping Uluru prepare the dough for bread, and the children were playing outside, Uluru asked thoughtfully, "Tephra, you speak to me, and to the children, but I wonder why you do not speak to Strata or even Foehn. You do not even answer their questions."

Tephra was startled by her direct question. "I am—" She was about to say "betrothed" but was not even sure she still was. Still, it was safer to act as if she were, and avoid offending The Always further. "I am betrothed. I cannot speak with a man until after I am mated. It is part of the mating preparation."

"Ah! You are promised to another! Is he handsome? He must be for you are very beautiful."

Tephra felt her face grow warm, and she bowed her head.

Uluru smiled, "Have you loved him a long time?"

She did not know how to answer, for she was not sure of the Barchan meaning of love, so she said only, "We have been friends since we were little more than babes. And yes, he is considered one of the most handsome in our village."

"Since you were babes! That is a long time to be in love." Uluru laughed. "How long have you been promised?"

She explained that Graben had asked to court her the year before, and that in the fifth moon he had claimed her as his betrothed. "We were to be mated soon, but now—" Tephra hung her head, shaking it slowly back and forth. "There will surely be no mating. I have brought dishonor and shame to my clan and to his, and to my village." She turned away from Uluru saying, "I will look to see that the children are alright." Using her walking stick, she limped to the doorway and looked out at the children playing in the yard, mentally returning to that day Strata found her on the plateau. Although she had to admit he had shown her nothing but kindness, she wished Strata had never found her. Once again, she berated herself for ever thinking she could rescue the animal and be able to return to the caves. Yet deep inside she knew she could not have endured hearing its pitiful bleating and knowing it would die. What other course could she have taken?

CHAPTER

15

At dawn, on the day after Graben learned that his betrothed was alive and in a Barchan dwelling, he went to Tor and Ogen. "Come with me to the game fields," he requested urgently. Once there, out of hearing of any other villagers, he reluctantly pleaded, "Fellow Drumlins, I am going to the Barchan settlement to rescue Tephra. I am asking you to come with me, but will not hold it against you if you cannot go with good conscience."

Ogen replied, "Tor has told me of the Barchan's visit to the Hammada, and I have been hearing many rumors. You are not only my cousin, but also my good friend. I will gladly go with you to uphold the honor of Drumlin Village. Olivine's mother has said our mating cannot take place while there is doubt that the caves are safe."

"I will be honored to accompany you," stated Tor, placing his hand on Graben's shoulder. "We must prove that our maidens are in no danger when they go to the caves."

"It is settled then," Graben said with relief. He had been uneasy about asking, yet knew he could not make the journey alone. "We will meet back here as soon as you can gather provisions. Bring your good hunting knives, for we may need to protect ourselves. I am not sure how long it will take to find the settlement, but it is believed the three Barchans who came to meet with the Hammada camped overnight in the woods north of the village. Perhaps we can follow their trail."

"It will not take us long to be ready to set out," Ogen stated, "but Graben, it will add more grief to our village when we are discovered missing."

"I have taken care of that. I have left a message for Kinber, asking him to tell Hevel that we have gone to Barchan to bring Tephra home. He will not get it until well after the midday meal, but that will give us time not to be halted in our plans."

Tor grinned, "You have planned well. But we should each return here by different routes. I will come by the river. Graben, return here straight through the village from your garden. Ogen, come by way of the low hills." The three strode off quickly to gather their provisions for the journey.

Graben returned to the dwelling he had prepared to share with Tephra, and quickly began putting together provisions for their journey to bring Tephra home. He was anxious to bring her safely back to Drumlin Village, but just as anxious to question her reasons for leaving the caves where she was supposed to be preparing for their mating. The thought of her being with the Forbidden Ones fueled his determination, and although he was aware of her injuries, he was certain that the Golith Trials had prepared him for the rigors of the return journey.

The three Drumlin men found the place where the Barchans had camped, and from there were able to trace their tracks to the rugged trail that led through the dense woods beyond the meadows, and up the side of the mountain where the woods converged with the Great Boreal Forest. The men found it rough going, especially in the dense forest, but Graben would only stop for a very short break, anxious to get to the settlement and back to Drumlin Village before dark. When the trail began to level off, Tor suggested they rest for a while before approaching the settlement. "We might meet with some resistance. We need to be rested and strong."

Graben agreed, and finding a grassy spot near the Cambria River, they sprawled out upon it, and fished in their packs for the dried meat, bread, and flask of cider they had each packed. After they had eaten and quenched their thirsts, Graben took his knife out of its sheath and tested its sharpness on a small plant growing nearby. With a nod of determination, he replaced it in its sheath, stood and gestured toward a narrow bridge. With Graben in the lead, they crossed it one at a time. Once they were on the other side of the river, they soon spotted a wide trail and followed it. Graben gave the others a reassuring nod when it was apparent they had found the trail to the Barchan Settlement.

Entering the settlement, Graben walked up to the only person he saw—an old man who was sitting on a worn bench outside a small hut. Graben thought at first that he was sleeping until he noticed the slight movement of the old man's mouth and an occasional puff of smoke from the pipe. Graben noticed that the pipe was intricately carved, and assumed the man might be someone of stature in the settlement. He bowed and asked, "Honorable sir, where will we find the dwelling of one called Strata?"

Without looking up to see who had questioned him, the old man replied in a lazy drawl, "Down the curved path, then take the path to the right. In the fourth hut, the dwelling of the healer, you will find Strata."

Graben was surprised that the old man answered so readily, and wondered if his sight had failed and therefore he could not see they were Drumlin. Following the directions of the old man, they quickly found the dwelling of the healer. Graben halted just outside the door and was about to call for Strata when he heard voices.

A man was speaking, but Graben could not hear clearly. Then, as they drew closer to the door, he heard the voice of an older man saying, "Yes, she will not be with us much longer. Just six, maybe seven more days, and she will be strong enough to risk the journey."

A younger male voice replied, "I thought as much. Tephra seems much stronger. She even took a few steps yesterday and sat out in Uluru's yard. I think the sun did her good, for the color was back in her cheeks."

At the sound of the Barchan male using his beloved's name and how tenderly he spoke of her, jealousy raged within Graben. He burst into the hut, "Are you the one called Strata? Where is she?" he shouted threateningly.

Startled from their meal preparations, the two men only turned and stared. Graben took a step toward the stove where the younger man was standing, and unsheathing his knife, held it in strike position. "Answer me, Barchan," he demanded, "Are you Strata?"

The younger Barchan nodded, "I am Strata."

"Where is the Drumlin maiden you stole?" Graben demanded,

"No one stole the maiden. She is at the dwelling of my sister, Uluru, where she has been well cared for. Put away your knife. I will take you to her. She is almost recovered and will soon be strong enough to journey back to your village."

"That is not for you to say, Barchan!" Graben spat out threateningly, keeping his knife at ready. "We have come to bring her back where she belongs."

The tall Barchan motioned for Graben to precede him into the yard. Graben walked out into the yard, glancing back to be sure the Barchan was following him, and informed Tor and Ogen, "He says she is at his sister's dwelling."

Graben, Tor, and Ogen followed Strata as he ambled along the trail to Uluru's dwelling. A few steps from the doorway the Barchan turned and faced Graben, and taking a deep breath, he said hesitantly, "You need to understand, Tephra is not strong enough for the journey down that rugged path. Foehn, the healer, says—"

Graben interrupted Strata by stepping towards him, holding his knife just inches from his face, and snarling, "Dare speak her name again and I will cut out your tongue! And do not try to prevent her from leaving your accursed mountain. We *will* bring her home this day."

"As you wish, but you are a fool. Because of her injuries, you will need to travel slowly. You will not make it out of the forest, much less down the mountain before nightfall." Even though Strata spoke quietly and calmly, Graben did not miss the loathing in the Barchan's voice, and the fact he had called him a fool. Graben lunged at Strata, pinning him against the outer wall of Uluru's dwelling.

"I have already told you, you have nothing to say in the matter. You are the fool if you think we will allow one of our maidens to stay here one day longer. She has already been soiled enough by your Barchan ways. You have dared to touch a betrothed maiden!" Graben growled through clenched teeth. As Strata struggled against Graben, Tor and Ogen stepped forward and, one on each side, held Strata against the wall.

"Graben! No!" Graben pulled back his knife and turned at the sound of Tephra's alarmed cry. "Do not harm Strata!" He watched as, aided by a walking stick, she limped toward them and said softly to Strata, "It is alright, Strata. I will go with them."

Graben turned abruptly and addressed her, his voice incredulous, "You speak to this man? To this Barchan?" He stepped toward her, and leaning close to her ear whispered threateningly, "The Hammada will hear of this and the many other decrees you have broken." He noticed that her hair was only partially bound, leaving several strands to fall in soft curls over her shoulders. He also noticed how lovely she looked with her hair that way, even though her skin was unusually pale.

Tephra hissed angrily at him, "I spoke only to save his life. *You* would have to answer to the Hammada for harming an innocent man."

"He is a Barchan!" Graben spat, taken aback at the angry tone in Tephra's voice.

"But still an enosh!" Tephra pleaded, her voice just above a whisper.

"Has he not touched you, carried you in his arms? By our laws, I would have a right to challenge him, and yet you defend him!"

Graben stared at Tephra accusingly. She sighed deeply, and shaking her head, looked down. He then exclaimed, "So, you do not deny it!"

Wheeling around to face Strata, he snarled, "You are challenged, Barchan! You have defiled a Drumlin maiden. You have stolen what was to be mine!" Anger and frustration, jealousy and suspicion churned within Graben—feelings so unfamiliar he was unable to curb them. Lunging at Strata, who was still being held by Tor and Ogen, he stabbed at him with his knife. His rage threw off his aim and the knife struck Strata's upper arm near the shoulder instead of his neck.

Before he could strike again, he felt Tephra's hand on his arm and heard her frantic voice pleading, "Graben, no! This is not our way!"

Graben sheathed his knife as he turned to face Tephra and said through clenched teeth, "Quiet! Do not lecture me about *our way*! Not after you have abandoned and even defiled our ways!"

Tephra slowly shook her head at him, her eyes full of tears, "It is not as it seems, Graben. It is not as it seems."

Graben noticed that several Barchans were gathering in the yard of Uluru's dwelling. He also noticed that Tephra was having difficulty standing, even with the aid of the walking stick, and both sobered him a bit. He led her to a nearby bench and motioned for Tor and Ogen to release Strata.

Suddenly, one of the smaller Barchans cried out, "He has cut Strata! He has drawn blood!" He lunged at Graben, his hands reaching toward his throat. Ogen quickly moved to protect Graben. Clenching his fist, he struck the smaller Barchan's jaw, causing blood to run from the corner of his mouth. The small Barchan staggered, righted himself, and then rammed his head into Ogen's belly. The blow caused Ogen to fall backwards, hitting his head on a log. He lay there a moment, then rose and tried to resume the fight with the small Barchan who was wiping the blood from his mouth and chin.

"No! Enough!" Tephra screamed, and the men pulled back. "Graben, Ogen. *This is not our way!* Two men are injured. No more, no more!" Sobbing deeply, she slowly shook her head.

A Barchan woman turned to the small Barchan, "Pingo, are you alright?" Pingo nodded, although he was rubbing his jaw. "Can you help Strata inside? Then go bring Foehn here quickly. Tell him Strata is injured, but tell him nothing else that happened here." Then she turned to Tephra, "Come inside Tephra, you need to rest your leg." Graben was about to object, but the woman looked at him and asked gently but firmly, "Can't you see she is in pain? Help me get her and your friend inside."

"Into a Barchan's dwelling? Never!" spat Graben with obvious contempt.

Tephra, still seated on the bench, grasped Graben's hand and spoke quietly, "Graben, I know you think I have shamed you, and I am sorry. But do not bring dishonor upon yourself by acting rashly. Ogen is hurt and Uluru has offered help. I know what we as Drumlins believe, but I also know that I have been shown much kindness here."

"Have they so ensnared your spirit that you defend them?" Outraged, Graben pulled his hand roughly from Tephra's, pointed his finger at her, and commanded, "You will come with me now!"

"I want to come with you, Graben. I want to go home!" Tephra looked at him pleadingly, as tears filled her eyes, "but I cannot walk. I can barely stand! And what of Ogen? Look at him—his head droops as he leans against Tor."

"You, I will carry. Tor will take care of Ogen. We leave now!" His kept his voice low, yet forceful and determined.

Foehn arrived and warned, "Ah, young Drumlin, you would do well to take caution. With two injured, your descent will go slowly. It will not be easy to—"

"I thank you for your concern," Graben interrupted with mocking politeness, "but we do not stay a moment longer on your mountain."

Foehn nodded, "As you will, but I must first check the maiden's wound and change the dressing."

Uluru also pleaded with Graben, "Let her have some food. She has not eaten since early. She has had little appetite with the pain in her knee. We were just preparing a meal when you arrived. Let her take food and drink, and I will prepare a packet of food for your journey."

Graben glared at the woman and impatiently shook his head, "We will leave now!" Turning back to Tephra, he held out his hand. "You are betrothed to me. Come with me now, or the Hammada will know that you have forsaken the teachings of The Always. You know what that will mean."

"This is the one to whom you are betrothed?" Uluru asked Tephra, her tone doubtful. "It is sad that he does not care for you, for you spoke so kindly of him!"

Graben turned abruptly and glared at Uluru, "Woman, you speak falsely, putting vile thoughts in her head." Then, his voice hoarse with emotion, he said, "For years I have waited, longing for the day I would claim her as my mate. The day we were to be mated, I learn she had left—"

"Oh, yes!" Uluru confronted him, "your pride has been injured, so now you care nothing for *her* injuries, or even those of your friend. If it were possible, she should refuse you as mate!"

At these words, Graben moved threateningly toward her, his hand reaching toward his knife.

"Graben, oh Graben!" Tephra's voice was barely above a whisper, yet filled with so much anguish that Graben halted and turned to her. Her face was wet with tears, her eyes full of pleading as she stood and limped painfully toward him. In two strides, he went to her, caught her in his arms, and buried his face in her hair, his anger and resentment diminishing with the feel of her in his arms.

"My beloved!" He gently picked her up, cradled her in his arms, and spoke to Uluru quietly, "I will take her inside. See to her needs if you wish, then we will be on our way." Graben laid her gently upon the mat Uluru indicated, looked across to where Foehn was attending Strata, and walked toward the door. He stopped suddenly and turned back to Tephra, frowning as he once again noticed how her hair flowed softly on her shoulders. "Your hair—arrange it in the Drumlin custom," he ordered in a gruff voice, then turned abruptly and stepped outside. He rubbed his forehead, annoyed that she would even think to abandon the hair customs. Although he did not like her being in the Barchan hut, the confrontation with the Barchan and the long hike up the rugged trail had taken its toll, and he was relieved to have a few moments to rest before they attempted the return to Drumlin Village.

Uluru brought a plate of stewed meat and vegetables and a cup of mulled wine to Tephra. "Try to eat something. You will need your strength for the journey," she said gently.

"Thank you, Uluru." Tephra glanced over to where Strata appeared to be sleeping. "Will Strata be all right? Is his wound very deep?" she asked softly.

Strata opened his eyes and turned towards her. "Ah! She speaks! Do not worry, lovely one. Foehn is a worthy healer, and I mend quickly."

Tephra blushed at his words and turned her attention to the plate of food in front of her. She had no appetite, but knew she would need strength for the journey. After she had eaten a few bites, she put the plate aside and sipped on the mulled wine. Although not strong, it soothed and calmed her. She lay back on the mat and closed her eyes as Foehn came to her and tended her wound.

Uluru assisted Foehn as he dressed Tephra's wound with fresh poultice and wrapped her knee with a clean, soft bandage. "Try to get them to take rest as often as possible. Step carefully, for the path you must take is rocky and quite steep in places," Uluru advised Tephra. She helped her to stand, and handed her a crutch Foehn had fashioned for her from a forked tree branch. The forked section was padded with cloth and Uluru showed her how to place that part under her arm. "This will help, but still you must go slowly. Here, take this cloak against the cool night air."

'Dear Uluru, thank you for your kindnesses. I wish I could repay you somehow."

"You kept my little ones entertained with your stories and songs, and that I will miss. My chores were done so much faster," Uluru grinned at the Drumlin maiden. Then, whispering in a serious tone, she added, "There is one thing I would ask of you?"

Tephra looked at her questioningly, and whispered in reply "What can I do? You—and your family—you have all been so good to me, a Drumlin."

"Send me word of you from time to time?"

"How? You know that this place is—"

"Forbidden Mountain? Yes, I know. And we once believed you were a people far inferior to us. But Tephra," Uluru continued in a hushed voice, "Barchans and Drumlins are not the only peoples. There are others, and many Barchans are beginning to understand...."

Tephra was amazed at Uluru's revelation and stared. Uluru shook her head, smiled tenderly and said, "We will find a way to send word to each other." She put her arms around Tephra in a farewell embrace.

Graben stepped into the doorway and was shocked to see Tephra embracing one of the forbidden ones. He barked, "Tephra!"

"I-I am ready. I am ready to go home, Graben." She placed the support under one arm, and carrying the cloak over the other, limped to the door.

Graben took her arm and they crossed to where Tor and Ogen were waiting. He went to Ogen, knelt beside him, and placing his hand on Ogen's shoulder, asked quietly. "Are you able to make the journey down?"

"I am able with Tor's help. Do not concern yourself."

Graben thought Ogen's speech was somewhat slurred, as if he had consumed too much ale. "Are you sure? We can make camp outside of the village. You can rest a while, and we will return for Tephra at dawn. I will just make sure that Barchan returns to his own dwelling, even if I have to carry him myself." He had remained standing near the doorway, and had heard Tephra voice her concern for the Barchan. He had also heard Strata call her 'lovely one," arousing feelings of betrayal and jealousy once again, and he had to restrain himself from reacting.

"We will be in our own village by dawn." Ogen gave Graben an encouraging smile. Graben looked thoughtfully at Ogen, then at Tor.

"Ogen is right," Tor stated firmly. "We will be in our own village by dawn. I am anxious to be off this mountain."

Uluru walked quickly over to Tor and Ogen and held out a pouch and a flask. "There is dried meat and bread in the pouch, and spring water mixed with a little wine in the flask. You may have need."

Tor looked questioningly at Graben and he shook his head, unwilling to accept anything from the Barchans. Tephra put her hand on Graben's arm and whispered, "Please. Do not offend." He grudgingly nodded, and Tor gave Uluru a slight smile as he accepted her offering. Tephra said gently, "Thank you, Uluru. May The Always hold you in his favor for your kindness to his people."

Graben strengthened his grasp on Tephra's arm and led her toward the trail, with Tor and Ogen following. No one said anything for a long while as they made slow but steady progress away from the Barchan settlement. When they reached the narrow bridge over Cambria River,

Graben said, "Tor, let Ogen rest here while you help me get Tephra across. Then I will help with Ogen."

Graben tucked Tephra's crutch under one arm, and holding one of Tephra's arms securely while Tor held her other arm, the two men carried Tephra across the bridge. After leading Tephra to a small boulder on which she could sit and rest her knee, the two men returned to help Ogen cross to where Tephra waited. They then continued on the trail that led down the mountain.

They had not gone very far when Ogen suddenly gasped, "Graben, hold up. I must rest. My head aches more with every step."

Graben guided Tephra to one of the trees that bordered the trail so she could lean against it for support, and then he went quickly to Ogen. "Of course, my friend, it is time for a rest." He helped Tor settle Ogen in an area of fallen pine needles, using his own cloak as a pillow for his injured friend's head. "How about some of the food the Barchan woman provided? Or some good Drumlin cheese and bread? We have some left."

"Maybe just some water with a little wine. I do not think my belly will hold food just now."

"Tor, help me see to Ogen." Tor gave the flask to Ogen, and then poured water onto a strip of cloth he had torn from the hem of his own tunic. Graben and Tor helped Ogen turn so that they could place the wet cloth on the lump at the back of his head. Once he was settled, Tor pulled Graben aside, "I am becoming more concerned about Ogen's injury."

Graben nodded, and while the others rested, walked ahead several paces. When he returned he announced, "We will rest a while longer. The steep part of the trail is just ahead, and going down it will not be easy with Tephra's injured knee."

Shortly after they were back on the trail, the path became more rugged as they had known it would. Though they had slowed their pace considerably, Tephra found it increasingly difficult to manage the rough terrain. At a particularly rocky section, she lost her balance in spite of Graben's hold on her arm, and almost toppled forward. She dropped the crutch and grasped frantically at Graben. He quickly scooped her up in his arms, and called back to Tor, "Be watchful of Ogen. The path is treacherous in places; more than we noticed on the way up."

As Graben carried Tephra in his arms down the uneven trail, he recalled something Kinber had said. The Barchan called Strata had carried Tephra in his arms from the plateau to the Barchan healer's dwelling. Once again, he tasted the bitter bile of jealousy, and held Tephra closer.

All four were exhausted when, just before nightfall, they made their way into the dense woods on the lower slopes of the mountain. Not only did Graben carry Tephra most of the way, but Ogen had leaned heavily upon Tor as his head was throbbing more intensely. Graben motioned for the two men and Tephra to sit down.

"I do not think it wise to continue. We will rest here tonight, at least for a while. Tor, help find a comfortable place for Ogen and Tephra to rest near that clearing where we can safely have a small fire." Graben and Tor used their hands to gather up fallen leaves and pine needles into two piles and then helped Ogen and Tephra to the places they had prepared. Once the two were settled, they set about building a fire.

There had been no conversation during the trip, only a word of caution now and then, and there was no effort at conversation now. Tephra kept silent, for she did not know what to say to Graben. It was clear he was angry and suspicious, and she had conflicting feelings about the actions and attitudes he had exhibited in the Barchan settlement. They were alien to the Graben she had grown up with and had come to care for. He was always competitive and ambitious, but had never shown such anger and violence.

Graben brought her a slice of bread and a small piece of cheese, and stated in a cold voice, "I am warming some of the wine and water that the Barchan woman gave you. It will warm you and help you to rest. We leave well before sunrise to meet the Hammada at the Stone." After that one moment when he had pulled her into his arms at Uluru's dwelling, he had become distant and cold. He saw to her safety on the trail, but there was little kindness in his efforts.

Tephra looked into his eyes to see if there was any caring left there, but saw only determination. She finished the food and wine he brought, then lying down and pulling the cloak over her head, tried to swallow the hard lump in her throat as tears filled her eyes. "I do not know this Graben," she thought. "He frightens me. I think this Graben would have killed Strata if I had not stopped him." Certain that Graben is convinced she had betrayed him—and in the gravest ways—she wondered if he still cared for her. She whispered to herself, "If only I could talk to him, tell him—tell him everything. But he is closed to me. And Tor—Tor who is also Sedi's friend—will not even look at me." Again, she struggled with her conflicting thoughts, wishing she had not rescued the lamb, which was not a lamb at all but one of the Barchan's goats. She tried to imagine what the Hammada would say. "Oh, Grandmother!" she whispered, curling herself into a ball and pulling the cloak tighter as the thought of bringing shame to her grandmother threatened her with feelings of despair.

Forcing herself to take deep breaths, she struggled to put aside such disturbing thoughts and to think instead of Uluru and her children. She brushed away her tears as she recalled the times she would sing to them, and play with them on the mat Uluru had made for her. Her thoughts drifted back to one afternoon as she sat entertaining the children with songs from her childhood. Strata had come into the dwelling with his cousin, and when she heard the voices of the men, she stopped singing and looked up. She saw that Strata was watching her intently with a slight smile, his blue eyes twinkling.

He sighed and shook his head, "I am sorry to interrupt your song. Please continue. Your voice is—" he paused, cleared his throat, then continued, "—very lovely."

Tephra shook her head, but managed a small smile. She motioned to the children to bring the wooden blocks they had been playing with earlier, and began helping them build a fortress. The children had quickly picked up on her gestures, learning that when an adult male was in the hut, she would not speak. Tephra was amused that the younger two, the twins, had begun to adopt her silence at those times.

Though she deeply longed for her own family, she knew she would miss Uluru and her children. She also knew that her future was very uncertain, and had to admit the possibility she may never see her own family again. All was dependant on what the Hammada would rule concerning her time on the forbidden mountain.

Taking several quick breaths, Tephra forced herself to stop dwelling on such uncertainties, and instead, turned again to thoughts of Strata. She wondered at the feelings Strata had begun to stir in her each time he looked at her, or when she would overhear him asking Uluru or Foehn about her knee and whether she needed anything. She thought back to the fear that had raced through her when she saw the blood pouring from the injury Graben had inflicted with his knife. He was a Barchan, a forbidden one. She should not feel happy when he smiled at her or enjoy his gentle, playful teasing. Exhausted from the journey and from trying to sort through her many conflicting emotions, she fell asleep remembering the last time she had seen Strata's grin and twinkling deep blue eyes.

CHAPTER 16

Graben added more wood to the fire and went to where Tephra was sleeping. "Tephra, wake up," Graben said as he gently patted her shoulder. She blinked her eyes and looked up at him. He handed the crutch to her and helped her stand and move closer to the fire. After helping Tor move Ogen closer to the fire, he portioned out the remainder of the bread and cheese, and handed Tephra the flask of watered wine. He urged her to eat quickly, saying it was time to finish their journey.

Just as dawn broke, the four made their way into the clearing where the Wise Ones were gathering at the Hammada Stone for morning prayers. Graben helped Tephra to the ground and motioned for Tor to help Ogen to rest as well. "Watch over them," he said to Tor. "I will approach the Hammada."

He turned and briskly walked the few yards to the stone. At the edge of the stone Graben knelt, and striking his breast with his right hand he called out, "I, Graben of the Clan of Earth-Tillers, beg to be heard by the Hammada."

Turning around at the sound of his voice, the Wise Ones gave him inquisitive looks. Karst walked to the edge of the stone, "You may speak."

Graben gestured toward Tephra, Ogen and Tor. "I, that is, Tor, Ogen and I, have rescued the maiden Tephra of the Clan of Shepherds from the Forbidden Mountain. We bring her to the Hammada for scrutiny."

Karst looked at the three who rested on the nearby grassy slope, and then looking back at Graben, said sternly, "So, you admit you went where Drumlins are forbidden to go."

"Yes, to rescue the maiden who was betrothed to me, Wise One," Graben answered defensively, yet taking care to speak with respect.

"You knew that there was an agreement with the Barchans that when the maiden was able to make the journey safely, four men chosen by the Hammada would go to bring her back to our village."

Graben nodded, "Yes, Wise One, I knew of the agreement."

"And yet you led two fellow Drumlins up to a place forbidden?"

"I did not trust the Barchan. I was afraid for my betrothed." Graben answered emphatically. Then, aware that perhaps his tone had been disrespectful, he added in a more courteous tone, "I also judged that the longer she was with the forbidden ones, the more tainted she would become, and would have a longer time of Purification."

"That was not for you to judge!" Karst declared, startling Graben. "Do you doubt the wisdom of the Hammada? And if you had consulted the Hammada, as you should, you would have learned that after further consideration, it had been decided that on this day a wise matron, accompanied by two strong men, would make the journey. The matron would stay with the maiden Tephra, to protect her and care for her injury, until she could safely make the journey. Yet, you risk further injury of the maiden by taking matters into your own hands."

Graben knew he had to show remorse for his actions, yet he truly was not sorry he had gone to find his betrothed, especially after he had encountered the Barchan male who had carried her. And, he was not sorry he had wounded that man.

"Graben, you, Ogen and Tor will have to undergo scrutiny and Purification as well," Karst said. Graben was shocked. He stood and took a step toward the stone, but Karst raised his hand and declared, "You were on the Forbidden Mountain, and went of your own free will. Each of you will have a hearing, and the Hammada will make a judgment on Purification."

Turning to Kame, Karst said, "Go see to your granddaughter. Take her to your dwelling, and return to us here. We will take counsel with The Always until you return."

Kame went with Graben to where the other three waited. Going first to her granddaughter, she knelt beside her and enfolded her in her arms. Looking toward Nunatak Peak, she spoke with deep emotion, "All my gratitude to The Always! I knew my child would be returned to us." Then she turned to Graben and inquired, "Ogen. He is injured?"

Ogen attempted to sit up and before Graben could answer, replied in a slurred voice, "Oh, Wise One, it is just a lump on the head."

"Graben," Kame said quietly, with a touch of alarm, "hurry back to the stone. Ask Karst to send Hevel immediately. This boy needs the healer's care."

Graben sprinted to the stone and led Hevel the healer to where Ogen lay. Hevel asked Ogen a few questions, listened intently to his responses, and examined the lump on his head. The healer then turned his attention to Tephra. He unwrapped the bandage on her knee, gently touched the swollen area, and then spoke to Graben and Tor. "Go to my shelter. Bring two litters and two men to help carry Tephra and Ogen."

Graben and Tor returned with two young men and the litters Hevel had requested. Karst had accompanied them. The healer looked up at Graben and Tor and said, "You two will take this young man to my dwelling." Addressing the other two men, he said, "The maiden will go with Kame to her dwelling."

Karst asked, "Is Ogen's injury serious?"

Hevel stood and led Karst away from where Ogen and Tephra were resting. "His eyes, his manner of speaking tell me yes," he answered. "He will need careful watching and all my skills and potions, and of course, the prayers of the Hammada."

Graben had followed them, anxious to hear how Hevel would answer. On hearing the seriousness of Ogen's injury, he rubbed the back of his neck, swallowed hard, then asked in a whisper, "He won't—he won't—*die?*"

"I will be truthful with you," Hevel turned to Graben and looked at him intently, "Yes, he could die, or he could be up and about in a few days. It depends on how he was injured. Graben, tell me exactly how he was injured."

Graben looked at Tor and, ignoring the uneasy feeling in his belly, told the healer that Ogen tripped over a stone, fell and hit his head on a log. He said that Ogen had seemed all right at first, then he admitted that on the journey down the mountain, Ogen had gradually become dizzy and the pain in his head increased. Graben deliberately left out the fact that there was a scuffle, that Ogen was knocked down forcefully, and that he, Graben, had wounded a Barchan. He knew neither of his friends, nor Tephra, would reveal the truth—it was too much of a risk.

Karst turned his attention to Tephra. "It seems Kame was right about her granddaughter," he said gently. "She never doubted you were alive." To Kame he said, "Go straight to your dwelling. Do not answer any questions the villagers may ask just yet. See to her needs, and then return to the Hammada Stone. A tribunal will be called." Karst then looked intently at Graben, Tor, and Tephra and in a stern voice, said, "You are not to speak to anyone, except to your mother and father. You may tell them what you wish, but do bind them to silence. You are thus bound."

Graben helped Ogen onto the litter, and he and Tor carried him to Hevel's shelter. After getting Ogen settled on a cot, he paused at the door, trying to summon the courage to ask Hevel if he should go to Ogen's parents. The thought of telling them of Ogen's injury caused an empty feeling in the pit of his stomach, but yet he knew it was his duty to tell them. Hevel said to tell Ogen's parents only that he had been injured, was resting comfortably in Hevel's hut, and Hevel would send for them the next day. Walking with heavy feet, Graben made his way to Ogen's family dwelling and gave them Hevel's message.

Kame helped Tephra bathe and dress in a clean shift, then cleaned and redressed her wounded knee. She brought her a mug of strong broth, a slice of bread, and Tephra's favorite millet cakes spread with honey, and placed them on a low table next to the cot where she rested. Kame's silence troubled Tephra somewhat, but she was exhausted from the journey down the mountain, so she welcomed the time to rest and refresh herself before she answered the questions she knew would be asked of her. She watched as her grandmother went to her prayer rug, her lips moving in silent prayer. After a few moments of prayer, Kame picked up her crystal-tipped staff and held the crystal toward the window so that it caught the slanting rays of the early morning sun. As the crystal began to glow a deep rose color, Kame gave a sharp intake of breath.

Tephra whispered hoarsely, "Grandmother?"

The old woman put a finger to her lips, went to her cupboard of herbs, and took down several jars and small bags. She then put a small pot of water on the stove to heat and added a pinch or two of each herb. After adjusting the flame, she turned to Tephra and said, "Rest. I must go to the Hammada Stone."

Tephra reclined on the cot and tried to rest, but her anxiety would not allow her to close her eyes. She knew the Hammada were likely considering her fate, and she bit at her lip to stop its trembling. Kame returned with three of the Wise Ones, Moraine, Eolia, and Kenǽ, and Tephra hugged herself tightly to stop trembling, for she suspected they were there to question her. After Kame poured the herbal tea into four small mugs, each woman took a seat on the prayer rug. Kenǽ motioned for Tephra to come sit in the center of the rug facing Kame, but Kame held up her hand and pleaded, "Wise Ones, may we permit the maiden to remain on her cot, allowing for her injury?" The three nodded, signifying it was allowed, and Tephra gave a shaky smile of gratitude.

Kame closed her eyes, took a deep, cleansing breath, and uttered a prayer. Tephra could not make out all of the words, but understood enough to feel assured it was a prayer for wisdom. The four Wise Ones lifted their mugs, took a drink of the tea, and placed the mugs near them on the floor.

Moraine looked at Tephra and said, "Maiden, called Tephra of the Clan of Shepherds, you are now to undergo scrutiny regarding your apparent violation of the decrees and traditions of the Village of

Drumlin and of The Always. We will hear and examine your accounting of the time from your entry into the Cave of Solitude to the time Graben brought you to the Hammada Stone with Tor and Ogen. We will ask questions which you must answer truthfully and completely. Do not omit anything, no matter how small or unimportant it may seem to you. What you heard, what you observed, and what you thought, must be made known to this tribunal. The Always will not be satisfied with less than total openness. Do you understand?"

Tephra took a deep breath, and answered, "Yes, Wise One, I do understand."

Led by the questions of the four Wise Ones, Tephra recounted her actions and her observations as Moraine had instructed. Kenæ and Eolia seemed especially disturbed that there were periods of time that Tephra was confused about, particularly the time she spent in the hut of Foehn and Strata. She worried that they doubted her truthfulness, but she knew in her heart she had answered all of their questions completely, except two times. When they asked about the Barchan man who had found her, she said that while it was true he had carried her, it was only because she could not walk and he carried her to the Barchan healer. She denied that there was anything improper in his manner toward her; but did not mention how kind he was and how his eyes looked when he smiled at her. When asked about Ogen's injury, she licked her lips, swallowed, and answered with the version she had heard Graben give, for she assumed Tor would give the same answer.

Often one of the Wise Ones asked a question that had already been answered, or asked Tephra to clarify or give more details. Tephra noticed that they asked some questions more than once, but phrased them differently. The women seemed most intent on scrutinizing her time in the shelter of Foehn, and when exactly she was brought to stay with Uluru. Tephra was becoming restless and at some of their questions bit her lip to calm herself before answering with a composure she did not feel. She was determined to show that she was cooperative and hiding nothing.

It was almost dark when the scrutiny was completed and Moraine stood and spoke authoritatively, "We have heard your accounting of your time on the Forbidden Mountain, and your explanation of how and why you ascended the mountain. We will each go to our own shelters and meditate. Before dawn tomorrow we will meet at the Stone, and together we will pray and be guided by The Always as to what we should recommend to the Hammada." The four bowed to each other, and Moraine, Eolia, and Kenæ left Kame's small dwelling.

Since they had paused only twice to take a little nourishment of bread, cheese, and watered wine, Tephra felt drained and exhausted. She had nothing to do now but wait. Her story was finished, and her fate was in the hands of the Hammada. She looked at her grandmother who was still standing in her place on the prayer rug, her head bowed low. Tephra suppressed a cry and rubbed her clammy hands on her shift as she whispered hoarsely, "Grandmother?"

The old woman lifted her head and gave a small smile. "My child, my dear child," she said as she came to sit on the edge of the cot, and then pulled Tephra into her arms. Tephra longed to find comfort in her beloved grandmother's arms, but instead she heard the heavy pounding of Kame's heart and sensed her grandmother, too, was afraid. "I spoke truthfully, Grandmother," Tephra said shakily, trying to reassure herself as well as Kame, "Do you think I will be banished?"

"Your words were true—that I know—but I sensed you neglected something, and I fear the others did also. Was there something you left out, child? I cannot help you if—"

Tephra interrupted, "It is only—only that I, well, I do not understand why the mountain people are forbidden. They showed me much kindness, and the woman I stayed with told me her brother risked much coming to tell you I was alive and how I was injured."

"Tephra, tell me again about the Barchans. How many were around you, spoke to you?"

Tephra took a deep breath, and said slowly, "There was the healer—Foehn was his name—and his son. No, no it was his grandson, the one who found me and carried me to the healer. And the woman I stayed with—the healer's granddaughter—her name was Uluru, and she had three children. Oh, and—and the grandson's friend, another young woman."

Kame was silent a moment, her head bobbing up and down, before she said, "Hmmm, the healer, the young woman, and the woman and her children will be of little concern. But, I must warn you, the time you spent in the hut of the healer when the grandson was there, and that he carried you in his arms, I am afraid the Hammada will find most offensive."

"Even though—even though I explained how it all came about? There was nothing I could do! And for this I will be banished?" Tephra asked in a shrill voice.

"Oh, child! I will not give you false hopes. There are things in your favor, so if you are banished, it will likely be only a short time of Purification."

"My mother, my family! Do they know I am here?"

"Word has been sent to them. Your mother will come in the morning. Now, we will have a bowl of soup and you will get some rest."

"You must rest also, Grandmother, you look tired. I am sorry I have troubled you."

Kame kissed her granddaughter on her forehead and went to prepare the soup. After they had finished the light meal, the old woman put a fresh dressing on Tephra's wound; then she sat beside her on the cot for several moments, lovingly stroking her hair. When Kame went to her own cot, Tephra noticed how weary she seemed. Squeezing her eyes shut and swallowing the lump in her throat, she whispered a prayer of remorse to The Always. She was unable to keep from trying to imagine what the Hammada might rule, so she lay awake, twisting at her hair until exhaustion took over and she fell into a restless sleep.

CHAPTER

17

The next morning, Tephra awoke to the smell of baking bread. The smell revived her appetite and Tephra realized she was hungry for the first time in many days. She and Kame had just finished their breakfast of fresh bread, boiled eggs, and dried figs when Caldera arrived. As soon as she saw her daughter, Caldera began weeping with joy and relief. Kneeling next to Tephra where she reclined on the cot, she gathered her up in her arms. Tephra sobbed as she poured out apologies—most of which were incoherent—painfully aware of the anguish she had caused her family, and the anxiety of what may still come.

Tephra knew her mother had many questions that she could not answer at this time, so she tried to reassure her by squeezing her hand as she looked into her eyes and smiled. Caldera returned the smile and nodded in understanding. Tephra asked, "How is Breccia? Does she know I am home? Father and Sedi, they are well?" As they anxiously awaited the judgment of the Hammada, the two sought comfort in talking about ordinary things to distract their thoughts—the sheep, the tunic Caldera was making for Sedi, and how Breccia was learning to sweep the floor properly. The last made Tephra giggle at the image it brought to mind. At times though, the words ran out and Caldera sat on the cot with Tephra's head in her lap as she stroked her hair or rubbed her shoulders. It was past midday when the expected messenger arrived. Caldera was to help Tephra get dressed in a simple shift and see that her hair was neatly braided. The messenger also advised that if they had not taken their midday meal, they should do so as the hearing could be lengthy, but neither Caldera nor Tephra could manage more than a bite or two of bread and a few sips of tea.

Tephra's knee was still too painful to allow her to walk very far, so two men of the Hammada carried her on a litter to the Hammada Stone, while Tarn and Caldera walked alongside. Once at the Stone, Tarn carried her to the center where a small bench had been placed so that she could be spared putting weight on her knee. Karst then spoke to her parents and the villagers who had been summoned to hear what the judgment would be. Many rumors had been circulated among the villagers, and Karst—considered the wisest of the Wise Ones—was responsible for seeing that false rumors were put to rest. It was important to the way of life in Drumlin that truthfulness be upheld.

Tephra looked up as Karst held his staff out over the villagers who were gathered in the clearing in front of the Stone. Calling them to silence, he said, "People of Drumlin Hills, this day we gather to pronounce a judgment on one of our daughters." At these words, Tephra winced and cast her eyes downward, staring at the hem of Karst's robe as he continued. "The Hammada has heard the testimony of Tephra of the Clan of Shepherds. It is understood that she, on her own, made her way to the plateau, which separates the Village of Drumlin from the Forbidden Mountain. And she did, of her own will, leave the Cave of Solitude during her preparation for the Mating Ritual with Graben of the Clan of Earth-tillers. She testified that she heard the cry of a lamb and was able to see the lamb struggling to free itself from a thorny vine. She felt it was her duty as a shepherdess to rescue the lamb before it would be killed by wolves or starve, entangled as it was in the thorns. Once she had freed the lamb, she tried to return to the Cave of Solitude, but fell and suffered a severe injury to her knee. Though injured, she still attempted to return to the cave, but the only safe passage led her up to the plateau. A Barchan man found her near a stream there."

Tephra winced again, biting at her lip as she heard the murmur of alarm that spread through the gathering of villagers. When the murmuring quieted, Karst resumed his narration, "The Barchan took her to his grandfather, the village healer, who tended to her injuries. After consulting with the chief of the settlement, the man who found her came to let us know she was alive and unharmed except for the injury to her knee. The Wise Ones have, under the guidance of The Always, heard and considered the maiden's accounting of her journey and her time among the Forbidden Ones. We have also heard what Graben observed when he went to the Barchan Settlement to rescue his betrothed. The laws of our people state: 'One who ascends the Forbidden Mountain and dwells among the people of that mountain, called Barchans, becomes unclean and is no longer fit to live among the people of Drumlin'."

Although Tephra knew the law as well as anyone in the village, upon hearing it stated by Karst, she found herself almost gasping for air. She had barely noticed the murmuring of the villagers, and was startled when Karst silenced them by thumping his staff on the stone.

"However," the Wise One stated loudly, "there is a provision that allows one so defiled to be reconciled through a Rite of Purification, if the Hammada determine that the circumstances of one's violation were not serious enough to deserve Rite of Banishment. It has been determined, and now decreed, that the maiden Tephra must go through the Rite of Purification in Partial Banishment. The terms will now be put to the maiden Tephra."

Tephra sat nervously twisting at her long braids during Karst's pronouncement, not daring to look at the villagers, but instead focusing her gaze on the leader of the Hammada. Relieved that she was not to be fully banished, she let out a long slow breath and waited anxiously to learn what terms Karst would name. He turned to her and said, "Maiden Tephra of the Clan of Shepherds, daughter of Tarn and Caldera, you will dwell in the shelter of Kame, a wise, esteemed member of the Hammada." At these words, that she would be with her grandmother, Tephra felt a rush of relief, but that relief quickly diminished upon hearing Karst's next words. "No one of the Village of Drumlin will be allowed to visit or have any exchange with the maiden Tephra during her time of purification. The maiden's family members are bound by this isolation also."

Tephra's eyes filled with tears and a knot formed in her throat, shaking her head slowly in disbelief as she thought, "Not see Mother or Father! Not be able to talk with Sedi, or play with Breccia? No!"

Karst turned to face the villagers again and informed them, "The maiden will undergo strict supervision from Kame, Moraine, and Eolia for a period of three moons. They will see that her days are filled with labor, study, prayer and meditation. They may advise the Hammada if the terms of Purification should be altered, if sufficient reason is given. She will, of course, not take part in any of the village ceremonies, festivities, or gatherings. Any villager who attempts to interfere with the seclusion of the maiden Tephra will be chastised. The maiden will now go into seclusion, and the people of Drumlin will remain here until she is secured inside the shelter of the Wise Kame."

Graben had been listening intently to the words of Karst. He was greatly disturbed by the pronouncement of Partial Banishment, for he did care for Tephra. Yet, he also experienced a sense of justification; after all, his whole life had changed when she left the caves. He was to be mated and had worked hard to prepare a more than suitable dwelling for one of the loveliest maidens in Drumlin. Why had she gone after that animal? Why had she let that Barchan carry her, touch her? She had even spent the night in his dwelling. Oh, he knew her knee was severely injured, but still he felt cheated, and anger filled him. He did not know where or how to direct his anger. He stalked off to his garden and began pulling weeds, tearing them out of the ground so viciously that he pulled out some of the young vegetable plants with the weeds.

"Graben! Graben?" he heard Tor call out. "I came to see how you were accepting the pronouncement against Tephra. I can see you are upset, as you should be, of course. What did you expect? Tephra—"

"Do not speak to me of this!" Graben barked. "By this time I would have been mated. We would be sharing the dwelling I had prepared for her. She would be sleeping by my side each night! Now...." Graben shook his head in frustration as he clenched a fistful of dirt and held it up, staring at it. He then crumbled it, letting it sift through his fingers, as he said in a voice hoarse with anguish, "This, this is what has become of my life plans."

Tor grasped Graben's shoulder and said, "After her time of banishment, you can still be mated to her. She will be reconciled."

Graben threw off Tor's hand and stood abruptly. "She was touched, carried in the arms of that Barchan! She left the caves, when she was supposed to be preparing for our mating. And why? To rescue a lamb?" The bitter taste in his mouth was evidenced in his bitter tone.

"You are angry, but you will feel differently in time. After the Rite of Purification—"

Graben shook his head and clenched his jaw, silencing Tor. How could Tor suggest that he, Graben of the Earth-Tillers and this year's Golith, be mated to one who had been among the forbidden ones and was now banished?

"It seems I have no words of wisdom or comfort, my friend. Speak to Karst. Ask for guidance. For now, go to your family."

CHAPTER 18

Graben, Tor, and Ogen were brought before the Hammada to answer for their unlawful journey to the Forbidden Mountain. Hevel the Healer examined Ogen and pronounced that he was not well enough to undergo scrutiny by the Hammada, so Ogen was excused and taken back to Hevel's hut. Graben and Tor were each questioned separately regarding the planning of the trip to the mountain, their encounter with the Barchans, and how Ogen obtained his injuries.

Graben was sent to wait in Hevel's hut while Tor was questioned. Anxious about how Tor would answer the questions of the Hammada, he paced back and forth near the cot where Ogen was resting.

"Graben, sit down. Talk to me. Your pacing is unsettling," Ogen complained.

"I am in no mood for talking. I am sorry my pacing is unsettling. My mind is unsettled!" Graben raked his hand through his hair, then restlessly clenched and unclenched his fists at his side.

"What is worrying you, Graben?"

"What if Tor and I do not say the same things? It could be bad for both of us!"

"Hevel won't let them question me, but I would tell them you did not force me to go with you. And I could say …."

Graben noticed Ogen's confused frown when he paused, and he knew Ogen was trying to remember the events on the mountain. He noticed too that Ogen winced and covered his eyes with his hand. The sick feeling in his gut returned as once again the sound of Ogen's head hitting the log echoed in his memory. The knowledge that he had not told the truth about his friend's injury ate at his conscience. Many times he had tried to justify his actions to himself, but the guilt kept nagging at him. Going to the cot, he knelt, put his hand on Ogen's shoulder, and said, "It's alright. You are injured, and you would not be if I had not asked you to go with me. Rest, my friend. I will sit over in the corner there and wait for the Wise Ones to call for me."

When Hevel returned with Tor, he checked on the sleeping Ogen. "Has he had any pain?" the healer asked Graben.

"He did not complain. But when he was trying to remember something and then could not, he frowned as though it hurt his head to try, and he covered his eyes."

Hevel nodded, worry adding to the wrinkles on his forehead. After placing a wet cloth over Ogen's eyes and forehead, he led Graben to the stone. Karst motioned for Graben to kneel in the center of the Wise Ones and asked him to pledge on his honor and on the honor of his clan that the accounting he was about to give was true.

Graben struck his breast with his fist, looked up at Karst and said, "I do so pledge."

Karst looked intently at Graben and warned, "The Always does not look favorably on those who speak untruths."

Graben nodded in agreement and tried to ignore the cold, hard knot in his chest.

"Is it true that although knowing the Wise Ones of our village were making plans to go to the maiden Tephra, you did conspire with two young men of our village to go among the Forbidden Ones?" Karst began the questioning in a stern voice.

"Yes, it is true, but—"

Karst held up his hand, "You may be given a chance to defend your actions later. And did you consult any of the Wise Ones, or even an older, more mature male of our village, before you made your own plans?"

"No, I consulted no one."

"Were you aware that to ascend to Barchan Mountain, the dwelling place of the Forbidden Ones, was a violation of the decrees of The Always?"

Graben hesitated before answering, "Yes, but I—"

"And therefore you knew that to violate such a decree would bring dishonor upon you and your clan?" Karst interrupted, his voice harsh and demanding. "And you were also aware that those who went with you would bring dishonor upon themselves and their clans as well. Is this true?"

"O Wise Karst," Graben pleaded, "I did not think about..."

"Ah!" Karst broke in again, "So you admit that you acted rashly, and without thought?"

"No!" Graben shook his head, and said emphatically, "I *did* think about what I was going to do."

"Did you spend time in prayer and meditation with The Always?" Graben's mind was whirling, thinking how to answer when Karst thumped his staff on the stone and accused, "It seems you did not, for even one so young and untrained in the ways of meditation would not have acted so carelessly."

"Yes, Wise One," Graben said quietly, and bowed his head to show submission.

"Concerning Ogen and Tor, did they take part in the planning?"

"They took no part, Wise One. I did all the planning. I told them I was going, and I asked them to go. They insisted on going with me as they did not want me to go alone."

"You did not force them in any way?" Karst's tone was severe.

"No, I did not force them," Graben maintained, struggling to keep his voice even. "I told them if they could not go with good conscience, I would not hold it against them."

"Well, at least you were honorable in that," Karst admitted grudgingly, then pointing his finger at Graben, asked, "Do you admit that your rash actions caused harm to one of your own village—one you call friend?"

"I deeply regret Ogen's injury," Graben answered with sincerity.

"Tell the Hammada exactly how Ogen was injured."

"I-I could not see clearly," Graben stammered, "but it seemed he turned too quickly and tripped, causing him to fall and hit his head on a log."

Karst frowned and stroked his beard thoughtfully. "Ogen's wound is near the back of his head, meaning he would have had to almost fall backwards. Is there more you can say?"

Graben swallowed and tried to moisten his mouth, which had gone dry. He let out a sigh before saying, "I was talking to the Barchans, telling them we had come to take Tephra home to Drumlin."

"I see," said Karst, the doubt in his voice unmistakable, "and the Barchans were agreeable to letting the maiden return to her village with you?"

"Not at first. But I was insistent."

"Graben, the three of you had your hunting knives with you when you returned. Why did you carry your knives with you?"

"For protection."

"From?"

"From dangers along the trail."

"And from the Barchans?"

"Yes, if necessary," Graben answered defensively.

"Was it necessary, Graben?" Karst narrowed his gaze at Graben.

Graben stood tall as he answered, "No, for I showed them that we were prepared to fight for one of our maidens."

"You would have wounded another enosh?" Karst spoke slowly, emphatically.

"If I thought they had defiled my betrothed, it would have been my duty," Graben answered firmly. He squared his shoulders defensively, and as he thought of Tephra in the hut of the Barchans, clenched his fists at his side.

"Now Graben," Karst interrupted his thoughts, "do you have anything else to add to this hearing—anything that may justify your actions?"

Graben looked at Karst, and struggling to keep his voice even, pleaded with the Hammada, "Was it not my right to re-claim my betrothed from the Forbidden Ones? Was that not even my duty as her betrothed—to protect her? The longer she remained with the Barchans, the more defiled she would become!" Striking his chest with his fist, he spoke through clenched teeth, "We would have been mated had she not gone with that Barchan!"

"Graben! You *are* aware that your betrothed was injured, and could not walk. We, the Wise Ones of Drumlin, heard her accounting. She is under Partial Banishment, as we deemed that a suitable chastisement for her purification. Now, return to Hevel's hut and wait there while the Hammada consider."

Graben returned to Hevel's hut to find Tor squatting with his head on his arms. Tor looked up when Graben entered, and Graben could see he was worried. Hevel entered a moment later and after freshening Ogen's cloth, returned to the stone without speaking to either young man. Graben adopted Tor's pose, and the two waited in silence while the Hammada deliberated.

Tor was called to the stone to hear what chastisement he would receive, and then Graben was called. When Graben learned that he would be bound to the dwelling of his uncle Shael for two moons, and be counseled by two men of the Hammada, he looked at Karst unbelieving and argued, "I am to be banished for saving my betrothed from the Barchan?"

"You dare question the judgment of the Hammada?" Karst took a few steps toward Graben and said in a controlled voice, "You would be wise to hold your tongue on this matter. Return to your family until Shael calls you to his dwelling to wait out your time of banishment."

Graben was filled with jealousy and anger toward the tall dark-haired Barchan. He could not be sorry he had wounded him; therefore, he could not show the necessary remorse to appease the anger of The Always, or convince the Hammada of the rightness of his actions. He walked to his mother's dwelling seething with resentment, his jaw and fists clenched.

CHAPTER 19

Tephra was curious when Kame returned one evening and without her usual word of greeting, went straight to her cupboard and began taking down several tins of herbs. After putting a kettle of water on the stove to heat, she measured pinches of several herbs into a clay teapot, returned the tins to the cupboard, and then came to sit next to Tephra on her cot. Taking one of Tephra's hands in both of hers, Kame said, "I have come from a hearing. Graben and Tor were called before the Wise Ones to answer for their unlawful journey to Barchan. Graben was banished to Shael's dwelling for two moons, and Tor was banished for one moon to the hut of Hevel, to help care for Ogen."

Tephra absorbed the news about Graben, unsure of how she felt about it. Although she doubted Graben would have taken his banishment humbly, she asked anyway, "How did Graben react?"

"It was noticeable he was upset—even angry. He questioned the judgment, and it was obvious Karst was struggling to keep calm."

Tephra was silent for a moment then asked, "Grandmother, how is Ogen?"

Kame sighed deeply before answering, "His eyesight is getting worse, and he has said he will refuse to ask for betrothal to Olivine."

"Oh, no! Dear Olivine!" Tephra felt an ache in her throat and tears of sympathy for her friend stung at her eyes. "But, Grandmother, is he really that ill?" she asked, though unsure if she wanted to hear the answer.

"Hevel says there are times when he can't remember simple things, and he has headaches so severe he cannot tolerate light or noise and even refuses food."

Tephra closed her eyes and bowed her head, trying to block out the memory of seeing Ogen fall hard against the log when Pingo attacked him in defense of Strata. She agonized over the thought that if Graben had not stabbed Strata, Pingo would not have tried to attack Graben, Ogen would not have hit Pingo, and Pingo would not have lunged at Ogen, causing him to fall.

She also recalled what Graben had told Karst—that Ogen had tripped over a stone and had hit his head on a log. He had also left out the fact that he, Graben, had wounded another enosh. Again, she wondered about the man who had come to bring her back from Barchan Mountain. He was unlike the Graben who had come to her dwelling as her brother's friend, and then later, had come to court her. The Graben she saw on Barchan Mountain was quick-tempered and unreasonably jealous, a contrast to the charming, yet serious-minded young man who had asked her to be his mate.

"I am sorry to bring you such news, my child. I know you want to go to your friend. If you wish, I will send word to her that you are thinking of her and are sad for her." Kame put her arm around Tephra's shoulder and suggested, "We should offer petitions to The Always, you and I together?"

Tephra chewed on her bottom lip, and fighting back tears, nodded; then, as Kame began chanting one of the ancient prayers, she cleared her throat and joined in the chant. The prayer was one begging The Always to look with favor on those they held in their hearts, especially those who were most in need. When they had completed the prayer, Tephra hugged her grandmother, and looked at her with a grateful smile. Singing often lightened her mood, and although her heart still ached for Olivine, the chanting had soothed her somewhat.

Even though she was allowed to dwell in Kame's hut, Kame often had other duties to attend to, and Tephra was left alone for long periods of time. When Kame was there during the day, one of the other matrons was there also. In the evenings, Kame and Tephra would meditate together, singing the poem-songs and chanting the ancient prayers for Tephra's purification and reconciliation. However, there was very little time for conversation, and Kame was well aware that Tephra longed for the company of people her own age. She was given some chores each day, but still the maiden grew restless, as there was little she could do without causing pain to her knee. She wove baskets and mats, shelled peas, and mended garments sent to her by her mother. Tephra would put on a smile when Kame would return from some errand, yet there were several times she noticed the maiden's eyes were red from weeping. It grieved Kame to see her dear granddaughter in such a state; however, without breaking the decrees of the Hammada, there was nothing she could do beyond the occasional hug and reassuring smile.

One morning after prayers with the other Wise Ones, Kame, Moraine, and Eolia asked that special permission be given for Tephra's parents to visit for a brief time. Moraine and Eolia assured the assembly that Tephra had been very agreeable and humble during the prayers and was doing well at her studies. Kame stated with certainty that Tephra did the chores given to her in a timely manner and without complaint. The others agreed that it would be allowed as long as Kame and two other of the Hammada were present. Kame was delighted to see the joy on her granddaughter's face when it was announced.

"Moraine and Kenǽ will be bringing your parents to share the midday meal with you tomorrow, and," Kame added with a grin, "Breccia and Sedi also!"

When her family entered Kame's shelter with the two Hammada, Tephra clung to her father, weeping with remorse and apologizing for the disgrace she had brought to her clan. Tarn's eyes brimmed with tears as he tried to console his daughter. "My lovely songbird, it will all be well. You were heard and judged by the Hammada, and are serving your time of Purification. Kame and the matrons attest that you are behaving as you should. Your standing in the village shall be restored and all will be as it once was. You will see."

Kame was delighted to see that Tephra's appetite had improved. Reveling in the comfort of having her family near, she ate a decent meal for the first time. After the meal, she sat smiling contentedly while her parents, Sedi, and Breccia talked about the everyday goings-on in the village. Their brief visit left Tephra with a quiet happiness that lasted well into the next day, and brought comfort to Kame as well.

CHAPTER 20

In the Barchan Settlement, the news of the visit by Drumlin men had spread quickly, though Foehn and Uluru had tried to minimize the violence. Strata remained in his sister's hut for several days and due to her nourishing meals and Foehn's care, the wound inflicted by Graben was healing quickly. The weakness in his arm troubled him, but his grandfather had assured him it would grow stronger as he gradually used it more. Kaoli visited often, and could see that Strata had something more on his mind than how his arm was healing. He was restless at times and at others seemed lost in thought. One afternoon, after he had been short tempered with little Pilli, Kaoli caught the unmistakable look of aggravation on Uluru's face as she sent the children to play outside.

"Is your moodiness and restlessness because your arm pains you?" she questioned sharply.

"It is bothersome that I cannot move it as before..." he answered, then frowned.

"So much that you snap at Pilli? That is not like you, Strata."

Strata bowed his head and grinned sheepishly, "I am troubled about the Drumlin maiden; wondering if her knee has healed."

"Troubled?" Kaoli said skeptically, "Nay, Strata, I think you care for her more than you should. Hmmm?"

Strata grinned, "It was noticed?"

"And not just by me. The children were asking if Tephra was going to be sharing your dwelling with Foehn or if you would build her a new one," Uluru said teasingly.

"We both know it is impossible. But yet, what you have observed is true. There is caring in my heart for the Drumlin maiden."

"And I think she came to care for you, too." Kaoli said matter-of-factly.

"I have to know that she is well, or if she is suffering some punishment for being on the 'Forbidden Mountain.' I am thinking of going to Drumlin Village—"

"No! No, Strata," Uluru said firmly.

"I agree with Uluru," Kaoli nodded, "that is most unwise."

"Kaoli, Uluru, do you see I cannot be at peace until I know? I will find the one called Kame, Tephra's grandmother. I will go to ask about the man who hit his head, and will ask about Tephra."

"Have you spoken to Foehn about this?" asked Kaoli, "And Augur, what will he say?"

Uluru shook her head and sighed, "Oh, Strata, I see by your face you are determined, so I will only add, be cautious. You always were a stubborn one!"

"I will be careful. I have given this much thought. Kaoli, you and Pingo will go with me," Strata turned to Kaoli, his voice and eyes pleading. "We will bring gifts."

"My brother," Uluru went to Strata and placed her hand on his face, "if you must, then plan carefully. Realize that you could bring further harm to Tephra. You know she was betrothed to the man who came for her. It would be most unseemly for a strange man, a Barchan, to go to her village and ask about her."

"I would do nothing to cause her harm!"

"No, not willingly. But, Strata, your caring for her is plain to see," Kaoli warned. "Perhaps I should go alone."

"I understand," Strata said with a deep sigh. "Kaoli, you will speak for me. I will be silent, but I must go and hear for myself."

"Then I pray the Almighty One go with you. And with you, Kaoli, for this one can be stubborn," Uluru said seriously, then smiled as she affectionately patted his cheek. Turning to Kaoli she requested, "Send word that I and the children miss her."

Kaoli nodded reassuringly, "I will send your words, Uluru, and I will watch out for Strata."

After three days of secretive planning—for they were unsure of how the people of Barchan would react—Kaoli, Strata and Pingo began their journey down to the Drumlin Hills. Before the sun rose, they met at the edge of the settlement, each carrying enough provisions for two days. They dared not take the trail that had led them to the Hammada Stone, but a much longer one that would put them near the meadows and the southern-most end of Mosken Lake. Their plan was to approach one of the shepherds and inquire about Tephra.

When they arrived at the lake, Strata saw two young maidens on the hillside watching over a small flock of sheep. He pointed them out to Kaoli who suggested, "I will go down to them. They will not be so frightened by my approach as by yours."

Walking slowly toward the Drumlin maidens, Kaoli waved her hand and smiled. "Greetings, maidens! May I approach you?"

The taller of the two maidens looked up at her greeting, signaled to her companion—who walked quickly to the other side of the flock—and motioned for Kaoli to approach.

"I am Kaoli. You need not be concerned, I come as a friend."

"You are not Drumlin," the maiden stated with concern and a bit of alarm. "Where do you come from?"

"I come from Barchan Mountain. I have come with the man who found the Drumlin maiden injured on the plateau. He and his sister are my cousins. It was in her dwelling that the maiden stayed while our healer tended her injury. We only come to ask if she is well, and if her injury has healed as it should."

"That is very kind of you. I am Esker," the maiden replied with a puzzled expression. "Yes, she is healing slowly, but she is well."

"And the young man who was injured when the men from your village came to find her? Is he well?"

Esker answered, "His injury was more severe than thought at first. It will be longer before he is well."

"We are sorry to hear of that." Kaoli said in a kind voice. She then paused a moment before asking, "The man who found the maiden on the plateau wishes to have a word with you. May I motion for him and his friend to approach?"

Esker signaled to the younger maiden to join her, and after whispering something in her ear, gave a hesitant nod. Kaoli waved to Strata and Pingo. The two men immediately left the thicket where they had been concealed and walked toward the maidens.

"Greetings, I am Strata, and this is Pingo."

"I-I-I am Esker, and this is my sister Creta," Esker stammered, as she stared at the tall Barchan man.

"Esker," Strata repeated, "Do you have knowledge of the Drumlin maiden called Tephra."

Esker nodded, "She is my cousin."

"Esker has told me that Tephra is healing slowly, but is doing well," said Kaoli.

"We are pleased she is doing well," Strata said, smiling broadly.

"But the young man is not healing as their healer feels he should," Kaoli added.

Strata's smile turned to an expression of concern and he said, "I am sorry to hear of it."

Kaoli asked, "When you see your cousin, will you tell her that we came to ask how she and the young man are healing?"

Esker lowered her head and said in a voice tinged with sadness, "I am not allowed to see her."

"Then, she has been banished?" Kaoli asked.

Esker looked up, surprise evident in her expression, and then answered flatly, "Yes, for a time, but it is only partial banishment. She is confined to her grandmother's dwelling." Esker suddenly put her hand over her mouth as if regretting her words and glanced around cautiously. She slowly removed her hand and said quietly, "I should not be—"

"Yes, we understand. We will go," interrupted Kaoli. "Thank you for what you have told us. Foehn the healer and my cousin, Uluru, who took care of Tephra, will be glad to know she is healing."

Strata pleaded, "Is there no way you can see her? If you can get word to her, will you let her know we came to see if she is well? Oh, and let her know Uluru's children miss her."

Esker smiled shyly at the tall, rugged Barchan, "Maybe I can find a way to let her know. Now, please go before someone from the village should come this way."

The three Barchans gave a slight bow as a way of leave-taking, and walked quickly back the way they had come.

Esker motioned for Creta to come closer and said quietly, "The strangers were the Barchans who found Tephra on the forbidden mountain. The tall man's sister took care of her, and then those three traveled down the mountain to let the Hammada know she was alive!" Creta's eyes were wide with a mix of wonder and fear. Esker understood her young sister's look of alarm, and said reassuringly, "It is alright. They came here to find out if Tephra and Ogen were well." As an afterthought Esker added, "Creta, I do not think we should tell anyone about their visit today. I have a feeling it would not be good for Tephra." Creta nodded in agreement, and the rest of the day the two maidens frequently talked about the visit and how sincerely concerned the three Barchans seemed. Both maidens, however, were puzzled by such actions from Barchans.

Esker also was concerned about her cousin. She missed her company and the sisterly companionship they had shared on the hillsides with their sheep. She longed to hear her lovely voice singing poem-songs. Esker looked for an opportunity to approach Kame alone so that she could ask her about Tephra. The next day after returning from the meadows, she saw Kame leaving her dwelling. Walking quickly towards her, she called out, "Grandmother Kame! May I speak with you?"

"Esker! How are you and Creta faring with the sheep?" the old woman turned toward Esker with a grin and held out her arms to embrace her.

Returning the embrace Esker said, "Oh, the sheep are not too much trouble, but Creta sometimes daydreams and well, you know." Esker sighed, then asked, "Grandmother, may I ask about Tephra?"

"Of course you may ask, child. Her knee is healing as it should, although it does pain her at times." Then lowering her voice to a whisper, she continued, "But her heart is heavy with uncertainty and loneliness, and," Kame shrugged her shoulders and sighed, "well, it is very trying for her to have to be inside and alone so much."

Esker's heart went out to her cousin. Knowing how much Tephra loved being out on the hills with the sheep, Esker wondered how she could bear being in Kame's small dwelling for so long. "Will you tell her that I asked about her, and that Creta and I miss her? Maybe it will help her to know that we think about her."

Kame tenderly stroked Esker's cheek, smiled, nodded, and continued on her way. That night Esker slept little, but instead kept tossing and turning, thinking, "I must see her. Surely it could be arranged."

The next evening she approached her grandmother again, pleading, "Is there some way I can see Tephra? Perhaps with you and the matrons present?"

Kame put an arm around her young granddaughter's shoulder in sympathy. After a pause, she said, "I think the Hammada might approve a short visit. In the weeks since the Hammada's ruling, the matrons have been quite pleased with the sincerity of her purification prayers, her prayers for Ogen, and her willingness to appease The Always. Mind you, it is an unusual request, but I will ask. Someone will come to you and bring you to her when it is time, but do not be too hopeful, my child."

Esker hugged her grandmother in thanks, and skipped to her own dwelling for the evening meal.

Two days later, just a short time after Esker and Creta returned from the meadows, Eolia and Moraine arrived at Esker's dwelling to escort her to Kame's for her visit with Tephra. Esker was admonished not to ask questions about anything her cousin witnessed or experienced while on the Forbidden Mountain.

"Oh, there is much we can talk about," Esker said happily as they walked to Kame's dwelling. "We will talk about things like the sheep, and Creta, and how big my baby brother has grown, and oh, lots of things!"

Tephra embraced her cousin with happy tears in her eyes. Holding Esker's hand, she led her to sit on the cot beside her. Kame and the two matrons sat on the prayer rug across the room, sipping tea and taking turns whispering the ancient prayers. Esker and Tephra had been made aware they would also be listening to their conversation to ensure all was proper.

"How is the flock this season?" Tephra asked. "Oh, I think I miss them almost as much as I miss my family and friends!"

Esker replied, "Oh, the flock is doing well. There is nothing unusual to say about them. Ol' Black Tail is as stubborn as ever!"

Tephra smiled at the memory of the old ram, then asked anxiously, "Have you seen Olivine? Kame says Ogen's injury has not healed as it should."

"That is true. His injury is more serious than first thought. Now he has broken courtship with Olivine."

Tephra closed her eyes and shook her head sadly, "How is Olivine taking it? She must be heartbroken!"

"Oh, Tephra, I wish you could go to her! I know you are best friends. Olivine is so sad—she thinks they may never be mated. She does not even want to see her other friends."

"I do not think the Hammada would allow a visit from one who is not of my family."

"It is unlikely," Esker replied, then reluctantly said, "Tephra, Graben is under Partial Banishment for two moons."

"Kame told me the evening after Karst made the pronouncement," Tephra said.

"When he left the Hammada Stone after his hearing he was very angry," Esker answered, "and I think the Wise Ones noticed."

Tephra nodded and said, "Yes, Kame told me."

Esker noticed she bit her lip and looked very sad. Changing the conversation, Esker asked, "What do you do all day when you are alone here?"

Tephra showed her the baskets she had woven, and the new one she was working on, and said, "See the pattern on those two? I am trying to put both patterns into one basket by using different sizes of reeds and adding thick twine. I also do the mending for Mother and Grandmother Kame, and I help Grandmother with other chores as long as they do not cause pain to my knee."

Esker had been trying to think of a way to let her cousin know of the visit of the three Barchans, so she suggested, "I know your fingers can get tired and sore from the weaving; mine do. What if you could draw, or sketch? I could show you some marks, and you could practice. Maybe I would be allowed to visit again. Here, look."

From her apron, Esker took a scrap of parchment on which she had sketched a rough image of a tall man, a shorter man, and a small young woman. They were standing next to a young maiden with a staff and near her were two sheep. In the background was a large mountain and a line was drawn from the mountain to the maiden and sheep.

Tephra studied the drawing and exclaimed, "Oh! Is that—?"

Esker put her hand on Tephra's arm and her eyes darted toward Kame and the two matrons.

Tephra nodded. "I could never copy these marks," she proclaimed, then said more softly, "But, I like what you have shown me.…" Tephra smiled and bowed her head as her face turned a deep pink. She picked up the basket she had been weaving, and said, "See, the heavy twine makes this part stronger so I can still use the small reeds here and the basket will hold its shape better."

Too soon the matrons announced that the visit was over, and the two cousins clung to each other in parting. Esker promised, "I will return as soon as allowed, and I will help you learn to draw some simple things."

Later that night, Tephra's face felt flushed when she recalled Esker's sketches and what they told—Kaoli, Strata and Pingo had come down to the hills to ask about her! She recalled the times Strata had teased her good-naturedly, had complimented her singing, and the times she had caught him just looking at her with a gentle smile on his face. Still, she was astonished that he would make the journey down the mountain to ask about her.

Had Graben asked about her? Even though he was in Partial Banishment as well, he could have asked. Surely Kame or someone else in her family would know if he had. Did he no longer care for her? He seemed so annoyed when they were coming down the mountain. Was he still angry? Were they still betrothed? Would he wait for her banishment to be over? Or did he feel she had brought too much dishonor to his clan?

These and more thoughts and questions tumbled around in Tephra's mind. During the day, when her knee would allow it, she paced in circles inside Kame's small dwelling, trying to find some peace. "If only I could walk on the hills and meadows with the sheep," she thought, "maybe there I could find some comfort." But she knew neither the Hammada nor her injured knee would allow such a pleasure.

CHAPTER 21

It was now near the end of the seventh moon, and there had been no rain since a small thunderstorm during the time Tephra had been on the Forbidden Mountain. Twice in one moon, dark storm clouds had formed to the northwest, holding promise of needed rain, but a high wind blew the storms further east. Thunder could be heard in the far distance and lightning was observed over Nunatak Peak, but no rain fell on the Drumlin hills. Farmers had the exhausting task of carrying water from the streams, which were getting dangerously low. The people grumbled and began to complain to the members of the Hammada, hoping that powerful prayers to The Always could relieve their toils. Karst called a village meeting, assuring the people that many prayers had been offered. He tried to reassure them that The Always, as his name implied, was always there for them and had always answered their prayers.

Several were not satisfied with this pacifying answer, especially the clan of earth-tillers, to which Graben belonged. One of the most outspoken was Shael, Graben's uncle and a member of the Hammada.

"The Always is displeased with the people of Drumlin," Shael proclaimed loudly. "But what have we done to displease him so greatly that he would not send rain for our crops and leave us to starve? It is not the *people* of Drumlin, but *one* Drumlin who has displeased The Always! And what have our Wise Ones done to appease the anger of The

Always? Does the defiled one not live in comfort with her grandmother? Does she not sit in idleness while we break our backs carrying water in an effort to save some of our crops?"

Karst tried to calm Shael, but another villager spoke out, "Shael has spoken aloud what many have been thinking. The defiled maiden has brought shame to her clan, to the clan of earth-tillers, and to our village. She has brought this drought upon us, as has the Hammada, by not following the laws of our village—the laws given to us by The Always."

Kame stood up suddenly and began to chant in a loud and ominous tone,

> *Beware of changes in the now!*
> *The rock will split, the rift will go deep.*
> *Fast the streams will flow;*
> *then the shift, and blood will flow!*
> *Nunatak is glowing as a fire.*
> *The Always has spoken to me....*

"And what does The Always say about your granddaughter, the defiled one you are comforting?" Shael interrupted in a rude tone, pointing his finger at Kame. Then he looked at Karst and challenged, "Where is the punishment due to such a one? You who are the wisest of the Wise Ones, where is your wisdom in this matter?"

Again, Karst tried to calm the outraged crowd. "Please, let us not hold anger toward one another. You know that the Hammada considered long before judgment was passed on the maiden. It was the decision of all the Hammada."

"That is not true!" Shael argued, "There were some against such leniency."

Eolia, one of the wise matrons and Kame's friend, answered, "You are spreading harmful rumors. You are saying this because of your nephew, Graben. He brought dishonor to your clan by going against the Hammada and was placed under Partial Banishment. Many witnessed his anger, though he tried to hide it, when his punishment was announced. The maiden's testimony was seen to be truthful and open, and she has accepted her punishment and has shown remorse."

Karst held his staff over the people and said, "The Hammada have been watching the signs from Nunatak even more closely since the maiden's return. We have considered the prophecies of some of our most esteemed members, and we admit there are new signs that alarm us. We are in frequent communion with The Always."

What Karst said was true, and even Kame was at times torn between love for her granddaughter, and the signs she had seen in Nunatak, along with the prophecies that had been repeated. She, too, wondered if the judgment against Tephra had been severe enough to appease The Always, even though Tephra had been most cooperative. And there was something else that troubled Kame—Tephra and Graben, and even Tor, seemed to be holding a secret. Why had Graben said nothing in Tephra's defense? Why had he never asked about his betrothed since her return; never asked about her injured knee and how it was healing? True, his mother had asked, but not Graben himself.

The Hammada spent many long hours in prayer and meditation as they discussed the drought and the complaints of the people of Drumlin. Several of the villagers harbored ill feelings toward Tephra, and that ill feeling was spreading. Quite a few were even exhibiting contempt for her family and clan. A rift, born of suspicion and fear, and fueled by the heat and drought, threatened the peace that had so characterized Drumlin Village. Several of the Hammada were uncertain which course to take; however, it was clear that some action must be taken. Finally, the Wise Ones were ready to announce a decision they knew would be extremely painful for some to hear.

Two days later, as the sun was setting, and the heat had eased, all the villagers were assembled at the clearing as instructed by the Wise Ones. The Hammada walked in procession to the large stone dais, two of them assisting Tephra as she walked with the aid of a walking stick. When she arrived at the stone, she was seated on a small bench in the center, the Hammada flanking her on each side. Karst walked to the outer edge of the stone and held out his crystal-tipped staff to quiet the murmuring villagers.

"My dear people of Drumlin," Karst began, "we gather this day to witness a Declaration of Banishment toward Purification. It has been determined that Tephra of the Clan of Shepherds will be banished to the outland for three moons for reason that she ascended to the Forbidden Mountain and, although she did have an injury that made it impossible for her to walk, she was indeed carried by a Barchan man to his settlement, thereby breaking her pre-mating rituals. Also, she did live with Barchans, the Forbidden Peoples, in their dwelling. We have come to this decision to further appease The Always so that our crops will receive the rains needed before they are damaged beyond help." Karst paused a moment as the villagers reacted to his words. Some, especially the clan of shepherds, were shaking their heads in disappointment and sorrow, yet many villagers were voicing their approval of the ruling.

He lifted his staff again, and continued with the details of Tephra's banishment. "Early tomorrow morning, four of the Hammada will escort the maiden to the hut in the outland. Three matrons—Eolia, Moraine, and Kenæ will alternately visit the maiden, one every three or four days, being certain that she has adequate food and water. They will give her certain chores to do, and will lead her in the meditations necessary for her further purification. At the end of the three months, the maiden will undergo scrutiny to determine if she is ready to re-enter into full participation in village life. Today she will be allowed to go to her family dwelling and to share their evening meal, after which she will be returned to the dwelling of her grandmother, Kame. You are reminded that if you should meet the maiden on her way to or from her family dwelling, or to the outland, you are not to approach her or to address her. Now return to your dwellings and pray that The Always will now look kindly upon us once more." Karst turned to Kame and instructed her to escort Tephra back to her dwelling as soon as the villagers had cleared the area around the stone.

Kame knew her granddaughter would be sent to the outland before she arrived at the assembly at the Hammada Stone. Yet, when she actually heard the words spoken by Karst, it was as though a heavy weight descended upon her. She had kept her eyes downcast, not daring to look at her granddaughter for she feared her own emotions were too near the surface. As the last of the villagers walked from the clearing, Moraine, who was standing next to Kame, nudged her arm. With a slight movement of her hand, she motioned for Kame to look at Tephra. The maiden's face was pale and she was sitting quite rigid with her hands clasped tightly in her lap.

As the last villager left the clearing, Kame and Moraine went quickly to her. Kame whispered gently, "My child, it is time to return with me to my dwelling." Tephra stood shakily, looked at her grandmother, and collapsed. Moraine managed to kneel and catch the maiden's head before it hit the stone floor. Hevel went to his hut as fast as his old legs would move and brought back an herb-scented wet cloth and a cup of water mixed with a little sweet wine. He wiped her face, neck, and arms with the cloth as Kame lightly slapped the maiden's wrists until she took a deep breath and tried to sit up.

"Easy. Go slow, maiden." Hevel instructed, as he and Kame helped her to sit on the stool. "You fainted, but you are not hurt. Here, sip this a little at a time." He handed her the cup of water and wine. Still trembling, Tephra took a few small sips from the cup, and then drained it in one gulp.

She handed the cup back to Hevel, saying in a hollow voice, "Thank you, Hevel." With her eyes downcast, she addressed Kame in the same flat voice. "Grandmother, may we go to your dwelling now?"

"Yes, child, if you are sure you can walk?"

"I can walk, Grandmother." Tephra picked up her walking stick with one hand and held out the other toward her grandmother. Kame took hold of Tephra's arm and gently guided her from the stone and onto the path to her hut. Moraine walked on the other side of Tephra, watching her closely for any sign she might faint again, as the maiden was still quite unsteady.

Kame's old heart was pounding, and she was fighting to control the urge to weep and collapse herself, but knew she had to be strong for her dear Tephra. The two women managed to get Tephra to Kame's dwelling, and convinced her to eat a few bites and drink some tea. Kame knew Tephra had barely slept the night before, so the tea was brewed from herbs and roots to help her relax and hopefully take a short rest before she would be escorted to her family shelter for a late evening meal. As Moraine was leaving to go to her own dwelling, she motioned with a jerk of her head for Kame to follow her outside.

"Kame, my old friend, I am filled with worry for you. After Tephra is taken to the outland, I should come stay with you a day or so."

"Ah! I have never felt my years so much as today. I will welcome a visit from you anytime, but it is not necessary to stay with me."

"As you wish, as you wish. But do not forget, I am your friend."

The two women embraced and Moraine went to her own dwelling. When Kame went back inside, she found Tephra had fallen asleep. "It is good she sleeps now," Kame thought, "tomorrow night she may well find it difficult to sleep in a strange place."

CHAPTER
22

At the prearranged time, four male members of the Hammada escorted Tephra to her family dwelling. When she entered, she saw that Caldera and Tarn had decided to treat this visit as a festive time and was glad for the sake of Breccia. The table was laden with Tephra's favorite foods and colorful ribbons hung from the doorway. When the meal was finished, the table cleared, and the remains of the meal put away, Tarn helped Tephra to a bench in the adjoining room. There she was presented with several gifts.

"This is for you to carry things in," said Breccia as she handed Tephra a sturdy woolskin pouch trimmed with small pieces of colorful ribbons. "Father and I made it for you," she smiled proudly, "and Sedi helped too."

"All I did was add the leather strap," Sedi said, winking at Breccia.

"You are allowed to bring some personal things to the outland," Caldera told her daughter. "The shoulder strap will make the pouch easier to carry."

"And I said it needed pretty ribbons for my pretty sister!" Breccia said proudly.

"There is a new hair comb in the pouch," Caldera said, "and take this, a warmer sleep shift for the nights may soon turn cool." Tephra did not miss the quaver in her mother's voice as she handed her the folded garment.

"The pouch is lovely, Breccia! Thank you, all of you," Tephra smiled, trying to blink back tears.

Tephra could tell that Caldera, Tarn, and Sedi were attempting to keep conversation limited to pleasant topics, but Breccia went to Tephra and asked in a sad, tear-filled voice, "Tephra, why do you live with Grandmother? Why is it you do not stay at our dwelling? And why does Sedi say we will not see you for a long time? Are you going back to bad mountain?"

Even though she was with her own family, Tephra's face flamed red with embarrassment. How could she answer her little sister when it was difficult to explain it to herself? Tarn rose from his place at table and went to stand behind Tephra. Placing his hands lovingly on his daughter's shoulders he said, "Tephra did a bad thing when she went to the bad mountain, even though it was because she got lost. Breccia, what does mother or father make you do when you do a bad thing, like that day you were running near the rocky part of the stream?"

"Mother made me sit in corner for a long time, and—and Sedi would not tell me a story! But I did not mean to run by the rocks. I was chasing a butterfly."

"Yes, and so you did not think about where you were running, and that you could easily fall and be injured. Well, it is something like that for Tephra," Tarn explained. "She did not mean to go on bad mountain. She took the wrong trail to rescue a lost lamb. So she—"

"She has to sit in corner for a long time," the child finished in a sad voice. Then she brightened, and suggested excitedly, "Why can't she sit in corner at Grandmother's, or she can sit in my corner!"

"Breccia," Sedi spoke gently, "Sister must go to the corner for grown-ups, for she is too big to sit in a child's corner."

Breccia jumped up from her stool and ran over to Tephra, throwing her arms around her. "I am sorry you have to sit in corner for such a long time!" she cried. Then, looking up to her father, she asked, "Can Tephra have my ribbon doll in her corner? I know I can't have Ribbons when I am bad, but Tephra will be in corner such a long time!"

Tephra, touched by her Breccia's generous offer of her favorite doll, was torn between laughter and tears. "Oh, my dear little one!" she said, "I cannot take Ribbons, she is your favorite, but you can loan me another."

"No, no!" Breccia shook her head. "You have to take Ribbons. You made her for me, and if you have her, you will come home faster because you know I will miss you both." Tephra, not knowing what to say in reply, picked up Breccia and held her close.

Sedi winked at Tephra and said, "Breccia, since you are letting Tephra take Ribbons to her corner, don't you think she should sing a song for you in exchange?"

Breccia lifted her head and smiled up at Tephra, "Oh yes! Please Tephra? It has been a long time and you have not sung for us!"

Tephra smiled, wiped her tears, and took a few sips of water. "Yes, little one, I will sing for you, and I will take Ribbons with me to my corner. When I look at her, I will remember this night. Let me think, what shall I sing? How about, 'Where Do Birds Go?'"

At Breccia's excited nod and broad smile, Tephra stood and began singing in her clear, soft voice the song she had often sung to the children of the village.

> *Sometimes when the rains fall*
> *I have wondered,*
> *Where do the birds go*
> *When it thunders?*
> *They build their nests*
> *In trees so tall,*
> *In their nests, they'll get wet,*
> *So where do they go?*
> *To a hole in a tree,*
> *Or under a bush,*
> *In places much too small for me!*
> *Sometimes when night is falling,*
> *I think about,*
> *Where do butterflies sleep*
> *When the stars come out,*

And the flowers close their petals.
Do they find a place to rest?
Yes! They fold their wings
And hide under a leaf,
With a ladybug or two for a guest.

As Tephra sang, Breccia performed the hand motions Tephra had taught her, smiling up at her big sister all the while. Tephra was deeply moved by the loving look on her little sister's face. At the end of the song, Tephra held out her hands to Breccia. The child clasped her hands tightly, and Tephra suggested, "Let's play a game while I am away. Every night, as soon as the sun slips from the sky, you sing this song to your dolls, and I will sing to Ribbons. It will be as though we are together. Would you like that?" Breccia's eyes opened wide as she nodded with enthusiasm. With appropriate but depressing timing, the four Hammada came to escort Tephra back to Kame's hut.

Tephra hugged her parents and Sedi, and knelt on one knee to hug Breccia, whispering a reminder to sing their song at sundown. Tephra picked up the bag Breccia had given her, with the doll tucked safely inside it, and walked out of her family dwelling with two Hammada in front of her, and two behind. She paused and looked over her shoulder at her family dwelling, swallowing hard to hold back tears. "Three months," she thought, "it is warm tonight, but it will be cold when I return to this place. The seasons will change, and that will make it seem longer."

Kame was standing in the doorway when the Hammada returned Tephra to her dwelling. Nodding respectfully to the escorts, Kame led Tephra inside and closed the door. Taking the bag from Tephra's hand, the older woman put in a tiny bag of ground herbs.

Kame put her fingers to her lips and whispered, "Only a pinch in a cup of warm water. Add a few drops of honey to take away the bitterness." Tephra looked at her grandmother questioningly, and Kame explained, "It will be strange at first. It will not be easy to sleep at night, so far from the village. But you must rest to stay well. Use a little less of it each night, for there is only enough for three or four nights. Now, come with me."

Kame went to the prayer rug and knelt, grunting a bit at the discomfort in her old knees. Tephra tried to kneel, but her grandmother motioned her to stand. "No, that knee is not yet ready for kneeling." The old woman bowed her head and mumbled a few prayers. She then took some ointment from a small pot and rubbed it into the maiden's injured knee as she murmured more prayers. She cautioned, "Tephra, walk only a little way at a time. In between, rest the knee upon a soft cushion. I will send one with you. If the knee throbs, rub on this ointment. Yes, just as I have been doing, and it will continue to heal as it should. Here, put this into your pouch."

Kame easily recognized that her granddaughter was trying to control her emotions by pretending indifference. She placed a hand on Tephra's shoulder, and gave a gentle squeeze as she said, "Listen carefully, my dear one, I know you are trying to be brave, perhaps for your old Kame? Yes? However, it is very important that when you are taken to the outland you allow what I know you must be feeling to show. Otherwise, the Hammada will think you are not truly repentant." Tephra nodded her understanding and Kame pulled her close to her, in a gesture to give and receive comfort. Kame gently suggested they both try to get some rest, although it was difficult to let go.

Graben and Tor, both recently released from Partial Banishment, had been at the back of the crowd as the judgment against Tephra was pronounced. Graben had stood with his arms folded across his chest, his face expressionless. Annoyed that he did not feel the justification he had hoped for, he stalked off toward his gardens, muttering under his breath. He was still consumed with jealousy and anger toward the tall Barchan. He could not be sorry he had wounded him, and many times wished the wound had been more severe. Doubts about

Tephra's accounting of her time on Barchan Mountain led to feelings of betrayal so strong that he was often left with a hard knot in the pit of his stomach. Given his feelings, he could not do all that was necessary to appease the chastisement of The Always, and therefore, he could not find peace.

Both he and Tor knew they had offended The Always by going up to the Forbidden Mountain and that their actions had caused injury to one of the Barchans and to Ogen. Later that afternoon as they were fishing, Tor tried to talk to Graben about his attitude. "Graben, I can easily see that you are still angry with Tephra," he said, "but as the Wise Ones have explained, it is wrong to hold on to anger. The Always may withhold his favor—"

"Do not speak to me of this!" Graben snapped, and silenced Tor with a stony glare. Graben knew Tor was right and had the right attitude, although he would not admit it. Still, when he recalled the way the Barchan had spoken to Tephra and the concern she had shown for the man, his whole body tensed up and he could feel his pulse racing. His life in Drumlin had not prepared him to deal with such violent emotions.

Tor had not known what to say to his friend. Neither had he known what to say to his cousin Olivine as she had wept in his arms when it was announced that Tephra had been declared departed, wept with joy when her best friend was found to be alive, and then wept again at the pronouncement of her banishment. Most heartbreaking of all was when she wept her anguish at Ogen's deteriorating eyesight. Tor left Graben to fish alone and walked to his family dwelling lost in his own questions.

After their evening meal, he asked his parents if they knew when someone had last been under banishment. His father replied, "Never in my memory."

After a moment his mother said, "I do remember old Grand-dam telling a story about a young man who had been banished to the outland. He lived in a tiny hut on the northern edge of the village. At first, he was brought food by a few of the Hammada; then he began to provide for himself by growing a little garden and trapping rabbits and other small animals in the woods nearby."

Tor asked, "How long was he banished? Was he ever restored to life in the village?"

"Ah! No, it seems he had grown so accustomed to being alone in the years he was banished that when he began to become part of village life. Even though it was gradual, he could not bear the noise or the closeness of the people. And he had not spoken aloud in so long that he could barely speak at all, only a hoarse whisper."

"Mother, that won't happen to Tephra?" Tor asked fearfully.

Tor's mother smiled, "Not likely. You forget, it is only three months of banishment and three of the matrons will be visiting her, instructing her every few days. How is Graben taking this?"

"He's angry—angry at the Barchans, and angry at Tephra; although I am sure he still cares for her, even longs for her."

"He will need to watch his behavior, lest the Hammada judge he questions the guidance of The Always. How was Ogen when you last were at Hevel's?"

"About the same. Hevel would never let me visit with Ogen for long—I mostly did chores for the healer. I think that is because Ogen is not well and it is more serious than we thought. All I know is that his eyesight is getting worse, as are the headaches, and Olivine told me he sometimes has numbness in his right arm."

"So she has been to see him. That is good."

"Not so good, Mother. The last time she visited, Ogen told her he would not ask for betrothal until he could meet her at the dwelling they would share as a whole man."

Tor's mother bowed her head and whispered something Tor could not hear clearly, but understood that it was a prayer to The Always. He kissed his mother's forehead, bowed to his father, and went to his own part of the dwelling. As he lay on his mat, he recalled the journey with Graben to the mountain to rescue Tephra. Tor was still shaken by the brief but fierce conflict with the Barchans, and astonished by the actions and attitudes his friend Graben had displayed on the mountain. He was deeply troubled that Graben had not told the truth about Ogen's injury, and he was angry with himself. He was, after all, just as guilty, for he had lied to the Hammada through implied agreement with Graben's version. A deep anxiety overtook him in that moment, but now he knew it was too late to change the situation.

CHAPTER 23

Just after dawn the next day, four of the Hammada escorted Tephra to a tiny hut on the far northern edge of the village. Tephra walked in the midst of the four with all the grace and dignity she could summon, except for the tears that began to flow as soon as she said goodbye to Kame. In spite of the tears, she kept her eyes straight ahead, her shoulders squared, and her delicate hands folded tightly below her breasts as she tried to stop their trembling. Over her shift she wore a long, hooded robe of brown, coarse cloth, and the beribboned pouch was slung over one shoulder. One of the Hammada carried a small gong which he sounded every few steps so that the villagers would know of their progress through Drumlin village.

A thicket of briars, trees, and shrubs formed a barrier between the meadows of the village and the area known as the outland. The door of the outland hut faced the thicket, and vines covered most of the walls so that it appeared to blend into the dense woods behind it. As Tephra entered the tiny hut, she turned and bowed to the four Hammada as she had been instructed. One of the Hammada, Kenæ, entered the hut and placed the basket she had carried on a small table near the center of the room; then she went to join the other Wise Ones who waited just outside the doorway. The four said a prayer of blessing over Tephra and closed the door of the hut. Tephra was aware they would return to the village and report to Karst that the maiden was now in the outland.

She also knew they would report how she had wept silently on the walk there, and that Kame would now know she had heeded her warning that she should not hold back her emotions. She did not want to cry. She wanted to show that although she had done no wrong, she was bravely accepting her banishment. Instead, the thought of the next three months all alone filled her with such dread that she could not swallow the hard lump in her throat and the tears had come unbidden.

Tephra stood near the doorway, gave a deep sigh, and looked around the hut that was to be her home for the next three months. In the corner to her immediate left were four shelves, one above the other, where she assumed she could place her personal belongings. On the top shelf, which was about shoulder height, was an oil lamp. In the far left corner stood a small cot with a roll of bedding at one end. She went over to it, slipped the strap of the pouch over her head, and laid the pouch on the cot. Directly opposite the doorway was a small shuttered window, half opened. Stepping over to it, she opened the shutter wide, and looking out the window, saw a small open meadow with a few late-flowering plants and one small tree. Beyond that were trees that grew thicker and more lush until there seemed only blackness beyond.

Leaving the shutter open to let in more light, Tephra went to the tiny stove to the right of the window. On the shelf above the stove, she found a pot for heating water or perhaps making a soup or stew, a small teapot, a tin of flint sticks, two mugs, and two small shallow bowls. She assumed there were two bowls and mugs for the visits of the Wise Ones. To the right of the stove was the table on which Kenæ had placed the basket. Tephra lifted the cloth over the basket and saw that it contained just enough provisions for three or four days: a small loaf of bread, a jar of honey, a small tin of tea leaves, some dried peaches, three eggs, and a chunk of hard cheese. Two low stools were nested under the table. To the right of the entrance to the hut was a curtained doorway. Tephra pulled the curtain aside to reveal a small chamber that held a bucket, wash bowl and cloths where she could wash up and relieve herself.

Going over to the cot, Tephra took the items out of her pouch and put them away. Her clothing, including the brown hooded robe, she folded neatly and put on the lowest shelf. On the top shelf next to the oil lamp, she put her hair comb, the ointment for her knee, and the little pouch with willow twigs for cleaning her teeth. She smiled as she placed Breccia's doll Ribbons on the second shelf. The pouch of herbs to bring on sleep she carefully hid in the doll's skirt. Reeds for basket weaving and two skeins of wool had already been placed on the third shelf, and beneath the bottom shelf, where she had put her clothing, was a small loom for weaving cloth.

To avoid giving in to the desolation she felt, Tephra took some reeds and began to weave a basket. As she worked she began to quietly sing some of the poem-songs, but after a few attempts, the sound of her voice in the small hut, so far from her family and friends, seemed strangely odd to her own ears. Songs of joy, which she thought might lift her sad mood, seemed unsuitable; while ones that are more solemn threatened to bring on weeping. Thinking a change of scenery was needed, she strolled out in the meadow and picked a few flowers. When she returned to the hut, she put them in water in one of the mugs and placed it in the center of the table, but noted they did little to brighten the hut.

At midday, she went to sit under the small tree as she ate a meager meal of cheese, fruit, bread, and water. The meal was satisfying, but not the heartier meal she would have needed as a shepherdess. She was delighted to discover that tiny, bright blue hummingbirds and several varieties of butterflies frequented the flowering bushes, and a small brown and yellow songbird seemed to favor the tree. The remainder of the day, Tephra alternated between working on the basket she had begun that morning, while enjoying the small visitors to the flower bushes, and taking short walks in the meadow. Twice during the day, she remembered to rub Kame's ointment into her knee and rest it as she had been instructed.

As the sky began to darken, Tephra lit the oil lamp and carried it into the alcove to wash up for the night. Carrying the lamp to the table, she changed into her sleep shift, folded her day shift and placed it on the shelf with her other clothing items. She took her hair comb from the shelf, unbraided and combed her hair, replaced the comb, and arranged the bedding on the cot. She then picked up Ribbons and the herb pouch, laid Ribbons on the cot, and went to the stove to heat water for a mug of the herb tea Kame had given her to help her sleep. When the water was warm enough, she poured some into a mug, dropped in a pinch of the herbs, added honey to the brew, and sipped it slowly.

She said her night prayers to The Always, blew out the oil lamp, and holding Ribbons close to her, sang "Where Do Birds Go" as she had promised Breccia. Even with the herb tea, Tephra found it difficult to fall asleep. When she was in the Cave of Solitude—how long ago it seemed!—she was alone, but never had she experienced this deep loneliness and isolation. It flooded over her in a giant wave as she once more contemplated the three months of days and nights ahead of her. Tears welled up, but she quickly brushed them away, determined to endure her punishment with dignity.

As Tephra awakened the next morning, she was at first puzzled at her surroundings, and then the awareness of her situation made her want to close her eyes again and slip back into her dreams. Instead, she arose, said her morning prayers, put on water for tea, and went to make use of the small chamber. After a breakfast of a boiled egg, bread, and tea, she took up the weaving loom and a skein of wool. The rest of the day, she spent much as the day before, sitting under the small tree weaving baskets and working the loom, and walking in the meadow.

As the sun set behind the tall trees, she went inside, lit the lamp, ate a bit of bread and cheese, drank a cup of Kame's special tea, and washed herself. Before blowing out the lamp, she sang her night prayers; then picking up Ribbons, began singing "Where Do Birds Go," but before she could complete the song, a thick lump formed in her throat. Hugging the doll close, she wept until she fell asleep exhausted, waking the next morning with swollen eyes and an aching head. Going into the curtained chamber, she splashed water on her face, soaked one of the linens with water, and returned to the cot, placing the wet cloth over her forehead and eyes.

Tephra arose again only when her stomach was rumbling with hunger, her headache only slightly better. She added some twigs to the small stove, lit it, and heated water for tea while she changed into her day shift. She brewed the tea strong, sweetened it with a dollop of honey, and took a long drink of it. Feeling a bit better, she ate some bread and dried peaches, and walked out to the meadow and to the tree. This tree, which she thought she recognized as a cherry tree, was quickly becoming her sanctuary, the small hut often too confining after having spent most of her days on the hills and meadows with her sheep. She would bring reeds with her as she sat in the shade of the tree, hoping the small meadow with the cherry tree would bring some of the familiarity of home to her.

The next two days went by in much the same way, and by her fourth day in the outland hut, she doubted she had any more tears left to shed. She was weary of waking up each morning with a headache, and she was still finding it difficult to settle into much of a routine. She had become accustomed to the discipline of a shepherdess and being outdoors most of the day. Now the confinement of the hut, and no regimented schedule, she was becoming restless and irritable. One of the Hammada, Moraine, arrived that morning and announced she had brought fresh bread, cheese, and a small pot of stew made with vegetables and deer meat. She expressed surprise when she found Tephra lying on the cot with the wet cloth over her eyes and inquired if the maiden was ill.

Tephra sat up and keeping her eyes downcast replied, "Not ill, Wise One, just my head aches."

"Come, sit. I will make some tea. Have something to eat. We will have a lesson this morning, then we will share the stew at midday. Perhaps you will feel better." Tephra ate the last of the bread that had been brought on her first day in the outland shelter and drank the tea Moraine had brewed for her, grateful for the kindness in the woman's tone. Now it was time to begin the lessons necessary for the purification requirement. While Tephra did not particularly want visitors at this time—she wanted more than anything to return home—she dutifully followed the directions of the Wise One. The lessons began with a time of meditation on the favors The Always had bestowed upon Drumlin, followed by a history of the Drumlin people, and a reviewing of the rules of behavior for the people of Drumlin.

Three weeks passed, and Tephra's secluded life in the outland began to take on a pattern of sorts. Every three or four days, just after their morning prayers, one of the Hammada would arrive with fresh provisions which varied on each visit. Some days there would be millet cakes that were flavored with figs, other days there would be wheat bread, or tiny cakes made of ground corn and sweetened with honey. The Hammada always sent fruit and vegetables—a peach or two, a handful of berries, or a small melon; carrots, a green squash with yellow stripes that Tephra particularly liked, or tiny spinach leaves; and sometimes even a couple of eggs or a chunk of cheese. The portions were small, but were still sufficient for Tephra's needs, particularly as she had little appetite. The Wise One would also bring a small pot of stew made with vegetables and either lamb, deer meat, or chicken which she and Tephra would share for the midday meal. These stews, Tephra suspected, were provided by either her mother or Kame, for the taste was so familiar. While she usually ate other meals rather absentmindedly, these stews she ate slowly, relishing every bite and recalling times with her family. For a few moments, she felt less isolated from her former life in Drumlin village—her life before she found herself on the Forbidden Mountain and in the dwelling of Barchans.

CHAPTER

24

One morning as Esker was dressing to go to the meadow to relieve Elos and Alem, she recalled the dream that had awakened her. In her dream, she and Tephra had taken a late evening walk together. Tephra had suggested taking the trail to Mosken Lake. At a place that was opposite Cambria Falls, Tephra had stopped and was staring at the falls. She slowly raised her hand and pointed to the right side of the falls where they partially obscured the entrance to the Caves of Solitude.

"Tephra?" Esker said quietly, "What is it? What are you staring at?"

Sighing, Tephra replied in a monotone, "I went into that cave a Drumlin maiden promised to a man of Drumlin. I knew what my life was to be. Now, I am no one." In the dream, as Esker was wondering what she could say to her cousin, the image of Tephra slowly vanished and Esker stood alone by the lake. Esker called out to her, but her voice simply echoed back from the caves and the mountain slopes. She awoke with tears in her eyes and a feeling of deep loss.

She had no appetite for breakfast, causing her mother to ask, "Esker, are you not well? Should I send Creta to tell the boys to stay a little longer with the sheep?"

"No, Mother, it is just—" the young shepherdess sighed, "I had a strange dream about Tephra, and I miss her!"

"Shhh! Yes, and I, too, miss her, but be very careful when you speak of her that no one outside of our dwelling should hear you."

Esker nodded in understanding, then said, "Mother, please send Creta later. I would like to be alone for a while. I will feel better then."

Etah nodded in understanding, "I can use Creta's help till midday. You will mange by yourself till then?"

"I am almost as good with the flock as—"

"Yes, I am sure you are. You were a good apprentice to her," Etah said, giving her daughter a proud smile. She urged Esker to at least take along a small millet and fig cake in addition to her usual midday meal in case she got hungry later. She then kissed her cheek and said, "May The Always grant you a pleasant morning, my daughter."

Once out on the low hills with the flock, Esker could not help but recall one of the days on these same hills with Tephra. It was the day they had both teased Graben about his chances of being named Golith at the Huntsman Trials. Esker was fairly certain she detected a hint of anger in Graben's voice at the very thought they could doubt his ability to win. Her thoughts then dwelt on something she had overheard when Kame visited Etah shortly before Tephra was sent to the outland. Esker was about to walk into the cooking area of their dwelling but stopped when she heard her mother ask, "What of the betrothal?"

"I am troubled that Graben has not come to ask about Tephra," Kame had said with a deep sigh. "His words and actions seem to doubt her innocence, even though she was his betrothed. He was always so proud of her. Now, it is as though she is nothing to him, except bitter herbs."

Thinking over Kame's words, Esker wondered, "Was it his bitterness and doubts that helped send my cousin to the outland? His clan leader—his uncle Shael—asked that she be banished, for they blamed her for the drought." This notion caused an uneasy feeling that she could not easily set aside. "I will ask Kame about it tonight," she said softly, then turned her full attention to leading her flock to a place in the meadow where a few scattered trees lent a bit of shade, and the grasses were thick and lush.

As she had been taught, Esker often scanned the area around her for any signs of danger for the flock. When she looked toward the distant lake, she thought she saw a movement near the lowest slopes of the plateau wall. She shielded her eyes against the glare of the mid-morning sun on the water, and looked intently toward the slopes. Yes, there was definitely something moving near the shallow end of the lake. As a precaution, she began to turn the flock in the opposite direction, nearer to the village and closer to help if it should be needed. The sheep were enjoying the lush grasses and the shade, and Esker had to prod a few with her staff to get them moving, bleating in protest as they did. Once she had managed to get the sheep turned, she looked back toward the lake and was alarmed to see that the figure was sprinting toward her. Suddenly she realized there was something familiar about the figure.

The figure waved, and Esker waved back as she recognized Kaoli. She smiled to herself, certain that the petite Barchan maiden had returned to ask about Tephra. Kaoli slowed as she came closer to the flock, and stopped a few feet from Esker. "Greetings, Esker. Are you well?"

"Yes, Kaoli. I am well. And you?"

"I am well. I come to ask about Tephra. She is well?"

"Her knee has much improved. She can walk without the crutch now, though not very far at a time."

"Ah! That is good!" exclaimed Kaoli. She then inquired, "Is she still dwelling with her grandmother, has she been able to return to her family, or perhaps she is mated by now?"

Esker took a deep breath and replied simply, "No."

"No? Esker, I can see by your expression there is more to answer than 'no'." Kaoli reached out and gently placed her hand on Esker's shoulder.

At the kindness and concern in the young Barchan's voice, Esker's eyes filled with tears. She tried to explain, "Tephra is—oh—I do not know how to say it so you will understand, or even if I should. I may be saying more than is allowed." The young Drumlin maiden put her hands over her face and bowed her head and shoulders in frustration and uncertainty. After a moment's consideration, Esker stood upright, removed her hands from her face, took a deep breath, and began her explanation. "There were many who blamed Tephra for the drought in our village, and for Ogen's eyesight failing and his headaches, which were sometimes very painful. He ended his courtship with a maiden who is cousin to Graben—the man who was to be mated to Tephra—and now...."

"Are he and Tephra no longer to be mated?" Kaoli asked.

"I do not know. Graben does not, well...." Esker hesitated. She did not know to answer, as she was not sure of Graben's intentions now, so she simply said, "Whether Graben and Tephra will be mated, I do not know. I think only The Always knows that."

"There is one thing more I must know about Tephra," Kaoli said, "Strata wants to know if she still sings." At Esker's puzzled expression, Kaoli explained, "Tephra would sing little songs to Uluru's children to entertain them, or to calm them to sleep, and often Strata would overhear her songs. I think I told you, Uluru is his sister, and it was in her dwelling Tephra stayed while her knee was healing."

"I do not know if she still sings. There is no one for her to sing to, not even her sheep. Perhaps she does still sing her prayers, but...." Esker sighed and shook her head.

"What do you mean, there is no one for her to sing to?" Kaoli asked with concern.

Esker took a deep breath and said in a sad, quiet voice, "Tephra has been banished to the outland."

"Oh, Esker! No!" Kaoli's cried out, her voice filled with compassion. "Thank you for telling me, Esker. I will go quickly now. I know it would not be good for anyone of your village to see us talking together."

"I am glad you came. My sister will not come until midday, so all is well."

"I would like to come again, to know that Tephra is well, if you do not mind?"

Esker reached out and took Kaoli's small hands in her own, saying, "Thank you for coming to me. It shows you are friend to my cousin. I can ask to be alone another day so we can talk."

"I can return here in two days, if that is agreeable. If not, it will be a week or two before I can return."

"I will arrange for Creta to return to the village after the midday meal on the second day from today," Esker suggested, even though she was puzzled that Kaoli would want to return so soon, as surely there would be no more news of Tephra.

Kaoli smiled, saying, "May the Almighty One look kindly upon you, Esker." The Barchan maiden turned and ran back the way she had come.

Two days later, after Esker and Creta had shared the midday meal, Esker sent her sister on an errand she had pre-arranged with their mother. Esker had noticed her mother's hesitation and pleaded, "Mother, I miss my cousin. I just want the afternoon alone."

"Alright," Etah agreed as she gently touched her daughter's cheek, "I remember being your age—sometimes you just need to be alone with your thoughts. I will make up an excuse for Creta to return early. But promise me you will be very watchful."

That afternoon, Esker watched over the flock alone, glancing expectantly toward the lake for any sign of Kaoli. She had quickly become fond of the small dark haired Barchan maiden. She was grateful for the caring that Kaoli and the two Barchan men had shown for a Drumlin. She was also somewhat amused by Kaoli. The Barchan maiden moved so silently, ran so swiftly, as though she barely touched the ground. She had a manner of speaking that was unusual to Drumlin ears, yet surprisingly pleasant. When she finally caught sight of the Barchan maiden, she was startled to see two men with her. As they drew closer, she recognized the men as the ones who had come with Kaoli before.

The two men stopped at half the distance to the flock, while Kaoli continued walking briskly to greet Esker, "Greetings, Esker! Are you well?"

Esker smiled at the now familiar greeting from the Barchan maiden. "Yes, Kaoli, I am well. And you?"

"Yes, I am well. Strata and Pingo made the journey with me. If you are not at ease with their presence, I will signal for them to wait for me near the lake."

Esker thought only a brief moment before replying, "It is good. I know they were kind to Tephra, and risked much to journey here to tell our people she was alive. Tell them they may come closer."

Kaoli waved to the two men, and they quickly walked to where Kaoli and Esker were standing. Smiling broadly, Strata addressed Esker, "Greetings! You are well, Esker?"

"Yes, I am well. I trust you are both well?"

"We are well," answered Pingo.

After a brief time of awkward silence, Kaoli rolled her eyes and said to Esker, "Strata has a gift for Tephra. Is there a way to bring it to her?"

"Oh, no," Esker shook her head, "She is allowed no visitors. Except for one of the Wise Ones, who goes to her hut from time to time, and I cannot ask them."

"There must be some way to get this to her," Strata said, as he reached into the pouch slung over his shoulder and pulled out what appeared to be a bundle of cloth. He carefully unwrapped the cloth to reveal a small woodcarving. Esker stepped nearer to get a better look at Strata's gift. At his nod of encouragement, she took it from his hand. It was a small bird with its head up, its beak opened as though in song, and it was perched on a small flowering branch. The bird and branch, both realistically carved from wood, rested on a small, smoothly polished wooden stand.

"This is wonderful! Who—?" Esker could barely phrase the question. She had never seen anything like it, and due to her talent for drawing, she could truly appreciate the workmanship.

Kaoli explained, "Strata is an excellent wood carver—although he mostly builds stools, tables, and such."

Esker, still nearly speechless with awe, managed to ask, "You carved this for Tephra?"

"I saw a bird singing early one morning, and wanted to carve it. It reminded me of Tephra. Now that I have heard she has been sent to a hut away from her village, I hoped …" Strata shrugged and looked down at his feet.

Esker smiled at his sudden shyness, "I understand."

Kaoli looked at Strata, then in pretended frustration, said, "He hoped the little bird would remind her to keep singing even if she has to sing to the birds."

Strata's sheepish grin confirmed Kaoli's words, and Pingo asked quietly, "You will bring this to Tephra for my friend Strata?"

Esker stated firmly, "You do not understand. No one of our village, other than the three Wise Ones, is allowed to go there, and the Wise Ones would never allow such a gift. They would know a Drumlin did not carve this! No one but the Wise Ones may go there. It is forbidden by our laws!"

"Not forbidden to Kaoli," Pingo declared boldly.

"It is true," Kaoli said firmly, "I am bound by no such laws. Besides, I have promised Strata I would somehow get this to Tephra. Will you tell me how to find her?"

"I don't think Tephra sings much now. Maybe this will cheer her." Esker thought only a moment about whether it was right or wrong for her to tell Kaoli how to find Tephra. She simply cautioned, "You must be very careful. Every few days one of our Wise Ones brings food to Tephra's door. I think it is usually early in the morning, but could sometimes be later in the day. If one of them should find you there ...." Esker shook her head.

"I understand," Kaoli nodded, "I will be careful. And do not worry about Tephra. I will visit her as often as I can. I will tell her that you care for her. It will do her good to know that someone from her village thinks kindly of her."

Esker nodded and smiled at Kaoli; then finding a twig, bent down and in a small area of dirt, sketched a map to where Tephra was now dwelling.

"Yes, I know how I can find her now. Thank you, Esker."

Esker glanced at the two Barchan men, and said sternly, "Kaoli, you, and *only* you, go to Tephra—no one else."

Kaoli placed her hand on her chest, saying, "I pledge to you, Esker, and to the Almighty One, I alone will go to Tephra."

Strata and Pingo bowed to the Drumlin shepherdess, turned and walked toward the lake in long, quick strides. Esker placed both hands on Kaoli's shoulders, saying, "I no longer think of you as just Barchan. You are now a friend. May The Always look with favor on you."

Kaoli smiled and placed her hand on Esker's shoulder, and responded, "And on you, my Drumlin friend." She then sprinted to catch up to Strata and Pingo.

After a moment, Esker focused her attention on her sheep, although it was difficult. She assured herself all was well with her flock and began to wonder what the Hammada would do or say if it became known she had told Kaoli how to find Tephra. Would she be banished also? Esker was relieved she had arranged that Creta would not be with her when the Barchans came. No one need know about their visit, or know that Kaoli would soon find her way to Tephra's outland hut and would be bringing a gift from the tall Barchan man. Tephra's banishment had left Esker feeling confused and uncertain. She, as much as anyone, knew Tephra's love for all animals, especially the sheep, and so she also knew Tephra would go to any lengths to save one of the little ones. It was great misfortune that in rescuing the lamb from danger she had climbed to the boundary of the plateau, was badly injured, and then rescued by one of the forbidden ones.

It was late in the evening the next day by the time Kaoli, Strata, and Pingo returned to their Barchan settlement, and they each went directly to their own dwellings to rest from their long journey to the Drumlin hills. The following morning the three met in Uluru's dwelling to plan Kaoli's journey to the Drumlin outland. Before the next dawn, the two men would go with her most of the way, but would remain safely out of sight. Once Kaoli had completed her errand, she would return to them and they would accompany her back to Barchan settlement.

Strata was anxious for Tephra to receive his gift, but he was also concerned for Kaoli to make another strenuous journey so soon. He suggested, "Kaoli, perhaps it would be best to wait, to rest a day before going."

"I will rest today, and before dawn tomorrow I will be ready to go," Kaoli insisted. "Uluru is preparing food for us--even some of the little cakes that Tephra liked." She added teasingly, "If you are too tired, I will go alone!"

Strata smiled at the energetic young woman. "Go rest. You need to be strong, for this journey will be even longer for we must take a different route—one that will bring us to the other side of the mountain and to the edge of the outland, away from Drumlin Village." Strata wished he could see Tephra and see her face when she was presented with the carved bird, but he respected the laws of her village and would do nothing to bring about further chastisement for her. He did not think of what the people of his settlement would say about his caring for a Drumlin maiden. Foehn, Uluru, Pingo, and Kaoli seemed to not only accept Tephra, but had come to care for her as well. He gave no thought to anything beyond that.

CHAPTER 25

That night, as Kaoli rested in preparation for her journey to visit the banished Drumlin maiden, Tephra lay on her cot in the outland unable to sleep. She recalled the events that had led to her solitude in the small hut outside the village: the Ceremony of Change where Graben had spoken for her, finding the kid, injuring her knee, Strata carrying her back to Foehn's hut, and her time in the dwelling of Uluru. She thought about the ancient teachings, and tried to make sense of them. Tephra could not help thinking of how much the Barchans were like her own people, and recalling how much she enjoyed listening to Strata's deep musical voice as he told Barchan folk tales to Uluru's children. There was a kindness in him, Foehn, and Uluru that denied the warnings she had heard about the Barchans. The peoples she had seen did not seem the coarse and barbaric peoples of the tales she had heard all of her life. She finally drifted into sleep remembering the gentleness with which Strata had carried her back to his grandfather's hut.

Tephra awoke later than usual and had just changed into her day shift when the matron Kenǽ arrived. Tephra put on water for tea, then busied herself putting away the provisions the matron had brought while the water heated. Kenǽ inspected the baskets and the cloth weaving Tephra had completed since the last visit, then sat at the table. Tephra poured tea for the both of them, and offered Kenæ a millet cake as she took one for herself. Kenæ gave Tephra a stern look, saying, "I have had my morning meal. Have you not eaten?"

"No, oh Wise One, it was a long time before I could fall asleep last night, so I woke late this morning."

"Hmmm," the woman said suspiciously, "Did you say your night prayers? Had you done all that was required of you that day? Hevel said you are to be walking a little three or four times a day so that your knee will become strong again."

Tephra answered, "Yes, Wise One. I have done all that is required at the times of day I should—the prayers, the chores, the walks." Her loneliness and restlessness, and the conflicting thoughts of last night, made her feel irritable and she found it difficult to maintain a submissive attitude.

Kenæ sipped her tea while Tephra finished eating the millet cake and drinking her own cup of tea, then she began the lesson. Tephra attempted to put all of her attention and energy into the lesson, hoping the Wise One would be satisfied with her progress and leave shortly. She wanted to walk out in the meadow and be with the birds and other small animals. They were becoming quite accustomed to her presence, and would now and then venture close enough to peck at a breadcrumb or fruit seed Tephra purposely let fall nearby. It amused her that when she sang one of the psalm prayers, they remained nearby.

"Maiden?" Kenæ asked, frowning, "speak up, I cannot understand what you are saying." In a surprising touch of compassion, she reached across the table and held Tephra's hand. "Perhaps it is being so long alone with no one to talk to. You have forgotten to speak up, especially to old ears. You are tired? You are not ill?"

"No, Wise One, I am not ill," Tephra smiled kindly at Kenæ, "It may be as you say—it is a long time alone with no one to talk to."

Kenæ nodded, "Yes, yes. We will end the lesson for the day." She stood, looked around the small hut as if checking to see all was in order, and then walked to the door.

Tephra hurried to open it for her, and asked, "Wise One, my grandmother, Kame—is she well?" The Wise One smiled kindly, nodded, and made her way back to the village. Tephra knew she would return to the Hammada Stone and inform the other Wise Ones about her visit. She hoped Kenáe was satisfied with her responses and that her report would be favorable.

Tephra quickly picked up some reeds for weaving and went out to the place in the meadow that had become her sanctuary. After completing a small basket, she stood, stretched, and began walking. Each day she had walked a little farther from the hut, and by this time had entered the sparsely wooded area at the far end of the meadow. Today she ventured deeper into the woods until she could barely see the hut, and remained there for a time, pretending she was in the woods near Mosken Lake and far from the hut in the outland. She recalled the times she had picked wild blackberries with Sedi and Graben, each eating handfuls as they picked. They had laughed at each other as their faces became smudged with the juice of the dark berries. Smearing the berries on each other's faces they would then laugh until tears formed in their eyes.

Tephra smiled at the memory—but it suddenly turned to anguish. "Graben!" she cried out, as memories more recent and painful came to her. Why had he never come to ask about her injury? Why had he not sent word as to his intentions? Why had Olivine not asked about her? Even though she was only allowed that one meal with her family, and the short visit from her cousin Esker, it was permitted for others to send messages when she was confined to Kame's dwelling. She knew that Graben had not even gone to visit Sedi. She sank to her knees in the fallen leaves, weeping and crying out, "Graben! Why? Olivine? You were my closest friends!" In a voice choked with tears, she whispered, "You did not speak for me—I would have for you! I did you no wrong! I did you no wrong—yet I am banished! No one may speak my name, not even the Wise Ones who come to give me lessons and bring food. I am no one."

As Tephra whispered the last words, "I am no one," a feeling of numbness came over her. She stood somewhat shakily, brushed the leaves from her shift, and walked slowly and deliberately back to her sanctuary. She began another basket, experimenting with the design by alternating reed widths within standard weaving patterns, and braiding thinner reeds into one. She was completely absorbed in her weaving, a welcome relief from the thoughts and memories that plagued her last night and earlier this day. It was past midday, and still she worked unhurriedly and meticulously, taking short walks every now and then to stretch her legs. She stood, and finding she was light-headed, realized she had not stopped for the midday meal or to say the prayers prescribed as part of her banishment and purification.

Tephra picked up the baskets and reeds, returned to the hut, and went to close the door. As she did so, she wondered why she bothered. No one was nearby and the Wise One, Kenǽ, had already come and returned to the village. Still, she always made certain the door was closed and latched when she was inside, leaving it wide open only when she went into the meadow. She lit the small oil lamp, and lit the stove thinking to prepare a simple stew that would serve as her missed midday meal and her evening meal as well. She prepared the stew from a few of the vegetables the Wise One had brought that morning, adding a small chunk of dried venison for flavoring the broth.

The stew was gently simmering on the stove when Tephra was startled by a soft tap-tap on the door. Thinking she imagined it, she shook her head and began unwrapping the apple bread Kenǽ had brought. She cut a small slice to enjoy after the stew, and then again she heard the tap-tap, a little louder, as a soft voice called, "Tephra! It is Kaoli!"

Stunned, Tephra froze a brief moment before going to the door in two strides, hoping, and yet afraid to hope. She opened the door slowly, just a crack, as she peered anxiously through the small opening. Seeing it was truly Kaoli, she swung the door wide. "Kaoli!" she said hoarsely, as tears welled in her eyes.

"Will you ask me to enter?" the Barchan maiden smiled.

"Oh! Yes, oh, please!" Tephra exclaimed with joy, moving aside to let her friend enter. As soon as Kaoli had stepped into the small hut and Tephra had closed and latched the door, the Drumlin maiden heartily embraced her Barchan visitor. Bewildered, she wiped away her tears and asked, "Kaoli, how did you know I was here?"

"Esker."

"Esker?" Tephra asked, quite confused.

"I went to find her on the meadows, to ask if you were well," Kaoli said, then laughed, "Oh, Tephra, I have brought you a gift." She carefully handed a small package to Tephra who took it hesitantly.

Puzzled, she asked, "What is it? Who—"

"Untie the string and unwrap it!" Kaoli said giggling.

When Tephra saw the lovely little bird perched on an apple blossom branch, all she could say was, "Oh-h-h!" in wonder. After a moment, she looked at Kaoli questioningly.

With a mischievous grin Kaoli responded, "From Strata. He carved it. He is an excellent woodcarver. He said he was watching a bird singing and it reminded him of you singing to Uluru's children. He said to tell you—wait, yes, I recall his words, 'Tell the lovely Drumlin maiden I hope this reminds her to keep singing.' He said to tell you, 'Singing when one is sad draws out the sadness. Then, peace can come into you, and soon, joy will follow.' It is an old Barchan saying, but a true one."

Tephra felt her face grow warm and said, "Drumlins have one very like it." She gently turned the wooden carving over in her hand. "It is beautiful. The little bird looks almost real," she said in awe. "Please tell Strata thank you. I do sing sometimes. I sing to my little sister at night." Noticing Kaoli has confused expression, Tephra explained about Breccia's doll Ribbons, Breccia's favorite song, and how they promised each other they would sing it at sundown and know each was thinking of the other. Then, with a downcast expression, she said, "I probably should not keep Strata's gift. I do not think it is allowed."

"Tephra, is it true that you see no one from your village, not even your mother?"

"No one comes, except one of our Wise Ones who comes every few days."

"Yes, Esker told me."

"Kaoli, no one else from my village is allowed. And I cannot go beyond the hedge fence that is the boundary of the outland just beyond the door." Tephra gestured toward the doorway and gave a false little laugh, "The people of the village are protected from me by the woods between the hedge fence and the village."

"Oh, Tephra!" Kaoli said, compassion evident in her voice, "I will come again as soon as I can."

"Your people will not mind? It is a long journey, and you must have had to cross the river...." Tephra felt a sudden lightheartedness at the possibility of visits from Kaoli, yet she was concerned for her safety.

With a twinkle in her eye, Kaoli giggled, "I will not tell them!"

"But, they will miss you, and wonder where you have gone!"

"They are used to my strange ways," the Barchan maiden said matter-of-factly.

"What about your family?"

"Strata, Pingo, and Foehn, and my grandfather, are the only family I have known."

"I know Strata is your cousin."

"He is more like an older brother. He has always watched over me." Then she giggled, "They know I have come here. Strata and Pingo came with me down the mountain, and will again if I want to visit you."

Bewildered, Tephra asked, "They are near?"

"Not very near. They are in the deep woods, a little way up the mountain. I am to return to them before sunset. We will rest in a lean-to shelter there overnight, and at dawn we will cross the river and return to our settlement."

"Kaoli, I do not know what to say, or how to thank you for coming so far. The journey cannot have been easy. You came to comfort me. You, and Pingo, and—and Strata." Tephra was deeply moved.

"You could offer me something to drink—and a little food if you have enough to spare," Kaoli suggested in a teasing voice.

"Of course!" Tephra suddenly remembered the stew that was gently bubbling on the stove and went to stir it. "I have made a stew. It is a simple one, and there is only a little, but we will have that with some special bread and tea." After carefully placing Strata's lovely carved bird in her pouch, Tephra ladled stew into the two bowls, cut another slice of the apple bread, and put water on to heat for tea. She then poured water from a pitcher into the two mugs and gestured for Kaoli to sit on one of the stools.

The two young women ate in silence at first, then Tephra asked, "Kaoli? You have no other family, just your grandfather, Strata and Pingo?"

"No, no one else. But it is a story for another time. This is good stew," Kaoli said, and Tephra understood not to press further, even though she was curious. Kaoli finished the stew, and as Tephra poured their tea, said, "I will return, Tephra, but only if you say it is good for me to do so. I would not wish to cause you to stay longer away from your family."

"I will think of a way to let you know the Wise Ones have come earlier, and it is safe for you to come. But, Kaoli, it is such a difficult journey! I cannot encourage it!"

"I come because you are alone, and because there are those in Barchan who care for you. They want to know you are well. I also come so that I can go to Esker and tell her that I have visited you. She will be pleased to know that you are well. She called me 'friend,' so I come for my friend Esker," Kaoli stated matter-of-factly, and smiled in her amusing way.

"I am glad you and Esker are friends." Tephra went over to the cot where Ribbons lay, and sighing she said, "I have thought of a way to let you know it is safe to come here. I just hope Breccia will not be angry with me for taking a ribbon from her doll, but it is all I can think of to use." Getting the small knife from the shelf near the stove, Tephra cut a length of blue ribbon from the doll's dress. "If it is safe, I will tie this onto a twig on the cherry tree in the meadow. Come, and I will show you which one to look for."

The two went out into the meadow, and Tephra walked over to the cherry tree. "Up here," she said, "on the side away from the hut. From which direction did you come? Can you see it from there?"

"Yes, I am sure I will be able to see it. I have good eyes." Kaoli clasped Tephra's hands in her own. "I must hurry now."

Tephra bent to kiss the small Kaoli on the cheek, whispering hoarsely, "Thank you, Kaoli, and thank Pingo, and of course, Strata. You have made me feel joy for the first time in weeks!" She touched Kaoli's cheek tenderly and said in a teasing voice, though tears came to her eyes, "Only seeing my family could bring more joy than your visit, my little friend."

Kaoli laughed her musical laugh, and ran toward the thick woods, and to where Strata and Pingo waited. Tephra thought how much Kaoli reminded her of Strata—the deep, dark brown hair and clear blue eyes, and their laugh, so similar.

When Kaoli was out of sight, Tephra went back into the hut, cleared away things from the meal she and Kaoli had shared, and worked on her weaving loom a while. Even though the sun had just slipped beneath the horizon, she washed up and changed into her sleep shift. Taking Strata's bird from her pouch, she sat it on the cot next to Ribbons, cleared her throat, and sang "Where Do Birds Go?" twice. She then picked up Ribbons and sang a song of joy to The Always as she managed a few slow dance steps in the small space between her cot and the table. She thanked The Always for the kindness of the "forbidden ones," even though she felt a bit guilty for encouraging their friendship—a thing forbidden by Drumlin Laws, and certainly more serious since she was under banishment. As she sang her thanks for the gift of the little bird that Strata had sent, she smiled as she felt her pulse quicken at the thought of him. Suddenly tired from the many varied emotions she had experienced that day, she lay down on her cot and fell asleep with one arm around Ribbons, and Strata's bird cradled in the other hand.

Kaoli was well aware that Strata would be anxiously awaiting her return, and was not surprised when he approached her from a ways off. "How was your visit with the Drumlin maiden?" he asked hurriedly.

"It went very well. She was surprised, and I think happy to see me." Kaoli answered as they walked to where Pingo had been waiting.

"Did you give her the bird I carved?"

"Yes." Out of the corner of her eye, Kaoli could see Strata staring at her intently. Quite certain that he was waiting to hear Tephra's reaction to his gift, Kaoli decided to tease him for a while by pretending more tiredness than she really felt. "I am hungry, and glad I can rest now!" she exclaimed, sitting down on the forest floor.

Strata quickly served Kaoli some of the rabbit stew Pingo had prepared, and helped her prepare a bed of fallen leaves and pine straw on which to spread her coverlet. She lay on her side propped up on one elbow, and watched with amusement as Strata paced back and forth. Finally, he asked again, "Did you give her the bird I carved?"

Clenching her jaw to keep from smiling, Kaoli replied, "Yes, as I already told you."

"Did she like it?"

"What? Oh, the bird. Yes, I think so."

Strata paced back and forth a few more times, then stopped and asked, "Did she *say* anything?"

"Oh, did she say anything? Only, ummm, only that she thought it was beautiful, and looked so real."

"Did you remember to tell her?"

"What?" Kaoli continued to tease, but seeing that she was close to going too far, she laughed and said, "Yes, Strata. I told her you wanted the bird to remind her to sing, even when she was sad. I even remembered the old saying."

"That is good," Strata said, nodding, still standing near Kaoli.

She grinned, sat up, and patted the coverlet next to her. "Strata," she said as if to a small child, "sit down!" She knew he was eager to hear more about her visit with Tephra. She told him about the meal they shared, about the song Tephra had promised her little sister she would sing every evening, and she explained about the doll. She said, "Tephra seemed delighted that you and Pingo had made the journey with me, and twice she reminded me to thank you for the carving." With a sly grin, she added, "I am sure that she blushed as she said your name."

Strata's broad grin affirmed what Kaoli had suspected—the tall Barchan man deeply cared for the lovely Drumlin maiden. Although Kaoli was slightly amused by this revelation, it also caused her concern. Even though Tephra seemed to care for Strata, their caring could likely bring much unhappiness. Kaoli sometimes doubted the wisdom of continuing to visit Tephra, but the thought of the Drumlin maiden all alone for so long troubled her, and she knew she would return to the outland hut often.

CHAPTER
26

One day Tephra realized she had now been living in the outland for six weeks, although many days it seemed she had been there for several months. She was sitting on her cot mending one of her shifts when she heard a knock at the door. Thinking it may be Kaoli, as it was not time for a visit from one of the Wise Ones, she went quickly to unlatch the door. Saying, "Greetings! Please enter," she swung the door wide.

Seeing not Kaoli, but her grandmother and Moraine, she was startled at first, then threw her arms around Kame, crying, "Oh Gram-mo, Gram-mo!" reverting to the name she had called her grandmother when she was just learning to talk.

Kame returned her granddaughter's embrace, held her at arm's length and said gently, "Put water on for tea. I have brought my special blend you like so much. And your mother sends a warm cloak, for the days are getting cooler." Kame then addressed Moraine, "Just put the basket on the floor near the table, but first take out the loaf of my special brown bread. We will have that with our tea."

"Ah, you look well, child," Moraine said to Tephra, "a little thinner perhaps?"

"I am well, thank you, Wise One." Tephra's hands shook as she dipped water from the pail into the small pan, excited at seeing her grandmother, yet anxious because she did not think Kame would be allowed to visit. She took down the two mugs from the shelf, and turned to see Kame take out a mug from the large pouch in her shawl. Tephra stood at the table while the two matrons sat on the stools. The three drank their tea and enjoyed the honey-sweetened bread in silence, and then Kame motioned for Tephra to sit on the cot.

Tephra went to her cot and sat watching her grandmother warily; wondering how it was the Hammada allowed Kame to visit her. Kame sat silently for a few moments, her eyes closed, her lips murmuring a prayer. Taking a deep breath, she looked at her granddaughter and began, "Tephra, I asked Moraine to come with me for there is much to tell you, and it is necessary that another Wise One be present when things of the village are shared with one in the outland. This was allowed as the Hammada assumes you will be returning to life in the village. It is to prepare you for that day that we are here."

Tephra swallowed and folded her hands, gripping them tightly to stop their shaking. There was something in Kame's voice that made her uneasy. In a near monotone voice, Moraine began a narrative of some of the happenings in the village as Tephra listened intently.

"Ogen is now well enough that he was allowed to leave Hevel and go to his own family dwelling. Tor visits him often, as does Olivine. Graben brings vegetables to Ogen's mother and helps with chores that Ogen can no longer perform. He will not let anyone else help with the chores, and still he has his chore of overseeing his family's gardens. Yet he never visits with Ogen—a fact which some of the Hammada find disturbing.

"Ogen still suffers from headaches, his eyesight is not improving, and he has longer and longer bouts of dizziness. Often he must spend the entire day on his cot in a dark corner of his dwelling. At those times he becomes withdrawn and moody, refusing to see anyone except his father."

Moraine paused and took a deep breath before continuing. "After consulting Karst, Shael, and Hevel, Graben went to your father and ended your betrothal. He told Caldera and Tarn he did not want the courting gifts returned or to be repaid for them. He told Sedi he would always be his friend, but if and when you returned to your family dwelling, he would not visit if you were there.

"Olivine has been heard by many to say she does not know anyone named Tephra, and was trying to forget she ever did. Olivine has stopped acknowledging greetings from any one of the clan of shepherds. She has made it plain that she blames you for Ogen's injury."

During most of Moraine's narration, Tephra had sat quite still, and with her hands tightly folded, stared at a spot on the floor—until the part about Olivine. Tephra began trembling and shaking her head slowly from side to side. She looked up at Kame and with tears streaming down her face, cried in a hoarse whisper, "But she is my best friend!"

Kame went to sit next to Tephra and held her as she wept. Then, after wiping the tears from her granddaughter's face, Kame put one arm around Tephra, and kissed her forehead. As she stroked her hair with the other hand, she said in a soft, consoling tone, "In time, my pet, in time, her heart will heal, and she can then forgive. You are always in my thoughts, my dear child. I am sad to leave you now, after what you have learned, but the Hammada was very gracious to allow me to come with Moraine, and we were granted only a short time." She hid her face in the waves of Tephra's unbound hair and whispered, "Your mother says you are always in the caring thoughts of your family and you are not as alone as you may feel." Kame stood, nodded to Moraine, and the two returned to the village.

Tephra felt almost dizzy from all that Moraine had related. She felt flushed, yet cold at the same time. She shivered and pulled the lamb's wool coverlet around her. It seemed like everything she had ever known was gone. "Oh, Graben! You still think I broke our vows," she whispered, as she recalled Moraine's words. Graben's actions Tephra could understand, but not Olivine's! They had kept each other's secrets since they could talk, trusting no one else with their confidences. The entire village was often amused by the fact that one was rarely seen without the other. They were often seen helping each other with chores so they could be together.

After the first shock, Tephra's sense of loss became too deep for tears. She lost sense of time as she thought over what Moraine had told her. The dimming light inside the hut was her only reminder of the lateness of the day. She stumbled to the door, opening it to let in the last afternoon rays of sunlight. It was warm out, yet she was still shivering so she put water on the stove to heat for tea. When the tea had steeped, she broke off a piece of the brown bread, picked up her mug of tea, and went to sit in her favorite spot under the cherry tree. She sat there until the last rays of sun left the sky, nibbling at the bread and sipping the tea. She then found her way into the darkened hut, closed and latched the door, and stumbled to her cot. Not bothering to change into her sleep shift, she wrapped herself in the coverlet, and lay curled up on the cot until dawn broke. Moraine's words echoing in her head allowed only an hour or two of broken sleep.

For the next two days, she went about her chores wooden-like, spending as much time as possible sitting under her favorite tree and weaving intricately patterned baskets. On the third day, she looked up from her place under the tree to see Kame and Moraine walking towards her.

"Tephra?" Kame said softly.

Tephra sighed deeply, picked up her weaving materials, and made her way to the hut. She went to put water on for tea, but Kame called to her, "My child, leave the tea alone. Come, sit." Kame motioned for Tephra to sit next to her on the cot, while Moraine sat on one of the stools. "Are you well, my child?" her grandmother asked.

Tephra shrugged then leaned against Kame, her head resting on her shoulder. "I am well, Grandmother, just… sad."

"Oh, my child! And now there is more I must tell you." Kame paused, looked at Moraine, and said, "No, this I alone must tell."

Tephra moved to look into her grandmother's face, fearing what she would hear. The old woman took Tephra's hands into her own and spoke tenderly, "Ogen has died from his head injury. Yesterday, he suddenly became very dizzy and had a severe headache. He lay down with one of Hevel's scented cloths over his eyes and forehead. When Parra, his mother, went to see about him, he did not seem to be breathing. She sent at once for Hevel, but it was too late. Ogen had departed."

Tephra was shaking her head back and forth slowly, whispering, "No, not Ogen! No, no."

Moraine then informed Tephra, "The Closing of the Ritual of Parting will be day after tomorrow, early in the morning. The Hammada have said you may stand on the outside of the clearing to observe the ritual, and then you may pay respects to Ogen's clan."

"I will stand with you if you wish," Kame offered.

"Yes, please. I would like that." Tephra's voice was barely above a whisper.

On the day of Closing for Ogen, Kame met Tephra at the hedge fence. She was carrying the white head-covering which was required for all females over twelve years old to wear at Parting Rituals. Kame arranged the covering on Tephra's head and the two walked silently to the edge of the clearing. Ogen's body lay on a low bier in the center of the Hammada Stone, while his family sat on stools behind it. Ogen's body was wrapped head to toe in white cloth, and then draped with a cloth of his clan's colors.

After Karst's opening prayers, the family stood and moved to the edge of the Stone in front of Ogen's body. The villagers filed slowly past in silence, stopping only long enough to turn to Ogen's parents and bow in respect. Parra, Ogen's mother, stood almost motionless, no tears escaping from her eyes, and barely acknowledging her neighbors as they paid their respects. However, the young man's father, Uyot, returned each bow as he blinked tears from his eyes. When Kame and Tephra, the last in the procession, approached the stone, Parra looked directly at Tephra. Her voice cold and even, she said hoarsely, "Defiled one! You have no place here. Because of you, my son has departed. Leave us. Leave this village. You will no longer find welcome here!"

Tephra, stung by Parra's words and the coldness in her voice, stared unmoving at Ogen's body on the bier. She recalled quite vividly seeing Ogen fall, and then, on the journey down the mountain, seeing him become more and more disoriented. Yet, she could not believe he was departed and tears filled her eyes.

Uyot placed his hand on his mate's arm, saying tenderly, "Parra my mate, Kame and her granddaughter are here to pay respect. Ogen would not—"

Before Uyot could complete his statement, Parra turned and went to kneel by the body of her son, her cold anger giving way to deep grief as her body shook with sobs. Uyot bowed to Kame and Tephra, and hurried to console his mate. Tephra watched as Uyot sat cross-legged next to Parra, gently pulled her into his arms and held her close as they wept together.

Tephra felt their grief and sobbed with them. Then she looked at Kame, shook her head, and ran, half stumbling, her vision blurred by her tears, back toward the hut in the outland. Her knee, unaccustomed as it was to running, began to ache, and as she limped through the small opening in the hedge she could not keep her balance. Her arms and legs were scratched by the sharp twigs. She managed to hobble through the door and fell upon her cot, sobbing with pain, grief, and remorse.

Tephra looked up as she heard Kame's voice, "Your knee is overworked. I will get Hevel."

"No," Tephra sobbed, "Do not leave me, Gram-mo!" and stretched out her hand toward her grandmother.

Kame sat on the cot and pulled Tephra's head into her lap, stroking her back and chanting one of the ancient songs—a song of the love and tenderness of The Always for his people. She then encouraged her granddaughter, "Do not dwell on the words of a grieving mother. She will forgive one day."

"Ogen! Oh, not Ogen. He was Sedi's friend. Olivine …!"

"I know. I know my child. It is hard when one so young—and a friend—departs."

Kame found cloths and using cool water, gently wiped away the blood from Tephra's scratched and bleeding arms and legs. She then dampened another and wrapped it around Tephra's knee. "I do not have the herbs needed for healing. I will ask the Hammada to send Hevel. Try to rest the knee and put cool cloths on it until then."

"Can you stay a while longer? Do not leave me yet!"

"For a while, my pet. Only for a while."

At midday, Kame prepared a light meal for the two of them, yet Tephra wanted only tea. When Kame had cleaned up after preparing the meal, she came to sit by Tephra on the cot. Tephra was glad for her grandmother's company, yet after her plea asking her grandmother not to leave, she had said nothing. How could she put into words the guilt she felt over Ogen's death, and the conflicting thoughts about the choices she had made?

"Tephra," Kame spoke softly, "I must return to the village now. Try to rest."

Tephra nodded and gave her grandmother a weak smile. Kame kissed her granddaughter's forehead and walked through the doorway. Tephra continued to lie on the cot, staring at the ceiling as silent tears streamed from her eyes. As darkness began to fill the hut, she glanced over to the shelf that held Strata's bird. She stared at it until the light faded, then closed hold her swollen eyes and drifted into a restless sleep.

CHAPTER 27

Late summer rains had insured that many crops would produce close to their normal yield, and also gave relief from the searing heat. The village of Drumlin was busy with the harvest, taking time out only for Ogen's Day of Parting, and giving little thought to the maiden of the clan of shepherds who had now been two months in the outland. Still, her clan had not forgotten her, and they were already preparing for her homecoming. The three Wise Ones, who had routinely brought provisions to Tephra and had tutored her in the lessons for her purification, were called to give testimony before the entire Hammada and any villagers who desired to hear the accounting.

The Wise Ones—Moraine, Kenǽ, and Eolia—spoke of the meekness and cooperation of the maiden. She had performed all the chores given to her, and they were well done. She had even made more baskets than required, and had, according to Kenǽ, created some very unusual yet pleasing designs, further proof that the maiden had not been idle.

Moraine testified that she often asked about the people of Drumlin, and seemed to be quite sad at not being part of the village life. When questioned, Eolia stated that Tephra showed no signs of rebellion.

Hevel the Healer had twice gone to the outland hut at Kame's request to examine Tephra's knee, the second time at Kame's request after Ogen's Day of Parting, and he was called to give an account of his observation. "The maiden has suffered physically from her disobedience of Drumlin laws and customs," the healer began. "Her knee was badly injured, not once but twice, during her journey to the Forbidden Mountain. It has taken a long time healing, and yet it will likely not be as before the injuries. None of you can deny that one of her gifts, and her joy, was dancing the ritual and ceremonial dances. Now, because of the injury, it is likely she will never be able to dance again."

At this statement a murmur ran through the people, for it was true that none could deny the grace and heart the maiden brought to the dances. Tephra's mother stepped forward, "Hevel, what did my daughter say when she was told this?"

"Caldera, the child wept and said, 'It is a harsh punishment The Always has sent me. Yet, I must accept his wisdom'."

Kame raised her staff and added, "She turned to me and said, 'I can still sing my songs to The Always, but I will forever be sad I can no longer dance for him.'" Kame had to hold back her own tears as she caught sight of Caldera, tears streaming down her face upon hearing the words of Tephra.

Siluria was standing with Mica and Olivine at the edge of the clearing, apart from their clans, as they were not yet old enough to have any say in village affairs. Siluria shook her head and exclaimed, "Not be able to dance! She was the best of all of us. Even my mother said she did not recall anyone who danced as good as T—uh, she did. I miss her so!"

Olivine frowned and stated, "I can easily take her place. I am almost as good as she was. We don't need her."

Siluria argued, "We do! Even though she was to be mated, she could still have helped us, and even teach the younger dancers."

Mica, who was of the same clan as Ogen, said, "We all know Tephra helped us be our best!"

Olivine spat, "Do not say her name! She you speak of is nothing to me!"

"She was your best friend," Siluria pleaded, "How can you ignore her when she returns?"

"It will be easy," Olivine retorted in a stern voice. "I can never forget she caused the death of my Ogen! I would be mated by now. Better she had remained on that mountain." She turned on her heel and walked away.

As Mica watched Olivine walk away, she said, "I, too, am grieving for Ogen, but I am glad Tephra will be returning soon." She turned to Siluria and confided, "Did I tell you that when I mentioned to Olivine that I would be glad to see Tephra again, she did not speak to me for several days?"

"Olivine is putting all the blame on Tephra, when it was Graben who asked Ogen to go to Barchan," Siluria stated, shaking her head in annoyance.

"Do you think there will be many who object to Tephra returning?" Mica wondered. "She will soon have spent the three months as was decreed."

"I am sure Ogen's family and Graben's clan will not welcome her return."

"Graben is still angry with her?" Mica asked.

"It seems he is either angry or gloomy every time I see him. Even Tor rarely seeks his company. Look, Karst is raising his staff." The maidens abandoned their conversation and turned to look towards the stone, curious and anxious to hear the Hammada's ruling.

The Hammada had heard objections from Ogen's and Graben's clans, and had spent time in meditation, but they could not see sufficient reason to delay Tephra's return to village life any longer than the three months. Karst raised his staff and announced, "The maiden Tephra of the Clan of Shepherds will in one month be returned to her family dwelling and will resume her duties as shepherdess. According to the testimonies given, she has done all that was required for her purification—she has shown remorse, has suffered, and The Always has shown favor on the village of Drumlin by the bountiful harvest."

Many of Graben's and Ogen's clans were disappointed in the ruling, but their grumblings were drowned out by the joyful shouts of the clan of shepherds. Many villagers of other clans went to Tarn and Caldera, expressing their happiness that a daughter of Drumlin would soon be returning to village life.

⁂

Twelve days before Tephra was due to return to her family and village life, Kame, Moraine, and Eolia paid a visit to the outland hut to bring provisions. Tephra hugged her grandmother, bowed politely to Eolia and Moraine, and said, "I will put water on for tea,"

Kame smiled and announced, "We have brought a treat, Tephra. Put away your provisions."

The four enjoyed Kame's special blend of herb tea and Caldera's peach tarts, while Tephra told them about the flowering plants she had found in the nearby woods, and that she planted them in the area near the wild cherry tree. "I even dug up a small seedling tree, and planted it. I do not know if it will grow, as I do not know plants the way Graben does, but—" she stopped, realizing when she said Graben's name that she was babbling to cover her nervousness.

"Well," said Moraine, "I think we should take a look at this flower garden you have made."

Kame, grinning, suggested, "We will have our look on our way back to the village. Tephra, the Hammada has set the day for your return to your family shelter and life in the village. Eleven days after today, Moraine, Eolia, Kenæ, and I will come for you just before sunset. Karst and Hevel will meet us at the edge of the clearing. There will be prayers, of course, and then we will escort you to your family dwelling. The next day you will join Esker and Creta on the hills with the flock."

Tephra was elated that a definite date had been set for her return to her family, yet she also experienced a sense of uneasiness.

Kame asked, "You are frowning? When I expected a big smile?"

"I know that Graben and Olivine, and their clans, will not welcome me, but what about the other villagers?"

Kame assured her, "All of your own clan is ready to welcome you with love and warmth. They know how much you cared for the sheep you tended. You have been missed, dear one."

Tephra smiled and hugged her grandmother, "Then I shall be content with my family, my clan, and my sheep."

After Kame and Moraine had gone back to the village, Tephra tied the blue ribbon on the tree limb to let Kaoli know it was safe for her to visit. Two days later, as Tephra sat weaving under her favorite tree, the Barchan maiden came skipping across the meadow from the direction of the deep woods. "Kaoli! You have come!" Tephra exclaimed, quickly rising to embrace her friend.

"As I told you I would. Besides, I would have to answer to Strata if I did not come to see that you were well. And you do look better than the last time I was here."

"I have news, Kaoli," Tephra smiled. "I will be going home to my family in two weeks!"

"Oh! That is good news," Kaoli smiled, and then frowned, "So, soon you will soon be mated?"

"I do not think I will be mated for a long time. Graben has ended our betrothal."

"Oh!" Kaoli said happily—then more soberly, "Oh, I am sorry Tephra. Are you very sad?"

"I guess I am sad that Graben and I may never even be friends again. And, I am very sad that one maiden, who was always my closest friend, now says I am nothing to her. But I am happy to be going back to my family, and I will be a shepherdess again on the hills with my sheep."

"I am not Drumlin, but Tephra," Kaoli spoke tenderly, "I will always be your friend."

Tephra grinned, "We are both enosh! That is enough!"

"Enosh? What is that?"

"Oh, how do I explain? I think it means we are both from what were once the same peoples."

"Yes! Augur speaks of the Ehud, a people once united before—"

"—Before the rift." Tephra finished. "My grandmother has spoken of this. And," Tephra bowed her head and said solemnly, "she has prophesied there is to be another."

"Another? What does she mean?" Kaoli asked, her forehead wrinkled in such concentration that she looked quite comical.

Tephra shrugged, indicating she was not sure herself, and then she giggled, "Oh, Kaoli! I am sorry, but what a face you made!"

"It is alright," Kaoli smiled, "Strata says I always make a funny face when I am thinking hard or don't understand something."

"And how is Strata?" Tephra asked, her voice soft and low. Slightly embarrassed, she added quickly, "And how is Pingo and Uluru and the children?"

Kaoli answered frankly, "He says he misses the Drumlin maiden he rescued. He misses her singing."

"Oh-h-h!" was all Tephra could say as she felt her cheeks grow warm.

"He wanted to come here with me, but Pingo said he should wait until you asked for him."

"Oh, Kaoli, he cannot, I—" Tephra stammered. "It is too dangerous. If you were found here, it could be explained, but not Strata," Tephra warned with an emphatic shake of her head.

Kaoli nodded, indicating she understood, and said, "I came once before, and waited for a time, but did not see the blue ribbon."

Tephra frowned and then with a deep sigh, told Kaoli about Ogen's Day of Parting, and how she had caused more pain to her knee. "It was several days before I felt like walking out into the meadow." Kaoli reached out and squeezed Tephra's hand. After a moment or two of silence, the two began sharing bits of life among their respective people until time for Kaoli to return to Barchan.

CHAPTER 28

The days passed slowly for Tephra, although she kept busy weaving baskets, perfecting her skills at the loom, and walking in the woods. There she would watch the birds and be reminded of Strata's gift and his request to 'sing even in your sadness.' Inspired, she would sing the poem-songs of The Always, even making up her own poem-songs.

When the day came for Tephra to return to her family, Kame, Moraine, Kenæ, and Eolia arrived late in the afternoon to escort her. Kame lovingly braided Tephra's long hair while the other women made certain the hut was left in order with no food remaining to attract scavenger animals. Tephra had already packed up her shifts and cloaks, Breccia's doll Ribbons, and Strata's carving of the bird. She had carefully wrapped the bird in one of her shifts, not wanting to answer questions about Strata's gift. After the door had been closed behind them, Tephra glanced toward the wild cherry tree that had been her place of solace during her three months in the outland. Silently bidding it farewell, she realized that in many ways she would miss the tree and the small garden she had planted around it. She would also miss the visits of Kaoli, and she wondered how she would ever be able to visit with her Barchan friends again.

After the prayers with Karst at the edge of the clearing, the group made their way to Tephra's family dwelling. Tephra was overjoyed to see that most of the clan of shepherds had gathered in the yard. There were tables filled with food and garlands were draped over the doorways. Her parents, Sedi, and Breccia greeted her with warm embraces, which were politely interrupted by Mica and Siluria who were impatient to be with their friend again.

It was well after dark when all the clan had left, but Mica and Siluria remained. Tephra had offered to help her mother with the chore of cleaning up, but Caldera, stroking her daughter's face, said, "Go—be with your friends. We will be together later."

The three maidens sat on a wood and stone bench outside Tephra's dwelling, with Tephra in the middle, her two friends holding her hands. They were silent for a while, no one knowing quite what to say, but Tephra found their hands comforting. Clearing her throat with a little cough, Mica spoke first, "Tephra, Siluria and I, well, we thought we should—um—things are, uh, things are different, and we do not want you to be shocked or hurt."

"Oh, Mica!" Siluria said abruptly. She then turned to Tephra and said gently, "Tephra, you have to know Olivine will ignore you. She pretends she never knew anyone named Tephra. She, and Ogen's family—well some of them anyway—blame you for Ogen's death."

"I know." Tephra said softly.

"There is more," Siluria continued as she caringly placed her other hand on Tephra's arm. "You know that Graben ended the betrothal to you. But, even though Drumlin law says he must wait one year before he can court another, he and his mother, and many of his clan, are petitioning the Hammada to not hold him to that time. They claim *you* ended the betrothal by going up to Forbidden Mountain, and therefore the betrothal was not binding."

Mica squeezed Tephra's hand and added, "Te, Enoht is being very insistent. His mate is most in favor of her own daughter, Catera, as a mate for Graben."

"Oh, no!" Tephra cried out.

"I am sorry Tephra! I know you and Graben—"

"Oh! It is not that. You did not know. Sedi had quietly asked Catera's father for courting privileges just a day or so before he was injured. Catera was delighted, and Enoht also, but her mother wanted her daughter to be mated to one of the earth-tillers. So, after Sedi was injured, and it was known how seriously, Catera's mother insisted there be no courtship, although Catera was heartbroken and wept and begged. Enoht helped her to sneak away late one evening and she came to talk to Sedi. My brother told me he held her in his arms as they both cried. I know Sedi hoped that one day he would be allowed to court Catera."

"Ah-h-h! Poor Sedi!" exclaimed Siluria. "Poor Graben, also, to be mated to one with such a mother!"

"Siluria!" Mica admonished. "Think of Tephra," she said, putting her arm around Tephra's shoulder.

Tephra shook her head, "It is alright, Mica. Since the day that Graben brought me down from that mountain, I have known he would not want me for his mate."

"Did he say something to make you think so?" asked Mica.

"No," Tephra answered, "Just the way he looked at me and spoke to me. I think he thought I had broken my vows. He—" Tephra shrugged her shoulders, not knowing how to explain.

"Tephra," Mica asked hesitantly, "will you, or can you, tell us what made you go up to the plateau? We have heard rumors, and some things we were told by the Hammada. We are your friends and we hope you can tell us. I need to understand what happened to Ogen. Olivine thinks I did not care for him, one of my own clan. Can you tell me the truth about what happened?"

"The truth?" smiled Tephra. "Yes. You two, and my family, are the only ones who have asked without judging me first. I will tell you tomorrow. Now, I must go in to be with my family." She stood and held out her arms to embrace her two friends. Siluria and Mica each held her close and promised they would return tomorrow after the evening meal.

Tephra went to be with her family, embracing them each again. Her parents had been sitting at the table drinking herbal tea and asked her to join them. She poured a mug for herself, then took Ribbons out of the pouch she had carried from the outland hut, brought it to where Breccia was playing, and put it on the floor next to her. Kneeling next to her little sister she said, "Thank you for letting me have her while I was away. Did you remember to sing our song?"

"Well, I did at first and then sometimes I forgot," Breccia admitted, lowering her head.

"It is alright, little lamb. Now we can sing together." Tephra felt a pang of guilt for the times she had been too upset to sing after promising she would.

Breccia broke into tears, pushed the doll away from her, and ran to Sedi. Tephra looked up at Sedi questioningly. He shook his head as he comforted Breccia. Tephra rose and returning to the table, looked at her parents and asked quietly, "Why did Breccia start crying?"

Her father took a drink of his tea, gave a deep sigh, and answered, "Breccia has been so excited about your coming home, that she could not help talking about it with her friends as they played together. It seems one or two of them said things that upset Breccia."

"What things, father? And why did she shove Ribbons away?" Tephra took a deep breath, trying to calm the uneasy feeling in her stomach.

"One of the children told her you had to go away because you were dirty. I think the child meant 'unclean.' When Breccia answered that you had to go sit in a corner far away and that she had given you Ribbons so you would not be lonely, the child said that since you were dirty, Ribbons would be dirty too. Don't take it too hard, dear one. Children hear bits of things, and they do not understand what they hear. Sedi has been trying to help Breccia make sense of all that has happened, but it is much for her young mind." Tarn put his arm around Tephra and patted her shoulder, adding, "It is good to have you with us again."

Caldera stood and Tephra went to her. "Mother, thank you for letting me visit with Mica and Siluria. It was good to know I have at least two friends in the village."

Caldera pulled her daughter to her and held her close. After a long pause, she held her at arm's length, and looked into her eyes. "Twice I thought I had lost you. First, when we thought you had fallen into Mosken Lake and departed. Then, when you had to be judged, I feared you would be banished forever," she said, as tears began to form in her eyes.

"I am sorry. I am sorry for all the worry and trouble it has caused you. Can you believe that I did not think that by trying to save a lamb I would cause so much heartache?" Tephra began to feel weak and sat down on a stool near her mother. "I think I should wash up and get some rest. I suddenly feel very tired."

"You are pale, except for a few more freckles, and you are thinner," Caldera observed. "Perhaps the provisions sent were not enough?"

"They were enough, Mother. It is only that at most times I had little appetite."

"Get some rest, my love. You must be on the hills with Esker tomorrow morning. I am afraid you will still be watched closely by the Hammada, and some of the villagers will be watching, ready to find fault," Caldera said, her voice tinged with bitterness. Hearing this rare emotion in her mother, Tephra felt distressed that she was the cause of it. While she was preparing for sleep, she had to keep blinking back tears as she thought of the hurt she had caused her family. "Somehow," she whispered to herself determinedly, "I will make it up to them!"

CHAPTER 29

Out on the hills with the flock once more, Tephra felt more alive than she had in months. Esker and Creta had run to meet her as soon as they saw her figure come over the nearest hill, and they greeted her with hugs. Creta pointed out the newest lambs, and Esker told the story of how one of the lambs broke its leg trying to jump over a fallen tree. "Creta cried and had to go with Elos as he carried it to Hevel," Esker said. "The healer made a splint for it and kept it in the yard behind his hut until it was healed. Creta went every day to pet the animal and to help feed it. When it was able to return to the hills, it was days before it would stop following Creta so closely that she would get angry at it!"

Tephra laughed at Esker's telling of Creta and the lamb, but to keep Creta from being embarrassed by Esker's story she said, "Oh, Creta, I am so proud of you! I am happy to hear you care so much for the lambs. It is the sign of a good shepherdess." With this, Tephra recalled with clarity the sight and sound of the animal that was caught in the briars on the terraced trails. Once again, she realized she could never have ignored the animal's cries.

When Tephra returned to her family dwelling that evening, she was smiling contentedly. As she hung up her cloak and went to warm up near the cook stove, Caldera called her over to the table where she was preparing potatoes to cook for the evening meal. Assuming her mother had called for help with the meal, or for some other chore, she asked what she could do to help. Caldera shook her head, "Tephra, Siluria left just a short time ago. She said she would return after the evening meal."

"I am sorry—I hope it is alright that she and Mica visit with me for a while. Mother, they want me to tell them why I was found on the plateau by the Barchans. I know I could not speak of it before, but now, it is alright?"

"Yes, I think it would be allowed now. And your friends deserve to know the truth from you. I am glad they asked."

Only moments after Tephra had helped her mother clean up following their evening meal, Siluria arrived alone. Tephra was waiting for her outside on the bench where she had sat with Siluria and Mica the night before. The torch outside had been lit, and when Siluria came near, Tephra could see that her eyes were red as though from crying. She went to her immediately, "Siluria? Is something wrong? Where is Mica?"

Siluria's eyes filled with tears, which she quickly brushed away. "Oh, Tephra, I tried to talk to Mica, but others have been saying things to her, and now—oh I am so sorry—now *she* says she does not know anyone named Tephra! I begged her to come, to hear what you were going to tell us. She said Graben had come to her and he asked her how she could remain your friend after you had caused the death of her cousin. He told her you defended the Barchan who caused Ogen to fall and hit his head. He said that you had lived in his dwelling when you were on the mountain, and that you spoke to him and even allowed him to touch you and carry you in his arms."

By the end of Siluria's narration, Tephra had stumbled to the bench and was trembling all over, hugging her arms to herself. "Why? Why does no one believe me? I did not break my vows!" Tephra spoke insistently, although her voice was barely a hoarse whisper. Siluria walked quickly to the bench and put her arm around Tephra. "I will listen, Te. I already believe you would never betray Graben."

Tephra took a deep breath and began the narrative of the events from the time she saw the animal entangled on the ledge to the arrival of Graben, Tor, and Ogen in Barchan Settlement. She ended her account by saying, "The Barchan man carried me against my will when he found me on the plateau. I could not get away from him because my knee was badly injured. He carried me to a healer in their settlement. At no time was I alone with the young Barchan man. He never spent the night in the same dwelling where I stayed. In fact, he carried me to his sister's dwelling so I would be more comfortable. It was his sister who took care of me. There were no Barchan men in her dwelling. I only spoke to the Barchan man when Graben came to bring me back here. And that was because he and Graben were arguing, and so I told him I was going with Graben."

"The Barchan was trying to keep you there?" Siluria asked alarmed.

"No, he was trying to warn Graben that my knee was not well enough for the rough trail down the mountain, and that it could be dangerous." Tephra did not give the full account of the altercation between Graben and Strata. She knew from Kame that Graben and Tor had not told Hevel or the Hammada the truth, and Tephra had kept their secret. Harming another enosh was a serious offense, and was unheard of in Drumlin Village. Disagreements were settled with a council hearing, or if needed, the entire Hammada, before they could became violent. Tephra knew if the Hammada discovered Graben had lied to them—had harmed another willingly and had lied to Hevel about the cause of Ogen's injury—he would be severely punished, and very likely be banished for a long time. She was deeply hurt by his suspicions and his distrust of her, but, after spending three months in the outland, she knew she could never want such a punishment for anyone. Besides, with all the rumors that were being spread, she doubted anyone would believe her if she did reveal Graben's secret.

"But Tephra," Siluria exclaimed, "they are Barchans, the Forbidden Ones! Yet you speak kindly of them."

Tephra placed her hand on Siluria's shoulder, and said, "I know. But they were nothing like I imagined, or nothing like we have been told they would be. When I first saw them, I was so frightened. I was afraid they would harm me somehow. When he offered to take me to his healer, I was stunned. When I fell, and made my injury worse, he showed kindness and concern. I was frightened because I could not walk, and I was afraid I would die on that trail, and all I could think of was getting back to the caves. But then, later, when he took me to his sister, well, she was so kind, and her children, too. Then the man and his cousin made certain the Wise Ones knew I was alive, even though it could have been dangerous for them."

"I do not know what to say. They truly do not seem like the Barchans we have been told about," Siluria said in a puzzled tone. She rubbed her forehead in concentration, and continued, "I know you told our Wise One's the truth, but yet, there are many who believe what Graben and Olivine are saying." Siluria bowed her head, then choking back tears she said, "Tor has said he is thinking that we should not be courting as he is Graben's friend, and I have said that you are still my friend. We had a big argument about it."

"Oh, Siluria! No!" Tephra pleaded. "If Tor breaks the courtship, then—"

"Yes! I know! It will be only Noll, and I am sure he will ask for betrothal."

Tephra inquired caringly, "So, you feel the same way about Noll as before?"

"Noll has been considerate and thoughtful during his courting of me, but I still remember how he used to make fun of me, and once played a cruel trick on me."

Tephra knew Siluria was quite fond of Tor. She buried her face in her hands as guilt and shame overwhelmed her once more. "I am so sorry, so sorry! What can I do?"

"Tephra, I do not blame you. You have always been kind to me, even when others were not. I will always be your friend."

"No, Siluria, no! Do not let Tor break courtship. I know you care for him, and he would be a good mate for you. Do not visit me again. Just knowing you believe me is enough."

"But, Tephra—"

"No, Siluria, please!" Tephra sobbed, holding her stomach as though to stop the ache inside. "I cannot be the cause of you being mated to one you do not care for. Olivine has lost all caring for me. She blames me for Ogen's death, and in a way, she is right. Now Mica says I am nothing to her. Please, do not say you never knew anyone named Tephra. Just talk to Tor and tell him you will no longer visit me so he will not break courtship with you."

Siluria eyes filled with tears as she said, "That would mean never seeing you again! Tephra, I don't—"

"Promise me, please?" Tephra pleaded again, her face wet with tears as she looked at her friend. "I will know you think kindly of me, and that will be enough."

"I will promise," Siluria reluctantly agreed, as she tenderly wiped the tears from Tephra's face, "only if you are very sure."

Tephra whispered hoarsely, "Yes!"

Siluria sobbed as she replied, "I will think of you every day, and I will petition The Always to show you favor."

Tephra stood, held out her arms to Siluria, and the two clung to each other until Tephra pulled back gently and said, "I will always be your friend, Siluria."

After Siluria returned to her own dwelling, Tephra remained sitting on the bench. Tarn came out and sat next to her, pulled her head down on his shoulder, and held her while she wept. Finally, she took a deep breath and bent her head to wipe her eyes on the hem of her shift. After a moment, she turned to Tarn and pleaded, "Father, I want to go to Grandmother."

Tarn nodded his understanding and said, "Go get what you need. I will tell Mother."

When Kame opened her door and saw Tephra and Tarn, she looked closely at both and nodded in understanding. Tarn kissed his daughter on her forehead, and left her in Kame's care. The old woman gently put her arm around her granddaughter's shoulders and led her inside. She removed Tephra's pouch from her shoulder, laid it on the end of one of the two cots in the room, and motioned for Tephra to sit down as she put water on to heat for her special tea. Sitting next to her granddaughter, she took both her hands in her own and began softly chanting prayers. Kame poured a mug of tea for them both, and as she handed a mug to Tephra, she could sense that her granddaughter was calmer in her presence.

"Tephra," she said as she sat across from her, "tell Grandmother."

Handing the half-finished mug of tea to Kame, Tephra told her about Mica and Siluria, and about Breccia and the other children. Kame listened intently, nodding at times to indicate she understood.

"You are surely exhausted from your first day back with the flock, and the emotions of the evening," Kame said. "Lie down while I seek the comfort of The Always for you." Kame helped Tephra remove her cloak, and covered her with a soft woolen coverlet. She went to her prayer rug, assumed the posture for deep meditation, and glanced over at her granddaughter, noting that her eyes were still filled with tears. Kame closed her eyes and after a few moments, was in deep meditation. Suddenly her eyes opened wide, she gasped, and in a low, trembling voice prophesied,

> *The rock will split, the rift will go deep.*
> *Fast the streams will flow;*
> *then the shift, and blood will flow!*
> *Blood will flow like the streams!*
> *It has begun.*
> *It has begun with deceit and secrets.*

The next morning Kame had fresh apple bread and a pot of strong tea brewing when Tephra awoke. After they shared the morning meal, Tephra put on her cloak and prepared to join Esker and Creta with the flock. Kame walked to the door with her, embraced her, and said with a reassuring smile, "My child, all things are done toward a purpose. Just remember The Always, and look to Nunatak."

Kame watched as her granddaughter walked towards the pasture and the sheep. "Words from The Always come more often of late," she thought to herself. "I must understand what they mean. I cannot protect her, cannot protect Drumlin, until I do." Going back inside and closing the door, she returned to her prayer rug and began the ancient chants for wisdom.

CHAPTER 30

Weeks had passed since Tephra's return from the outland. One chilly day, after the evening meal, Tarn announced that Tephra would be going earlier to the flock the next morning. Cooler days brought a change in the activities of the village, particularly the shepherds. The young men stayed with the flock overnight while the weather was warm enough, and the maidens relieved them in the morning. Now that the nights were getting colder, the maidens would take the flock out just after the frost had melted and the young men would relieve them around mid-afternoon. When the frost began to fall close to midnight, the young men would bring the flock in to the sheep pens. Cold nights were dangerous for shepherds and their sheep, for then the wolves were hungrier and braver. The predators had learned over time that when the temperatures drop, the shepherds became drowsy and the sheep moved closer together to sleep. This change in the shepherds' schedule meant Tephra, Esker, and Creta were home earlier in the day. The only exception was when the rains were heavy, or would turn to sleet or snow—then the sheep remained in the sheltered pens where both shepherd and shepherdess took watch turns, for even there the flock was not entirely safe from predators.

With the two young shepherds out with the flock, and Sedi unable to help due to his injured leg, Tarn and Elek, Esker's father, had often depended on the help that Graben volunteered. Since he had ended the betrothal to Tephra, Graben no longer came to help the shepherds, meaning the two older men were often quite weary at the end of the day.

More than once, Tephra overheard her father grumbling about the difficulties of bartering with certain clans. The grain farmers, who were distantly related to the earth-tillers, had asked for more wool than last season. Tephra was not surprised that certain vegetables, which Caldera usually traded for at a bargain from Graben's clan, were now a higher price and a lower quality. Elek had the same problems when he went to have tools repaired. Ogen's father was reluctant to make the repair and bartering was difficult. Each time Tephra heard the difficulties her clan was facing, she winced with an inner pain, knowing she was somehow the cause of it all. She resolved to do all she could to help her parents, even taking on extra chores after coming in from the hills.

Esker and Creta often complained of having to be on the meadows so early, and Tephra often felt like she had just closed her eyes when it was time to arise. Yet, she still loved watching the sunrise over the mountain and seeing the colors reflected on Nunatak Peak. Young Breccia liked the change in her sister's schedule. Since Tephra had to arise so early, she had to go to sleep at the same time Breccia did, especially with the extra chores she had undertaken. Now Breccia did not feel so left out and alone. She and Tephra cuddled together on the sleep mat they shared for warmth on chilly nights, and sang together "Where Do Birds Go?" before Tephra fell asleep.

One night as Tephra was getting her sleep shift from its shelf in the tiny room she shared with Breccia, she picked up her pouch and took out the bird Strata had carved for her. She had never shown it to anyone, and rarely took it out of its pouch, which she stored under her shifts. She knew Breccia was giving long goodnight hugs to their parents and to Sedi, so she felt it was safe. As she ran her fingers tenderly over the bird's back, she smiled, sighed deeply, and placed the bird back into the pouch—but not before Breccia's sharp eyes had seen it.

"What is that, sister?" the child asked as she ran over to where Tephra stood.

Tephra knew she would have to satisfy the child's curiosity, but did not want to give too much information, so she simply said, "It was given to me by the people on the mountain who found me when I was hurt and who helped me get well enough to come home."

"Can I see it?"

Tephra sat down on a low stool near the shelf and held the carving in her palm so that Breccia could see it clearly.

"Ooooo!" the child exclaimed, "it looks just like a real bird!" Frowning, she looked up at her sister and asked, "Why did they give you something so pretty? Aren't they bad people?"

"I don't know, dear one. The ones who helped me did not seem like bad people." Tephra put the bird back in the pouch and thought of the Barchans who had been kind to her.

Lying down on the sleep mat, she held out her arms to her little sister. "How about if you sing the bird song to me tonight," she suggested. "I don't think I've ever heard you sing it by yourself."

Breccia yawned as she crawled under the coverlet, and said, "I will try." Tephra turned down the lamp and held the child close. Breccia began the song, singing softer and softer, until the words were unintelligible and she fell asleep. Although her body was tired, Tephra lay awake—her mind kept running through all the events from the night she and Graben were betrothed up to her returning from her three months of banishment. As tears seeped from her closed eyes, she tried again to understand her many conflicting feelings. She knew she would always miss Graben's friendship, because by now she doubted he had any feelings left for her. She was happy to be back home, but it felt as though her only friends were the Barchans who had cared for her, and they were still "forbidden."

The next morning, Tephra relieved Elos and Olin a little earlier than usual, sending them back to their shelters even though Esker and Creta had not yet arrived. She found comfort in being alone on the hills with the sheep and walked around the flock, looking over each animal for cuts or matted fleece as she had been taught to do. Creta arrived alone and announced that Esker would be coming a little later. Tephra was puzzled, but did not question Creta, sensing that Creta would not, or could not, answer. The two walked, watching the flock in silence until Esker arrived and walked with them. Esker had said nothing to explain her late arrival and did not even greet her cousin as was customary. Tephra looked at Esker, and catching her eye, gestured for the two of them to walk a short distance from Creta. Esker nodded agreement and told her sister that she and Tephra would walk around to the other side of the flock.

When they were out of hearing of young Creta, Tephra asked, "Esker, why are you so quiet this morning? Are you well?"

Esker stopped, looked at the ground, and slowly shook her head. "You are my cousin and my friend. I have wanted to be like you all my life. I still remember the first day I was apprenticed to you—I was so happy. You have always been so kind, so patient with me and how forgetful I can be. I do not wish to hurt you, Tephra, ever." Esker wiped away tears that had pooled in her eyes and resumed walking.

Tephra reached out and held her cousin's hand. "Esker, your words are very sweet and I know you mean them, but why do you say them to me now? Something troubles you."

In short choppy sentences, as she tried to keep from crying, Esker told how two of her friends—one from Ogen's clan, the other from Olivine's—had said they could no longer be friends. They had said, "Your cousin is unclean, defiled. That means anything that belongs to her, or anything she touches, is also unclean, defiled. We do not want to be your friend, or we might become unclean."

"Oh, Esker!" Tephra cried out. "They are such children! They do not understand. My time in the outland means that I am clean again. I am no longer 'defiled' and the Hammada has proclaimed it so!" She sighed deeply. "But it seems very few in Drumlin have accepted what the Wise One's have declared, and I know why."

"Why?" Esker asked as she squeezed her cousin's hand in a caring gesture.

"It is because of the death of Ogen, because Olivine is so sad now and has broken friendship with me. But also because Graben ended our betrothal and he is much admired in Drumlin. Since he refuses to believe that I did not break my betrothal vows, many others doubt it also."

"I believe you did not break your vows to Graben, Tephra. And the Hammada must have believed you too, or you would have had to stay in the outland for longer."

Tephra smiled tenderly at her cousin, and suggested they go back and walk with Creta. As they continued their work, Tephra found her thoughts constantly dwelling on her family and how her attempts to rescue a lamb had led to such unrest in her village.

A few mornings later, as Tephra was about to leave for the pasture, Caldera called to her and asked if she would return a little earlier to stay with Breccia. "I must go to Kame's and to Moraine's for some healing herbs. Breccia is feeling very cross this morning and complains of her belly. I do not want to leave her with Sedi if she is ill."

"Yes, mother. I am sure Esker and Creta will manage the flock just fine."

Just before midday, Tephra left the pasture to return to her shelter. When she arrived, her mother was ready to leave on her errands. "Sedi is in his room working on a new loom and cording comb. He was relieved you were coming home early. He is trying to finish it before Father comes home." She sighed and lowered her voice, "I think he feels useless sometimes, and he hopes with these new tools he can be more helpful. Breccia is in the main room on her play mat. She is curious about what Sedi is working on, but do not let her disturb him." She kissed Tephra on the forehead, and hurried out the door.

Tephra went to Breccia, suggesting several activities they might do together. But Breccia was sullen and shook her head at all of them. Tephra, growing impatient, asked, "What would you like to do? What would make you feel better?"

"Dance for me!"

Tephra was startled at the request. "Little one, Hevel has said I cannot dance because my knee has not healed as it should."

Tears sprung to Breccia's eyes and she whined, "But who will teach me to dance?" Then she sniffed, frowned, and asked in a challenging voice, "You can walk, so why can't you dance?"

Tephra was briefly taken aback by her young sister's question. She thought a moment then gave a little laugh and exclaimed, "You are right, dear Breccia! I can dance some of the steps if I do them slowly. And I can teach you some of the easier steps."

Breccia cheered in delight, and Tephra clapped out a slow rhythm, which the child quickly learned. As they clapped, Tephra performed a slower version of the steps to one of the ritual dances. She kept her steps simple, her movements slow and guarded so that very little stress would be placed on her knee.

As she went into a slow turn, she was startled by a sharp, mocking voice. "Hah! I thought you were unable to dance!"

Tephra spun toward the voice, lost her balance and stumbled. Her breath caught in her throat at the sight of Graben as he walked to her in two long, quick strides. His right hand grasped her left hand, which she had thrust outward for balance, while his other hand clasped her right shoulder.

At that moment, Tephra heard Sedi call out, "Graben! What is this? Tephra, are you alright?"

Graben quickly removed his hands from Tephra and turned to face Sedi who was leaning on his crutch and looking from one to the other, his face registering both confusion and suspicion. Graben answered sharply, "What is this? That is what I was asking your sister. I caught her dancing! Yet, Hevel the Healer had pronounced before the entire village that she was no longer able to dance because her knee injury was so serious." His tone was derisive and challenging.

"Tephra? You are not hurt?" Sedi questioned, "I heard you and Breccia clapping, but—"

Tephra shook her head in frustration, and said with a calmness she did not feel, "My little sister said that since I could walk, I could also dance. She was right. I can dance, but *only* the slow moves and the steps which do not put stress on my knee." She took a few steps to sit on a nearby bench, and winced in pain, revealing that her abrupt turn had indeed caused stress to her knee. "I cannot possibly keep up with the steps for the ceremonial dances; therefore, I can only dance to amuse my little sister," she said with restrained fury and a touch of sarcasm.

She looked up at Sedi and he looked at Graben and jerked his head in the direction of his room, indicating for Graben to follow, but

Graben shook his head. "I will return another day, when I am certain *she* is not here."

Tephra winced again, this time at the words Graben spoke and the coldness of his tone. Limping slightly, she hurried toward the door and reached for her cloak. As Graben opened the door to leave, she said quietly but firmly, "Graben, I wish to talk with you," and preceded him out the door.

When he had closed the door behind him, Graben said, "Sedi has been my truest friend for many years. I am trying to keep what you have done from spoiling that."

"What I have done? So, you continue to believe that I broke my vows to you? I have told the truth about what happened on the mountain. Have you?"

Graben retorted, bitterness evident in his tone and narrowed eyes, "You forget. I *heard* you, as did Tor, as you asked if that Barchan would be all right, although I had every right to attack him. There was more than polite concern in your voice. I heard you speak his name—more than once—and saw the way you looked at him. I also saw the desire in his eyes when he looked at you." He took a step toward her, and said through gritted teeth, "*That* truth you left out when you spoke to the Hammada."

Tephra had never been in a confrontation such as this, and she was unprepared for the emotions it aroused. She wanted to lash out at him for doubting her, for lying to the Wise Ones, and for allowing the blame for Ogen's death to fall on her alone. She bit her lip as tears of anger and frustration filled her eyes and flowed down her face. She took a deep breath and through clenched teeth, said, "I did not betray you, and I have kept silent about your actions on the mountain. You insisted that I leave Barchan with you even though you knew my knee was still badly injured. It is because of your jealously and your pride that my knee has not healed as it should and I can no longer dance the ceremonial dances. How dare you come into my family dwelling and upset my little sister with your accusations, and—" she stopped and said no more. She feared she would lose all control and say things that might cause more harm to her family and her clan, for she could not trust Graben's reaction. Before he could respond or react, she walked quickly inside, closed the door firmly, and went to the wash room. There she took a few deep breaths, splashed water on her face and blotted it dry.

Sedi met her as she came out of the wash room and said quietly. "I will stay with Breccia. I have calmed her with some story, a simple explanation and she is playing in my room. If she does not see that you have been crying, she will ask no more questions. I heard angry voices. You are not hurt?"

Tephra shook her head and smiled at her brother, whispered a heartfelt thank you, and went into the room she shared with Breccia. Going straight to the shelf that held her pouch, she took out the little bird, sat cross-legged on the sleep mat, and pulled the coverlet around her shoulders. She cradled the carving in her hands, closed her eyes and breathed deeply in and out, attempting to calm herself. When she heard the sounds of her mother busily preparing the evening meal, she rose, put away the bird, smoothed her hair, and went to help with the meal. She ate very little, and even though she was aware of the concerned looks from her mother, could not bring herself to speak of the incident with Graben. She did not think Sedi would say anything either.

After the meal, Tephra went to her mother and suggested, "Go sit with Father. I will clean up in here and then will help Breccia wash up." She was especially tender with Breccia as they prepared for sleep that night. She played a simple game with her, and sang a silly song as they snuggled together on their shared sleep mat. After Breccia fell asleep, Tephra kissed her tenderly on her pink cheek and whispered, "Yes, my pet, I can dance."

CHAPTER
31

The days became shorter and colder, the nights longer, and the snowfalls more frequent, which meant even less outside activities. Tephra went out on the hills as often as the weather would allow; other times she would accompany her father to the sheep pens to help with the sheep, although at first he objected. She hoped that if Graben knew she would be out, he might start visiting Sedi again. He told her Graben had only come once or twice since that day he had found Tephra at home. Sedi was becoming moody and irritable, missing the company of his friends. He had taken Ogen's death hard, and had been relieved that Tor and Graben still came to see him, trying to include him in whatever activities his injured leg would allow. Now, however, it had been weeks since Graben had been to see him, and Tor had paid only one brief visit on his way to complete an errand for his father.

One morning, while Tephra and her father were working in the sheep pens, he said, "So quiet. Did you not sleep well?"

She shook her head and attempted a smile, still recalling troublesome dreams that awakened her several times. Then she bit her lower lip, frowned, and twisted one of her braids as she said, "Father, I would like to go stay with Grandmother."

"You have talked with her about this?"

"No, Father, but I think she will approve."

"Tephra, why is it you are asking this?"

"Father, I would still be helping you, and going out with the flock, but I am the reason Sedi is so irritable," Tephra paused and looked up at her father. "His friends do not include him for they do not want to be where I am. Breccia also has been hurt by what some children say. Even Esker has heard things that wounded her. I also know that you and Mother have had trouble at market. If I am away, maybe it will be better for everyone."

"Ah, Tephra!" Tarn said, smiling at her tenderly as he placed his hand on her shoulder. "Kame's hut is only at the edge of the village. I doubt staying there will make a difference. You are our daughter and you belong with us. People will get over all this soon. Things will be as they once were, you will see."

"Father, I do not think so. I respectfully ask to go to Kame's. I need to go. I have no friends. And now, with so many thinking I broke my vows, no one will want to be mated to me, so I will bring even more dishonor to my clan. Wise Kame will pray with me, and help me make sense—" Tephra broke off, swallowing hard and blinking back tears.

Tarn went to her, put his arms around her shoulders, and in a voice filled with compassion, said, "Tomorrow you will go to Kame. I will go speak with her, and I will talk to your mother."

Tephra remained at Kame's dwelling until near the end of the third moon. The weather had changed—the snows were melting from the lower mountains and the streams swelled. During her time with Kame, Tephra had confessed all her fears, her questions, her anger, and her confusion to the heart of her wise grandmother. The two had spent many hours in prayer to The Always, and sat in silent meditation awaiting his answers while enjoying moments of peace. The day before the traditional First Grazing, Tephra announced to Kame that she had made a decision, but asked if she could bring the matter before the Hammada.

Seven days later, the Hammada called the entire village to gather in the clearing to hear an announcement. Just after sunset, the torches were lit on the Hammada Stone and around the clearing, and all the villagers were sitting with their clans, including Tephra's parents. Tarn held his arm around Caldera's shoulder and both kept their eyes focused on the grass in front of them. Karst raised his crystal-tipped staff to signal for silence, cleared his throat, and unrolling a small scroll, began reading:

"To the Peoples of the Village of Drumlin Hills: The maiden called Tephra of the Clan of Shepherds has entered into voluntary banishment. The maiden made this decision of her own free will after a long period of prayer and meditation led by her grandmother, the Wise Kame. The maiden also had the counsel of the entire Hammada. She had become well aware of the division among our village, of the ending of life-long friendships, of arguments and disagreements that went unsettled, and of increasing unrest in the marketplace.

"The maiden Tephra believes that she is the cause of the rift, of the split that had been prophesied by the Wise Kame. This prophecy, which was made only in the presence of the Hammada and never elsewhere proclaimed, was therefore unknown to the maiden. The maiden avows that she has correctly, honestly related to the Hammada the events and circumstances of her journey to the Forbidden Mountain and her brief stay there. The maiden Tephra deeply regrets that her actions, though innocent in their intent, have caused the death of one of our village, and heartache to many. She goes away from Drumlin out of love for her people, convinced that her continued presence here would not allow the rift to be healed. She goes to be alone, to meditate, and to pray to The Always for healing among her beloved People of the Village of Drumlin."

⚭

There was stunned silence during Karst's reading of the announcement, and at the end of the reading, there was much murmuring among the clans. Those of the shepherd clan sitting nearest Tarn and Caldera reached out to touch their arms or shoulders in a consoling gesture. Tarn could hear some of the women around them sniffling. He heard the shocked voices of some expressing outrage that the Hammada would agree to send away one so young, one with so many gifts that would benefit her clan and her village. Other voices reached his ears also, villagers who said it was right that she should go away. Some who heartlessly said she should never have been allowed to return. Tarn acted as though he did not hear the cruel remarks. He just held Caldera closer as her body shook with silent weeping, knowing she heard the spiteful words also. Karst allowed a time for the villagers to react, and raising his staff, again asked for silence.

When the villagers had quieted, Karst stated, "The maiden has already left the Village of Drumlin. At sunset last evening, she bid farewell to her family, and many of her clan. Just before sunrise this morning, her father, Tarn of the Clan of Shepherds, escorted her there himself, accompanied by Kame, Elek, and Eolia."

Tarn stood, walked to the stone, and spoke to Karst, "Honorable Karst, I would like to speak to the village." Karst nodded, and Tarn stepped up on the stone, turned and faced the villagers. In a voice clear and strong, yet filled with emotion, Tarn addressed the villagers. "It was against my wishes and the wishes of her mother, my mate Caldera, that she go away. As her father, and as she is not mated, I could have forbid it. We did, I admit, argue much. Finally, my daughter, my beloved Tephra, made a declaration in the presence of Karst and her mother and me. These are her words—words I will never forget: 'I must go away so peace and unity may return to Drumlin. I now renounce Drumlin, and all its laws, customs, and traditions. I will, however, continue to pray to The Always for the beloved village of my birth. My name is to be stricken from the list of villagers, and no one may speak my name from this day on.' These were her own words." Tarn bowed his head and coughed as he struggled to keep his emotions in control, then looked up and focusing his gaze on the clan of earth-tillers, continued, "Her mother and I must now forget that we had a daughter named Tephra. Her brother and her sister, and her entire clan, may never speak her name and must forget her also. I ask you, fellow Drumlins, could you? Could you forget your own child?"

As Tarn stepped down from the stone, Caldera and Sedi, aided by Elos, were there to meet him. Several villagers from the clan of shepherds and from other clans as well, came to console them. With true humility, Tarn thankfully received their words of praise for the dignity he showed as he spoke to the villagers. One of the villagers, Siluria's father, asked if he and some of his kinsmen could have the honor of escorting Tarn and his family back to their dwelling. Tarn and Caldera could only nod and smiled gratefully, their emotions too raw for words.

While the villagers were at the Hammada Stone hearing Karst's pronouncement, Tephra was in the outland hut, preparing a meager evening meal. When Tarn, Kame, Elek, and Eolia escorted Tephra to the hut, Kame carried a large basket full of bread, jam, honey, cheese and eggs. Tarn brought bags of ground wheat and millet, vegetable seeds for planting, a few small garden tools, a spool of heavy twine, and a weaving loom. Tephra's own thick woolen coverlet, a large tin of teas, and a pair of warm boots made by Sedi were carried by Eolia. Elek brought a second coverlet and a large fold of cloth sent by Caldera, Tephra's small sewing basket, and a thick handful of reeds for weaving baskets. In her shoulder pouch, Tephra carried three day-shifts and her night shift, her hair comb and ribbons, willow twigs, the carving of the small bird, and three skeins of wool. She carried a warm cloak over one arm, and a bow and sheath of arrows was slung over the other shoulder. Before Sedi's injury, he had taught her to hunt with the bow, and she had been practicing, with Sedi coaching her, over the past two weeks so that she would be able to hunt for small game. No one would be bringing supplies to Tephra this time. For several years, she had been learning from Caldera how to make bread and small cakes, and she would grow her own vegetables. Her mother was worried how she would sustain herself, but Tephra was certain this was what The Always required of her, and he would help her survive.

She had spent the day arranging all the supplies, and making the tiny hut more comfortable. As she unpacked her pouch, she discovered two decoratively woven panels that had hung on one of the walls of the room she shared with Breccia. She smiled, knowing Caldera had slipped them into her pouch. She hung one from a peg on the door, and laid the other on the table to hide the roughness of its surface. In the late afternoon, she had taken a walk in the meadow. The wild cherry tree was holding on to a few blossoms, and she had broken off part of a small, low-hanging branch and placed it in on the woven panel. She wished she had brought more reeds for weaving baskets, then shook her head and smiled, thinking, "And what will I do with all those baskets?" The maiden felt a peace she had not known in almost a year.

CHAPTER 32

Tephra knew the Golith Huntsman Trials would be soon, and then would follow the Festival of the Fifth Moon. She recalled former festivals when she would dance with the other maidens, and felt a pang of regret. Remembering the singing of the ancient poem-songs with the entire village, she smiled. However, the memory of last year's festival was muddled by all the events that happened afterwards. She would recall the anxiety of being lost on the plateau, and all the events and emotions that followed, and she would cringe inside.

Although often lonely, Tephra kept busy with her vegetable garden and the flowering plants she had transplanted from the woods, and weaving cloth on her small loom. At midday, when the weather was mild and the ground dry, she would sit in the shade of the wild cherry tree, look toward Nunatak Peak and meditate as Kame had taught her. After eating a light meal, she would stroll through the woods, looking for berry vines, roots, and leaves for healing. Each day or so, she would wander a little farther into the woods. After a while, she observed that the land took a slight incline.

One day she noticed that several strides ahead was a small clearing, about twice the size of her tiny hut. On the other side of the clearing, the land, thick with Boreal Pines and broad-leafed oaks, rose abruptly. She saw something shining, reflecting light at the far edge of the clearing. She quickened her pace, and came to a small pool fed by water trickling from between a layer of rocks. The water was clear and reflected the blue sky and the color of the trees around it. She was delighted to find this source of fresh water, which meant she would not have to depend on catching rainwater or have to ration quite as carefully. She went quickly back to her hut for a bucket and returned to the small pool to dip a supply of fresh water. Soon, the pool became one of her favorite spots in the forest. Some days she would take her midday meal to the pool and would meditate with the trickling sound of the water as background.

On one visit to the pool, Tephra was certain someone had been there since her last visit. There was a footprint on one side of the pool, yet she knew she had not walked on that side of the water on her last visit. It alarmed her at first, but then she had a daring but encouraging thought—Kaoli. The footprint was small enough, yet why would Kaoli be there?

Early the next morning as she worked in the flower garden she had planted, Tephra looked up and gasped as she saw a blue ribbon tied to a low branch of the tree. Her heart beat fast with excitement as she touched the ribbon—she was certain it had not been there a couple of days ago. She hurried back to the hut, returned with a blue hair ribbon from her pouch, and tied it next to the one already on the tree. At midday, she went into the hut to get the food for her meal. When she returned, she almost dropped her mug of water when she saw Kaoli sitting under the tree and grinning broadly.

"Kaoli! How did you know I was here?" Tephra asked as she sat the basket containing her meal on the ground, and went to embrace her visitor.

"Esker told me," Kaoli replied, then giggled and said, "We have all thought of you often, and wondered how you were. Do not tell him I told you, but Strata was going to go to Esker himself to ask if you had mated the one who came to take you from our settlement. We all told him it would not be good for him to go, but that I should go. Until the weather was warmer, he would not allow me to risk the trails. I hid and watched from the trails below the plateau for several days, but never saw you, only Esker and Creta.

"One morning Esker was alone with the sheep, so I went to her. She was happy to see me, and right away she told me that you were here in the outland again. She said she wanted to explain, but was afraid someone would see me, or that Creta would return before I was out of sight. So, I hid behind some rocks and bushes while she stood close by and told me how you came to be here. " Kaoli stopped to take a deep breath and continued with a confused look on her face. "Esker said you wanted to come here, that you offered to come to make peace in your village. Were the people of your village so very disturbed by your time on Barchan Mountain?"

Tephra thought a long moment before answering Kaoli. She did not want the Barchans to think ill of her people, yet she knew Kaoli deserved some kind of answer. "A few of my village were angry with me and blamed me for the death of one of the men who came to bring me back. Others thought I had betrayed my betrothal vows. These villagers made trade difficult for my family. It is not easy to explain to one unfamiliar with the ways and laws of Drumlin."

Kaoli nodded thoughtfully, then said, "I like your cousin. She truly cares for you. Tephra, she misses you so much."

Tephra did not know what to say. She was glad to see Kaoli, but her heart ached to think of those she cared for back in Drumlin Village. She hesitantly asked, "Did Esker say anything about the people of the village? How are my parents, and Sedi and Breccia?"

"Your family is well, although they miss you. Esker said that if I saw you to tell you that some of the people who had been saying unkind things were now friendly again. A young man named Col came to help your father with the sheep pens when Esker's father was ill with a fever. I think Esker is fond of Col."

"Col? Well maybe he's grown some since last I have seen him. He is of the clan of blacksmiths. He was always shy, and was teased because he was small. All the blacksmiths have been large men." Glad to have someone to talk to, Tephra spoke with a bit more animation than was usual.

"Tephra?" Kaoli asked, concern evident in her voice, "When will you return to your village? If people are being kind again, you could return?"

"I do not think I can ever go back. I have—as I understand Drumlin laws—I have said I am no longer Drumlin. My name cannot even be spoken in the village."

Kaoli shook her head slowly as tears filled her eyes. She frowned, looked up at the ribbons on the tree, and said, "If you are no longer Drumlin, then it should not matter that I visit you; unless someone still comes here to bring you food?"

"No one comes. My grandmother, her friend Eolia, and my father, who walked with me here, brought enough to last until I could provide for myself. That is how it had to be."

"But, you will be here all alone in that tiny hut, with no one to talk to? What do you do all day?" Kaoli was outraged.

"You forget I was here for three months," Tephra said calmly.

"But at least someone came every few days, and they brought food. And then I came when I could, but to be here forever?"

"Come—come inside with me. I was about to take my midday meal. I will make us tea, and we can share a meal." Tephra picked up the basket and gestured for Kaoli to go ahead of her into the hut.

Kaoli looked around the small space and commented on the small changes Tephra had made: there were two wall hangings, a woven cloth on the table, the shutters on the high window had been taken down and scrubbed clean, and a new curtain hung over the doorway to the small chamber. She picked up Strata's carving of the bird from the shelf where it was sitting next to a small basket that held Tephra's hair comb and ribbons.

Grinning, Kaoli said, "You have made this old hut into a more proper dwelling. I see you brought Strata's gift with you. He will want to know if you remember to sing."

"Things were so—so different when I went back after the banishment. I did not sing for a long while, except to my little sister." Then Tephra smiled and said, "Now I sing the psalm prayers to The Always every day and sometimes make up my own poem-songs, even though there is no one to hear them but the birds, and a few squirrels and rabbits."

"Then I can tell Strata that you still sing," smiled Kaoli, as she poured tea into the two mugs.

The two shared a meal of millet cakes, young baby carrots, and Kame's special tea while Kaoli shared bits of news about Uluru's children. As soon as they had eaten and cleaned up the mugs and plates and shook out the tablecloth, Kaoli announced she needed to hurry back. The two young women embraced and Kaoli promised she would return.

A few days later as Tephra was at the pool washing one of her shifts in the trickling water, she heard a rustling sound behind her. Thinking it might be a rabbit, she wished she had thought to bring her bow and quiver. As she slowly stood and turned to see what animal had made the sound, she was startled and delighted to see Kaoli walking toward her—and following close behind, was Strata.

"Greetings!" Kaoli called, "See who has followed me!"

"Gr-greetings!" Tephra stammered.

Strata replied with his usual light, teasing tone, "Greetings, maiden!"

Tephra realized she was still holding her dripping wet shift, so she folded it, wrung out the water, and looking at Kaoli, said, "I have to hang this in the sun to dry."

After an uncomfortable few moments of silence, Strata asked, "Would you show me your gardens? Kaoli has told me about them."

Tephra, still slightly dazed at Strata's presence, simply nodded and led the way to her gardens and the tiny hut, trying to understand if she was happy to see Strata, or just happy to see anyone. "Of course," she thought to herself, "I am always happy to see Kaoli." She considered, "I am no longer Drumlin. I am no longer betrothed. Perhaps now it is permitted for me to speak to Strata."

Strata complimented the way she had arranged the small flowering plants around the cherry tree. "A small bench would be a good thing for sitting under the tree," he suggested. "It could fit just there, and you could see the flowers, and you would have a nice view of the sunset as well."

"I usually sit on that patch of soft grass under the tree at midday. Of course, only when the ground is dry."

Strata looked up at the tree and pointed, saying quietly, "Look, a bird bringing food to young ones in that nest."

"I see!" Tephra said softly. "The birds seem to like this tree. I have to be careful when I sit under it."

Strata chuckled lightly, "Yes, I guess that could be a problem."

Tephra smiled up at him, amazed at how easy it was to talk to this man. The bird in the tree reminded her of Strata's carving and she stammered, "Oh! Um, I—I, I—I want to tell you thank you for the carving of the bird. It is lovely."

"I thought, I thought you ...." began Strata, then cleared his throat. "Well, I hope it reminded you to sing. Kaoli did tell you?"

"Yes, she told me," Tephra smiled. "And, and yes, it did remind me, for there were times when I would think I had no reason to sing."

"Tephra, maybe you should hang that out to dry," Kaoli said, reminding Tephra of the wet shift still in her hand. Tephra draped the garment over a length of heavy twine that ran from the hut to the tree, wondering if she should invite Strata into the hut. Yes, of course she should. He and Kaoli were her friends, and Strata's presence was no longer forbidden.

"I can make tea, and I have some wild blackberry cakes I made yesterday," Tephra offered as she gestured to the door of the hut. "I found a vine of the berries in the woods a few days ago. I put in a little honey to bring out their sweetness."

As Tephra prepared the tea and set out the two mugs and plates, she felt embarrassed as she realized there were not enough dishes. She glanced up to see Strata looking at the shelf where the carved bird sat next to her comb and ribbons, and felt the blush creep up from her neck and onto her cheeks. She also saw that Strata's large frame filled the tiny hut, and yet he did not seem uncomfortable. While the tea steeped, Tephra asked about Uluru and the children. She learned that the youngest had just gotten over a fever, and that Uluru was soon to be mated. The man's mate had died two years before and had left him with a little girl the age of Pilli, Uluru's oldest daughter.

"Uluru is very happy. She cares deeply for this man. She has seen what a good father he has been, and also how he cared for his mate when she was so ill with a fever," Kaoli told Tephra. "Uluru says she knows they will find love together."

Tephra was pleased to hear about Uluru. "She was so kind to me. I hope they—I hope they will be very happy together." Tephra was unaccustomed to hearing the word 'love' expressed so casually.

The tea was ready and Tephra put the basket of blackberry cakes on the table between the two plates. She gestured for Strata and Kaoli to sit on the two stools, and she poured their tea. "I had a cake before going to the pool," she said, not wanting to admit there were only two plates and two mugs.

As Strata and Kaoli enjoyed the cakes and tea, Tephra asked about Foehn and Pingo. Afterwards, Strata went to the open door and stood looking out at the woods that separated the outland hut from the village. Kaoli offered to wash the plates and mugs, and suggested Tephra and Strata go wait under the cherry tree. Just as the two stepped out of the doorway, Strata turned and spoke softly to Tephra, "Kaoli told me that you left Drumlin, and that it was your decision to leave. She said that you asked to return to this hut so that peace might return to your village. She says you can never return. Is that true?"

"Yes," Tephra replied, not looking at Strata but at the woods, "most of what she said is true. There are ways one can return, but I think it is very, very difficult."

"What would you have to do to be able to return?"

Tephra slowly shook her head, sighed and said, "There is nothing that I can do. People of the village must request it, and there are many steps, although I cannot think on that. I cannot hope for that, or I will find no peace. I am sorry I cannot explain more, for there is much I am not sure of. And some things I am certain would never happen."

Strata reached out his hand to touch her shoulder, then hesitated. "Am I allowed to touch your shoulder in parting?"

Tephra felt her face grow warm as she looked up at him and smiled, "It is allowed now."

Strata placed his hand gently on her shoulder, saying, "Be well, Tephra. May we come again?"

"Be well, Strata," Tephra replied, and struggling to keep her voice even, said, "And yes, you are both welcome to come again."

Tephra walked with them to the pond, and holding Kaoli close, whispered, "Thank you, Kaoli." She watched them until they were out of sight, then looking up towards Nunatak Peak, she flung out her arms and whispered a joyful "Thank you" to The Always.

The day was warm and bright and Tephra was preparing a midday meal to take out under the tree when she heard a soft tap at the door. Tephra opened the door and was delighted to see Kaoli standing there holding a basket, and behind her stood Strata, grinning broadly.

"Greetings!" the tall Barchan said, "you did say we could come again?"

"Oh! Yes, of course, um …" Tephra stammered, "um, uh, come in, please." It had been over two weeks since the two had last paid a visit to the outland hut, and Tephra had been hoping they would return soon.

Kaoli, giggling softly, set the basket on the table, and began unwrapping pieces of pottery—a plate, a mug, a bowl. "Just in case you have visitors!" she smiled broadly.

Tephra felt awkward at first, then she laughed, gave Kaoli a quick hug, and said, "Then I hope this means you will surely visit again!"

Strata gave a fake cough and Tephra looked up to see he was still standing in the doorway. He said almost timidly, "Come outside, Tephra. I brought a little something for your garden."

Tephra tilted her head to one side, looked at him suspiciously, then followed him out the door and around to the flower garden. Strata stopped and gestured toward the tree. Tephra gasped as she saw a wooden bench sitting under the tree, not on her favorite grassy spot, but just where Strata had said a bench could fit. She walked quickly to the bench, and slowly brushed her hand over the smooth wood of the seat, and then the back of the bench with its pattern of a leafy vine carved in low relief.

Not knowing what to say, she gazed up at the tall Barchan who stood looking like a small boy with his hands behind his back, rocking on his heels, and sporting a silly grin. Tephra shook her head, threw her head back, and laughing out loud, put her arms out to the side and danced a few light steps around her garden. She stopped in front of the bench, sat down, and looking at Strata, motioned for him to sit next to her. His grin became a shy smile as he sat beside her and said, "I have made many things for other people—sometimes because they hire me, sometimes as a favor to a friend—but my woodworking has never caused anyone to dance!"

"Tephra was the best dancer in Drumlin," Kaoli informed Strata. "Esker told me."

Tephra blushed at Kaoli's comment, then she stood up and looked down at the bench, frowning in concentration.

"Is—is something wrong?" Strata asked.

"I am wondering how you carried this down a rough trail, and through the thick woods."

Strata laughed. "It would have been very difficult, all of one piece, but the bench is made of several pieces. I carried them down the trail with Pingo's help. Through the woods, it was not so difficult, as Kaoli carried some of the pieces. Once we were in the clearing by the pond it was put together, and then Kaoli and I carried it here."

"Oh!" Tephra said. She then asked, "But where is Pingo?"

"His mother needed him for some errand," Kaoli answered. "He hurried back to the settlement."

"But it is such a long way! Surely he would stay where you will rest tonight?" Tephra asked with concern, recalling that when Kaoli had visited before, she mentioned they had rested overnight somewhere along the trail.

Strata laughed, "As soon as Pingo gets to the trail above the woods, he will run. You have never seen anyone run as fast as Pingo. He lives on the outside of the settlement. He will be home by dark." Tephra could only smile and raise her eyebrows.

Looking carefully at the bench again, Tephra said musingly, "Some of the Drumlin woodsmen make stools and tables, and work shelves. They help build our dwellings or help to add a room when the family grows too large, but I have never seen anything like this!" Tephra paused, then frowned. "I think in Drumlin it would be seen as, well, maybe wasteful of time? All of our tables and such are well made, and very sturdy, but they are only rubbed smooth and polished with oil from one of the trees in Drumlin Woods." With an appreciative sigh, she ran her hand over the carving and said, "They are not carved like this."

After a moment of awkward silence, Strata responded in a low, soft voice, "If my bench brings you pleasure, then my time was not wasted."

Tephra looked at him to see if he was teasing her, but his expression was tender and serious, and she felt the pulse in her neck race. She suddenly felt awkward, and to change the mood of the moment, suggested they go inside for the midday meal.

Kaoli went to the basket she had brought and took out a block of cheese, six boiled eggs, and three small loaves of bread. "I thought this time we should bring something to share," she said smiling proudly.

Tephra returned her smile, saying, "We will have a feast, for I have fresh vegetables!"

As the items for the meal were laid out, and Tephra poured water into their mugs, Strata looked around and laughed. "I should also make a stool so that we can all sit for our meal!" he proclaimed.

Tephra frowned, then with a small laugh said, "We can take the table outside under the tree, and bring one stool. Both are low enough, and with the bench, we will each be able to sit and enjoy our feast."

The food and dishes were gathered into baskets by Tephra and Kaoli, while Strata carried the table and placed it in front of the bench. While he went back for the stool, Tephra spread the cloth she had woven on the table, and helped Kaoli set out the food and dishes. Tephra and Strata sat next to each other on the bench and Kaoli sat on the stool across from them. As the three enjoyed their meal, Strata told an amusing story about an argument Foehn had with an old woman of the settlement. Tephra giggled, then sobering, said, "I am wondering what Uluru and Foehn think of your visits to me here. Are they not afraid for you to be so near Drumlin Village?"

Kaoli looked at Strata and grinned. "They both understand we would not be kept from visiting you," she said. Then giving an exaggerated wink, she added, "I would have come alone, but Strata insisted I needed him to protect me on the trail."

Strata smiled sheepishly, then stood and after a lazy stretch, announced, "I am afraid we need to start on our way back. We must reach the lean-to before dark."

"Thank you both for today," Tephra said, as she wondered if it was reluctance she heard in his voice. "And Strata, thank you for the beautiful bench!"

Strata acknowledged her gratitude with a wide grin, picked up the table, and carried it back into the hut. Kaoli brought the stool while Tephra packed the dishes into the basket and brought them inside.

"Thank you for the meal," Strata said, standing awkwardly in the doorway.

"You are welcome," Tephra responded softly, "and thank you both for the dishes, and the food you brought." Kaoli and Tephra exchanged a quick hug, Strata gave Tephra his usual wink and grin, and the two Barchans walked toward the woods.

That night, as Tephra lay on her cot thinking about the afternoon spent with Kaoli and Strata, she was overwhelmed with feelings of guilt. "I was happier today than I have been in a very long time. This is wrong! I am outcast from my people, my family, even though I chose it," she thought as her throat tightened and tears filled her eyes. "I wish I could talk to Kame. I am doubting everything again."

Tephra got up from the cot, lit the lamp, and wrapped a light cloak around her as the night was cool. She paced around the hut recalling the decisions she had made, and why she had made them. Tephra stopped pacing and pressed her clenched fists to her forehead. In anguish she cried out, "Oh! How many times must I go over this, to Kame, to Mother, to the Wise Ones, to myself? I cannot change any of it. I have been punished—banished!—and still many in my village believe Graben's lies." Pacing again, she thought of the many villagers who were once friends, but had scorned her family and her clan. She realized with further clarity that she had to leave, had to forsake Drumlin, for her presence was unsettling to so many. She had accepted that she would be living a life of loneliness, of even hardship. "But now," she thought, "now I have friends again, someone to talk to every now and then. That they are Barchan does not matter—they are enosh. No. I will not feel ashamed. I will, instead, give thanks to The Always for the friendship of Strata and Kaoli." Feeling resolved, the maiden knelt on the hard-packed earth floor and with true sincerity, chanted a psalm of thanksgiving for her Barchan friends and a psalm of blessing for Drumlin Village.

CHAPTER 33

Esker and Creta were taking their midday meal in the shade of some scrub oaks, as the day had grown quite warm. The heat had also drawn the flock to the shade, so the two maidens had spread their meal cloth between two low-hanging branches so as not to be disturbed by the animals. The sound of their occasional soft bleating was interrupted as several sheep made sudden sounds of alarm. Esker rose quickly and looked to see what had disturbed them. Her anxiety turned to relief as she recognized the small form of Kaoli lightly skipping toward the trees. "It is Kaoli!" she said to her sister, as she waved and walked out to meet her.

"Greetings, Drumlin maidens," grinned Kaoli.

Esker returned her grin, saying, "Greetings, Barchan maiden. It has been many weeks since we have seen you. You are well?"

"Yes, I am well. And you and Creta look well, so you must be." Kaoli waved to Creta who was lying on the meal cloth and savoring a fresh peach. "Your cousin is well also," she said, keeping her voice low. "You do not need to be distressed about her. Strata and I have visited her twice."

"She is not too lonely? I cannot think of her all alone so far from her family and her friends, and all the things of the village she must be missing. The Festival of the Fifth Moon was not the same. I missed her dancing, her singing—I just missed *her*. Even though I had Col to celebrate with, I still missed her," Esker confided quietly as she brushed at a tear.

"I think sometimes she is lonely, but she has many things to keep her from thinking about how lonely she is."

"In the outland? I have heard the hut is very small and crude. What can she find to do all day?"

"She has planted flowers and flowering plants near a small tree. There are always birds in the tree, and butterflies around the flowers, and she has a small vegetable garden. She has made the tiny hut into a very pleasant place. I saw it before, and she has worked very hard."

Esker clasped her hands together and said, "I will give thanks to The Always tonight. I have worried about her so! Thank you, Kaoli."

Kaoli smiled and gave a little bow. "And how are the people of Drumlin? Are things any better since Tephra went away?"

Esker thought a moment before answering, "I think so. There are still a few who are angry with her, but they cause no real harm. Olivine, who was always trying to tell everyone what to do and how to do it, is still trying to stir up trouble. However, most villagers just feel sorry for her because she cared so much for Ogen. She was already acting as though they were betrothed, although he had not yet asked."

"What about the one who was betrothed to your cousin?"

"Graben? I always thought that—um, that to be courted by him showed the favor of The Always, but now I see he is full of self-importance. He used to tease her when they were children, or sometimes take no notice of her at all. Until he asked for courting rights, she thought he just saw her as Sedi's little sister—although I think she cared for him almost as much as she cared for Sedi."

"Then, she was happy when they were betrothed?" Kaoli asked.

"She never said so, but then, it is not proper for a maiden to say so until the day of betrothal. Only then is she expected to show her joy."

"Not even to her cousin?"

Before Esker could answer Kaoli's question, Creta called out, "Esker, shall I shake out the meal cloth now?"

"If you are finished with your meal, yes, please do so," Esker answered her sister. Then she frowned and replied to Kaoli's question, "I did ask her one day, but she did not answer."

"Hmmm," Kaoli said, wrinkling her forehead and pursing her lips. "So, how is Graben now that she has gone away?"

"He is still courting another maiden, I think. But, he goes to see Sedi much more now. Breccia told me she heard Graben say he was not sure he wanted to be mated to Catera," Esker said, then smiled broadly. "The little girl once whispered to me, 'I think Graben still wants to mate with my sister, but she had to go away.' And I think the child may be right."

"I see. But do you think your cousin would accept him as a mate?"

"If she were still living here in the village, if she had not gone away, she would likely have no choice. If the father and the Wise Ones agree, the maiden must obey her father and the Wise Ones."

Kaoli and Esker talked a while longer, sharing and comparing the customs of their respective people. When Kaoli said she must now hurry back to help her grandfather, Esker hugged her close and whispered, "Thank you, my Barchan friend, for looking after my cousin, and for bringing me news of her. It will bring much comfort to her family."

After Kaoli said goodbye to Creta, Esker watched as she half-walked, half-skipped her way across the meadow.

That night, Sedi was in his room working on a leather tool pouch. He looked up as his mother said in a quiet voice, "Sedi, we have had news of Tephra." Both of his parents were standing in the doorway and he could see tears in the eyes of both, yet both were smiling.

Puzzled, Sedi asked, "News of Tephra? How did you hear?"

Caldera entered the room and sat on a stool near Sedi, and Tarn stood behind her, his hand on her shoulder.

"One of the Barchans came to your cousin," answered Tarn.

"Barchans came to one of us?" Sedi asked disbelievingly.

"Yes," Caldera said smiling, "and it was so good to hear that she is well!"

"How would Barchans know that my sister is well?" Sedi was filled with suspicion.

"It seems a young maiden of Barchan Settlement, who had helped Tephra when she was healing on the mountain, learned that she was in the outland and went to see her," Caldera answered. "The young Barchan has even brought food to her!"

"So," Sedi said, not at all pleased with what he was hearing, "she allows Barchans to visit her." He was thoughtful for several moments, looked sadly at his parents and shaking his head, stated with finality, "Then, she truly has abandoned her people. She has turned away from all that is Drumlin. I have only one sister, Breccia."

"Oh, Sedi!" cried Caldera, "Can you not be a little happy that she is not entirely alone, with no one to see about her and no one to see if she has enough to eat? I worry so—what if she became ill? Who would know?"

"She made the choice;" Sedi said flatly, "no one forced her."

"No, that is not true!" Caldera said vehemently, "She *was* forced—forced by people who believed lies."

"Mother," Sedi said in exasperation, "my sister was on Barchan—"

"Say no more, my son," Tarn appealed, "we have no need to be reminded of it all. Our daughter said she willingly broke no vows, committed no wrong against the laws of Drumlin or The Always. We believe her. She is your sister; how can you doubt her?"

"Graben tells it differently," Sedi spoke defiantly. "He has told me he had begun to think she never wanted him as a mate. He told me how she spoke to that Barchan man, and how she was so concerned for him."

"What do you mean?" asked Tarn, concern evident in his tone.

"Graben also said he heard the Barchan speak to her in a way that was far too familiar. He was greatly disturbed by the Barchan's words."

Tarn and Caldera looked at each other. Sedi knew they both wanted and needed to continue to believe in the innocence of their daughter, but were obviously troubled at Sedi's words.

"My son," Tarn looked at Sedi and said gently, "Graben is angry. He cannot forgive her for leaving the caves, no matter what her reasons were, and he does not try to understand."

Caldera added, "There is something else you must know. Tor's mother told me that he seems deeply troubled. She has heard Tor mumbling in his sleep, but she cannot make sense of what he says. She was sure, however, that she understood him to say Ogen's name, and then something about Graben and a knife."

Graben had told Sedi of the fight with the Barchans and the truth about how Ogen was injured, and had sworn him to secrecy. Sedi was disturbed by what his mother had told him concerning Tor and did not know how to respond. However, to keep from worrying his parents further, he said with a sigh, "It is just that it is so strange without her here. I miss my sister. And I can see that Graben is so unhappy."

Caldera smiled at her son and said, "We understand—he is your friend." Then, she said thoughtfully, "I do not think Graben wants to mate with Catera. He knows you cared for her—and still do I think—but their clans are much in favor of it. Catera is lovely, and even though your father and I approved of her as a mate for our son, she is not our Tephra."

Tarn smiled at his mate, "No, she is not. Our daughter is much like her mother. I do feel sorry for Graben."

Caldera leaned toward her son and kissed him on the forehead. Tarn gave Sedi's shoulder a gentle squeeze, wished him a good night's rest, then he and Caldera went to their room.

Preparing for sleep, Sedi turned down the lamp and adjusted his position on his cot. He lay in the dark, not able to close his eyes for he was much troubled by what his parents had told him about Tephra's visitors. With many thoughts going through his head, it was a long time before he could fall asleep.

CHAPTER 34

The following morning Graben did not go to the gardens, but instead sent word that he was not feeling well. After a troubling dream, which he could only recall in bits and pieces, he had awakened well before dawn and had spent the morning pacing in his dwelling—the one he had prepared for Tephra. As he paced he talked to himself, his voice low and raspy. "She should be here with me, not all alone in that hut! She was the loveliest maiden in all of Drumlin—and the perfect mate for me. She would have sung for me the way she sang to the children. Ah! The way she moved when she danced!" He recalled vividly the way she had danced the night he had asked for betrothal, and he ached with longing for her. He groaned aloud, imagining how she would have danced for him alone in the dwelling he had built with his own two hands just for her. Tor, Noll, Ogen—they all offered to help, but—no!—he had to do it all by himself. It had to be perfect—the best dwelling in Drumlin for Golith and his mate. After all, Drumlin's best hunter deserved Drumlin's most desirable maiden. He fell to his knees as he realized he could never mate with Catera. "She is lovely," he said quietly, "but not for Golith, no, not for Golith." Then, with firm resolve, he cried out, "Tephra! You *will* be my mate!" He would go to the Hammada. He would beg them to allow her to return, to return to him. "I forgive you, Tephra, I forgive you," he whispered hoarsely.

The Hammada proclaimed she was no longer unclean. Why did he not accept it?

Graben covered his face with his hands as he wept bitter tears of regret, rocking back and forth on his knees. As he wept, the thought came to him, "I must talk to Sedi. He will help me plan how to bring his sister home." After a few deep breaths, he forced himself to rise, go to his wash basin, and splash water on his face. He brushed at his hair with his hand and, filled with renewed confidence, said, "Yes, I will go to Sedi."

When Graben arrived at Sedi's dwelling, it was near midday. Caldera met him at the door and informed him that she and Breccia were going to bring some broth to Kame as the old woman had caught a summer cold. "You and Sedi will have a quiet meal," she said. "After we see to Kame's needs, Breccia and I are bringing a midday meal to share with her father."

Graben was relieved that the he and Sedi would be alone. Sedi was sitting on a stool at the table, his crutch leaning against a nearby wall. He gestured for Graben to have some of the food Caldera had left, and after taking a few bites himself, said, "I am glad you came today, there is something I must tell you."

"Ah, Sedi!" Graben said excitedly, declining the offer of food with a wave of his hand. "I came here to tell you I am determined to go to the Hammada. I will challenge them to find something, *anything* in our laws that would let me bring Tephra back to Drumlin! I know I never want another for my mate. You must help me plan—"

"Wait," Sedi cautioned as he reached out and placed a hand on Graben's arm. "I have heard from my sister," he said, being careful to keep his voice low. Graben gave a short gasp, and stared at Sedi. "But, before I tell you," Sedi continued, "you must swear to me—swear on Nunatak Peak—that you will not tell where you heard this, or mention any of the names."

Graben frowned, and as his pulse quickened with dread, he quickly raised his hand in a sign of pledge. Sedi continued, "A young Barchan maiden—the one who first brought word my sister was alive—went to my cousin bringing news of Tephra." Sedi's voice took on a sarcastic tone as he said, "It seems she is quite happy in her outland hut, for the Barchan maiden visits her from time to time, and even brings her food."

Graben looked at Sedi in astonishment. "Are you certain it is only the Barchan maiden who visits her?" he asked suspiciously. "She is young to be making such a journey alone."

"I only know what I told you," Sedi answered flatly.

Graben stood and walked to the doorway and back again, running his fingers through his hair. Shaking his head slowly from side to side he groaned through gritted teeth, "No, no! This ruins everything. I cannot believe she allows those people to visit her, or accepts anything from them."

"I know how you feel, my friend. My own sister allowing and maybe encouraging the visits of Barchans…."

"Sedi!" Graben muttered hoarsely, as he grasped his friend's hand, "If the Hammada should find out she allows them to come to the outland hut, they would never permit her to return to me!"

"I am afraid there is nothing to be done now, my friend," Sedi said in a consoling tone. Then, in a voice tinged with bitterness, which was not lost on Graben, he said, "Ask for betrothal to Catera. She will make you a good and faithful mate."

"Catera should be your mate," Graben answered soberly. "I think she still cares for you."

"Even though I desired her, it would never be. Her mother!" Sedi put a hand on his forehead as he shook his head back and forth.

Graben gave a short, derisive laugh, and said, "Ah, yes, her mother. Oh no!"

"Fear not, for her mother likes the handsome Graben of the Clan of Earth-tillers!" Sedi attempted a smile.

"Thank you for trying to cheer me up," Graben said with a hint of sarcasm. "I must go."

"I am sorry, Graben. I, too, am troubled by Tephra's actions. My sister is truly like a stranger to me now."

"Thank you for telling me before I made a fool of myself before the Hammada," Graben said with a bitter smile and a shake of his head.

Giving a farewell nod to Sedi, he quickly returned to his shelter where he picked up his spears and knives, and headed to the game field. There he threw knife after knife, spear after spear at the targets, each throw potent with rage at the thought of the tall Barchan going to Tephra's outland hut. When his anger and sense of betrayal had settled into vindictive sense of purpose, he went to find Tor. He found him outside his family dwelling cleaning fish and packing them in salt.

Graben called out to him, "Tor!"

Tor turned with a jerk, and with a startled look on his face, said, "Graben? Hard work in the garden today, or have you been swimming? You are soaking wet!"

Graben related to Tor all that Sedi had told him concerning Tephra. Then grasping Tor firmly by his shoulders, he said through gritted teeth, "She has been bewitched, I know it. I cannot believe she would accept those mountain people as friends." Sighing deeply he added, "You and I both know she loved Drumlin far too much." He removed his hands from Tors shoulders and smacked a fist against his other hand as he said, "Tor, I was convinced the Wise Ones would let her return, now that the unrest in the village is settling. But not now, not if they should discover she is visited by Barchans."

Tor frowned, nodded and said, "Yes, the village is much as it was before. However, how do you know this about Tephra? Who told you?"

"I have sworn I would not repeat what I heard. I have just broken that pledge. I also pledged I would not say who brought the news to me, and that pledge I will keep. This much I will say," Graben looked up toward the mountains and stated with confidence, "Tephra is not the only maiden who has been with the mountain people. Other maidens are being bewitched by them. Tor, I am afraid even Siluria is not safe!"

"Are you saying Siluria has been visited by the mountain people also?" Tor asked in alarm.

"That, I do not know." Graben purposely left Tor's question open to speculation.

"What can we do? Should we tell the Wise Ones? Go to Karst?"

"And what will they do?" Graben asked with a derisive laugh. "Pronounce a decree? Hah! And that will keep our maidens safe? No, it is time for action. Here, I will help you finish packing those fish. Then, we go find Noll and some of the other young men, and even Col and his friends."

Graben and Tor went throughout the village, talking to all the young, strong men of Drumlin—even the ones who were mated—spreading the fear that the maidens and even the young matrons of the village were in danger from the Barchans.

"The forbidden ones have dared come down from their accursed mountain and have already bewitched at least two, possibly three, of our finest maidens," Graben told each young man while Tor stood by his side and nodded in agreement. "One of those maidens was so bewitched she cast herself out from Drumlin, and she was truly one of the fairest! We must challenge the Barchans. I ask you to help me avenge the corruption of the one who was my betrothed!"

Two young men, Talus and Olin, readily agreed to assist Graben with his challenge. They said they would help spread the word that the maidens and young matrons were in danger from the Barchans. Olin had been mated for only one year, and insisted he would not allow one of the "forbidden ones" to corrupt his mate. Devon, mated two years now, was at first reluctant, but at the urging of Olin he agreed that action did need to be taken.

At Graben's request, Col and Tor stealthily made their way to the outland hut to see if any of the Barchans were there. When they returned to the village, they reported all they saw and heard to Graben.

"We watched a while and did not see Barchans, but we did see Tephra tending to her flower and vegetable gardens," said Tor.

"And not only was her hair was unbound," Col added, "but she was singing a psalm of joy to The Always."

With a baffled expression, Tor remarked, "For someone all alone, she is very cheerful."

Graben looked toward Barchan Mountain and said decisively, "Tell the men to gather on the game field at sunset."

CHAPTER 35

Graben addressed the nine men who had assembled on the game field. "Men of Drumlin, I am certain that a Barchan called Strata is responsible for the threat to the maidens and young matrons of Drumlin. He bewitched and defiled the one who was betrothed to me. Col and Tor have discovered that she is still under his spell. What's more, there is proof that there are two other maidens who are being led astray by the forbidden ones." He paused as the men looked at one another in alarm. "This man Strata must be brought to stand trial before the Hammada as an example to all of Barchan," he continued, as he stood feet apart, fists on hips, looking at each of the men in turn. "As the strongest men of our village, it is our duty to ascend Barchan Mountain and capture this man who threatens the peace of Drumlin. The Hammada will see that he is punished as a sign to other Barchans. They will be reminded they are forbidden to come onto Drumlin land." Graben paused, and lowering his voice, gave an impassioned plea, "If you are willing to go with me to Barchan and bring him to face our Wise Ones, meet me here before sunrise tomorrow morning. We must end this threat to our way of life." He then assured them that by the time they arrived at the village, most Barchans would be in their dwellings having their midday meal. This would allow them to reach the man's dwelling with very little hindrance from anyone of the settlement. After a brief moment of hesitation, the men all agreed to accompany Graben, then each returned to his own dwelling.

At sunrise the next morning, the men arrived carrying their hunting knives and fishing spears or axes. Following a narrow, rugged trail near the outland, they reached the Cambria River and found the bridge. After crossing, they searched for any trails, other than the main one that Graben recalled, that might lead to the Barchan Settlement. Finding several, they chose three that seemed the most traveled, and Graben directed each group to a trail, hoping each would lead to the settlement from a slightly different direction. Graben, Col, and Olin would enter the village first, using the main trail. Although Graben was fairly certain he would remember, he would ask of whatever Barchan he met the way to the healer's dwelling, where he assumed Strata would be found. The men were directed to proceed cautiously, calling no attention to themselves, unless they heard the agreed-upon signal from Graben.

Graben saw an old man sitting outside a hut. He was whistling a tune and whittling a pipe from a piece of wood. "Old man, is this the trail that will take us to your healer?" Graben asked politely.

The old man rose and pointed down a side trail, then he resumed his whittling. As the old man began whistling a strange shrill-sounding tune, Graben at first gave him a suspicious glance, but then assumed he was just strange.

Graben motioned to his men and they followed him down the trail. At the first dwelling they came to, a woman stepped out of the doorway, and seeing the Drumlin men with their spears and axes, she gave a yelp of fear and ran back inside. The men continued down the trail, keeping watch for signs that the woman's cry may have alerted the settlement. At the next dwelling, a man was standing in the doorway. He called out to them, "What do you want here? You are not Barchan!"

"We are looking for the healer," answered Graben, striving to keep his voice cordial. "Where can we find him?"

"What business do you have with our healer that you come with spears and axes?"

"The healer is sheltering a man who defiled one of our maidens, and is leading others astray. The man is to stand trial before our Hammada," Olin answered.

"Hammada? Then you must be Drumlins. We are not bound by your laws! Leave our mountain."

"We will leave as soon as we have the Barchan we came for," retorted Col.

The man shook his head, went inside his dwelling, and closed the door. As the men rounded a bend in the trail, they were confronted by four Barchan men. Most held large knives or axes, some large heavy clubs. Walking slowly, they formed a circle around Graben and his two men. One man, shorter than the rest, but with a stout muscular build, stepped forward and glaring at each of the Drumlin men in turn, said in mock politeness, "Well, visitors bearing knives and spears, what is it you seek here? We welcome all who come in peace."

Graben sneered at him and answered sarcastically, "We seek our good friend, Strata."

"Ah, Strata! Well, he is also *my* good friend. If I see him, I will tell him you were looking for him. What name shall I give?" the Barchan asked again with false cordiality.

"Tell him it is the one who put a knife in his arm," Graben replied through clenched teeth, "and is sorry it missed his heart!"

At Graben's words, the Barchan men tightened their circle, moving in closer to Graben's men who had turned to face the Barchans, their weapons ready.

Col called out, "Just take us to him and we will leave your mountain."

"You make threats against one of our best men, and you think we will just hand him over to you?" The short, stout Barchan gave a derisive laugh. "Go back to your wise ones and tell them Arbo has refused your kind request."

When Graben tried to push his way past Arbo, he grabbed Graben's arm, twisted it behind his back, and swiftly pulled a large hunting knife from its sheath at his waist. Holding the knife tip to the top of Graben's ear, he snarled, "Will you hear better with one ear, Drumlin? I said leave our mountain."

Graben glared at him defiantly, then inwardly winced as he felt the sting of Arbo's knife tracing a thin line of blood from the top of his ear to his jaw. Before Graben could react, Col lunged toward Arbo with his axe, but the Barchan defended himself by throwing his knife into Col's upraised arm. Col dropped the axe as he cried out in pain and clutched at the knife that was embedded in his arm. Graben sounded the signal to the other teams, pulled his knife and slashed at the unarmed Arbo. Olin, holding up weaponless hands, signaled for a truce and went to help Col. He led Col away from the other men, tore a strip of cloth from his own tunic, carefully removed the knife from Col's arm, and wrapped the cloth around the wound.

Noll had arrived with two other Drumlin men, Talus and Devon, and both Barchans and Drumlins were watching each other warily to see who would strike first. Suddenly there was a shout from farther up the trail, "Graben! We've found him!"

Graben backed away from the unarmed Arbo and started walking in the direction of the shout. Arbo warned, "You will not take Strata from this mountain unless he wants to go. No one makes Strata do what he does not want to do."

"We will see," Graben stated flatly, not looking at Arbo, but at Col and Olin.

Graben, Noll, Talus, and Devon walked up the trail with the Barchans following. When they reached where Tor and his men had gathered, Graben looked around and asked, "Where is he?"

An old man stepped through the door of a nearby hut. Graben recognized him as the healer who had tended Tephra's injured knee. The old healer said, "We do not have a Drumlin maiden here. Why do you come looking for Strata?"

"He is here?" asked Graben, addressing the Drumlin men as well as Foehn.

Foehn nodded. "He is here."

Tor affirmed, "Malik saw a young boy and asked where we could find him. The boy led us here."

"Strata!" Graben called out in a challenging voice, "Do not hide like a frightened little boy. Come out and face me, or we will—"

Graben said no more as Strata stepped into the doorway behind Foehn, placed his hand on the old man's shoulder, and said gently, "Go inside, Grandfather." The Barchan looked calmly at Graben, crossed his arms, and leaned casually against the door frame. "The maiden you seek is not here," he said in a flat voice. Then in a bitter, accusatory tone he said, "You know where she is, for you and your village sent her there."

"How do you know where she is?" Graben snapped as he glared at Strata.

"I told him where she is now living." Graben turned quickly toward the voice of a woman.

"You told him? How is it you know of things Drumlin? Who are you?" asked Graben sternly.

"I am Kaoli, and I only know that there is a lovely maiden named Tephra who lives alone in a tiny hut *outside* of Drumlin," she said smugly.

"You are forbidden to approach a Drumlin," Tor said in a threatening tone.

"According to your laws, the maiden Tephra is no longer a Drumlin," Kaoli said matter-of-factly, shrugging her shoulders.

"We are here for Strata!" Graben said determinedly, as he turned to face the Barchan. With a confident stare, he barked, "You will come with us to be tried before our Wise Ones."

"No," Strata stated firmly, "you have nothing to hold against me."

"You defiled a betrothed Drumlin maiden. You bewitched her with your strange herbs and your spells. You touched her and carried her against her will, causing her to break her vows!" Graben angrily spat his accusations.

Strata took a few steps toward Graben, his arms still folded across his chest. Looking Graben straight in the eye, he said in a cool, even voice, "I carried an injured maiden here to my grandfather who tended to her injury. He fed her nourishing broths, and wiped her head with cool, herb-soaked cloths to soothe her fever. I then carried her to my sister's hut, as it is not fitting for a maiden to be in a dwelling with men who are not her family—not even in Barchan Settlement. So, yes, I touched her. You are a fool, Drumlin! You would rather I left her lying there as a meal for wolves? I say again, you are a fool."

As Strata turned on his heel to go back into the dwelling, Graben lowered his head and lunged at him, ramming his shoulder into the Barchan's back. The force of the blow caused Strata to stumble and strike his head against the frame of the door. Arbo and another Barchan ran to Strata's aid. Arbo threw himself at Graben, knocking him flat on his back, then sat on his chest and pinned his arms to the ground. The force of Arbo's attack knocked the wind out of Graben, and with the weight of the Barchan on his chest, he was struggling to breathe.

"Stop! Let him up! He can't breathe," pleaded Col, who had, with Olin's help, now joined the others and was cradling his injured arm.

"He can breathe enough to nod that he will leave Barchan Mountain and take all of you with him!"Arbo snarled.

Graben nodded, and Arbo released his hold on Graben's arms, stood and held out his hand to help Graben to his feet. Refusing the help of the Barchan, Graben took a few deep breaths and struggled to stand on his own. Tor went to him to offer his help, but Graben again refused with a shake of his head and a wave of his hand. Although he was still feeling the effects of Arbo's attack, he did not want to appear weak. He stood, turned, and walked down the trail away from the settlement. Tor and the others followed in silence as they descended the mountain and returned to Drumlin Village.

When they reached the edge of the village, Tor offered, "I will take Col to Hevel. Graben, maybe you should come also."

"I have no need of Hevel," Graben said glumly. "Take Col to him. Tell him what happened." Turning to the other Drumlin men, he said with as much dignity as he could summon, "The rest of you, return to your dwellings. I will have to answer to the Hammada for Col's injury, and the fact that I failed to bring the Barchan back to stand trial before them. None of you will be held to blame. You acted honorably." With a curt nod, he walked briskly to his dwelling.

The following morning, Graben approached the Hammada just as they had finished their dawn prayers. He bowed and asked to speak to the Wise Ones. Karst gave his consent, and Graben told them how he had led several men of the village up to Barchan Settlement with the intention of bringing the one called Strata to the Hammada to stand trial. "I am convinced he bewitched the one to whom I was betrothed, and that he defiled her. I am also certain that he was attempting to bewitch and defile other maidens of Drumlin. I regret that I failed in my attempt to bring him to you, and that Col was injured in the attempt."

"Is the injury serious?" Karst asked.

Hevel the Healer stepped forward and reported, "Tor brought him to my hut last evening. He is still sleeping. The knife wound was deep, and needed to be cleaned and stitched closed. I had to give him a sleep potion."

"His arm will heal?" Graben asked anxiously.

"In time," was Hevel's blunt reply.

Karst was silent as he leaned upon his staff and, for what to Graben was an uncomfortably long time, looked up toward Nunatak Peak. Karst nodded slowly, then giving Graben a stern look, motioned for him to kneel. "Graben of the Clan of Earth-tillers," Karst began, "once again you have taken Drumlin matters into your own hands. You have stirred up fears among the men of the village and encouraged them to ascend to a place forbidden. You will stay in Hevel's hut for two weeks helping him care for Col. You will also go to his family dwelling and perform the chores that Col cannot now do. You will present yourself to my dwelling before dawn and just after sunset each day for prayer and meditation, and you will, of course, still be responsible for your duties in the vegetable gardens. Do you understand?" Karst pointed at him, and Graben did not mistake the annoyance and controlled anger in Karst's tone.

"Yes, Honorable Karst," Graben answered, looking at the ground to avoid the look in Karst's eyes, "I understand."

"Now, go to your dwelling and return here at midday, prepared to stay at Hevel's hut until you are told you have made reparation."

As Graben walked to his dwelling, he thought over what he would say to his mother and to his Uncle Shael. He had seen the scowl on Shael's face as he gave the report of his return to Barchan. He went first to his dwelling, then to his mother's for he hoped to tell her himself before she heard it from Shael.

As he feared, his mother bit her lip as tears filled her eyes when he told her of the events of that day. Her voice quavered with disappointment as she asked, "Why did you not talk this over with me or Shael before you went off on your own?"

"Because he is still mourning the loss of that banished maiden and he can't think clearly," Graben jerked his head toward the sound of Shael's voice—a voice filled with contempt. Apparently he had come into the dwelling as Graben was talking to his mother. "She is not worth it, Graben," Shael spat. "Oh, she may have some charms, but not worthy of you. Not worthy of our clan. I will be keeping an eye on you, and I will be speaking to Karst. I will hear if you are not doing all that is required." Shael nodded to Vena and abruptly left the dwelling. Graben mumbled an apology to his mother as he kissed her cheek, picked up his few belongings, and returned to Hevel's dwelling.

Within the first few days, Graben realized that Karst had planned his days so he would have no time to "stir up fears among the men of the village," for each night he fell upon the cot in Hevel's hut exhausted. To add to his misery, his shoulder still ached from ramming it into Strata's back.

CHAPTER 36

Kaoli helped Foehn bring Strata inside so that he could tend to his head wound. Strata kept insisting he was fine, but Foehn had him lie down in a darkened area of their dwelling. Foehn quickly applied cloths soaked in a healing tea to Strata's wound to keep the swelling down. "How does your head feel?" he asked Strata.

"It hurts a bit, with sort of a pounding pain."

"Open your eyes. Look at me." Foehn peered at Strata then nodded and asked, "How does your belly feel?"

"A little hungry. Why?"

Kaoli rolled her eyes, then said to the healer, "Foehn, ask him about his back. He seemed to be in pain when he moved."

"Well?" asked Foehn.

"It is a bit sore when I move around."

"Tell me when I touch where the pain is," instructed Foehn.

"There," Strata said as he winced, "must be about where that Drumlin rammed into me."

"The head wound will need to be stitched, but a poultice will help that ache in your back," Foehn assured him, as he went to prepare the things needed to tend to Strata's injuries.

The rest of that day, and into the next, Strata slept off and on, with Kaoli and Foehn taking turns caring for him, watching for signs that his eyesight changed or that his stomach could not take food. Late in the morning on the second day, Strata was more alert, so Kaoli asked Foehn if it would be all right for her to go to Uluru's dwelling. She returned around sunset, and as soon as she entered the dwelling, Strata called out to her.

"It is good you came," Foehn grumbled. He has been asking for you, whining for me to trot over and bring you here."

"Kaoli!" Strata said impatiently, "I want you to get Pingo and go see that Tephra is all right. I fear what Graben will do, or may have already done. See if she needs anything."

"Well, it seems you are well enough to order people about," Kaoli said, half teasing, yet taken aback by his tone.

"I would go myself but that old medicine man threatened to give me a sleeping potion if I even thought about it again," Strata said, glaring at Foehn, then winking.

Kaoli shook her head and smiled, "Very well. You may be right to worry about Graben. I will go find Pingo now, to see if we can leave at first light tomorrow. We will return as quickly as we can." Then going to Foehn, she said in a voice just loud enough for Strata to hear, "Give him a sleeping potion if he gets to be too much trouble." She giggled and ran off to find Pingo.

Tephra was working in her vegetable garden early one afternoon when she heard a familiar voice call out, "Greetings!"

Turning towards the woods she was surprised to see Kaoli and with her, Pingo. She wondered why Strata had not come, but said nothing about it. She offered them refreshment, and they went inside as she poured out three mugs of water, and removed a cloth from a basket of small cakes.

"They are my usual, made with blackberries," she said as she held the basket towards them, indicating they should take one. Bringing their mugs of water and the cakes, they went to sit in the flower garden.

Pingo laughed when he saw the bench and said, "I helped Strata carry the pieces. Him just whistling all the way. I was breathing hard!"

Tephra felt her cheeks grow warm at the mention of Strata's name. "How is he?" she asked.

"He sent us to see that you are alright. Wanted to know if you needed anything," answered Pingo.

Kaoli took a deep breath and asked, "Has anyone from Drumlin been to see you?"

"No!" answered Tephra, surprised at the question, "you know they cannot." She was confused as to why Kaoli would ask such a question and her stomach quivered with alarm. "Tell me what has happened."

Kaoli told her how Graben had come to Barchan settlement with two or three groups of Drumlin men, demanding to know where they could find Strata. "They were determined to bring Strata to Drumlin to stand trial before the Wise Ones," Kaoli said. "He said it was because Strata had bewitched and defiled you. A few of the men got into a fight. One Drumlin's arm was badly injured by a knife, and some Barchans had small injuries—"

"Was Strata injured?" Tephra interrupted.

"Not too badly."

"How did it happen?" Tephra asked anxiously.

"Strata was angry—angry that they had sent you away and angry at the things Graben accused him of. He asked Graben if he would rather you had been left injured on the trail for hungry wolves to find. He called Graben a fool, and Graben attacked him. Strata has a head wound and a very sore back, but he is healing quickly. Foehn is well pleased."

Tephra stood and paced around the bench, then stopped with her fists clenched at her side. Looking toward Drumlin village, she said angrily, "Strata is right. Graben *is* a fool!" She turned to face Kaoli and said insistently, "Take me to Strata. It will only take me a moment to be ready." Tephra hurried into her hut, not waiting for Kaoli's response.

Tephra made sure everything was in order and the vegetables wrapped and put out of the way of small scavengers. She put away her garden tools and went out to water a few plants. Going back inside, she put her sleep shift, a day shift, her hair comb, willow twigs, and hair ribbons into her pouch. The rest of the blackberry cakes were placed in a small basket. Looking at the carved bird, she thought a moment, stroked its back, and left it on the shelf. With a light cloak draped across one arm, the pouch slung over her shoulder, and the basket of cakes on the other arm, she walked out to where Kaoli and Pingo sat waiting on the bench. "I am ready. Take me to Strata," she said.

Are you sure you want to go up to Barchan Settlement?" Kaoli asked Tephra. "It is a long way."

"Very sure," Tephra replied firmly, and began walking toward the mountain trail.

It was after sunset when the three made their way through the woods, up the steep mountain trail, and arrived at the lean-to shelter Strata had erected when Tephra was first sent to the outland hut. They had to rest a few times when her knee would start to ache from the climb up the steep trails, and Tephra had grown irritable, knowing she was the cause of their slow pace. Kaoli suggested they rest there for a few hours. Tephra was impatient, and started to protest, but then realized she was quite tired and needed to rest her knee.

At Tephra's insistence they awoke before dawn, and with the aid of a torch made by Pingo, the three arrived at the bridge over the Cambria River just after sunrise. Tephra paused and looked at the bridge warily. Kaoli took one of her hands, and with a reassuring smile, she slowly led the way across. Near midday they had reached the main trail to Barchan. As they walked through the settlement to Foehn's dwelling, she was aware of the unfriendly looks from a few Barchans. After hearing about Graben's visit to the settlement, she was not surprised at their expressions, and was glad Kaoli and Pingo were with her.

At the door of the dwelling Pingo said, "I should tell them Tephra is here." Grinning broadly he added, "Don't want Strata to faint!"

Tephra walked into Foehn's hut as soon as Pingo announced her. She looked around the room, and quickly went to Strata, exclaiming, "You are hurt!" Kneeling on the mat next to him, she removed the cloth from his head to inspect the injury herself. The swelling had receded, but she winced at the sight of the stitched wound and the purple and green bruising. "Pingo, fetch a fresh cloth. This one is warm." She turned back to Strata and asked, "How is your appetite? Are you tolerating food?"

"Grandfather," Strata teased, "I think this maiden doubts you have been taking good care of me!"

Afraid she had offended Foehn, Tephra turned to him and said apologetically, "Oh! Foehn, I am sorry, I was just—"

Foehn chuckled, "Do not fret, my dear. I am happy to have some relief. He can be a bear when he's hurt. And he is restless because he cannot work or walk about."

"And you putter about, muttering to yourself, then leave me alone for most of the day!" Strata pretended to complain.

"Then it is good that I came," Tephra smiled, "Poor old bear!"

Strata opened his mouth as though to respond, but said nothing as Tephra and Kaoli giggled and Foehn gave a hoot of a laugh.

"Hah!" laughed Pingo. "She called you 'old bear'! Good for you." Strata glared at Pingo, and the little man clapped his hand over his mouth as with the other hand he gave a mock salute to Strata.

Foehn handed her a fresh cloth and as Tephra placed it on Strata's head, he gently put his hand on her arm. "You are alright?" he asked, concern evident in his voice.

"Yes," Tephra replied, then gave a little cough. "Better than you are," she attempted to tease, but her voice quavered at the expression on his face as he looked at her--an expression she had no name for.

She was relieved when Kaoli spoke up. "She said no one from Drumlin had been to the hut."

Strata frowned, and with a puzzled expression looked from Kaoli to Tephra. "No one? Then, why...?" he finally managed to ask.

"She had to make sure you were alright." Kaoli shrugged and rolled her eyes at Strata. "But now, I will take Tephra to Ululru's as it is getting dark. But I will bring her back early tomorrow."

"Yes, come early," offered Foehn, "and I will make my batter cakes."

"Foehn makes a bribe to you," Pingo said with a grin. "Makes best batter cakes in Barchan!"

"Oh! Then I will be sure to be here early," Tephra promised, smiling at Pingo. "Thank you for telling me."

Pingo bowed, said goodnight, and trotted out the door. Tephra picked up her pouch and the basket, and said goodnight to Foehn. She turned to say goodnight to Strata, but suddenly felt awkward, so she only smiled, and followed Kaoli to Uluru's dwelling.

The woman and her children welcomed the maiden warmly. After the evening meal, Pilli asked Tephra to sing for them, and when the children were finally settled on their sleep mats, she sang them a lullaby. Tired from the long walk, she said goodnight to Uluru and went to the sleep mat provided for her.

Early the next morning, Kaoli walked with Tephra to Foehn's dwelling, then left on an errand for her grandfather. After enjoying the batter cakes—which were every bit as delicious as promised—Tephra helped Foehn with his chores. She made certain the cloths on Strata's head were changed regularly, brought him mugs of water, helped Foehn pick beans in his garden, and insisted on helping cook the midday meal. When she began helping clean up after the meal, Foehn took the cloth from her hand and said quietly, "Go, sit with my grandson. You are better medicine for him than all my potions."

Blushing at his words, Tephra smiled shyly and went to sit next to Strata on the mat.

"I am glad you stopped fidgeting," he teased, "you were making me feel lazy!"

"You must rest, Strata. Besides, helping Foehn is one way I can thank him for his caring for me when I was injured."

Tephra was suddenly aware that Strata was looking at her intently, a tender smile on his rugged, handsome face. She looked into his blue eyes and as she did, experienced a pleasant but unfamiliar feeling. She looked quickly away, stood, and offered to help Foehn again.

Foehn shook his head and said, "When your knee was healing and you were with Uluru, I heard you sing to the children. I enjoyed hearing your songs. A song might brighten this dreary hut. Would you mind?"

"For you, Foehn, I would not mind," Tephra smiled warmly at the old man. She began singing one of the songs the children had liked best. It was a song about a grasshopper, a hopping-beetle, and a frog, and was a lively tune. As she sang she was delighted to see Foehn do a little dance step in time to the music. Worried another fast-paced tune would overly tire Foehn, she then sang a slow, sweet tune about a butterfly. As she sang, she danced in the small space, performing simple motions illustrating the words of the song and the graceful movements of a butterfly. At the end of the song, she slowly lowered herself to the floor, being careful to keep the stress off her injured knee. She folded herself into a semi-cross-legged position on the mat, then bowed her head and lowered her arms to her side.

"Ah, how lovely!" Foehn exclaimed, "You have brought joy to my old heart!"

"Uluru's children must be glad that you are here to sing for them once more," commented Strata.

Foehn chuckled and exclaimed, "And now you must dance for them, too!"

"Yes, I will dance for the children," Tephra said, smiling at Foehn, and feeling a bit surprised at herself that she had actually danced for Foehn and Strata. She rose from the mat and said crisply, "But now I must change that cloth." She brought a fresh cloth and placed it on Strata's head.

"How is your garden?" he asked.

Tephra talked about her two gardens, the abundance of blackberries and strawberries she had found this season, and how she had spotted a beehive. "I wish I knew how the beekeepers get the honey from the hive without getting stung," she said, wrinkling her forehead, "my supply is getting low."

Strata remarked teasingly, "Perhaps you could sing them a lullaby, and when they go to sleep you can take their honey!"

Tephra tried to pretend she was annoyed with his teasing but ended up giggling, and said, "Hah! When Foehn has pronounced you well enough, you can reach the hive after I've sung the bees to sleep!"

Foehn slapped his knee and laughed out loud, saying, "It will be worth walking that rugged old trail to see that!"

Tephra returned to Uluru's dwelling before sunset so she could help with the evening meal. When Tephra began to help with cleaning after the meal, Uluru suggested, "Tephra, go to the children. I know they would love to hear your stories and songs again. I can finish here."

Tephra looked at Uluru and was about to say she would finish the cleaning herself, but Uluru smiled and pointed to where the children were playing in the main part of the dwelling.

Pilli looked up and cried out, "Tephra! You will sing for us?"

She sang the song Foehn had danced to, and another that the children liked because they had learned to echo certain parts. Remembering that she had told Foehn she would dance for the children, she had them arrange themselves so she had a small space in which to dance to the song about the butterfly. When the dance was finished, and she was sitting on the floor in the final pose, the children clapped, then went to her and showered her with hugs and kisses.

"Tephra! That was beautiful!" Uluru exclaimed. "Barchans love to dance, but our ways are not nearly so graceful."

"Thank you," Tephra said humbly. "I had not danced in a long time because of my knee. The last time was for my little sister before I went to the outland."

Uluru smiled and said, "We are glad you danced for us. But now, children, it is time to get washed up and changed into sleep shifts." There were tears and grumblings at this announcement, but Tephra quieted them by promising if they did as they were told without complaining, she would come sing a lullaby when they were all on their sleep mats.

After the children were asleep, Uluru and Tephra enjoyed a cup of tea together while Uluru talked about her mating day that was a little over two weeks away. She told Tephra how the men of the village would carry her on a special chair to the grove in the center of the settlement where she and Basal would be pledged to one another. A feast, provided by all the matrons of the village, would follow the brief ceremony, and there would be music and dancing also.

Suddenly Uluru stopped talking and put her hand to her mouth. She said apologetically, "Oh, dear Tephra, I am so sorry! I am chattering about my mating day and you must be thinking about the mating day you would have had. How careless of me!"

Tephra assured her, "I do not mind, Uluru. I do not think it was meant to be. And I have found some contentment."

"I know Kaoli and Strata have gone down to visit you in the outland, but she has told me only a little about why you are there all alone. I pray one day soon you will find happiness." Uluru reached out and clasped Tephra's hand.

"Thank you, Uluru. I think I should get some rest. I want to see Strata before I leave early tomorrow."

"I understand it is a long walk and the trail is rugged and steep, but I would be so pleased if you would come for my mating day. I am sure Strata would go to walk with you."

"I would like that, Uluru. But," Tephra hesitated, "would it be alright with your mate, and the others of your settlement?"

"It will be alright." Uluru squeezed Tephra's hand to reassure her.

"Oh, but, it sounds so festive! And I have only these shifts," Tephra said as she gestured to the garment she was wearing.

"Hmmm," Uluru tapped her lips, her eyes brightened, and she grinned. "I have something you could wear. I will send Strata for you early, and you can change here."

Tephra bit her lip in effort to suppress a grin of excitement, then kissed Uluru on the cheek, feeling grateful for her friendship, and the invitation to return to Barchan Settlement.

Early the next morning, Tephra made her way to Foehn's dwelling with a warm, lighthearted sensation in her chest as she looked forward to returning for Uluru's mating day. She tapped at Foehn's door and heard Strata's greeting, welcoming her to enter. Entering the dwelling she looked around for Foehn but did not see him. Then she heard him in the back room of the dwelling and she went to Strata where he was resting. She knelt on the mat, and lifted the cloth to inspect the head wound. "The swelling is almost gone, and the color is much better, too," she said with satisfaction.

"Thank you," Strata said, "but can you say 'Greetings, Strata!' when you enter my dwelling?"

"Oh! Are you a bear again today, Strata?" she grinned at him.

"I am tired of lying about. Foehn is being an old mother hen. I am well enough to tend to myself, and I'll grow weak if I lie here any longer."

Foehn had returned and was standing by the mat. He said in a huff, "And if you should blackout on the trail, or the pain in your back hit you when you are working in your shop, you will wish you had listened to 'mother hen.' Hah!"

"Foehn, do you think he could walk around a bit? Just outside to sit in the sun? I will stay with him."

Foehn agreed that it might do Strata some good, so he was helped to sit outside on a bench with a cushion for his back. Tephra sat next to him, and Foehn brought them each a cup of tea and a biscuit spread with jam. As they sat enjoying Foehn's offering and the sun and light morning breeze, Tephra wondered if she was enjoying Strata's company too much. When they had finished the tea and biscuits, Tephra brought the mugs inside, told Foehn she needed to go back to her hut in the outland, and asked if he could send for Kaoli or Pingo to walk with her.

He answered, "Go to Uluru. She will send one of the children to find them. Thank you for coming, Tephra. It is good to see you walking about and looking well."

When Tephra told Strata she was going to Uluru's and why, he cleared his throat, and in a serious tone said, "You came to take care of me. You did not owe me that. I am grateful that you came."

She did not know how to respond to his gratitude, or how to remind him he had carried her to safety two times. Tephra smiled shyly and gently touched his arm, taking care to avoid looking into his eyes. "I must go to Uluru, she said, "but I will come to say goodbye before I go home."

Tephra returned with her cloak and pouch containing the items she had brought with her. She went in to say goodbye to Foehn and to ask if Strata should come inside as she was leaving. Foehn assured her Strata would be fine for a while longer. She walked to the door, paused, and turned back to give Foehn a kiss on his wrinkled cheek. He grinned broadly and laughed, "I have not been kissed by such a lovely maid in far too many years!"

Tephra giggled and went outside to say goodbye to Strata as she waited for either Kaoli or Pingo to arrive. Pingo walked up and announced as he gave a mocking bow, "I came to walk the maiden to the low woods. She will be safe walking with Pingo."

Tephra stood, turned to Strata, and trying to control the slight tremor in her voice, said, "Be well, Strata. And remember, you, Kaoli, and Pingo, are always welcome to visit." To lighten the moment, she gave a quick little laugh and added, "I am always home."

Strata's eyes met hers as he smiled broadly and said, "We will remember." He looked at Pingo and said in a serious tone, "Take care of her, Pingo."

Pingo nodded, bowed, turned abruptly, and started walking quickly toward the main trail. After a few steps, he looked back at Tephra who was several paces behind him. "I will not walk so fast. You have bad knee," he said apologetically. They walked in silence for most of the way, except for times when Pingo cautioned her to watch her step because of uneven places or fallen branches on the trail. When they reached the bridge, Pingo paused, and with a shy, sideways look, he held out his hand to her. Tephra took his hand and he held it firmly as they carefully crossed the river.

By sunset they had reached the lean-to shelter, and Pingo announced bluntly, "Strata said we wait here till sun comes up." They ate a light supper of biscuits, jam, and dried meats supplied by Pingo's mother, then spread their cloaks on the ground to rest for a few hours.

Before dawn, Pingo lit a torch and walked with Tephra as far as the pool in the woods, and after refusing her offer of refreshment, returned to Barchan Settlement. Tephra knelt by the pool, and cupped her hands together to catch water from the waterfall. After taking a drink, she splashed some water on her face. She went to the bench in the garden and rested a while after the long walk, recalling moments of her time with her friends in Barchan Settlement. When her stomach complained of hunger, she went inside to prepare a meal.

As she gathered things for her meal, she began noticing that some things seemed out of place. She wondered if someone had been there, or if she was just tired and imagining things. She first thought that perhaps it had been Kame or someone else from her family, but considering what she had learned about Graben and the other men attempting to bring Strata before the Hammada, she began to have suspicions. Could it have been Graben? Would he have come to the outland? A daring gesture, even for him, she thought. She shrugged off the idea, whispering to herself, "I'm just tired and not thinking clearly."

CHAPTER 37

The day was near for Uluru's mating day, and Kaoli was sent to walk with Tephra up the trail. For the past two days, Tephra had been watching and waiting, hoping Uluru would not forget to send someone to walk the trail with her. She had already packed her pouch with her sleep shift, a day shift, her willow twigs, and her hair ribbons. As soon as Kaoli tapped on her door, Tephra offered her escort a mug of water and a biscuit while she made sure the hut was left in good order.

When they arrived at Barchan Settlement, they went straight to Uluru's. Kaoli helped herself to a mug of water and politely refused the offer to stay for the evening meal, saying she promised her grandfather she would be home to share the meal with him.

After the midday meal the next day, which was Uluru's mating day, Kaoli returned to help both Uluru and Tephra dress and arrange their hair. Uluru was dressed in a long, creamy white, flowing shift. The top of the shift was caught at the shoulders with several colored ribbons that flowed down below the waist. Tephra gasped when she saw Uluru in her mating dress. Kaoli had combed out Uluru's dark brown hair, letting it fall sleek and soft down her back, except for one long braid that began on one side, continued draped across the top of the head, and then fell down the other side, the ends tied with white ribbons.

"Ah! You look beautiful!" Tephra exclaimed in a soft voice.

"Thank you," Uluru replied, her eyes twinkling. "Now it is time for you to try the shift I found for you."

When Kaoli held up the shift, Tephra sighed, "Oh—it is lovely."

Tephra stepped into the soft, butter-colored shift that was tied at one shoulder with green and blue ribbons, leaving the other shoulder bare, the skirt flaring to just below her knees. A woven sash of green, blue, and yellow ribbons accented Tephra's small waist and flattered her subtle feminine curves. As Kaoli combed out Tephra's hair, she parted it high on one side, noting how it fell almost naturally that way. Tephra reached for a ribbon to braid part of her hair, but Uluru shook her head, saying, "You do not need the braid or the ribbon. Your hair is so lovely."

Kaoli said, "It is time for us to make our way to the grove. The men will be here soon to carry Uluru there to meet her mate."

Tephra followed Kaoli as she led the way along the trails of the settlement to the grove. In the center of the grove was a large, raised, square wooden platform. Railings were on three of the sides, and on the other side, two wooden steps led up to the platform. Tall wooden poles were spaced along the sides of the platform, and ribbons and garlands of flowers were draped from pole to pole. Tables and benches were set up around the outside perimeter of the platform, leaving the entrance clear. On one side of the grove was a smaller, higher square platform with five steps leading up to it. There were also tables on either side of the small platform. The people of Barchan Settlement were gathered in the grove, standing in small groups and talking quietly.

Tephra heard the sounds of music and turned to see the musicians as they entered the grove and stepped up onto the square platform. The tempo of the music slowed, and at Kaoli's gesture, Tephra turned to see Strata and five other Barchan men bearing Uluru in the mating chair. As they reached the platform, they carefully lowered the chair to the ground. A man walked to the chair and held out his hand to assist Uluru from the chair. Kaoli whispered, "That is Basal, Uluru's mate." Together they walked hand in hand up the steps to the large platform, circled the platform once, then went to the center. Strata helped an old man with a very long beard up onto the platform. Kaoli whispered to Tephra that this was Augur, the Chief of the settlement.

Augur placed one hand over the joined hands of Uluru and Basal, and in a spoke in a loud, hoarse voice, "Basal, if you desire to be mated to this woman, declare it to all gathered here."

Basal responded heartily, "I, Basal, declare before all gathered here that I desire to be mated to this woman, Uluru."

Augur then spoke to Uluru, "Uluru, if you desire to be mated to this man, declare it to all gathered here."

Uluru smiled and said in a voice clear and strong, "I, Uluru, declare before all gathered here that I desire to be mated to this man, Basal."

Placing his hands on their shoulders, Augur proclaimed, "The Almighty One has heard, and the people of Barchan have witnessed: Basal and Uluru are now mated and will dwell together for the rest of their lives. May the Almighty One bless them with love for each other."

The people cheered as Basal and Uluru circled the platform again, and the musicians played a short, sweet-sounding melody. After the music ended, Basal shouted, "We are mated! Feast to our happiness!"

Tephra watched as women of the settlement brought out bowls and platters of food and placed them on the tables on each side of the musicians' platform. The Barchans lined up to fill their plates, laughing and talking. Tephra was so intent on observing all the activity around her that she jumped at the sound of Strata's voice. "Would the lovely Tephra sit with me at the feast?" he asked with a smile.

She looked over at Kaoli who gave her a wink and an impish smile. "Yes," she said, smiling up at Strata, "I would like that."

He had been standing with his hands behind his back, and at her response held out two plates and two mugs. "Every dwelling brings food to the feast to be shared among all, but each person brings their own plate and mug."

Tephra took one of each and asked, "No forks?"

"Don't need them. All the foods can be eaten with the fingers. A tradition that started many years ago when a few young men, and a couple of old men too, had a bit too much ale and started throwing forks at a tree like they were knives."

Tephra giggled as she imagined the scene Strata described, "A good tradition then!"

He smiled, looked at her, cleared his throat, and said softly, "You look wonderful."

"Uluru made the shift for me," she said, looking down at the dress to avoid looking at Strata.

He cleared his throat again and suggested, "We should get some food before it is all gone!"

When she saw all the food, Tephra did not think that even such a large crowd could consume it all. Most of the foods were very much the same as those eaten by the people of Drumlin, but some things looked unfamiliar. She took only a few food items, as she was a little nervous and afraid she would not be able to eat very much. Strata kept trying to add food to her plate, but she would move her plate away and he would put it on his own plate instead. There were kegs of ale, a vat of a light berry wine, and one of water. Tephra was about to dip water into her mug, but Strata insisted she at least try the wine, so she allowed him to fill the mug half full.

They found two places at one of the tables, but ended up sitting across from each other. Tephra felt awkward sitting next to a skinny young lad who kept sneaking adoring looks at her, while on her other side was a matron who kept up a constant chatter with the young matron next to her. Tephra and Strata ate in silence, for the matron's prattle made conversation between them almost impossible.

When Tephra had eaten her fill and had drained the last of the wine from her cup, and Strata had managed to eat all that he had piled on his plate, he looked at her questioningly. She understood, nodded, and they both picked up their plates and mugs and went to a large tub where the dishes were being washed and stacked aside by three young maidens. As Strata handed the maidens their plates and mugs Tephra noticed carvings on the bottoms of each, and that the maidens stacked the four dishes together on a table alongside other stacks of dishes. She assumed someone from each dwelling would gather the dishes after the feast.

The musicians had taken up their places as Strata and Tephra were bringing the dishes to be washed, and now the music began. Uluru and Basal danced together to a lovely slow melody, then suddenly the music stopped and was replaced with a fast-paced tune. The newly mated couple began clapping in time to the music and to Tephra's amazement, began doing a rather quick step as they clapped their hands, slapped their thighs, and clapped each other's hands. The crowd applauded the newly mated couple as they stepped off the platform. Someone handed them each a mug of ale which they drank thirstily as other couples stepped onto the platform and danced to a variety of tunes from fast paced to slow and rhythmic.

A time or two Strata gestured for Tephra to dance with him, but she shook her head vigorously. In the Village of Drumlin, maidens and young men did not dance together, but she simply said, "I do not know the steps they are doing." Later, as the musicians played a slow sweet melody, he asked again. She thought a moment, realized that she was no longer in Drumlin, and had already left behind some of the customs— such as wearing her hair down. She shyly placed her hand in his outstretched one, and let him lead her onto the platform. He placed her hands on his shoulders and then placed his hands on her waist. She found she quickly picked up the steps, as they were not too different from those she performed as a ceremonial dancer, and soon moved with confidence.

When the song ended, Strata walked her to the edge of the platform just as a fast-paced tune began. He looked at her questioningly but she shook her head and mouthed, "My knee." He nodded that he understood, and they walked to a nearby bench and sat down.

As they watched the other dancers, Strata pointed out several people of the settlement. "See that tall bearded man dancing with Kaoli? He is my uncle," he said, "and the maiden with the blue sash is Pingo's cousin. Ah! And there is my cousin Gabbro dancing with his mate Corrie." She also learned from Strata that most of the strummed instruments the musicians played were very similar to the ones in Drumlin, but that one of the instruments was played by drawing a wooden rod across the strings. Tephra found the sound of it very pleasing.

During a pause in the music, the people of Barchan chatted happily and filled their mugs from the various kegs. At the sound of a bell, everyone gathered around the perimeter of the large platform. Peering through the crowd, Tephra was surprised to see Foehn on the platform.

He held up his hand and spoke loudly, "Fellow Barchans! I am sure you have seen the pretty maiden with flaming hair in our midst this evening. She is from another place, and is a friend to Uluru, Kaoli, Strata, and to me. Uluru asked the maiden to attend her mating feast, and I hope you will welcome her." Tephra blushed as Foehn made his announcement and people applauded and turned to look at her, many of them smiling warmly. Several matrons, appearing to be the age of Uluru, came to welcome Tephra and to thank her for coming. Two of them commented that Uluru had spoken very kindly of her and that they were glad she had come to see Uluru mated.

Tephra, pleasantly surprised at their cordial reception, could not help blushing slightly as she responded to their greetings. As the voice of a matron called the crowd to attention once more, Kaoli, followed by Uluru's youngest, came over to Tephra and took her hand. Pulling her away from Strata and the rest of the crowd, Kaoli whispered guiltily, "Tephra, I am so sorry. I did not think to tell you. All the maidens and matrons bring a small gift for the new matron, and the men bring a gift for her mate. Uluru will understand, but some will wonder why you did not bring a gift. I just wanted you to know because this is the time the gifts will be brought up to the platform and given to Uluru and Basal."

Tephra felt awkward, but did not know what she could possibly give Uluru even if she had known beforehand. "What can I do, Kaoli? I do not want to offend your people."

"Butterfly dance, Tephra, butterfly dance!" a small voice called out. Tephra looked down at little Pilli, who was still holding Kaoli's hand. "Mother likes butterfly dance. She told me you dance like pretty butterfly. Everyone will like!"

Tephra frowned and shook her head uncertainly, but Kaoli squealed with delight, "Yes, Pilli! You are right. Your mother would like it if Tephra danced her butterfly dance—she would like it very much!" Looking at Tephra pleadingly, she said, "Our people love to dance, and they would love the way *you* dance."

"I don't know, it would be better with music, and the musicians would not know Drumlin songs."

"Come with me. One of the strummers is my good friend," Kaoli said as she pulled Tephra toward the musicians' platform. "Taruu!" she called, and motioned to one of the strummers, a young man who grinned broadly as he stepped over to Kaoli. "Taruu, this is Tephra, my friend. She is from another place. She does not know our customs, and I did not think to tell her to bring a gift for Uluru. Taruu, she can dance a lovely dance for Uluru, but she needs music. Can you play something she can dance to?"

Taruu shrugged his shoulders and asked, "Fast? Slow?"

Tephra said, "Somewhat slow. If I clap out a rhythm, would that help?"

Taruu nodded, and Tephra clapped out the rhythm and hummed the tune for her butterfly dance. Taruu began strumming on his instrument, and Tephra smiled and nodded as she continued to hum and to clap the rhythm. He asked, "Just that fast? Yes, it is much like a tune we know. I will ask Lian to follow my pace, and I will watch you and try to match your movements."

"Thank you, Taruu," Tephra smiled and placed her hand over her chest in a gesture of gratitude, then she and Kaoli walked to the larger platform. While all the gifts were being presented, Tephra recalled the many times she had danced the ritual dances in Drumlin. Remembering the thrill and joy she experienced from the dances, she realized how much she had missed dancing since her injury—really dancing, not just the simple dances she had performed for Foehn and Uluru's children. After the last gift was presented, Kaoli stepped up and whispered to Uluru and Basal who were sitting on a bench near the edge of the platform, surrounded by their gifts: simple, useful things such as a loaf of bread, a mug, a piece of cloth, a bag of seeds. Basal, Uluru, Strata, and Kaoli quickly moved the bench and gifts onto the ground next to the platform.

Uluru and Basal stepped onto the platform, and Basal held out his hand to Tephra as Uluru announced, "My friend, Tephra, is a lovely dancer. She will dance her 'Butterfly Dance' as her gift to me, and to my children. It is one they love."

Tephra took a deep breath to calm the sudden rush of excitement and nervousness and walked to the center of the platform. As she began clapping out a rhythm, Taruu began strumming, and she began the steps of the dance.

Strata watched in awe as Tephra moved across the platform like a gentle breeze, her arms moving as gracefully as butterfly wings. She circled the platform, at times lifting her foot behind her, and turning around on one foot. Bowing low as she completed the turn, she brought her foot down and forward, straightened, and then performed a light hop-step. At first, she seemed a bit nervous, but as Taruu and the other musicians followed her movements in almost perfect time, she seemed to relax, and her movements became more graceful. She circled the platform and repeated the steps, with a slight variation each time, and finished her dance by slowly lowering herself to the floor and bowing low in the final pose of the dance. After a brief pause, she stood—a little shakily, Strata thought—and looked over at Uluru, her eyes wide. Then, as the people of Barchan began their rhythmic applause, she smiled warmly and waved to her appreciative audience.

When she walked to the edge of the stage where he was waiting with Uluru and Basal, he quickly stepped forward to take her hand and assist her down the two steps. He wanted to tell her how perfect her performance was, but several people approached her with kind, appreciative words. He led her to the kegs and offered a mug of wine, but she insisted on water. He dipped water into two mugs, handed one to her, and looked for a bench where they could sit. Strata asked her how she had learned to dance like that, but he was unable to get much of an answer for their conversation was often interrupted by Barchans coming to greet Tephra and to compliment her dancing.

It was near sunset and the torches in the grove and along the trails had been lit when the newly mated couple slipped away to Basal's dwelling. In a few days, Basal and his daughter Kela would move into Uluru's dwelling, as it was larger, but for this night and the next, they would be alone. Kaoli was staying at Uluru's to care for Kela and Uluru's children until Basal and Kela were settled in the dwelling of Uluru.

The women and young children of Barchan began to make their way to their dwellings to wash up and prepare the younger ones for sleep. The men and the older maidens and lads remained to clear away the remains of the festivities. Strata walked with Kaoli and Tephra to Uluru's dwelling, carrying both Pilli and Kela, as they were exhausted from all their running about. To Strata's relief, Kaoli took the children inside, allowing Strata to say goodnight to Tephra alone.

Tephra spoke first, her voice soft, her smile warm, "Thank you for being with me. And for explaining your customs so I did not feel so out of place. I am sure I kept you from your friends."

"I am glad if I was able to make you feel more at ease," Strata replied, feeling a bit uneasy himself at the moment. He then added, "It was a good mating feast, don't you think?"

"It was wonderful," Tephra replied, smiling up at him. "I am so glad Uluru asked me to come. Now I think I should go help Kaoli with the children."

"And I should be helping clear the tables and benches."

"Good night, Strata."

"Rest well, Butterfly," Strata gently teased, and Tephra raised her arms and waved them in a fluttering motion as she danced inside to help Kaoli.

Strata grinned broadly, winked, and walked briskly back to the grove. As he joined the others in putting the grove area back in order, he began whistling happily. Gabbro motioned to Strata to help move a table, and when they had it in place, Gabbro remarked with a sly expression, "Tell me, cousin, does the cheerful tune you are whistling have anything to do with the lovely dancer?" Strata stopped whistling and flashed a bashful grin.

Tephra stayed at Uluru's dwelling to help with the children until Basal and Uluru had returned. Feeling that she was now more in the way than she was helpful, she prepared to return to her hut in the outland. Basal gave a little bow and assured her she was welcome to visit anytime she wished, which made Uluru smile and kiss him on the cheek. Tephra embraced the children, each one sniffling and trying to blink back tears as they told her goodbye.

As Kaoli was still helping Uluru and Basal merge their two households, it had been arranged that Pingo would arrive just before dawn the next morning to walk with Tephra to the woods. However, while Tephra was saying her goodbyes, Strata arrived and said, "Pingo has a sour belly from eating too many plums, so I came to walk with you."

"Poor Pingo," Tephra tried to sound sympathetic, but was glad that Strata would be walking with her. The shift she had worn to the mating feast had been carefully washed, neatly folded, and placed in her pouch, which she put over her shoulder. She had at first refused to take the shift, but Uluru and Kaoli kept reassuring her it had been altered just for her from one of Uluru's shifts that no longer fit as it should after bearing three babies. Tephra had graciously accepted it, knowing it would remind her of Uluru's mating feast.

As Tephra and Strata walked along the trail that led toward the woods and the outland, they passed the grove where Uluru and Basal's mating feast was held. When she saw the platform, Tephra smiled, knowing she would often think of Uluru's mating feast and would remember the feeling of dancing for her Barchan friend. At one point along the trail Strata stopped and pointed to a deep ravine on one side.

"Down there is where I found you when you tried to walk back to Drumlin on your own."

"I was so frightened," Tephra said, frowning and shaking her head at the memory.

"Of me?" Strata asked, his voice just above a whisper.

"Of everything," Tephra admitted, staring into the ravine, her voice quivering with emotion. "The lightening, the rain so hard and cold. And all that I had been taught about your mountain. I was afraid I would never find my way down, and then, afraid of what would happen to me when and if I did."

"Are you afraid now?" Strata gently touched her shoulder.

"No. I am unsure of some things, but not afraid," Tephra answered as she turned to look at him, her gaze even.

"Not afraid of the mountain and its people?" Strata grinned, taking her hand.

Tephra grinned back, "No, not afraid."

Their hands still joined, they continued most of the journey in an easy silence, speaking only when Strata pointed out something along the trail—deer tracks, a hawk sitting on a high limb watching for a meal, a vine of fragrant flowers winding around a tree trunk.

They only stopped once to rest and eat the bread, cheese and light ale Uluru had sent with them. When they reached the lean-to, Tephra paused, but Strata shook his head, "It is still light. I will make a torch when needed. You will be in the hut tonight." Tephra was puzzled at first, then nodded her understanding.

As soon as the sky began to darken, Strata made a torch from a fallen Boreal tree branch. With one hand firmly holding Tephra's arm, he led her safely down the rocky slopes and through the woods. The torch cast an eerie glow around them, but Tephra realized she was not afraid.

When they reached the hut, it was dark. Strata opened the door, took Tephra's pouch, and handed her the torch. He entered the hut, lit the lantern, and placed her pouch on the table. He took the torch from her, gently took her small hand in his large one, and with a slow smile, said, "Thank you for dancing with me."

Tephra felt a fluttering in her stomach as she noticed there was no teasing grin or wink as he thanked her. "Thank you for teaching me the steps. It--it is pleasant to dance that way," she said, suddenly shy again.

They both stood awkwardly for a few moments before Strata said, "I should go. Pingo may need me to help with his chores."

"You will stay at the lean-to?" Tephra asked, concerned that he would walk all the way back in the dark.

Strata nodded. "I will rest there a while."

Tephra sighed, feeling relieved, then with a barely suppressed giggle, said, "Tell Pingo I hope his belly feels better." Strata chuckled, slowly released her hand, and walked into the woods. Tephra watched until he was out of sight, and then walked to her hut, smiling contentedly. She carefully removed the other items from her pouch, but left the shift Uluru had made for her protected in it. Not bothering to change into her night shift, she washed her face, turned down the lantern, and went to her cot.

CHAPTER 38

Stretching and yawning, Tephra awoke the next morning feeling relaxed and lazy as she recalled the walk from Barchan with Strata. She rose from the cot and stretched again, then put water on to heat for tea. After a mug of tea and a slice of bread spread with honey, she set about doing her chores. She needed fresh water so, taking her soiled shift and other items that needed cleaning, she picked up her bucket and went to the pond to wash her clothes and to get fresh water.

Tephra remained at the pool longer than usual, enjoying the lyrical sound of the water falling from the rocks into the pool, and remembering her time in Barchan Settlement. Her stomach began to rumble, reminding her it had been a while since she had eaten. She filled her bucket, picked up the items she had washed, and returned to the hut and hung the garment out to dry, still smiling from the memories.

Her smile faded quickly as she went around to the door and found it standing halfway open. She was quite certain she had closed it securely. Once she had left it open while she went to the pool and on her return, was startled by a squirrel who was sitting on the table and munching a millet cake, so she no longer left it open when she would be out for a while. Entering cautiously, she halted, almost dropping the bucket of water as she stared in disbelief. Graben was sitting on a stool by the table, staring into the mug he held in his hands. He looked up as she entered, smiled, and placing the mug on the table, stood quickly and went toward her with his arms outstretched. She took a step back as he said in an affectionate tone, "Tephra, I came for you. I was worried when you were not here!"

"You—you came for me?" Tephra asked suspiciously as she moved to set the bucket on the table, keeping her gaze on Graben.

"Yes, my beloved," he cooed, placing his hand over his heart, "I came to tell you that I realize I may have accused you wrongly. I cannot stop thinking that if that Barchan had left you on the trail, wolves could have attacked you! He brought you to their healer so that you could return to me. I now understand that you only spoke to him when you were protecting *me* from harming another enosh and bringing the displeasure of The Always upon myself."

Tephra slowly shook her head and gave a sigh as she realized by his self-assured tone what he was saying. "So, Graben, you now risk the displeasure of The Always by coming to the outland to speak to one who is banished—one who has renounced Drumlin?" she asked crossing her arms and leaning her head to one side.

"I have been staying at Hevel's, taking care of Col—his arm was injured—doing all sorts of chores for Hevel and Col's family, working hard in the gardens, and getting up even earlier than usual to pray with Karst. I am so tired at the end of the day, I fall asleep as soon as I lie down on the hard mat at Hevel's," his voice was tinged with self-pity.

"Why do you tell me this?" Tephra asked, annoyed, and at the same time, wary.

"I know I can talk to the Hammada. I will tell them the truth about Ogen, and that I caused injury to another enosh. I have admitted I led Drumlin men up the mountains out of jealousy and suspicion—not once, but twice—and that the second time, Col was injured. I will say that all I accused you of, I now know to be lies. I will apologize to your clan—before the entire village. I will say that I am certain you would never have broken your vows to me, and that I was wrong to ever doubt your faithfulness." Graben's tone was pleading, but still his words sounded rehearsed.

Tephra listened intently, yet all the while doubting Graben's motives. "You will admit all of this?" she questioned, her voice tinged with skepticism. "Do you come here with the Hammada's approval? Ah! I can see by your downcast eyes they do not know you are here. So, without approval of the Hammada, you come to a place forbidden and speak to one cast out from Drumlin, and you think *you* can persuade them to accept me as a Drumlin once again?" She crossed her arms to hide her trembling hands because something about him being there in the outland hut was unsettling.

"I am sure the Wise Ones will listen," he pleaded with conviction, holding out his hands to her. "I am of the Clan of Earth-Tillers, the largest and most prosperous clan. Two of our clansmen are Wise Ones of the Hammada. And," he paused, lifted his chin, and with a self-satisfied smile, stated proudly, "I am Golith, two years now! Did you know that, my beloved? My marks were even higher this year than last. I will still be Golith to you!" Leaning toward her, he lowered his voice and said in a persuasive tone, "Think of it Tephra. You can still be mated to me!"

Tephra looked at him pityingly, sighed and holding her hands up, palms outward in a gesture of finality, said, "It is too late, Graben, much too late."

He smiled in the way she once found charming, but now seemed false. He reached for her hand, and caressed it between his two hands. "You said you would always be my friend, remember? And that I would always be yours," he said, reminding her of that day on the trail to the meadows.

She jerked her hand from his and held it behind her back, the other hand she pressed to her quivering stomach and began in a carefully controlled tone, "You have not been a friend to me, Graben. I can no longer call you friend! I suffered banishment because of your suspicions and your lies. If you had spoken up for me then, I would not have had to go away for three months. You never asked my family about me, never asked how my knee was healing. You ended our betrothal. Your clan refused to barter with my clan. Things were very difficult for my family. You—you even let Olivine turn against me, when if she had known you struck the first blow …." Tephra had to pause to control her emotions. The anger and resentment that she had held inside for so long were rapidly surfacing. Swallowing hard and taking a deep breath, she fought back the tears that threatened and said slowly and emphatically, "I willingly renounced my family, my friends, my clan, and my beloved Drumlin in hopes of bringing an end to the rift among the peoples I care about. The Hammada know why I did, but even they cannot change the decrees of The Always."

"Oh, Tephra," Graben said, attempting a convincing smile and extending his arms out to her, his palm upwards. "Now that the village is more peaceful, the Hammada may see your act of willingly leaving Drumlin as heroic, and—and as a sign of how much you truly love your people. They will also see it as a good thing that I have forgiven you and am now willing for us to be mated!"

Tephra shook her head slowly from side to side, then looked at him squarely. "Graben, I no longer wish to be mated to you," Tephra stated firmly, her arms held stiffly at her sides, her hands fisted. As she realized what she had said, and that she had finally had the courage to say it, a sense of relief flowed through her.

"The Hammada may rule it," Graben said with certainty and an air of conceit as he crossed his arms and sat on a nearby stool. "You know they were pleased that I would be mated to the loveliest maiden in Drumlin."

"You are so confident," she replied with restrained contempt, as she walked toward the window, opened the shutter all the way, and then turned back to face him. "And will they be pleased when they learn that you broke the decree that *no one* was to come here—*no one* was to speak to me?"

"They do not need to know I came here," Graben said in a conspiratorial tone, and a smile that was more of a smirk.

"So you would keep it from them? More secrets, more lies, Graben?" Tephra raised her eyebrows and crossed her arms. "I should not even be speaking with you. That is what was commanded of *me* when I agreed to forsake Drumlin—that I speak to no one of the village." She turned sideways so she did not have to look at him.

"Surely if there were a chance to be mated to me, and to live in the fine dwelling I have provided for you—" he said smugly.

Tephra shook her head, still not looking at him, and said firmly, "No, Graben, no. You have been no friend to me, or to the people I care about." Then, arms still crossed, she turned to face him, and said emphatically, "No. I will not, cannot be mated to you. Please leave my dwelling." She saw the cold, hard look in Graben's eyes and felt a tremor of fear, and was even more convinced she could never be mated to him. Not this Graben.

"You are refusing me, even when I can see to it that you can live as a Drumlin once again? You would rather live out your life here, alone, in this small, crude hut?" he asked incredulously, gesturing with his hands, apparently still unconvinced she could refuse him.

"Yes!" Tephra said emphatically, "Now please leave."

"Oh, I will leave, but first, answer this: Where were you when I arrived here? Where could you go?" his tone was challenging, suspicious.

Tephra took a deep breath, and answered flatly, "There is a small pool in the woods where I go to get fresh water every morning."

"And so that is where you were yesterday as well? But, I waited a very long time!" Graben asked skeptically.

Tephra answered bluntly, "I was at the mating feast of the woman who cared for me when I injured my knee."

"You went to Barchan Mountain? Again? Willingly?" Graben asked incredulously, his eyes wide.

"As did you! You went to harm another. I went to the mating feast of a friend." Tephra's voice was now angry and cold.

"You will regret refusing me," Graben said menacingly, his eyes narrowed.

"Go. Go to Catera," Tephra said in a quiet, firm voice as she pointed to the door. "She will soothe your hurt pride. Or better yet, talk to Olivine, as she cares nothing for me now, thanks to your lies. You two are much alike—you know nothing of friendship."

Giving her a threatening look, Graben stomped out the door. Tephra quickly and firmly closed the door and realized she was trembling and her knees were weak. Going to the table, she sat down wearily on one of the stools, reached for a mug, and dipped water from the bucket. Her hand was shaking and she became even more irritated when water sloshed onto her shift as she took a drink. Feeling overwhelmed with emotions, she brewed a mug of tea and went to sit on the bench under the cherry tree to try to sort them out. The tea soothed her, and as she was no less confused and irritated by Graben's visit, she went to her garden and began pulling weeds and deadheading some of the flowering plants.

CHAPTER 39

Graben went straight to his shelter, picked up his knives and spears and headed for the game field. There, at each recollection of the conversation with Tephra, and how she had scoffed at him, he threw with a calculated accuracy. "She had not been pleased to see me," he thought as he recalled her expression when she saw him in the hut. "How long had she remained on that mountain? If it was the woman's mating feast, where did she stay?" He realized she had seemed different, and her hair had not been fully braided. He stopped, retrieved his spears, and began throwing again as he said in a low voice, "The way she spoke to me!" Convinced it was the wickedness of the Barchans that had changed her; he muttered under his breath, "How else could she have refused me? I assured her I could talk to the Hammada. She could have returned to Drumlin!"

"Graben! What has happened?"

Graben spun around to see Tor sprinting toward him. He did not know what to say. He could not say he had gone to the outland to bring Tephra back, and that she had refused him. No, he could not admit that even to his good friend. He paused a while, catching his breath and thinking what to say.

Pretending a laugh, he gave a wave of his hand and replied, "Oh, just that Catera's mother told my mother that it would not be fitting for us to live in the dwelling I prepared for 'the outcast one' and that I should prepare another."

"So," Tor said, "you have decided to ask for betrothal to Catera?"

"Hah! It seems it has been decided for me, by Catera's mother and my uncle Shael," he replied with a grimace.

"You do not seem pleased. The way you were throwing those knives, you could throw your back out."

"You would be throwing knives too, if you had been betrothed to the most desirable maiden in Drumlin and she betrayed you," Graben said, clenching his jaw.

"My friend," Tor said thoughtfully, "I still have doubts that Tephra broke her vows. I know—"

"Say no more!" Graben interrupted with a growl. He looked down, shook his head and said sadly, "And yes, I too have doubts—and they will always remain just doubts."

"Try to forget her, Graben," Tor said sympathetically, "Catera can be very charming, and she adores you." With a light, teasing laugh, he added, "Build a dwelling far from her mother, and your mating could be a happy one."

Graben reached out and placed his hand on Tor's arm, "When will you decide to mate with Siluria? I think she prefers you to Noll, but he is determined to win her, or so I hear."

The two young men continued their discussion as Graben picked up his knives and spears. Graben put away the weapons and returned to Hevel's hut. Col would be returning to his family shelter the next day, but would not have full use of his arm for two or three more weeks. Graben's mother had asked him to return to the family dwelling when Tephra voluntarily went to the outland hut, but Graben decided he would stay in the dwelling he had prepared for Tephra permanently—at least while he built one for Catera and helped Col's family with chores.

That night as he lay on the mat he had thought he would be sharing with Tephra, he wept bitter angry tears at the memory of her rejection. His fists pounded the mat as in his mind he saw her in the tiny crude hut, smiling and content, her lovely hair flowing about her shoulders. He cried out in agony as he envisioned the Barchan entering the hut and saw Tephra going to him with a welcoming smile, her hands outstretched to him. After his imagination ceased torturing him, he fell asleep exhausted. He woke the next morning later than usual, with the imaginings of the night before still fresh in his mind. Soon those visions were replaced by another as he planned how he would make Tephra regret refusing him. That vision made him smile—and the smile was a bitter one.

While Graben was still sleeping, the Wise Ones were gathered on the Hammada Stone for their morning prayers and meditations and to see what prophecies might be revealed in the ice facets of Nunatak Peak. As they lifted their crystal-tipped staffs toward the peak and the sun began to rise on the far horizon, several gasps were heard among the group.

Eaolia cried out, *The rift is not healed! Nunatak reflects blood!*

Kame wailed, *Blood will flow this night! Beware of changes in the now ...*

Others murmured, for they too had seen the glow of red on the broadest facet of Nunatak. Karst called for more prayers, "We must heed the warning. We now pray that The Always will guide us as to how to protect our village. We have only begun to heal the rift that was. We must ask The Always what we are to do."

Late that evening, dark storm clouds gathered over Drumlin Hills. As lightening flashed across the sky and thunder rolled, the shepherds brought their flocks into the pens. Two shepherds would take turns at watch in the pens throughout the night. As Elos headed to the sheep pen at midnight, he thought he saw a shadowy figure running away from the pen. The rain was heavy and the night was dark, so he was unsure until a flash of lightening showed a glimpse of someone running toward a grove of trees. The figure appeared to be carrying something, but it was too far away for Elos to be certain. Going to Alem, the other shepherd, he found him sleeping in a corner of the shelter. When he tried to rouse him, Alem groaned and put his hand to the back of his head.

"Somebody hit me!" he said as he started to rise. "The flock suddenly became more restless, and as I was trying to see what was causing it, I felt something hit my head. Then I guess I passed out."

Elos related to Alem what he thought he had seen. It seemed unreasonable someone would steal a lamb, but the two shepherds counted the flock anyway. After each counted twice, they both came to the conclusion that someone had indeed stolen one of the young lambs. At Elos's urging, Alem went to wake Hevel and have his injury cared for. Now alone, Elos was troubled by what had happened and kept looking toward the grove of trees. With the darkness and the rain, however, he was unable to see anything.

CHAPTER 40

The next two days, Tephra went about her daily chores, happily remembering Uluru's mating feast. A few times, she recalled Graben's visit and how it had ended, but refused to dwell on it. She did wonder when Strata and Kaoli would visit again, but she knew it was a long journey, and Strata and Kaoli had responsibilities. On the third day after Tephra had found Graben in her hut, she left at dawn to go to the pool. She had just finished her morning prayers when Kaoli arrived with a coverlet draped over one arm, the other hand carrying a small basket. Tephra smiled and gave her a questioning look.

"I have brought Gidá's biscuits and a nice sausage to share," Kaoli explained. "And, I will stay until tomorrow morning, if you do not mind."

Tephra laughed and shook her head. "No! That is wonderful! But will that coverlet be enough for you?"

"Oh, I do not need much. I often sleep on the grass outside our hut on pleasant nights," Kaoli said, shrugging her shoulders.

After Tephra had washed and wrung out her shifts and cloths, she helped her spread them over then rocks to dry. The two sat near the pool, leisurely eating their meal and talking, until Tephra suggested they return to the hut and hang the garments in the sun. Tephra filled her water bucket from the flowing water and Kaoli helped Tephra carry the cleaned, but damp garments and cloths to the hut and hung them on the line.

As the two entered the doorway, Kaoli screamed and Tephra gasped and stared in horror, dropping the bucket of water. Blood was splattered on the walls, the shelves, the stove, and the cot. Tephra's hand flew to her mouth as she saw, lying in the center of the table, a lamb's tail. She backed out of the doorway pulling the stunned Kaoli with her, and running around to the garden. They sat on the bench, trembling and holding on to one another. Speechless, Kaoli looked questioningly at Tephra. Her voice a hoarse whisper, Tephra tried to explain, "It—it is like something from Drumlin's ancient tales. If a man insulted another and did not apologize, the offended man would wipe sheep's blood on the door of the man who had offended him. The blood would remind him that he needed to make amends." She paused and took a deep breath, "It is an old legend…."

"But, Tephra, who would do such a thing to you? And it is not on your door, but all over inside!" Kaoli's eyes were wide with disbelief.

Tephra rested her elbows on her knees and putting her hands over her eyes, said, "I do not know. I can only think there is more blood because he is not only insulted, but shamed and dishonored." She sighed deeply and looked up at the hut. "And if that is true, I can only think of one who would do this."

Kaoli whispered in a shaky voice, "Who, Tephra?"

Tephra hugged her arms to herself, lowered her head, and said, "Graben, or perhaps Olivine. Each may think they would have reason. There is much you do not know. Kaoli, you have been a good friend to me, and I should tell you, but just now I cannot."

"What are you going to do? It will take a lot of scrubbing to wash it all off, and then, there may still be the stains of it."

Tephra was suddenly frightened as she considered the anger that could have driven Graben to do such a thing. "He would have had to kill a lamb—one of my lambs! And he left the tail! He wanted to be sure I knew what animal the blood came from!" she cried out in a hoarse whisper. Turning to Kaoli, she wiped away tears with the back of her hand and pleaded, "Will you help me? I cannot possibly clean it all before dark, and I cannot leave it. The weather is too warm; the scent will attract scavengers."

Kaoli looked at the hut, then at Tephra, and putting her hand on Tephra's arm, replied, "Yes, of course. You are right. It must be removed soon."

The water bucket was now barely half-full, but that was poured into the wash bowl in the alcove, and Kaoli went to refill the bucket while Tephra began the task of cleaning away the blood. The two maidens took turns making repeated trips to the pool for fresh water, and still it seemed there was much blood left, or at least the stain of it. Tephra did not know what to do about the cot. The mat and coverlet were soaked in several places. Even the pouch had splatters of blood, and upon inspecting it, Tephra was relieved that the lovely shift Uluru had made for her had been protected. Her sleep shift, her other day shift, and her cloaks were heavily splattered. Kaoli had carefully carried the unsoiled shift out to the bench and had tried washing the pouch, but the stain remained. Strata's carving was dripping with the reddish sticky substance.

Tephra began to feel nauseous. She stopped to wash her hands in clear water and said to Kaoli, "I will see what I can find for us to eat and we can go sit out in the fresh air." Tephra found a loaf of bread in a basket that had not been splattered. The tin of tea and a jar of honey had been wiped clean, as had the stove. She was able to heat water and brew a strong pot of tea.

After they had eaten the bread spread with honey, and were sipping their tea, Kaoli asked, "Where will you sleep? Your cot is not fit to sleep on."

"I had not thought of that. I only thought of removing all that—" she gestured toward the hut, not wanting to say the word.

"Tephra, it will soon be getting dark. We must start back on the trail now. We can likely make it to the lean-to, and Pingo was to meet me there in the morning. Come with me. I know there is still much cleaning to do, but we can return tomorrow."

Tephra thought for a moment. "I suppose it is the only thing to do. I just want to get my hair comb and willow twigs and ribbons. At least they were untouched."

The two went inside and Tephra got the items she had mentioned. On an impulse, she also picked up the tin of tea, a small pot, a flask of water, and the tin of flints and placed them in the basket that had not been touched by the blood. Kaoli cautiously rolled up the shifts, cloaks, and coverlets so that she could carry them without her own shift becoming soiled. Tephra closed the door firmly and the two set out for the woods and the trail to the lean-to.

By the time the two had reached the forest where the trail inclined more sharply, the sun had set beneath the treetops and the forest felt shadowy and sinister, especially after what they had encountered in the hut. Tephra could not shake the image of the lamb's tail on her table. She thought how that lamb had been slaughtered as a token of revenge and she became truly frightened. When the sun had set even lower and the trail became more treacherous in places, Kaoli suggested they look for a pine branch to make a torch.

"I have flints. Try to find a branch," Tephra said as she began looking around. "There!" she called to Kaoli, "up there, caught on a forked limb is a small fallen branch. I think I can reach it." Stretching up onto her toes, she reached for the branch, but could not quite grasp it.

"Here," Kaoli offered, kneeling on one knee, the other bent, "stand on my knee and you will be able to reach it." Tephra put one foot on Kaoli's knee, and with one hand on her shoulder for balance, was able to reach the small pine branch. Using a strip torn from the hem of Tephra's shift, they were able to fashion a torch that, though faint, helped them to see the trail well enough to avoid any dangers. As the sky darkened even more and the shadows in the forest became deeper, the trail seemed even longer to Tephra. She breathed a deep sigh of relief when they finally reached the lean-to. Kaoli put the blood-soiled items a short distance from the lean-to and covered them with pine needles, while Tephra spread Kaoli's coverlet under the lean-to. Wishing they had more food to share, Tephra broke off two pieces of the bread—saving some for the morning—and spread it generously with honey. Both were exhausted from the trips to the pool for water and scrubbing at the bloodstains, so after washing down the bread with water from the flask, they stretched out on the coverlet. Kaoli turned on her side away from Tephra, and was soon snoring softly. In spite of her physical tiredness, Tephra lay wide-awake for a time, staring up at the stars twinkling through the tops of the trees. Her mind drifted through time, reliving certain events that had brought her to this point. When she could not hold her eyes open any longer, she drifted into sleep filled with confusing dreams.

Kaoli shook Tephra awake, saying it was dawn, and time they were on their way to the settlement. Tephra asked, "Wasn't Pingo supposed to meet you here this morning?"

"Yes, but sometimes he can get confused about time. We can go on. He will meet us on the trail. I am hungry, and there is not much bread left. He was to bring Gidá's biscuits and sausage."

In the clearing was a circle of stones prepared by Strata, Tephra managed to start a small fire and heat water for tea to accompany their small ration of bread. When they had eaten, and the fire safely extinguished, they started on the trail to Barchan Settlement.

As they rounded a sharp bend in the trail, Kaoli stopped and lightly grasped Tephra's elbow. "Look there," she said with relief and pointed to a tall figure in the distance, "Someone is coming for us, and it is not Pingo."

"Strata!" Tephra whispered hopefully, and began to walk faster. As the figure came closer, "It is Strata!" Tephra said with deep relief, and handing basket she was holding to Kaoli, ran, half limping, toward him as fast as her knee would allow. By the time she reached him, she was weeping from all the fears and anxiety she had been holding inside. She stopped in front of him, and looked up at him. Without a word, he picked her up in his arms. She was so frightened and so glad to see him that she willingly let him take her into his arms and she wept on his shoulder.

By the time they reached the bridge, Tephra had dried her tears, but kept her head on his shoulder, one hand holding onto his upper arm. He had been silent as he carried her, but now he gently set her on her feet, and with one hand on her cheek, said, "You are safe now."

Tephra was surprised that he asked no questions, but assumed Kaoli had given him some kind of signal, so she just smiled and nodded. Strata held her arm as they crossed the bridge, then went back to take the basket from Kaoli so she could cross safely. When he returned to where

Tephra waited, he took her hand and held it as they continued on the trail. Just at the outside of the settlement, he noticed she was limping, and again picked her up in his arms.

She started to protest, but he shook his head, winked, and carried her all the way to Uluru's dwelling.

Basal answered Kaoli's tap at the door and opened the door wide as he asked in alarm, "Is that Tephra? She is ill? Injured?"

Strata shook his head slowly, and carried Tephra to a bench next to the large meal table. He eased her onto the bench and sat next to her, one arm protectively around her shoulder. "Tephra's knee was paining her after the long walk. Pingo and I had gone hunting last night, and he told me he was going to meet Kaoli at the lean-to. He was skinning the rabbits he had trapped, so I set out to meet her."

"Uluru is getting the children cleaned up after the evening meal," said Basal, "but I can brew a pot of tea." While the tea brewed, he placed bread, jam, cheese, and a few plates on the table. Uluru came into the room and poured a mug of water for Tephra and Kaoli.

As Tephra nibbled at the bread and cheese, and took long drinks of the soothing tea, Kaoli described what she and Tephra had seen when they stepped into the doorway of the hut.

"Tephra, why would anyone do such a thing?" Uluru asked, her forehead wrinkled in concentration. Tephra shrugged her shoulders, shook her head, and then related to Uluru and the others what she had told Kaoli about the ancient Drumlin ritual.

Strata clenched his fists, and asked gently, "Tephra, you have some idea of who did this wicked thing?"

"Can't you guess?" Tephra asked solemnly.

"I think I can," Strata nodded, blowing out a long, frustrated sigh.

Uluru nodded, "I think I can, also. I admit I did not like him, but to do such a horrible thing! Why?"

Tephra looked at Kaoli, "I am sorry, Kaoli. I could not tell you before. I could not think about it then." She looked down at her mug of tea and, as though relating a strange disturbing dream, told them how she found Graben in her hut when she returned from the pool in the woods, how he had said he had come for her, had decided to forgive her, to believe her. Out of the corner of her eye, she saw Strata slowly shake his head from side to side, and bow his head low.

Tephra continued, realizing she was now even more puzzled by Graben's visit. "He acted as though I should be glad to see him. He told me he planned to go to the Hammada and plead for me to be received back into Drumlin. He said he would admit that he had lied, and that he was wrong to accuse me of betraying our vows." She paused, frowned and looking at each of those present in turn said, "But in truth, if he did admit he had lied, they would never listen to him then. But, he was too full of pride to see that. He even said he would not tell the Wise Ones he had gone to see me in the outland." She paused to take a drink of her tea, and then said with scorn, "Oh, he is Graben, of the largest and most prosperous clan, and he is *Golith*, two years now! The Hammada would listen. They would surely grant his request so that he, Golith, could be mated to 'the loveliest maiden in Drumlin.'" At her last words, said in a derisive tone, she shook her head in disbelief.

"So he now wants to be mated to you?" Uluru asked.

"What is *Golith?*" Kaoli asked, frowning in her peculiar way.

Tephra turned to Kaoli and smiled, "A Drumlin legend, a great hunter. It is also a story for another time." Then she looked up at Uluru. "I told him I did not wish to be mated to him. I told him that I could not even call him friend any longer, for he had not been a friend to me. He bragged that the Hammada would likely rule it. When I assured him I would rather live out my life alone and in that crude hut, he asked where I had been when he arrived the day before. He said he had come then and had waited a very long time." She looked down and toyed with her mug as she sighed and said, "When I told him I was here for Uluru's mating feast, he became very angry. He told me I would regret refusing him, and stormed out of the hut."

"So, because you refused him, he does this vile thing? What sort of man is he?" Basal asked, disgust evident in his voice.

Tephra shook her head, "He is not the Graben of my childhood—that much I know."

Before dusk of the next day, Strata, Tephra, Kaoli, and Pingo had made their way to the lean-to, bringing a strong soap to help remove the bloodstains. Tephra's shifts and coverlets were left behind so Uluru could wash them after soaking them overnight in water and a solution Foehn had provided. Basal helped Uluru pack food for several days, as most of Tephra's food stores were ruined, and Pingo's mother had offered two coverlets to temporarily replace her ruined mat and coverlet. Strata said they would rest for a few hours and then they would make the rest of the journey by the light of a torch.

When they arrived at the pool in the woods, Strata insisted the others remain there while he went to make sure the hut was safe. Seeing the damage that had been done using the lamb's blood, and seeing the lamb's tail that had been left on the table—neither Tephra nor Kaoli had had the stomach to remove it—Strata felt an uncommon rage build inside him. Lifting his eyes upwards and striking his chest with his fist, he whispered hoarsely, "Almighty One, help me! If I could find him I would do to him as he did to Tephra's lamb, and spread his blood over all of Drumlin!" Taking a deep breath to calm his wrath, he walked to the clearing near the pool and motioned to the others that it was safe.

The four set to work washing away the rest of the blood and scrubbing at the stains. Even though Strata put his fury at Graben into scrubbing at the stains on the walls and other woodwork, much discoloration still remained. Kaoli had brought a lamp of scented oil, and when they took their midday meal outside, she placed it on the table and lit the wick, hoping the scent of the oil would disguise the scent of blood.

After she had eaten her meal, Tephra brought the carving of the bird to Strata. It was still sticky with blood. "I am not sure of the best way to clean it," she said, "I did not want to damage all the details." He took the carving and as he began to wipe off the layers of dried blood, the head of the bird fell off onto the ground. Tephra looked at the head lying in the grass, and at the body still in Strata's hand, and the color drained from her face. Apparently the head had been severed and then placed back onto the body. The blood had temporarily held the head in place. Tephra clamped her hand over her mouth and half stumbled, half ran behind a tree.

Strata heard the sound of retching and started after her, but Kaoli grabbed his arm. "No," she said softly but firmly, "I will see to her." Strata picked up the bird's head and began cleaning both parts, wondering at the deliberate malice behind the act of severing the bird's head and leaving it for Tephra to find.

Kaoli helped a shaky Tephra to sit on the bench and brought her a cup of water. Strata went to sit next to her and put his arm around her shoulder while Kaoli spread the thick coverlet on the soft patch of grass.

"Come, Tephra," Strata said tenderly, "lie down for a while." She stood shakily and let him lead her to the coverlet where she laid down on her side, curling up in a near fetal position. "Pingo, bring the other coverlet," Strata called, "she is chilled." Strata draped the coverlet over Tephra as he said, "Kaoli, brew a strong mug of tea, and put in a spoon of honey. And bring a piece of bread." He sat on the grass next to her, watching her closely. Though the day was pleasantly warm, Tephra was shivering.

Kaoli brought the mug of tea and the bread to Tephra, and managed to coax her to sit up and drink some of the tea and eat a few bites of the bread. She put the mug within Tephra's reach and said, "Rest here a while. Strata, Pingo, and I will do more cleaning." Tephra smiled a weak smile, and nodded.

Tephra lay there staring up at the leaves of the tree, trying to consider what to do. "I cannot stay here," she thought, "I am too afraid of him. I would always be in fear he would return, and I do not know what he might do! Is it possible the Hammada would believe the lies he would tell? Could he get them to accept me as a Drumlin once again? And what about the villagers? Would they accept me? Oh, of course! They would accept Graben's mate! He is Golith!" She realized that she would be able to see her family if his plan succeeded, but to spend her life with him? No! Not even to see her family. She did not think he would believe her now, anyway, even if she were tempted to accept him so that she could see her family. He knew she had been in Barchan Settlement. He would always be suspicious, and she would always be afraid of him. No, all the caring she had once felt for him was gone, and with it, any respect. Only disgust and fear were left. "I am afraid to stay here," she thought again, "but Uluru's dwelling is crowded with her new mate and now four children. Kaoli's hut is small, and of course I cannot stay with Strata and his grandfather. No, I will have to overcome my fears." Thus determined, Tephra ate the remainder of the bread Kaoli had brought her, drained the tea from the mug, stood slowly and went into the hut.

Kaoli looked up when Tephra entered the hut and asked, "Are you feeling better?"

Smiling, Tephra nodded, "Yes, thank you. Thank you, all of you, for caring for me," and picking up a cloth, began to scrub at a shelf.

Suddenly Strata called in a gentle but authoritative voice, "Tephra, Pingo, Kaoli. Come outside." The three followed Strata out into the garden and he gestured for them to sit down. He paced as he spoke, "It is not wise for Tephra to remain here, for many reasons. The stains will always remind her, at least until the walls can be covered with something. The weather is already changing and soon the nights will become quite cold. Then, snows will come and the trail will at many times be impassable for us to travel and see if she is needs anything. *And*," he said emphatically, stopping to look from one to the other, "none of us feels that Tephra is safe alone in this hut—not after what we have seen here."

"Strata, I must stay here," she insisted. "There is no other choice. I knew when I came here I would be alone and that at times it would not be easy, but—"

"There is a choice. You come to Barchan," Pingo said decisively.

Tephra argued, "There is no place for me to stay in Barchan. I will not stay with Uluru. She is just mated, and with four children now. Kaoli, your hut is small, not much bigger than this one. I cannot be a burden to you or to anyone."

"I hear your arguments, but they are useless," Strata put his hand gently on Tephra's shoulder. He continued, "While we were at Uluru's and I heard about what was done here, I did not like the idea that you would remain in this place. When I saw how much you were disturbed by what had been done to the bird, I was determined you would not remain here. When Kaoli brought you a piece of the bread that Basal had helped pack for us, well, I thought of where you could stay," Strata grinned, seeming quite pleased with himself. Kaoli, Pingo, and Tephra looked at each other, and then back at Strata. He continued, "Basal's dwelling. He has brought his household to Uluru's. His dwelling is now empty, but for a cot, a stove, and few other pieces. You will be comfortable there."

Tephra shook her head, "And what about Basal? Have you thought he may have other plans for his dwelling?"

"Basal is a good man. He will do what is right. You staying in his old dwelling is right." Pingo said resolutely.

Tephra smiled at him, "Pingo, you sound very sure."

"Pingo is right, Tephra," Kaoli agreed emphatically. "Basal had no plans as yet for his dwelling. By the laws of Barchan, what belongs to Basal also belongs to Uluru, and so she has a say in what he does with the dwelling. He adores Uluru, so if he thinks it is what she wants ...."

Tephra stood and folded her arms tight around her waist. She paced around the hut and back to the garden, and stopping to face the others, announced in a decisive tone, "It is getting late. We will leave for Barchan as soon as we have what I need from here. I will talk to Basal and Uluru. If I am certain they are willing to let me live there, for a time, and if I can repay them somehow, then it will be so. If not, I will return here."

Without waiting for a response from the others, she picked up the light coverlet, went into the hut and began gathering items she would need to stay at Basal's old dwelling. Kaoli helped her as she packed the plates and mugs into a large basket, wrapping them in the coverlet, along with her wash bowl and water pitcher. The two small pots were placed in a smaller basket with her cutting knife and eating utensils. Going to the outside wall nearest the garden, she gathered her garden tools. As she did so, she spotted the bird carving. It had been cleaned, but the head was still detached. Handing the tools to Strata, she then turned and picked up the two pieces, cradling them in her hands as she looked at Strata. "You can mend it?" she asked hopefully. He nodded and smiled, and she tucked the bird in with the wrapped plates and mugs.

Strata and Pingo had packed what was left of the food Basal and Uluru had sent and had rolled up the thick coverlet. Strata took the large basket from Tephra and she carried the smaller one. Kaoli carried the basket of food and the coverlet, and Pingo struggled with the garden tools.

As they walked into the woods, Tephra looked back and cried out, "Oh, no!"

Strata stopped suddenly and, alarm evident in his voice, asked, "What is it?"

Tephra answered in a sorrowful voice, "My bench! My beautiful bench! I cannot leave it behind."

Strata let out an audible sigh of relief and stifled a laugh. "Tephra! We will return for it. I am pleased you do not want to leave it behind, but we cannot possibly carry it now."

Tephra looked at Strata and giggled in spite of the blush she felt creeping from her neck to her face. Immediately the others joined in the laughter, relieving the tension of the day as they began the journey up to Barchan Mountain.

Strata had to make a torch for the last part of their journey to the lean-to. The going was somewhat slower what with carrying Tephra's few possessions, so that it was nearly dark the next day by the time they arrived at Uluru's. Leaving the baskets and Tephra's other belongings on the bench or leaning against the outside wall of the dwelling, they entered and were warmly welcomed by Basal. Uluru had a hot meal waiting for them, and when each had made use of the wash room, they sat at the table and ate hungrily. Even Tephra found she had an appetite for the first time in two days. After they had eaten their fill, Tephra began washing the dishes they had used, but Kaoli took the cloth and said, "Go talk to Basal. I will send Uluru shortly. She just went to check on the children."

Tephra waited until Uluru returned, and with an encouraging nod from Kaoli, asked Uluru if she could talk to her and Basal. When they were seated in the other room, Tephra took a deep breath and asked Basal and Uluru if, in exchange for chores, she could live in their other dwelling for a time, or at least until the spring. Basal good-naturedly assured her that chores were not necessary, but Tephra insisted she somehow repay them. Uluru looked at Tephra, and giving her a knowing smile, wisely responded, "I can always use help with the children, as you know. Is there anything else you are skilled at? You will need food also."

"I can weave baskets—very strong ones, and weave on a loom, and my mending is much improved if it is a simple garment or repair."

Basal offered, "There is a small chicken coop behind the dwelling. There is a large one here, and it is difficult for me to keep both as they should be kept. I left two hens and a rooster there. If you are sure you can take care of them, you will have eggs, and soon, chickens for food or to sell."

"I have no experience with chickens," Tephra sighed, giving a slight shrug, "only lambs and children."

Tephra turned as Pingo spoke up, "I have much experience with chickens. I will teach you. It is not hard."

Tephra smiled at his offer, "Then I should pay you something for your time in teaching me."

"You can give me some eggs, when you have too many. And chicks too when you have too many."

Strata explained, "Pingo has the largest chicken yard and coop in the village. Only a few Barchans have their own chickens, so he provides many families with eggs and roasting hens."

As it was getting late, and all were tired, Tephra stayed at Uluru's that night. The next morning Kaoli arrived to walk with Tephra to her new dwelling. It had been left in good order by Basal, so in no time Tephra had put away her few belongings. As she was putting her things away, however, she found some items Basal had left behind. She began to set them aside, but Kaoli assured her that Basal had no need of them, and she would be welcome to make use of them. In the room she had chosen for sleeping and dressing, she found a wooden, lidded box that contained a coverlet. There was also a low cot with a thick sleep mat, several shelves, a small bench with a padded seat, and a small square table on which sat an oil lamp.

Pingo brought a message from his mother whom Tephra recalled meeting briefly at Uluru's mating feast. He bowed and said proudly, "Tephra must keep the two coverlets. Mountain nights are much cooler than nights on the low hills."

"Please tell your mother that I am most grateful," Tephra said, somehow sensing Pingo would be offended if she refused. Pingo gave a quick bow and went on his way.

As Tephra and Kaoli shared a light midday meal, Tephra became silent and looked down at her hands. She was thinking of her family. Little Pilli, Uluru's youngest, often reminded her of Breccia. Kaoli commented, "You seem sad."

Rubbing her hand over her heart, she said in a soft, quiet voice, "At times I miss my family so very much—it is like an ache deep inside. Then there are times when I am content, almost happy, and then I feel guilty. I wonder, 'Do they think of me? Do they miss me?' Yet, I hope they do not miss me or worry too much." She paused, swallowing and squeezing her eyes shut in an effort to hold back the tears that threatened. She continued slowly, dreamily, "I would like at least to see Mother and Father, and Kame. And Breccia and Sedi, and Esker also. I would like them to know I am alive still." Tephra rested elbows on the table and placed her hands over eyes. Choking back a sob, she turned to Kaoli and said as tears filled her eyes, "Oh, Kaoli, my mother wept so hard when I left, even though she said she understood why I had to leave. She said, 'That you do this for your family and village—Tephra, you are my ménani'. She has had to pretend she feels no sorrow, but instead, to be almost glad I am gone."

"That must be very hard for her! But, I do not understand, 'ménani'?"

"I am not sure I can explain. It is an ancient word, not used much anymore, but it was, it …. I felt it was something very beautiful and special for her to say to me." Tephra smiled, though the tears spilled from her eyes.

Kaoli nodded, squeezed her hand and said, "I must go see about grandfather. But I do not want to leave you feeling so sad. Will you be all right? I can come back in a little while."

Tephra smiled and nodded, saying, "Yes. I will be all right. Thank you, Kaoli. It helps that you are here with me now. Go take care of your grandfather."

CHAPTER

41

While Kame and the other Wise Ones gathered on the Hammada Stone for their pre-dawn prayers, Kaoli set out for the low Drumlin hills to watch for Esker. The Wise Ones lifted their staffs toward Nunatak as the sun rose over the horizon. As they watched the facets of the mountain peak, several of the Hammada gasped and Kame moaned,

Beware! The rift is upon us, the sign is fire!
It is fire on Nunatak!
Fire is the sign the rock will split,
And the rift will go deep.
What is will be no more;
what once was will come once more.

The old woman wept, and those that had seen the colors of fire on Nunatak murmured together, trying to discern what it meant. They had clearly heard Kame's prophecy, and this time, they knew she spoke with wisdom. Many were unclear as to the meaning of the words, but knew her warning was worth heeding; knew they must pray for wisdom and understanding.

Kaoli met Esker on the hills near midday, and after greeting her and asking about the sheep and Col, she said, "I came for Tephra. She is all right, but she really must talk to Kame. Something has happened, and Tephra had to leave the outland hut and flee to Barchan Mountain for a time." Kaoli saw Esker's eyes go wide with fear, and she took her hand and held in a light, reassuring squeeze. She continued, "On the day after tomorrow, Tephra will return to the hut in the outland to get some things she left behind. She will be there at midday, but cannot remain long. Can you get a message to your grandmother?"

"I will tell grandmother," Esker assured her. "I am certain she will find a way to go to the hut. Thank you for telling me about Tephra. I miss her so! But I am glad to hear that you are her friend."

Kaoli grinned. "I am glad I have two Drumlin friends—except," she frowned as she asked, "well, Tephra isn't really Drumlin anymore, is she?"

"So say the Hammada. But Tephra *is* Drumlin, and will always be. If you had heard the way she sang the poem-songs that tell of our history, our ancestors, and the way she danced the ceremonial dances—everyone thought she performed the dances better than anyone had in many years." Esker paused and looked up toward Nunatak Peak. Kaoli did not miss the faraway look in Esker's eyes as she continued, "My mother once said Tephra danced as though she was dancing just for The Always—as though her dance was a prayer. You would understand if you had heard her sing or seen her dance." Esker looked at Kaoli and shrugged as she gave her a friendly smile.

"I am beginning to understand," Kaoli said, remembering the way Tephra had danced at Uluru's mating feast. However, she did not think it wise to mention that to Esker. Placing her hand on Esker's shoulder, she gave a slight squeeze and said, "I must go now. Please, be sure Kame understands it is very important she goes to the hut. Be well, Esker."

"Be well, Kaoli. Thank you," Esker placed her hand on Kaoli's shoulder and returned the gesture.

On the arranged day, Kame made her way to the outland hut, being careful that no one could presume her destination. When she arrived, Tephra was digging up some plants and arranging them in a basket. Kame stood and watched her granddaughter for a moment before announcing her presence and thought to herself, "She is lovely and graceful still, but thinner. She does not eat well. I should have made my venison stew. She needs a hearty stew." She cleared her throat to announce her presence and walked closer.

Tephra turned at the sound, and began weeping and laughing at the same time. "Oh, Gram-mo!" she called as she ran, her arms outstretched, toward Kame. The two held on to each other for several moments, and then Tephra led Kame in the direction of the bench.

"What an unusual bench! Much skill is needed to make something so fine-looking," Kame exclaimed. "Made by one of the Barchans?"

"Yes, Grandmother, made by the one who rescued me."

Kame nodded, and smiled a knowing smile. "Will you offer your grandmother a cup of tea?"

"Before we go inside, there is something I must tell you," Tephra sat on the bench and gestured for Kame to sit beside her. She told her of going to Barchan to attend the mating feast of Uluru, about the pool in the woods, and how when she returned from washing and drawing water she had found Graben in the hut.

"Grandmother, Graben said he had come for me. He said he was certain he could convince the Hammada to allow me to return and be a part of Drumlin again. I think you know that he deliberately harmed the Barchan who rescued me, and that led to Ogen being injured. When I reminded him that he had doubted me, and had told lies about me, he said he was ready to admit he was wrong. I reminded him that he had harmed an enosh and had caused harm to two of his own people, and that he had lied about that also. He was quite certain the Hammada would forgive him. He boasted that since he was Golith two years now, and that he was of the largest and most prosperous clan, surely the Hammada would want him to mate with the 'loveliest maiden in the village.' I told him I did not want to be mated to him. I told him he had not been a friend to me, or to my family, and I could never be mated to him."

Tephra stood and paced in front of the bench, continuing her account of Graben's visit. "He laughed, saying surely I would not rather live here all alone. I told him that I would rather live all alone, and I told him to go to Catera. He was very angry. I was frightened, for I had seen his anger in the Barchan Settlement, but I tried not to show it. I told him to leave, and he told me I would regret refusing him, and stomped out the door."

Tephra paused, and Kame reached for her granddaughter's hand. Tephra took a deep breath, and continued, "When I went to the pool three days later, Kaoli met me there. She returned with me here, and when we opened the door, we saw blood was splattered almost everywhere inside, except for the table. But, in the middle of the table was a lamb's tail. I shiver when I think what might have happened if I had been in the hut when he came with the lamb's blood."

At hearing this, Kame began rocking back and forth, and uttered,

> *Beware! The rift is upon us, the sign is fire!*
> *It is fire on Nunatak!*
> *Fire is the sign the rock will split,*
> *and the rift will go deep.*
> *What is will be no more;*
> *what was will come once more!*

"Grandmother," Tephra whispered anxiously, "what does it mean?"

Kame did not answer, but instead looked up toward Barchan Mountain. She heard her granddaughter say, as though from far away, "Gram-mo, come inside. I will make us tea. The hut has been cleaned although many stains are still there." The old woman looked up, placed her hand in Tephra's outstretched hand, and let her lead her into the hut.

At the door of the hut, Kame paused, observing the stains that still remained on the walls. "Esker said you were staying in Barchan Settlement. You went there after finding the blood in the hut?" asked Kame, as she walked into the hut.

"Yes, I am staying in a dwelling that belongs to Uluru and her new mate. I do chores for them to repay them for letting me stay there, at least until spring."

While the tea was steeping, Kame sat on one stool, and motioned for Tephra to move the other one close to her. Looking into her granddaughter's face, she asked, "The Barchans have been good to you it seems? Are you happy with them?"

Tephra smiled, "Yes, they have been very good to me. Uluru made me a lovely shift to wear at her mating feast. She and her new mate are most kind to me. Her first mate died years ago just before the birth of her youngest. Kaoli, too, has been a good friend to me."

"I understand the trail up to Barchan Mountain is not an easy one. And then, one must cross the fast-moving river that becomes Cambria Falls. You travel this alone?" Kame's voice was filled with concern.

"Oh, no. Kaoli and Pingo or Strata make the journey, and I come and go with them when I am asked."

"So they brought you today? And will take you back there?"

"Strata and Pingo went to fill water flasks at the pool. They should be returning here soon. And Kaoli is waiting at a lean-to a ways up the trail." Tephra poured the tea and set out some little cakes. "Grandmother," she said thoughtfully, "you uttered a prophecy after I told you about the blood."

"There has been talk among some of the Hammada about the possibility of you being received back into Drumlin. The trade amongst the clans has improved, although one still hears rumors and there are still one or two clans who refuse to trade with our clan. It is only talk, and the Hammada does not move quickly on something as serious as this. It may be that the whole of the villagers would have to agree. One thing is certain—the colors in Nunatak have not only spoken to me, but to several of the Wise Ones. Many of the Hammada agree that for now, you may be in great danger here."

"Do they know what kind of danger?"

"I am certain some know, but having no real proof, it is difficult."

"I understand," Tephra said sadly, "Yet, I am most puzzled about one thing. The Barchans are forbidden people to us. We do not even talk of them—except sometimes older children would tell scary stories to younger ones—as Graben and Sedi did to me." Kame noticed a hint of a smile as Tephra revealed what Kame and all adults already knew, and Kame smiled in spite of herself. In a more sober tone, Tephra continued, "I was so very frightened when Strata found me and brought me to his grandfather. All our lives we are taught they are forbidden, even evil, but told never why. And we could not ask. Grandmother," Tephra frowned, confusion evident on her face, "why are they forbidden? Why was I called unclean simply because I was among them? They were kind to me. I must know if I am to live among them, if even for a short time."

Kame nodded slowly, closed her eyes and bowed her head. After whispering a prayer, she related all she dared or knew, for even the Wise Ones were not of one accord regarding what was fact and what was legend or myth. "I can only tell you what my great-grandmother told to me on the day I was betrothed to your grandfather. He was several years my senior, and there was already much talk he would be one of the Hammada. He and Karst were both being tutored by Juhen, who was, as you should know, one of Drumlin's most revered leaders."

At Tephra's nod Kame continued, "As I said, I can only tell you what dear old Bika told me. Nunatak Peak, the Footstool of the Always, we now know is ice-covered. But many generations ago, it was thought to be a cluster of giant crystals fallen from the Place of The Always. In the mountains below the peak were found smaller crystals of an unusual shape—the ones on the staffs of the Hammada. For those who look to The Always, the crystals were a gift, something sacred, a way for The Always to speak to and through the Wise Ones. That is why they are on our staffs. There were other peoples, other enosh, who did not pray to The Always. They also found crystals—though smaller ones—and to them the crystals had no meaning except for trade, and that was blasphemous to us. When our people tried to insist the crystals not be used for bartering, there was much fighting and bloodshed—something our people have always sought to avoid. Our ancient Wise Ones chose to keep our people separate from those who did not seek the guidance of The Always, and who used the crystals for bartering, and who seemed more inclined to settle disagreements with violence. The rest you know—how the Wise Ones, guided by The Always, led our people to the Drumlin Hills, where we have prospered and multiplied and lived peaceably."

Tephra had kept her eyes on Kame during her narration, but now looked down at her hands folded on her lap. "Some of what you have told me, I knew of. But, Grandmother, do the Barchans use crystals to barter? I did not see any. And why are we not told what you have just told me?" Biting her lip and frowning, she looked at her grandmother.

"Perhaps because it was thought that too much knowledge would bring too many questions that are best left unanswered." Kame shrugged and smiled lovingly at her granddaughter. Tephra stood and walked to the doorway, apparently lost in thought. Kame left her to her thoughts for a few moments, then invited, "Sit child, take some refreshment."

While the two were enjoying the tea and cakes, Strata arrived. He greeted Kame respectfully, accepted a cake, but asked for a mug of water instead of tea. Tephra dipped water into a mug and handed it to him. After he had eaten the cake, he took a drink of the water, and said with a grin, "Pingo is waiting at the pool. He likes the sound of the falling water."

Kame stood and motioned for him to sit on the stool on which she had been sitting. Rubbing her chin thoughtfully, she paced in the small space, then stopped and looked at Strata and then at her granddaughter. "Child," she began hesitantly, "you asked the meaning of the blood and the prophecy I spoke. Some I cannot explain, but this much I must tell you both. In ancient times when one Drumlin man was insulted by another, and when there was no reconciling, the offended man would wipe sheep's blood on the door of the man who had offended him." She paused, took a deep breath, and began pacing again. "Shedding the blood of another is forbidden by The Always. The spirit of the one who sheds blood is damaged and that person is no longer fit to live among Drumlins until such time as he is made whole again, purified. Even if the shedding of blood does not lead to death, purification is still required. Even if a Drumlin harms another enosh, one who is not Drumlin, a time of purification is necessary. Putting blood on the door of one who has insulted you—or harmed you or your family in any way and has refused to make restitution—is a reminder that to insult one of your own people and refuse to reconcile is almost as serious as shedding his blood. You see, to dishonor someone, to cause them harm, is to take away something of that person, to harm their spirit, and yours. Do you understand?"

Tephra nodded slowly and whispered, "Yes." While Strata looked at Kame intently and said, "It is not unlike the old traditions of Barchan. It is not hard to understand. But why would someone put blood all on the inside of Tephra's hut?"

Kame shook her head and looked down at the floor before answering, "I think he wanted to be certain she understood how deeply he was insulted, dishonored. His pride caused him to do something evil. In Drumlin, we do not kill animals unless for food. Even wolves, we try to frighten away before killing a creature that The Always has fashioned. That Graben killed a lamb solely for the purpose of …." She gestured toward the stains on the walls, slowly shaking her head and pursing her lips.

For several moments, no one said anything, and then Kame looked directly at Strata. He nodded slowly, and looked her in the eye. Some inner sight told her he was a good man—one she could trust, even though a Barchan. "Strata, come outside. Tell me about that bench you made," she said, indicating by her expression to Tephra that she intended to talk to Strata alone.

Kame walked to the bench and sat down. "You care for my granddaughter?" the old woman asked bluntly as she looked up, studying his face.

"Yes, Honorable One, I do. But I know I must give her time. She has had much to trouble her."

"She cares for you, I think, but I will caution her to consider carefully her actions. Often she has acted with her heart, and not considered well if what her heart says is wise. This had caused much heartache."

Strata nodded, and said assuredly, "I am not the only one in Barchan who cares for Tephra."

"Yes, she has told me of the kindness of your sister and her family."

"There are others of my settlement who have been kind and welcoming to her."

Kame lowered her head and nodded thoughtfully, then said, almost as a command, "Take care of her, Strata. It is not good, nor is it safe, for her to stay here any longer. I know your grandfather. If you are like him, I can rest easier about my beloved Tephra."

"As the Almighty One hears my words, I promise you I will look after your beloved Tephra."

Kame gazed at Strata intently. "Yes, I believe you will. May the Almighty One favor you highly, Strata."

"May The Always grant you peace, Wise Kame." Strata returned her gaze, and then bowed his head in a gesture of respect.

"This is a fine bench you made for her. There is nothing like it in Drumlin. Sit here while I speak with my granddaughter, then I must return to Drumlin before I am missed." Kame stood and walked toward the hut, paused, and turned back to Strata. "Send word of her to Esker from time to time." Strata grinned and nodded, and Kame went into the hut to speak to Tephra.

"Come child, sit and listen carefully to your old Gram-mo. You are right to go to Barchan. Remain there. You are not safe here, as Nunatak has revealed to me and to others. I will tell your family that you are safe. Now, you care for the tall Barchan?"

"Yes, I think I do, and I think he cares for me. It will take time before I know if, as the Barchans say, 'we will find love together'." Tephra said, blushing as she said the phrase.

"He does care for you. He has risked much for you. There is goodness and gentleness in him, and yet he is strong in mind and body. Graben, though strong in body, is filled with too much pride. Tell me, did you care for Graben?"

"Yes, I did care for him in a way. He was always my friend, even when as children he would tease me. He was Sedi's friend." She sighed, and her gaze going to the open doorway, said, "Sedi—I care so much for him! He was my friend as much as he was my brother. I think I thought of Graben the same way."

"You did not think you would 'find love' with Graben?"

"I know now that I never thought of that. He had asked for me. Father was greatly pleased. So, I would be his mate. It is the Drumlin way."

"Yes, yes," Kame nodded, and placing her hand gently on Tephra's cheek, she cautioned, "Do not let what Graben has done cause you to act without careful thought and guidance from The Always. As you said, it will take time. Now come, let us say our goodbyes. I must hurry back to Drumlin," Kame said, her voice sorrowful at knowing this would likely be the last time she could hope to see her granddaughter. Yet at the same time, she felt contentment in knowing her granddaughter would be safe and cared for in Barchan Settlement. She held Tephra to her as both wept silently, then wiping Tephra's tears with her hand, she chanted, "I pray The Always look favorably upon you, and guide you with love and wisdom. May he grant you peace and contentment." The old woman wiped her own tears with her sleeve, and returned to Drumlin Village.

Tephra stood taking deep breaths and swallowing back tears as she realized that in leaving the hut in the outland and going to live in Barchan, she was without a doubt severing all ties with Drumlin. She hugged her arms to herself and walked outside to where Strata stood with the bench he had taken apart. He was tying the parts into two bundles using wide strips of a strong cloth. Looking not at her, but toward the woods, he asked, "Are you ready to return to Barchan? Pingo should be here soon to help carry the bench."

"I have the things I came for. I am ready," Tephra answered. She felt a bit awkward, knowing that Kame had likely revealed to Strata her feelings for him. She was glad when Pingo arrived from the pool and she did not have to be alone with Strata. Her shyness around him returned and seemed to stifle their conversation as they walked the trail back to the lean-to where Kaoli waited. She had built a small fire and was roasting a rabbit she had caught in a trap. After sharing the rabbit and biscuits sent by Gidá, the four wrapped their cloaks around them, and got a few hours rest before heading back to Barchan.

They left just as the sun was barely up, arriving in Barchan Settlement in time for the evening meal Foehn had prepared for them. Then Strata escorted Tephra to her new dwelling in Barchan. She did not sleep well, still feeling the sorrow of saying goodbye to Kame, and all her conflicted feelings and doubts about her future.

Due to her restlessness, she had just awakened and dressed in time to hear a tap on her door. She was not surprised to see Strata, for he had assured her he would come to put the bench back together and to help her arrange the plants in her sitting yard. She was, however, surprised to see Pingo, along with his mother Gidá, who was holding a platter of biscuits. Tephra welcomed them warmly, and Gidá brought the platter to the table as Tephra poured four mugs of tea. After the men had eaten their fill of the soft, tender biscuits filled with plum jam, they went outside to re-assemble Tephra's bench.

Gidá, a small slender woman whom Tephra liked at once, welcomed Tephra to Barchan and assured her, "If you need anything at all, just tell Pingo. My son is devoted to Strata. One day we will have a long visit and I will tell you about Pingo and Strata. As I said, he is devoted to Strata, and since it seems our Strata cares deeply for you, Pingo will be your faithful servant."

A light blush came over Tephra's face, and she smiled warmly at Gidá, "Thank you. Pingo has been very kind and helpful."

"He is a good son, with a nature much like his father had. In his looks, though, he more favors me, except for his grin. Ah, whenever he grins, it is my dear old mate smiling at me from the Place of the Almighty One, for I must believe that good man is there. Come to my dwelling sometime. Bring your mending, we will talk, and I will bake more of these." Gidá kissed Tephra on the cheek, and said quietly, "The settlement is still talking about your lovely dance at the mating feast. And," she added with a sly chuckle, "about how well you and Strata danced together!"

Tephra could not help grinning, nor help the blush that spread up her neck and face. She thanked Pingo's mother for her visit and the biscuits, and walked with her out into the yard where Pingo and Strata were sitting on the bench they had just put together. Tephra picked up two of the garden tools and handing one to each of the men, began instructing them as to where she wanted the flowers planted. After they prepared the areas, Tephra placed the plants and watered them by dipping water from the bucket Strata had filled. Pingo had suggested a stone path leading between the plants to the bench, so he drew out lines in the dirt and pulled out grass and weeds from the desired spaces. "Tomorrow," Pingo said to Tephra, "I will show you where to find some flat stones. You choose some. I will carry for you."

"Thank you Pingo, you have been very helpful. Would you like some tea?" Pingo shook his head, gave a quick little bow, and walked toward his dwelling. Tephra paced around the garden, looking at the ground. She suddenly turned to Strata, swallowed the lump in her throat, and said with sincerity, "Strata, I do not know how to thank you for all you have done for me. You brought me to Foehn when I was injured, went to look for me when I tried to return to Drumlin, and brought me again to Foehn. You were wise enough to know I would be more comfortable at Uluru's dwelling and brought me to her. You made sure my family knew I was alive, even though you could not be sure how my village would receive you. You were badly wounded two times because of me."

Strata reached for her hand and tried to interrupt her words of appreciation, but Tephra insisted, "Please, Strata, let me say this. You sent that lovely carved bird to me, reminding me to sing. I know you sent Kaoli to visit me in the outland. You came to see me, brought me food, and that lovely bench. You have been the dearest kind of friend to me." Tephra smiled, and gave a nervous laugh as she brushed at a tear that had rolled down her cheek.

"So I should have left you to be meal for wolves? No, I could not, for I had never seen hair the color of yours. I had to keep you here, at least for a time," Strata teased.

"Strata! I am being serious. I am trying to thank you," Tephra pretended to scold.

"Alright, Tephra," Strata said soberly, "I will say 'You are very welcome,' and now I must to grandfather, see if he needs help before I go to my woodshop." Placing his hand on her shoulder and giving it a light squeeze, he said, "Be well, Tephra."

Tephra watched him walk toward his dwelling, and then went inside her own dwelling. After washing her hands, she went to the corner where she kept her weaving loom. She sat on a thick sheepskin mat and began singing one of the poem-songs of Drumlin as she worked at the loom.

CHAPTER 42

One week after Kame had met Tephra at the outland hut, all of Drumlin Village prepared to celebrate the mating of Siluria and Tor. Earlier that day, Siluria's mother and Eolia had brought Siluria from the Caves of Solitude to the dwelling Tor had provided for her. That evening, a feast was held in their honor. The grassy slopes surrounding the Hammada Stone were filled with villagers, and next to the stone, were tables laden with foods. While waiting for the arrival of the newly mated couple, the villagers visited with their clan or walked around, stopping to exchange a few words with other villagers. As the sounds of the strummers were heard, the people of Drumlin ceased their conversations and waited in respectful silence as Siluria and Tor approached the Hammada Stone.

When the couple stepped onto the stone, Karst raised his staff and announced, "People of Drumlin, Tor of the Clan of Fishermen and his mate, Siluria!" As the couple smiled and waved to their fellow Drumlins, they responded with applause and cheers and then formed a circle around the Hammada Stone. The strummers played a cheerful tune and the villagers stepped in time to the music as they circled the Stone, singing a traditional blessing.

After the music stopped and the villagers returned to their places, Tor and Siluria made their way to Tor's clan, the clan of fishermen, and invited, "Come feast in honor of my mate, Siluria." They then went to

Siluria's clan, the clan of weavers, and made the same invitation. The clans of the mated couple made their way to the tables of food, and after they had filled their plates, the other villagers lined up to partake of the feast.

As Siluria and Tor sat together eating, Siluria noticed that Tor kept glancing around. Finally she asked, "Tor, what is it? Are you looking for someone?"

"I don't see Graben," Tor answered quietly. "He has been very moody at times, but he told me he would be here to drink a mug of wine to our mating."

"Perhaps he is with Catera's clan?" Siluria suggested.

"I do not think so. Catera has been very upset. He rarely goes to see her. She saw Noll coming from the game field a day or so ago, and asked if he had seen Graben. He told her Graben had been at the game field, throwing spears, but he had said he was going to take his spears to the stream and spear some fish. So, she went to look for him there. When she got near the stream, she saw him sitting on the bank, just looking into the water. As she got nearer she heard him muttering, 'Tephra! My lovely dancer, lost to me forever! Why? I was Golith for you!' She said she was shocked to hear him say the name. She ran back to her shelter, weeping. She told Mica, who told Talus, and he told me."

"I thought he did not care at all for T—um, her," Siluria said, "After all, he seemed glad when she was outcast."

"Yes," Tor agreed, "it is true, he did seem not to care that she was sent to the outland. Not either time."

Siluria was uncertain about commenting further on the subject, so she suggested they finish their meal.

After the newly mated couple had eaten, they went around to each of the clans, inviting them to visit their dwelling and thanking them for celebrating with them. They found Graben with his clan, but he did not look well. When he stood and walked up to congratulate the couple, Siluria could see his eyes were red, and she thought his speech was a little slurred, as though he had drank too much wine.

Mica and Olivine went to the newly mated couple to offer their best wishes. Siluria embraced the two maidens, and thanked them for their gift of a water pitcher. As Siluria hugged Mica, she whispered, "I wish Tephra could have been here." Mica said nothing in reply, but before she turned to go back to her own clan, she mouthed to Siluria, "Me, too!"

When the feasting ended, it was getting dark and storm clouds were rolling in. Just in time, the tables were cleared and the villagers began to make their way to their dwellings as the first raindrops started to fall. Tor and Siluria ran toward their new dwelling with Tor holding Siluria's arm protectively. As the drops fell faster, he picked her up and walked quickly the last few yards to their door. They were both giggling as they entered their dwelling and grabbed cloths to dry each other's hair. Tor looked at Siluria and asked, "Are you pleased that we are mated?"

"You must know that I am!"

"I had hoped you were, but there were times during the feast you had a sad, faraway look."

"Tor, I am sorry. I know Graben is your best friend, but I miss—"

"I miss Tephra, also. It is all right to say her name when we are alone. I pray to The Always that she is well."

"We will pray together, my mate," Siluria said softly.

"I am worried about Graben. He was not one to drink strong wine, only a mug of watered wine or a mug of ale at times. I am certain that he was very drunk when we went to his clan."

"Then we will pray for Graben also," Siluria said.

Tor nodded, frowned, and Siluria sensed he wanted to say something and was trying to find the right words. Taking both of her hands in his, he said, "Siluria, you are my mate, and I should not keep secrets from you, but you must promise that it will remain our secret."

Siluria's throat went dry at her mate's words and his tone, but she managed to whisper, "Of course, I promise."

Tor took a deep breath and in a halting voice, told her the truth about what happened when he went with Graben to bring Tephra back to Drumlin. He told her about Graben's burst of violence and explained how Ogen was injured.

Siluria shook her head slowly as tears filled her eyes. "Tor! Everyone blamed Tephra for Ogen's death, but Graben—"

"No," he interrupted, and in a hoarse whisper admitted, "I am as much to blame, for I went along with his lie."

Siluria recalled what Tephra had told her about her time on the forbidden mountain, and thought about what Tor had just told her. She knew that there was kindness and a strong sense of loyalty in her mate, and she cared for him deeply. She also knew how persuasive Graben could be, and how admired he was as a leader amongst the young men of the village. Her caring for him meant she could forgive him for any part he played in Tephra leaving Drumlin, for he seemed truly remorseful. Stroking his jaw, she smiled up at him and said, "I am glad I can now tell you. I never wanted another for my mate. Nothing you have told me changes that."

Tor took her in his arms and kissed her tenderly.

The next morning Noll went to the gardens to see Graben, but was told he did not show up at the area of his clan's garden where he was to supervise the harvesting. Noll was concerned because Graben had partaken of far too much wine, and did not look well during the mating feast for Tor and Siluria. When he did not find Graben at his mother's dwelling or the one he had prepared for Tephra, he went to Shael.

"Graben was drunk with wine last night," he told Shael. "After the feast, I went with him to make sure he got safely to his dwelling. He was mumbling, but I thought I understood him say, 'Lost to me forever' and then he wailed, 'I sent her away. I let them send her away.' Shael, I tried to talk to him, but he got really angry and told me to leave him. As I was leaving, I saw him take out a jug of wine."

Shael was visibly upset, and sent a few of the earth-tillers searching the village, asking if anyone had seen Graben since the feast ended. Noll went to Tor and Talus, asking if they had seen him. Tor suggested they look in Graben's dwelling for any clue as to where he might have gone. As the three looked around the hut, Noll realized something was missing. "The coverlet is missing. Last night he was clutching it to him, but it is not here."

"Was it really thick and with a blue band?" asked Tor.

When Noll answered that he was sure it was as Tor described, Tor shook his head slowly, sighed, and said, "That was to be his mating gift to Tephra. He had it made extra thick, and chose the blue band, although it was more costly. It was made for the cot they were to share."

The men were puzzled as to where Graben could have gone. Going back to the vegetable gardens, they met with the men of Graben's clan and learned they had not found Graben, and no one they talked to had seen him. Graben's three friends looked in all the places they thought he might be, even their secret places they had as children. Noll and Tor went to Sedi and asked if he could think of any place Graben might have gone. Sedi suggested they look near a certain place along the stream where they once liked to go. The stream was wide, and along one side were boulders just the right height for a young boy to sit and dangle his feet in the cool water, or share confidences with a friend or two. A willow tree grew next to the boulders, its draping branches forming a perfect hiding place. Near the stream, Noll and Tor met two young boys on their way back from fishing. When the boys were asked if they had seen Graben, one hung his head, and looked side-ways at his friend.

"We-we left the feast early and came here to fish," one said hesitantly. "When it started to rain, we ran back to our dwellings. But, I saw a man going that way." The boy pointed in the direction of the woods that divided Drumlin from the outland.

The other boy added, "He must have been hurt or sick. He was wrapped in something—a coverlet maybe—and he could not walk very good. But he was too far away. I do not know if it was Graben."

Noll, Tor, and Talus looked at each other. "The outland hut," Tor said.

"We should get permission from one of the Wise Ones," Noll cautioned, "but...." They looked at each other, and in silent agreement the three sprinted toward the outland hut. When they arrived at the hut, the door was wide open. Entering, they found Graben passed out across the bare cot, clutching an empty wine jug in one arm. The coverlet was damp and clumsily wrapped around him. Noll tried to rouse him while Tor and Talus looked for flints to light the stove, and a pot in which to heat water. They were shocked that Tephra was not there, and wondered what could have happened to her and where she could have gone. The hut was a shambles—the table was turned over, a stool was smashed against a wall, and two shelves were partially ripped from the wall. Noll also noted the dark stains on the walls and brought them to the attention of the others. After finding a couple of flints, Tor and Talus managed to use pieces of the broken stool to start a small fire in the stove.

As Graben started to come to, he began shivering. "Help me move him closer to the stove," Noll said, "He must have come here in the rain. His clothing, his hair, and the coverlet are wet."

As they half carried, half dragged Graben toward the stove, he moaned, "She's gone. Gone to *him*. I sent her away." As the fire warmed him, and he became more awake, he looked up at Tor and said with resentment, "Leave me. Leave me here. Go to your mate."

"Graben. Graben, you can't stay here. You've already caught a chill," Noll said as though speaking to a small child.

Graben became almost violent, standing and charging at Noll, shouting, "Leave me!" Then suddenly he stopped, grabbed at his head with one hand, his belly with the other, stumbled out the door and vomited in the grass. He then slumped to the ground.

Talus suggested, "We should take him to Hevel. There are cuts on his hands that need tending to. Knock him out if we have to." The other two nodded agreement, but it was not necessary to knock Graben out, for he was too weak to argue. Talus ran ahead to alert Hevel, and with Tor on one side and Noll on the other, they managed to get Graben to the healer.

Noll told Hevel, "We found him in the outland hut, soaking wet and his arm wrapped around an empty wine jug. Tephra was nowhere in sight. Hevel, most everything in the hut was broken, and from the cuts on Graben's hands…."

Tor added, "It did not look like Tephra, or anyone, had been there for some time."

Hevel looked worried and strictly ordered the three to say nothing of the condition of the hut, or that Tephra was not there. "This matter

I will bring before the Hammada. Until then, you have seen nothing. Graben will remain here for a time. I will speak to his family. Go now, go about your duties. You did right to bring him here straight away."

⁂

The next morning at prayer, Kame listened warily as Hevel informed the Hammada of the condition in which Graben was found and the condition of the hut. He also alerted them to the fact that Tephra was not there, and, it seemed, had not been there for an undetermined amount of time. "The young man will remain with me in my shelter for several days yet," Hevel informed the Wise Ones. "He is not well. His mind wanders, and his utterings are often bewildering. He sits for a time staring at nothing, and will not be parted with the coverlet he was found with."

Karst asked, "Can you make anything of what he says?"

"No, Wise One, only he seems to blame himself for something. I would say a deep guilt is eating at him, but questioning him is useless now—perhaps in time."

Kame knew that now was the time to tell the other members of the Hammada of her visit to Tephra in the outland. Lifting her staff and clearing her throat, she said, "Honorable Karst, there are events I must bring before the Hammada." Karst bowed to indicate that she should speak, and Kame stood and began the narrative of all that she had learned from Tephra—how Graben had visited her in the outland, his proposal for bringing her back to Drumlin, his admission that he had harmed the Barchan, and had lied about Ogen's injury. "When Tephra told him she no longer wanted to be mated to him, Graben threatened her, saying she would regret refusing him." Kame paused a moment, then said, "Three days later, Tephra had gone to a nearby pool to draw water. When she returned to the hut, she saw blood splattered on the walls. In the center of the table, a lamb's tail was left for her to find." Many of the Wise Ones gasped in disbelief, but she assured them, "I saw the blood stains myself, so I do not doubt that what Tephra told me is true."

Shael kept silent as Kame related the incidents, but when she returned to her seat he asked testily, "Are you suggesting that my nephew Graben is responsible for the blood in the hut? What proof do you have?"

"I admit there may be doubts, but considering Graben's recent behavior, and the fact that twice he disobeyed Drumlin law forbidding one to ascend Barchan Mountain, we cannot assume he is innocent."

Shael rose and objected loudly, "Neither can you assume he is guilty! And what of your granddaughter? If she is not in the outland hut, where is she?"

"My granddaughter has taken refuge with those who cared for her when she was injured." Several of the Wise Ones gasped and began uttering prayers, alarm evident in their tone. Kame lifted her staff and stated firmly, "It was unwise for her to remain in the hut after the threats and the spilling of lamb's blood. And after the hut was recently left in ruins, I am certain she had no choice."

"Many of us were beginning to worry that the maiden was in some kind of danger after the recent prophecies," Moraine added matter-of-factly.

"Ah, Kame!" cried Eolia, her voice full of compassion. "Even though her life may have been in danger, I fear that with Tephra's return to Barchan Settlement she has severed any chance for return to Drumlin."

Kame nodded in understanding as a tear ran down her wrinkled face. Moraine walked over to Kame and placing her hand on her shoulder in a gesture of sympathy said, "Perhaps this is the rift the prophecy foretold."

"It is only a splinter of the rift," Kame said sadly, her voice barely a whisper.

Karst raised his staff and said solemnly, "Our village is in dire need of our prayers and our wisdom. Raise your staffs and call upon The Always."

The Wise Ones entered into prayer for Graben and for the village of Drumlin, and then one by one, they went to their dwellings, each one disturbed by what they had heard this day. Kame felt compassion for Graben, yet was deeply relieved that her granddaughter was safe in Barchan Settlement.

CHAPTER 43

In the three weeks that Tephra had been living in Basal's former dwelling, several of the maidens and matrons of the village had come to tap at her door and welcome her. Some brought gifts of food, or some household or decorative item they thought she might have use of. Kaoli and Pingo, and Uluru as well, had been quietly spreading word of the Drumlin maiden who had been rescued by Strata and now had to flee Drumlin. Most recalled her dancing at the mating feast of Basal and Uluru and had seen her with Strata. Due in no small part to the respect that Strata and Uluru held in the settlement, they seemed happy to welcome her to Barchan Settlement.

Tephra was deeply grateful for their brief visits and their apparent acceptance of her, a Drumlin. She mentioned this to Strata one afternoon when he came to sit with her on the bench in her yard.

Strata grinned, "I am glad so many are welcoming you." Then he frowned, and said, "Look at me, Tephra." Strata held both of her hands in his. "Graben threatened you, and soon after that, there was blood splattered all over the hut and a lamb's tail left on the table. Your grandmother told me—no, no, she made me promise—to see that you are safe. She felt strongly that you were in danger in the hut."

"Yes," agreed Tephra, "she told me that Nunatak had revealed to her that I was not safe in the outland. She encouraged me to come here. I felt it would be best."

"I know you must miss your family, and your people, your village."

"Yes, I do, so very much—but I had to leave. It was the only way to bring peace to my family, my village. My grandmother told me return *is* possible," she paused and looked at Strata's hands holding her own." If she is right and it is possible to return to Drumlin, I would have to return to the outland hut, perhaps for a long time. I could not remain here, or return here, ever, and no one from here could visit me. I would miss my Barchan friends, of that I am certain."

"Tephra, could you be happy here in Barchan Settlement? Could you live as a Barchan?"

"I know I have friends here. But could I live as a Barchan? There is much to learn of Barchan ways, I know, but—"

"You are not sure you would be happy here?"

"I am not unhappy here, Strata. But for me to give up Drumlin ways and live as a Barchan is not easy. It is not easy to give up my family and all I have ever known, now that I know it is possible to return."

"You think you would go back to the hut in time, perhaps when you and your grandmother felt it was safe?"

"I do not know, Strata. I do not know."

"I understand, although we Barchans are not as isolated as in Drumlin Village. We trade with those in other settlements and villages, and some have become friends. We are learning to accept their ways, and they, ours. Even while clinging to our own ways and beliefs."

"There truly are other enosh still? Uluru once told me there were others, but I only know of Barchans and Drumlins!" Tephra looked up, astonished at what she heard. "There really is much to learn about Barchan ways!"

"I am a patient teacher," Strata grinned. "But now I must go help Foehn with a few chores before the evening meal."

"Good evening, Strata," the maiden smiled.

"May the Almighty One grant you a good night's rest," he said in parting.

Tephra remained sitting on the bench for a long time, thinking over her conversation with Strata. She knew she deeply cared for him, and for his family, but how could she forget her family in Drumlin Village?

To return to Drumlin would be difficult for many reasons, if it truly were possible, and may take a very long time. "Somehow," she thought, "I must make a decision, and be at peace with that decision."

Tephra went inside her dwelling and had just begun preparing her evening meal when she heard a tap at the door. She opened it and saw Kaoli standing there holding a plate of biscuits and a jar of jam. "I bring peach jam and biscuits from Gidá. May I stay for evening meal with you?"

Tephra laughed, "If you do not mind boiled eggs and greens, you are welcome."

"With Gidá's biscuits and jam, it will be a feast!"

As the two maidens ate their simple meal, Kaoli shared the latest gossip going around the settlement. While they were cleaning up after the meal, Tephra asked, "Kaoli, would you do something for me? I need you to take me somewhere."

"Where do you want to go?"

"I need to go to the plateau where Strata first found me, the one that overlooks Mosken Lake."

"I will meet you after the morning meal. Eat a hearty one for it is not a short walk. And you may want to bring along something else to eat, and a water skin."

"You are not going to ask why I want to go to the plateau?" Tephra questioned with a teasing smile.

Kaoli shrugged, "You will tell me when you are ready." She gave Tephra a wink and a grin and said, "Thank you for the eggs and greens. I will be here early tomorrow."

Tephra rose early the next morning, and as Kaoli had suggested, breakfasted on a boiled egg, cheese, and one of Gidá's biscuits spread with jam. She brewed a strong tea, sweetened it with honey, and drank it as she filled a water skin and placed a biscuit, a slice of cheese, and a pear into her pouch. When Kaoli tapped at her door, she threw a shawl over her shoulders and was ready to go.

Upon reaching the plateau, Tephra stopped to refill her water skin at the pool at the edge of the stream, and continued walking to the edge of the plateau. She stood for a while looking out over Drumlin Hills, then down at Mosken Lake and over toward the Caves of Solitude. Turning to Kaoli she said in a flat, monotone voice, trying to control her emotions, "I would like to be alone for a while. Would you return to the settlement? Do not be anxious. It will not be difficult to find my way back." Kaoli gave her a puzzled look, but nodded and walked toward the trail that led back to the settlement.

Tephra continued standing at the edge of the plateau for a long time, her eyes taking in the distant hills and meadows where she used to walk and watch her clan's sheep. Tears flowed unchecked as she silently said farewell to the hills and meadows, the village, and the stream where she and her friends had waded or fished. "After all that has happened, would I want to go back to Drumlin if it were possible as Grandmother suggested?" she thought. "It would mean I would have to leave Barchan Mountain and live in the outland for a time, perhaps a long time. I would never see Strata, Kaoli, Foehn, Pingo, or Uluru and her family. I would never see Strata again." She looked out over the meadows and the village in the far distance, and tearfully said farewell to her family and her clan. "I will pray to The Always that someday we can be together again, and that you can meet Strata and his family." The vision she had of Barchans and Drumlins meeting in friendship, one she would not have imagined two years ago, made her smile. She knew she would keep this vision, this hope, for a very long time. Going to the stream, she knelt beside it and splashed water on her face. As she blotted it dry with a part of her cloak, a voice made her jump.

"You have nothing to fear. I am Strata of Barchan Settlement. What are you called, lovely maiden?"

Tephra stood and looked into the twinkling blue eyes of the tall, dark-haired Barchan as he reached out his hand. She did not think to ask him why he was on the plateau, or if he knew she would be there. Rather, she trustingly took his hand and said, "I am Tephra, also of Barchan Settlement. Will you walk me home?"

THE PEOPLE AND PLACES OF THE LEGEND OF TEPHRA

Adar (A dar) – a Drumlin male—Kame's deceased mate and former Wise One

Arbo (R bo) – a Barchan male

Augur (aw grr) – the Chief and Advisor of the Barchans

Barchan (BAR cun) – name of a mountain, and the people who dwell there

Basal (base ALL)– a Barchan male; father of Kela

Beda (BEE da) -- sister of Graben

Breccia (bree CHE uh) – a Drumlin; Tephra's young sister

Caldera (cal DARE uh) – a Drumlin woman; mother of Tephra

Cambria (CAM bree uh) – waterfall and river

Catera (cat era) – a Drumlin maiden

Col (coal) – young man of Drumlin; Clan of Blacksmiths

Corrie (KOH ree) – a Barchan woman; wife of Gabbro, a goatherd

Creta (CREE tah) – a young Drumlin shepherdess; Esker's sister

Devon (Deev on) – young man of Drumlin

Drumlin (DRUM lin) – village set in Drumlin hills; people who dwell there

Elek (EL eck) – a Drumlin male; Clan of Shepherds; Esker's father; brother to Tarn

Elos (EE lows) – young Drumlin shepherd; cousin to Tephra

Eolia (e OH le uh) – a Drumlin matron; one of the Hammada

Enoht (E knot) – a Drumlin; father of Catera

Enosh (E nosh) – a term meaning "human"

Esker (S kur) – young Drumlin shepherdess; Tephra's cousin

Etah (E tah) – a Drumlin woman; Esker's mother

Foehn (FOE in) – a Barchan male; village healer and elder

Gabbro (Gab row) – a Barchan goatherd; cousin to Strata

Gidà (gee DAH) – a matron of Barchan; mother of Pingo

Golith (GO lith) – a legendary huntsman from Drumlin history

Graben (GRAH ben) – a young man of Drumlin; Clan of Earth-Tillers

Hammada (huh MA duh) – the Wise Ones, ruling council and elders of Drumlin

Hevel (HEY vel) – Drumlin's village healer; one of the Hammada

Kame (KAH me) – Drumlin matron; one of the Hammada; Tephra's grandmother

Kaoli (kay O lee) – a young woman of Barchan; cousin to Strata

Karst (cars-t) – elder Drumlin male; leader and spiritual guide of the Hammada

Kenæ (KEY nay) – a Drumlin matron; one of the Hammada

Kela (KEY lah) – a young girl of Barchan; daughter of Basal

Kinber (KIN burr) – young man of Drumlin; apprentice to Hevel

Lahar (LAY har) – a Drumlin of the Clan of Toolmakers; father of Mica

Malik (Mal ick) – young man of Drumlin

Ménani (may NAH nee) – a gifted, unselfish being

Mica (MY cuh) – Drumlin maiden; daughter of Lahar

Moraine (MO rain) – a Drumlin matron; one of the Hammada

Noll (NOLL –as in doll) – young Drumlin man; Clan of Harvesters

Nunatak (NOON uh tack) – high, ice-covered mountain peak; "Footstool of The Always"

Ogen (OH gin) – young Drumlin man; Clan of Toolmakers

Olin (OH len) – young man of Drumlin

Olivine (OH live een) – a Drumlin maiden; Clan of Orchard Tenders; Tephra's closest friend

Parra (PEAR uh) – Drumlin woman; mother of Ogen

Paleo (pal A oh) – young boy of Barchan; son of Uluru

Pilli (PILL e) – young girl of Barchan; daughter of Uluru

Pingo (PING go) – a young Barchan male; friend of Strata

Sedi (SAID ee) – young Drumlin; Tephra's older brother

Shael (SHAY el) – Drumlin male; one of the Hammada; leader of Clan of Earth-Tillers

Siluria (sill LURE e ah) – Drumlin maiden; Clan of Weavers

Talus (TAY lus) – young Drumlin male; Clan of Woodsmen

Tarn (as in barn) – well-respected Drumlin male; Clan of Shepherds; father of Tephra

Taruu (TAY roo) – a young Barchan musician

Tephra (TEF rah) – a young Drumlin shepherdess; Clan of Shepherds; granddaughter of Kame

Topo (TOE poe) – Drumlin male; father of Siluria

Tor (tore) – young Drumlin man; Clan of Fishermen

Uluru (you LURE ooh) – a Barchan woman; sister to Strata

Uyot (OO yote) – Drumlin man of the Clan of Toolmakers; father of Ogen

Vena (VEE nah) -- mother of Graben and Beda

Thank you for reading!

www.ingramcontent.com/pod-product-compliance
Lightning Source LLC
LaVergne TN
LVHW091710070526
838199LV00050B/2334